**Carol Marinelli** recently filled in a form asking for her job title. Thrilled to be able to put down her answer, she put 'writer'. Then it asked what Carol did for relaxation, and she put down the truth—'writing'. The third question asked for her hobbies. Well, not wanting to look obsessed, she crossed her fingers and answered 'swimming'— but, given that the chlorine in the pool does terrible things to her highlights, I'm sure you can guess the real answer!

**Louise Fuller** was once a tomboy who hated pink and always wanted to be the Prince—not the Princess! Now she enjoys creating heroines who aren't pretty push-overs but strong, believable women. Before writing for Mills & Boon she studied literature and philosophy at university, and then worked as a reporter on her local newspaper. She lives in Tunbridge Wells with her impossibly handsome husband Patrick and their six children.

# HIS INNOCENT FOR ONE SPANISH NIGHT

CAROL MARINELLI

# RETURNING FOR HIS RUTHLESS REVENGE

LOUISE FULLER

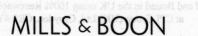

**MILLS & BOON**

First published in Great Britain 2023
by Mills & Boon, an imprint of HarperCollins*Publishers* Ltd,
1 London Bridge Street, London, SE1 9GF

www.harpercollins.co.uk

HarperCollins*Publishers* Macken House, 39/40 Mayor Street Upper, Dublin 1, D01 C9W8, Ireland

His Innocent for One Spanish Night © 2023 Carol Marinelli

Returning for His Ruthless Revenge © 2023 Louise Fuller

ISBN: 978-0-263-30669-9

Th[...] paper [...]en.

Pr[...] tricity

# HIS INNOCENT FOR ONE SPANISH NIGHT

CAROL MARINELLI

**MILLS & BOON**

For Anne and Tony

Love always

Carol xxxx

# CHAPTER ONE

'I CAN'T JUST upend everything and move to southern Spain!' Emily Jacobs shook her head at the impossibility of it all. 'I have commitments here.'

'No,' Anna corrected, nodding towards her daughter Willow, who was running ahead, delighting in the crisp snow and a visit from her godmother. 'I'm the one who has commitments. As of three months ago, you have precisely none.'

'But I told Gordon I'd stay until the business was sold...' Emily started, and then paused, because it was in fact the other way around. Gordon had told *her* that she could stay in the bed and breakfast they had run together until it was sold...

He'd said it as if he were doing her a favour—as if he were making some magnanimous gesture, letting her stay on.

In truth, they hadn't run it together. The business had belonged to his mother, and when she'd recently died Gordon had rather brutally broken off their engagement...

Emily had quickly found out that she was considered as staff.

Live-in staff.

She'd had her own room in the large residence, respecting Gordon's religious beliefs and his wishes to wait until they were married to share a bed.

Emily hadn't told her best friend that part.

Surely people would laugh—ask why she'd stayed when he so clearly didn't want her...

Only she'd been too close to make sense of those things.

With no experience to compare, all Emily knew was that his kisses had held no promise. If anything, they'd tasted of reluctance.

His hands had never roamed.

Only once.

And even then he'd abruptly dropped contact and told her she was 'on the chubby side'.

So she'd lost weight, only he hadn't noticed.

So she'd put it back on, and he hadn't seemed to notice that either.

Always shy and uptight, she had felt the little confidence she had possessed evaporate, and she'd swung between blaming herself for his lack of passion and reassuring herself that it would change once they married.

Now, on a bright February afternoon, with the sky so blue it might well belong to summer, she was starting to see things more clearly—Gordon had never wanted a sexual relationship with her and had simply used her as a front to appease his mother.

He had never wanted her.

Not for a moment.

And that was the reason why, despite being in a relationship for five years, and engaged for three of them, at the age of twenty-six she was a virgin.

'Willow, wait!' Anna said, dashing ahead to catch up with her energetic four-year-old, who was now running towards the frozen lake. 'Goodness…'

Emily laughed as her friend caught up with her child, but she didn't pick up her pace to catch up with them. It was nice to walk alone for a brief moment.

The time spent with her friend and daughter was actually refreshing.

Could she simply leave?

Take this rare chance and go?

An old university friend, Sophia, had called her just a couple of days ago with an offer. They'd kept loosely in touch via social media, but her call had come out of the blue.

'I'll need an answer soon,' Sophia had warned. 'I'm going on maternity leave and I want this sorted. Anyway, the brothers want a fresh perspective. They want to appeal more to tourists. Everyone in Jerez knows already how incredible it is… I showed Alejandro what you did with the website for that cottage where you work.'

Emily hadn't corrected Sophia and told her it was actually a bed and breakfast where she lived.

'He was impressed. And with the restaurant too…'

Since the break-up, Emily had been trying to get her website design business off the ground. Sophia's offer shot every ball out of the park. It was huge and utterly unexpected and, for the incredibly shy Emily, simply daunting.

This was not a simple job. Her potential clients wanted perfection and they were certainly willing to pay for it.

'Six weeks, with accommodation and transport,' Sophia had said. 'And there'll be a generous bonus if the website is up and running on time.'

The bonus was indeed generous—the whole package was. Worryingly so!

Emily only had two clients. Her business was supposed to be building slowly—not exploding with offers such as this. She felt underqualified and far too inexperienced and had fought not to say as much.

'Think about it,' Sophia had said. 'I'll need an answer by Monday.'

With such a big decision to make, Emily had taken an extremely rare day and night off to spend time with Anna, her most trusted friend. They had grown up together in a tiny English village and were sometimes mistaken as sisters. Not so much in looks—Anna's hair was paler than Emily's dark blonde, while Emily was curvy, Anna was slender, and where

Emily was timid, Anna was bold—but there was such a bond between them that at times it would be easy to assume they were sisters.

Anna and Willow were all the family that Emily had.

Was that why she'd been so accepting of the inadequacies in her and Gordon's relationship? Had she wanted a family so much that she'd chosen to settle for crumbs?

'Look at you!' Emily smiled at her goddaughter. She was wearing a coat and boots, a hat and gloves and huge ear muffs, due to some problems with her ears, but her teeth were chattering even as she pulled on her mum's hand to break free. 'You're freezing.'

'I don't care,' Willow said. 'I want to go and skate on the ice.'

'No!' her mother and her godmother said in unison.

'Those other children are…' Willow pouted as she was dragged reluctantly away. But she soon cheered up as they walked out of the park towards the village.

'She's too fearless…' Anna sighed.

'Like her mother!' Emily smiled. 'You used to go on the ice when we were little.'

'Yet you never did,' Anna said, turning her head. Emily could feel her eyes on her. 'You were always…'

'Chickening out?'

'I was going to say you were always sensible.'

'I wanted to go on it,' Emily admitted. 'I was just…'

'Scared?'

'Not so much of the ice cracking…' Emily sighed. 'I think I was scared of disappointing them.'

She thought of her mum and dad, they had been older than most of her friends' parents, and they had worried incessantly. Wrapping her up not in cotton wool, but in awful homemade cardigans, homemade scarves, homemade hats. Standing at the end of the drive wearing tense expressions if she was five minutes late home… While she'd been a little embarrassed at times, she'd felt so loved—but also so responsible for their happiness.

If ever there was a time to be brave and make changes Emily knew it was now, but despite being just out of a relationship and soon out of a home, she did have some commitments.

'There's the business sale...' Emily reminded Anna.

'Emily, you're not even going to get a share of the proceeds of the sale. You'll be left with nothing while Gordon will be off living his best life.'

Anna stopped talking then, clearly trying not to rub salt into her wounds.

Actually, there were no wounds.

She and Gordon's relationship had never been passionate enough for that.

'Tell him to take care of the sale of his own business,' Anna said. 'He's used you enough.'

Emily said nothing, just pressed her lips together so that her tense breath blew white out of her nostrils.

'Mummy, look!' a delighted Willow said as she ran back to them. 'Emily's a dragon.'

'Half-dragon,' Emily said, taking her goddaughter's hand on one side as Anna did the same on the other. 'Whole dragons breathe fire.'

'Are you really half-dragon?' Willow asked.

'I'm trying to be,' Emily said, and nodded, wishing she did have an inner dragon she could summon. A bit of fire to her spirit. Because as they tramped towards Anna's little home Emily knew that where Gordon was concerned she'd been more than a bit weak.

Where *everything* was concerned.

She should have resumed her studies in business and hospitality, but instead she'd taken the easier option and moved in with Gordon and his mother and worked in their family business.

It was nice to talk it through with Anna. Though Anna

could be rather blunt at times, Emily appreciated it, for there was a decision to be made.

'So?' Anna broke into her thoughts. 'You met Sophia at university...?'

'Yes.' Anna nodded. 'She was in the Spanish group I went to.'

It had been a part of university she'd loved. A group that had paired up Spanish students with those learning the language.

'And you've stayed friends?'

'A bit...' Emily nodded. 'Well, we follow each other online. She saw my photography there, and the work I'd done for the B&B website, and the one for that restaurant chain...'

'Things are starting to take off for you.'

They were.

Her purchase of an expensive camera body had been far from impulsive, and had been the most money Emily had ever spent at once in her life. Gordon hadn't exactly been encouraging, and she'd felt dreadful spending the money left by her frugal parents on something so extravagant, but she knew if she was going to make a career out of website design then she needed the best equipment she could afford.

Slowly Emily had saved and added to her camera with various lenses and lighting equipment, and she had bought a tripod that, even though it had been second-hand, was fiercely expensive and, she was now realising, rather heavy.

'Six weeks seems like a long time to update a website...' Anna said.

'Not really... It's for some vast sherry bodega in Spain.'

'Vast?' Anna checked. 'I thought a bodega was a deli?'

'Not in Spain! The vineyards are out of town, but the bodega is where the barrels are stored and the sherry matured.' She'd been researching it since the second she'd hung up on Sophia. 'There are restaurants, *tabernas*, and the building itself is like a castle. It's more than a website makeover—they want a new one from scratch, as well as fresh images...'

'"They"?'

'It's a family business—though I think it's mainly run by two brothers. When they're there...' she added.

'Meaning...?'

'They sound like two spoiled playboys.'

Alejandro and Sebastián Romero, from everything she could glean, were as good-looking as they were depraved.

'It looks as if the whole of the Mediterranean is their playground.' Emily took a breath. 'I don't think I'm anywhere close to qualified to do it. This is a multimillion-dollar empire—multi*billion*, even...' Emily's eyes went wide at the prospect of such a huge client. 'They want a completely fresh take... for their business to be looked at through untainted eyes...'

'Virgin eyes?' Anna nudged her. 'Well, that's not you...'

It was, though.

And she felt very lonely with her secret.

Despite being so close to Anna, there were things Emily simply could not reveal, so she gave a tight shrug.

'I don't know anything about sherry,' she admitted. 'Well, I didn't. I honestly thought it was an old ladies' drink. Mum and Nanny always had one at Christmas...' Emily smiled fondly when she thought back to her childhood. 'It's a massive industry over there.' She gave a shaky laugh.

'In Jerez?' Anna checked, pronouncing it as it was spelt and then correcting herself, as Emily had done earlier. 'Sorry... *Hereth*!'

Emily laughed. 'I never thought sherry could be...' She looked over Willow's head and mouthed one word. *Sexy.*

It was Anna who laughed now, perhaps at the thought of sherry being sexy. Or, more likely, at her rather uptight friend who couldn't even say the word. And not just because they had a four-year-old walking between them.

'How?' Anna asked.

'I don't know...' Emily admitted.

She wanted to go to Jerez. She'd read about the rival bodegas, the dancing ponies and flamenco dancers, and it fascinated her.

* * *

It had been a lovely day, and all too soon Willow was in her pyjamas and pleading for Emily to read her a story.

'Of course,' Emily said, heaving herself up from the sofa.

'Emily's got a lot of phone calls to make,' Anna said, and then added. 'You *are* allowed to say no.'

'In this case, I don't want to.'

Willow chose the book—it was a motivational one, telling little girls to dream big.

'I could be a dragon when I grow up,' Willow said as she lay back on the pillow. 'And blow fire…'

'You'd be a wonderful dragon,' Emily agreed.

But then Willow shook her head at the idea. 'I'd melt the ice, though, and then I couldn't skate.'

'True.'

'I think I'll be a princess and an explorer,' Willow said, thinking out loud, 'and maybe I can be a unicorn at the weekends.'

'That sounds brilliant!' Emily smiled, and was about to offer another story, but an afternoon of playing in the snow meant Willow was already half asleep.

'You look pretty when you smile,' Willow said, 'though you don't smile very much.'

'I know…' Emily nodded. 'I think I was born with a serious face.'

That made Willow laugh, but then she had a question. 'What will you be, Em?'

'What do you mean, what will I be?'

'When you grow up?'

*A Victorian spinster,* Emily thought, though of course she didn't say that.

'I'm twenty-six,' Emily settled for saying. 'That's pretty grown up.'

'Not for unicorns.'

Having wished her goodnight, Emily gently closed the door.

She could hear Anna, busy in the kitchen, but instead of heading straight down Emily sat on the stairs, grateful again for a moment of peace amongst friends.

Most of the photos on the walls by the stairs she had taken herself.

Willow's christening…her first birthday…

One tiny picture had the Jacobs and Douglas families together.

It had been taken at a fete in the next village, during the Christmas break of their final year at university… Anna's father had been the busy vicar, her mother the loyal vicar's wife.

Anna had told Emily that very day that she was pregnant and was terrified as to her parents' reaction.

Rightly so, as it had turned out.

Emily looked at her own father, so frail in a wheelchair, smiling for the camera without really knowing what was going on. Emily looked more carefully and could see the exhaustion in her mum's eyes. Just a month later she'd died.

*"'Now is the winter of our discontent…'"* Anna had said, given she'd been studying *Richard III* at the time.

Worse than a winter of discontent, though, Emily knew she had almost settled for a life of *almost* content.

There had been no contentment to be found in her lonely bed.

There was no contentment when you were in your twenties and being kissed by your fiancé as if you were some visiting great-aunt.

Emily didn't care that Gordon was undoubtedly gay. She just wished she'd known from the start, rather than waste five years wondering what was wrong with her.

Hell, they could have been honest friends, instead of faking a relationship.

*You stayed because it suited you!*

The thought she had been suppressing popped unwelcome into her head and Emily tensed as she faced it. Usually she'd stuff that thought right back down rather than admit to herself the truth—she hid from life. And always had.

As a child she'd been painfully shy, and having over-protective parents had felt like a blessing rather than a curse. She'd had the perfect excuse—that she couldn't take risks for fear of upsetting them. But, more honestly, she'd chosen not to take risks because they terrified her shy self.

It wasn't just in the big things that Emily held back. To this day she dressed conservatively and cut her own hair rather than sit in a salon chair and face scrutiny.

She checked her phone, her heart sinking when she saw it was Sophia, her rushed writing a mixture of Spanish and English.

Big NYC contract negociaciones. Los hermanos want the website changed. Permiso por maternidad from Monday, so need you there tomorrow. Puedes? Sophia

Tomorrow?

Emily re-read the message, her rusty Spanish telling her that Sophia was taking her maternity leave early, which meant there would be no one familiar to show her the ropes—and that was terrifying enough.

And Sophia's *'Puedes?'*—*'Can you?'*—was very direct.

She clearly wasn't going to plead—if Emily didn't want the work, then she'd have no trouble finding someone else.

Was she going to let another opportunity pass her by?

Emily wanted adventure and travel…

This was both.

And maybe, when the work was over, she might stay on in Spain for a little while longer and take care of another thing she'd long been neglecting.

Romance.

She wanted to find out how it felt to be kissed with passion.

As for sex?

She didn't know her own body, and she wanted to.

Yes, a holiday romance might just be on the agenda...

She sat for a few more moments and then made a call—only it wasn't to Sophia. Finally, taking a breath, she headed into the living room.

'I just called Gordon,' she said in a shaky voice. 'I've told him I'm moving overseas to take on a new job and I'll be leaving in the morning.'

'Yay!' Anna squealed, and jumped forward to embrace her, but Emily shook her hand to stop the contact, not quite ready to celebrate yet.

'He's very upset...' Actually he'd seemed more upset than he had been about the break-up! 'He said I should have given him more notice...'

'He gave *you* no notice,' Anna snorted.

'I'm going for it,' Emily said, her voice coming clearer now that her decision was made. 'I'll call Sophia now and tell her I'm taking the role.'

Emily did so, injecting enthusiasm into her voice to mask the terror she felt. 'I'll sort out the flights tonight...' She listened for a moment. 'Oh, that's fine. I'm hardly going to be there...'

They chatted for a few moments, and when Emily had concluded the call she filled Anna in.

'Sophia's hoping to meet me, but if not her husband will. Oh, and the apartment I was meant to be staying in has been booked by mistake—the flamenco festival is on—so I'm staying in the housekeeper's apartment.'

'With the housekeeper?' Anna screwed up her nose.

'I hope not!' Emily's head was spinning! 'It's all going too fast...'

'If you think about it, you'll never go.'

'True,' Emily admitted. 'Anna...' She looked up at her. 'I never wanted to go on the ice—it wasn't just because of my parents.'

'I know.' Anna smiled.

'And I have nothing to wear…'

The age-old problem was, in Emily's case, true. Her clothes consisted of stretch trousers and plain tops, all in muted greys and blacks. She wore the same all the time, as the trousers were good for crouching, as she had to for her photography. They were boring, practical.

'I actually have nothing to wear.'

'There are shops in Jerez! There are even hair salons,' Anna said.

Emily tensed as her friend teasingly touched a raw nerve. 'I've been looking it up while you read to Willow. It looks incredible, actually…'

It did.

Emily booked her flights, allowing for a couple of weeks' free time at the end. And when she should have been at home, packing her case and gathering together her equipment for tomorrow's flight, instead she looked at images of the stunning city that awaited her.

'I'm going to say yes to everything,' Emily vowed.

'And that starts with being able to say no,' Anna said. 'Just be yourself, Emily. It doesn't matter whether or not they like you, so long as they love your work.'

Anna was so bold, and Emily desperately wanted to be, so she nodded. 'I'm just…' She wanted to try new things, make up for the lost years. 'I'm just going to go for it!'

# CHAPTER TWO

ALEJANDRO ROMERO WOULD prefer this conversation, this day, this week, to be over.

Given it was late on a Sunday evening, it soon would be.

Not that Mariana would accept the end.

'You tell me our relationship is over in a *cellar*?' she shouted.

'I told you we were finished in December,' he responded calmly. 'It's February now.'

As well as that, it was hardly a cellar.

The Romero bodega was a short walk from the gorgeous Plaza de Santiago, with its churches and cafés and gorgeous shops and fountain. They stood under spectacular wooden arches in what had once been a church. The room was beautifully lit, with the moon streaming through a small stained-glass window. The location was coveted, its contents were worth millions, the archways spectacular, the artwork stunning—but, when Mariana regaled people with the tale she would, of course, say that Alejandro Romero had dumped her in a cellar.

For good.

Not that Mariana was listening.

*'Alejandro, si significo algo para ti, por favor no hagas esto.'*—'*Alejandro, if I mean anything to you, then please don't do this now.'*

'Now?' Alejandro demanded. 'Mariana, what do you mean "now"? I told you that we were through before Christmas...'

'But then we found out about your father.' She grabbed his jacket. 'At least wait until—'

'When?' he cut in. 'It will never be a good time for our families.'

'Your father is dying!' she wailed, but he stood there unmoved.

Alejandro loathed drama. Yes, drama—because it wasn't, nor had it ever been, a romance, and it was nothing to do with love.

'You are an emotional wasteland, Alejandro.'

He shrugged.

'Listen to me... Let him go to his grave thinking our bodegas will merge.'

'I would expect my father has another year,' Alejandro said. 'If he has surgery, it could give him even more than that. And I will tell you now, I don't intend to stay celibate that long.'

'You're such a bastard, Alejandro. It's always about sex with you.'

'Yes,' he said. 'And don't tell me you haven't benefited from our arrangement. I don't want marriage, Mariana. I don't want to play these family games any longer.' He removed her hand from his arm. 'Tell your family, and tell your friends, that we are over—because if you don't, I shall. I don't love you, Mariana.' He was blunt, but it was the truth, and nothing he hadn't said before. 'And you don't love me.'

'Which is exactly why we are perfect together.'

She ran a hand along his tense jaw and tried to push his thick black hair back from his eyes, but Alejandro removed her hand.

'You don't believe in love and I don't need it...'

She had an answer for everything, and, in many ways she was right. Alejandro did not believe in love. If it did exist, then he didn't want it. He'd seen what it had done to his father.

'Don't do this now,' she warned. 'You cannot do this to your father. It would devastate him.'

'Mariana, we're over.'

'Until the next woman you date gets stars in her eyes and doesn't know how to handle you. Until she starts wanting more. Then you'll realise how good we had it.'

She reached for his groin and he pushed her hand away. 'Go home,' he told her, peeling her off him as she tried to kiss him, her red lips too much for his dark mind tonight.

She smeared his face with her lipstick and then laughed as he pulled his head back.

'Go home,' he said again.

'I'll see you when you're lonely,' she sneered, before flouncing off. 'After the summer, maybe?'

'We're done.'

He stood in the semi-darkness, relieved that they were over but doubting himself as to the timing.

Alejandro knew he was—as Mariana had accused him of being—an emotional wasteland. He found life far easier to negotiate without emotions.

He worked hard and he partied harder.

And, while he did both vigorously, it was all with a certain air of dispassion that infuriated his lovers but impressed his associates and his peers.

*I don't care.* That was the message behind his dark brown eyes and his indifferent shrugs.

No one was allowed to get too close, and he rarely revealed his innermost thoughts.

His father though, was the opposite.

The news would indeed upset him.

Yet Mariana had spoken as if it might devastate him.

José Romero seemed rather more willing to lie down and die than fight at the moment, and Alejandro certainly didn't want to add to his malaise.

Alejandro could hear laughter and conversation wafting over from the fine dining restaurant in the main courtyard. He'd have to walk through it to get to his gated residence. But instead of heading for home he made his way to the front of the bodega and entered the rather exclusive Taberna Romero.

*'Hola!'* A waitress smiled a welcome, and so did a few cus-

tomers, but Alejandro just nodded—he was really not in the mood for polite conversation tonight.

The place was often packed, but it was especially so this Sunday night, when there were flamenco performers on stage. Glancing at the set list, he realised it was Eva performing.

The trouble with being at home, Alejandro thought as he slid into a seat in the booth reserved for the Romeros, was that there were rather too many exes.

Eva had been his first lover.

And that had been a *very* long time ago.

He heard the stamp of boots on the wooden stage and the tempo shifting as the lights dimmed further, but he barely looked up. Too many reminders tonight.

He could recall sitting backstage in Barcelona or Madrid as his mother performed—she'd long since outgrown smaller venues by then. He recalled, too, the accusations by his father when she came home...and then his dreadful depression when she no longer did.

His brother Sebastián and his sister Carmen loathed their mother with a passion, yet Alejandro could see his mother's side too.

If his father could just have been more accepting and understood her talent, her art...

And flamenco *was* an art.

He just couldn't bring himself to watch, so instead of looking at the stage he glanced around the *taberna*. It was mainly filled with locals, all looking forward to Eva performing, and there were several of her dance students in attendance.

And then he saw a woman who was definitely *not* a local.

It wasn't just her blonde hair that made her stand out, but the way she sat nervously, twiddling her hair, sipping wine, looking so out of place and just plain awkward. Her top was too tight, her hair had either been whipped by the wind or cut with a hand whisk, and he watched as she picked up a shot glass of *puré de guisantes* and sniffed it, as if trying to work out what it was.

She didn't quite hold her nose, but she knocked it back in one and then pulled such a face that he found he held his breath. Finally she gulped it down with a large sip of wine.

And then shivered.

Like a little dog shaking itself off.

And as her breasts moved her hair did too, and brought a rare smile to his features.

Next she tried to chase an olive with a fork, rather than pick it up with her fingers.

He saw the camera on the table beside her and realised that this was perhaps Emily Jacobs, the English woman who was here to do the photography and design for the new website.

He should go over and introduce himself, but he could not be bothered to make polite conversation tonight. Anyway, she looked miserable. She had now given up chasing reluctant olives, and looked as if she was about to leave just as the main act came on!

God, maybe he should have listened to Sebastián and used someone tried and trusted rather than go for the fresh slant recommended by Sophia…

But then she looked up.

Not at him.

She looked up to the stage.

He knew from the stamping, from the shouts of approval and from the dimming lights, that Eva was about to perform, and that she would be standing poised on the now-dark stage, but still he did not turn around.

Alejandro watched Ms Jacobs instead.

And he knew then that his much opposed decision to bring in an outsider had been the right one.

He watched as her expression shifted from weary to alert… how she sat up straighter in the hard wooden seat as the stage lights lifted and she witnessed for the first time true flamenco.

Her food was forgotten, her eyes wide and fixed on the dancer, her mouth open just a little. Her white shirt strained a little across the bust, and yet somehow her very plain outfit was subtly beautiful.

*She* was beautiful.

Gone was the slouch and the attempt to fade into the surroundings.

There was now an expression of rapture on her face that perhaps should have him turning to the stage and watching the performance.

Alejandro simply preferred watching her...

It was as close to magic as Emily had ever seen.

Her rushed journey to Jerez had proved incredibly long. There had been no Sophia nor her husband to greet her at Jerez Airport—just a man holding a sign bearing her name, who'd offered Sophia's apologies and given her an envelope.

The note had said that Sophia would catch up with her for breakfast tomorrow, but tonight she'd suggested Emily dine at the *taberna* and get a feel for the place. Also that Eva was performing.

Emily had had no idea what that meant.

She would by far have preferred to sit alone in the thankfully vacant housekeeper's apartment that she'd been shown to rather than venture out, but it would be for work.

More than that.

She'd been hungry.

As well as that, this was her new career—her long-awaited adventure. And so, before she'd changed her mind, she'd headed down to the *taberna*.

She'd asked for a table for one and then, a little overwhelmed by the menu, at the waitress's suggestion had ordered a selection of tapas.

A rather delicate selection had arrived, which hadn't quite matched her ravenous appetite.

There'd been a few guys quietly strumming guitars on

stage, and the atmosphere had been friendly, but sitting alone eating dishes best shared she'd felt awkward and exposed.

Emily had just given up on the tapas and had been reaching for her camera, ready to leave…when the magic had started to happen.

The stage had gone dark and Emily had looked up as the noisy venue had hushed. Either her eyes had become accustomed to it, or it was a trick of the lighting, but she could just make out the silhouette of a woman, centre stage, one arm raised above her head. And as the lights lifted Emily saw the woman's other arm moving slowly, making gentle waves, as if with a life of its own.

*This must be Eva*, she quickly realised. The performer Sophia had suggested she come to the *taberna* to watch.

Eva was stunning.

Her black curls were pinned up, her make-up dramatic and her neck taut and slender. Her dress was the same vibrant yellow as rape fields in summer, the fabric not unlike flowers moving in the wind. Emily sat high on her seat to get a better look, utterly transfixed as Eva commenced a slow, sensual dance.

It was spellbinding.

Eva clapped, making a sharp noise with the strike of her hand, and then she beat out the tempo with her black shoes and the men matched it with their music.

Eva smiled and growled and bared her teeth, portraying every emotion as she moved, demanding that the musicians match her changing moods.

The dancing pushed them on.

It was incredible.

There was nothing Emily could do but watch as Eva's elegant body and strong gestures held the entire room.

The noise of her shoes, the thunder of the men's boots and the increasing tempo from the guitars, as well as the percussion instruments two of the men held between their thighs, seemed to be building towards a crescendo.

Yet, they continued on.

Eva's claps were like whips being cracked, precise and demanding, and then suddenly more muted.

The men clapped too, now, as if urging her to new limits, attempting to exhaust her. And yet she refused to relent, striking the stage so fast that Emily felt as if she were caught in a sudden hailstorm, struck by a power she could never hope to override.

How, Emily begged herself, had she not known this world existed?

She wanted to move, to get up and dance as some of the customers were doing. She wanted to shout out and cheer like the other patrons. She could feel herself smiling, even taking a sip of her wine and raising her glass in appreciation at one point.

It was hypnotic, incredible… But then, as a woman stood up from a table to get closer to the stage, Emily briefly turned, and although the *taberna* continued to heave with music and dance, and the music poured forth, for Emily it all seemed to pause.

He stopped her with his gaze.

He wore a dark suit.

Some other patrons did too, but they were end-of-work-day suits, with jackets off, shirtsleeves rolled up.

Casual.

This man was far from that.

His tie was loosened, his jaw unshaven, and yet he was utterly immaculate.

And he was bold with his dark eyes.

Emily had never been looked at like that before.

Had never looked back at another person with such intensity in her entire life.

It truly felt as if it would be entirely appropriate for him to walk over to her right this moment, or for him to beckon her to him.

She sat there on the hard wooden chair, feeling the thunder of boots reverberating from the stage, and the patrons, but they were tiny jolts compared to the sheer effect of this man.

The music returned—it had never left—and her senses also

returned, as if a long drink was being poured, filling her from her thighs upwards, low, low in her stomach—which she held in. Not just because she all too often held it in—he couldn't see that anyway—simply because it was clenched and guarded against the heat of his stare. And still he filled her senses as the music played on. She could feel her breasts grow heavy in her bra, feel her throat too tense even to swallow.

And as for her mouth…

It felt too big for her face…her lips out of position. And without a word being spoken, with barely a moment between them, she was more turned on than she had ever been in her life.

It was the music, she told herself, dragging her eyes from his face. Surely it was the music or the effects from the wine?

Yet the carafe on her table was still almost full, she realised at a glance, trying to fathom what was taking place.

It was his beauty, she told herself as she reached for that final olive, stabbing it with a little fork and missing.

*Damn.*

She dipped some bread in oil and tried to pretend she could not feel a pulse where she'd thought none existed.

It startled her—to be in public and for the first time turned on. So much so that she wanted to dash to the loo…to escape. To flee from the rush of unfamiliar sensations and the intensity of a man she hadn't even met.

Emily simply reverted to type…

And fled.

*Mujeres*, it said on the door. There was a little picture of a woman in a flamenco dress, and Emily was grateful for it, because second language skills were not at the forefront of her mind at the moment.

It was empty—thank goodness.

Of course they were all still watching Eva perform.

She could hear the shouts and the music. It was the music that was affecting her so strongly, Emily told herself as she stood in the very pretty ladies' room.

There were huge mirrors on the walls with velvet chairs placed in front of them, as if it were some kind of dressing room. Emily stood there for a moment, taking in not so much the surroundings but her own reflection.

She wore the same black trousers and thin shirt that she'd left the apartment in.

That she'd left England in, come to that.

The same black court shoes…

Her hair was tangled and tied up, and her face, as always, was completely devoid of make-up.

Yet she was flushed.

Her lips were rosy, as if she'd been chewing them.

Her nipples were showing through her shirt.

And as she sat on a seat she noticed her dilated pupils and moist eyes, and felt as if something had been unleashed.

*It has to be the music*, she told herself.

Of course it was.

She kept trying to replay that second when everything had somehow shifted.

When the lights had dimmed?

Or was it when the clapping had started?

The stamping of boots, perhaps?

When she'd locked eyes with him?

The door opened and, ridiculously, she almost expected it to be the man whose eyes she'd locked with. Quickly she told herself she wasn't thinking straight—she was surely sleep-deprived, jet-lagged…

Sex-starved.

She laughed out loud at that.

Oddly, it didn't seem to be out of place, because the young woman who now came in laughed also.

'*Ella es brillante, ¿no?*'—'*She's brilliant, isn't she?*' the lady said, taking a seat beside Emily and rearranging her rather spectacular bust.

'*Sí,*' Emily agreed, grateful that she understood what had been said, but not quite brave enough to respond in Spanish. 'I've never seen anything like it…' Her voice trailed off, but it didn't matter.

'She is the best.' The woman looked down at her lovely bust and, happy with her cleavage, took some lipstick from her purse. 'I go to her workshop.'

'Do you?'

'We come here for practice some days…' She caught Emily's eyes in the mirror. 'Are you English?'

Emily nodded, feeling incredibly drab beside this gorgeous, confident woman.

'I'm Stella.'

'Emily.'

'And are you here for a holiday?'

'For work,' Emily said, and yet it felt as if she was lying.

It felt as if she was here on an adventure.

An adventure of her own.

But then common sense returned.

'Damn!' she said suddenly, and saw the woman start. 'Sorry. I left my camera on the table.'

'No problem.'

She felt a little more composed as she walked out. Eva had stopped performing, or was taking a break, because the music was softer now and the lights had gone back on.

And her seat was taken.

The tapas and wine had been cleared away and at her table for one now sat a carefree group of four. There was no handbag—and, worse, there was no camera.

There was a moment of panic—she'd been careless enough to lose her possessions on her first night in Spain—but then she felt an odd calm…a quiet certainty that *he* wouldn't have allowed that to happen…and she turned her head to the mysterious stranger.

There were her things. On the table where he sat.

She felt again that curious calm as, with a slight gesture of his head, he beckoned her over.

And, as easily as that, Emily went.

# CHAPTER THREE

'EMILY…' HE WAS POLITE, and thankfully he missed how startled she was that he knew her name because he moved to stand as she joined him. 'Sophia said that you were arriving today.'

It dawned on her then that he must be one of the brothers as he gestured for her to take a seat at his table.

No hard chair for a Romero, she thought as she took her place in a red velvet booth. And somehow, she managed to play it not cool—that would have been impossible with blood so hot it bubbled through her veins like lava—but at least she managed to appear outwardly poised.

'I'm Alejandro,' he said.

'The middle one?' she checked, trying to remember the little she knew of the Romero siblings.

'The reasonable one.'

'Good to know.'

'At least in comparison to the other two.'

She smiled. 'Sebastián and Carmen?'

'Sí.' he nodded. 'Would you like a drink?'

'I've had one,' Emily said. 'Or two…' She put her hands up to her cheeks, as if the wine was to blame for the flush to her face and neck.

He gestured to her camera and bag. 'The waitress brought your things over—she hadn't realised you were staff.'

'I didn't tell her…' Her hands reached for her beloved camera. 'For a second I thought I'd lost this.'

'No.' He shook his head. 'That wouldn't happen in here. Although it's a nice camera.'

'It's a bit...' She hesitated. 'Well, it felt a bit extravagant at the time.'

'But it's for your work.'

'Yes, but when I bought this it was really no more than a hobby.' She rolled her eyes. 'An expensive one. Almost all my baggage allowance was taken up with photographic equipment...'

Alejandro frowned just a little and it dawned on Emily that the Romeros, with their yachts and private jets, had probably never heard of a pesky little thing like baggage allowance.

'Well, you can always use this table if you need to be here to get photos of the stage or whatever.'

'Thank you.'

He was polite...almost formal. It was as if that odd moment when they'd stared at the other, when they'd locked gazes, hadn't happened. And really nothing *had* happened—just a look.

A look during which presumably he'd guessed the pale woman with a camera was his new employee.

It was her own mind that had gone wild.

He spoke with a rich Spanish accent. And, although perhaps it was the brighter lights as the stage was rearranged, his features demanded scrutiny. His eyes, framed perfectly with dark arched brows, were every shade of brown and vividly revealed, because the whites of his eyes were the clearest she had ever seen. His mouth was pale and his lips were full, and she saw a smear of red lipstick on one side of his mouth...

Why did that last detail sting?

It was no business of hers who he'd been kissing—and anyway, even if he wasn't her boss, Alejandro Romero was completely out of her league. She was only sitting with him because she was staff.

He sat back a little, holding his glass loosely with long fingers as he made polite conversation. 'How was your trip here?'

She thought back to a few hours ago, and it felt like light years away. 'It was fine…well, a bit rushed.'

He just looked at her.

'There was a long wait in Madrid for my flight to Jerez…'

'There are a lot more direct flights from Seville.'

'Really?'

'It's an easier route. I'm surprised Sophia didn't arrange that.'

'I booked my own flights.'

'That's right—I know she's been unwell. Was she able to meet you?'

'No.'

'So you haven't been shown around?'

'Not yet,' Emily said, as if it didn't matter—as if she hadn't felt terrified and alone as she'd sat in the apartment.

And now here she sat in a *taberna*, face to face with the most stunning man.

Both had been overwhelming—though the latter was nicely so.

'So where are you staying?' he asked. 'In Plaza de Santiago?'

'No, I'm staying here…on the property,' Emily told him. 'Apparently the usual accommodation is unavailable, so I'm in the housekeeper's apartment.'

'We're neighbours, then…'

'Neighbours?'

'The residence here is mine.'

'Oh…'

Gosh, she'd glimpsed the beautiful building behind huge arched iron gates, never for a second thinking it might be somebody's home.

'Usually the staff stay in one of our residences in the *plaza*,' Alejandro said, and then he gestured to the stage. 'But the flamenco festival is about to commence, and your accommodation must have been booked out by mistake.'

'So there isn't usually live entertainment?' Emily asked. 'This is just for the festival?'

'Oh, no, there's always live entertainment,' he said. 'But it's rare that Eva performs.'

'She's incredible.'

'Indeed… There's generally a few performances in the afternoons, but with the festival coming up there will be a lot more.' He looked at her then. 'At night, the list is more informal. Spontaneous.' He looked towards the stage. 'It looks as if some of Eva's students are about to perform.'

'I didn't realise just how big flamenco was here,' Emily admitted. 'I mean, I thought it was…' Her voice trailed off; she was not sure he would appreciate how little she knew.

'Thought what?' he prompted.

'That it was something just put on for the tourists.'

'Oh, no.' He seemed to take no offence at her naivety. Clearly he had heard it many times before. 'They love the traditions here,' he explained. 'There are a lot of *peñas*…'

'*Peñas?*' Emily checked.

'It's a local term. Kind of…' he sought a translation for her '…a flamenco club where *aficionados* go.'

'*Aficionados?*' she repeated, and then worked out what he meant without explanation. 'Enthusiasts?'

He nodded.

'And are you one?'

'Not particularly,' he said.

He looked up as a waitress came over to top up his glass and shook his head. Emily had the feeling he was about to go, but then he looked at her.

'Have you tasted our sherry?'

'No,' she admitted. 'I did try to get hold of some, but I live in a small village and…'

'It's fine.' He spoke in rapid Spanish to the waitress and soon a bottle was brought over, and also a cheese board.

But it was the bottle that held her gaze.

She'd seen it online, of course, but the photos hadn't captured its beauty.

*Yes, beauty.*

Its glass was black and the cork was sealed with an amber resin that trickled down the side of the neck like melted candle wax.

It was a work of art in itself—so much so that she picked it up and read the label.

The words *Bodega Romero* were branded into the glass, and even the label itself was stunning.

At first glance it looked like a flower—an orange poppy, perhaps, with a dark centre—but on closer inspection she saw it was a photo of a flamenco dancer. The orange was the ruffles of her dress, the black centre her slick black hair in a bun...

'It's gorgeous,' she said, and then put the bottle down, watching his long fingers skilfully deal with the seal and the cork. She was nervous, but nicely so.

*'Oloroso,'* he said. 'It is probably the sherry you are more used to.'

'I'm not a big sherry drinker. I...' She hesitated, deciding it would be rude to say that she couldn't stand the stuff. 'Well, I'm not really a drinker.'

'It's fine,' he said again. 'Did you like the tapas?'

'Yes,' Emily said politely. 'They were delicious.'

'All of them?'

She felt her lips pinch on a smile at the doubt in his voice and realised he'd possibly seen her before she'd seen him.

'Not the pea puree in a shot glass...' She pulled a face. 'I'm sure they were beautifully prepared,' she added hurriedly. 'I just don't like peas...especially when they've been liquefied.'

'So why did you drink it?' he asked as he dealt with the bottle's seal.

'It's rude not to clear your plate.'

'The chef's not that sensitive.' He smiled a lazy smile and his teeth were as dazzling as the whites of his eyes.

God, he was gorgeous—and it wasn't just that he was easily the best-looking man she'd ever seen. Despite the sheer thrill of him, she felt a rare but certain sense of ease in his presence.

His movements were smooth as he poured the drink and conversation flowed just as easily.

'Did you see the little silver spoon on your plate?'

'Yes.'

'It's there so that you can taste a little, then decide.'

'I'll remember that in the future.'

'Good.'

She wanted to taste just a little, Emily thought as she looked at that lipstick-smeared mouth and wondered what it might be like to be kissed by him.

It was a brief thought.

A pointless one.

He was completely out of her league and that wasn't being self-effacing—Emily was simply being real. This was a tasting—a chance to test the product—nothing else.

It was just this tiny part of her mind that was raising objections… Saying this was something else.

Their eyes locked again as he raised his glass. *'Salude!'* he said.

'Cheers.' Emily smiled and, knowing he was watching her as she took her first sip of Romero sherry, felt terribly aware of her own mouth. In the oddest way, she actually wondered if the glass might miss her lips.

He must think her a nervous wreck, Emily was sure, because it took her two attempts to get the glass there, interspersed with nervous giggles.

Alejandro did not think her a nervous wreck. Just nervous, shy, and—unlike the sherry—very sweet.

He watched her take a sip, and her blue eyes closed as she held it in her mouth. Alejandro, who spent a lot of his life introducing sherry in tastings, found himself turned on by what should be just the usual.

She swallowed, and then opened her eyes, and out bobbed the tip of her pink tongue.

'Wow!' she said, and then began to take another taste, but halted herself as the aftertaste hit. 'Oh…' She smiled at him. 'Perhaps I do like sherry after all.'

'Or you're just being polite?'

'It's gorgeous,' she said. 'Though I have no idea about wines and such, so please don't ask me to describe its taste on the website.'

'Don't worry—that part's already written. This is a full-bodied sherry.'

Why did everything sound mildly inappropriate tonight? He found that he was fighting not to glance down to her rather full-bodied breasts.

Instead, he looked at what she was holding in her hands— the amber resin from the seal.

'You get to keep that.'

Emily looked up.

'It's tradition,' he said.

'Oh…' She looked at the beautiful amber resin she held between her fingers and could see the trapped wing of a butterfly within. It was a little like the way she felt…

The way she'd always felt.

Trapped by her own shyness.

Simply unable to fly.

'Now, cheese,' he said. 'Assuming you like cheese?'

'I do,' she agreed and, slipping the seal into her bag, she watched as he sliced slivers of cheese and gestured for her to take up a fork.

She hesitated. 'Actually, I don't like goats' cheese…'

'Okay.' He didn't even look up from the cheese he was slicing.

He did not know just how momentous a thing it was for Emily to state her preference.

'What about ewes' milk?'

'I don't know,' she admitted. 'It sounds dreadful, but…'

'It's soft…sweeter…'

Oh, 'the usual' was proving so much more difficult tonight.

She was telling him she was, in fact, starving, and that the tapas hadn't really sufficed.

'I didn't have time for breakfast, and there was nothing much left on the trolley.'

'The trolley?'

'On my flight,' she said, smearing creamy cheese over a delicate cracker. 'By the time they got to me all the sandwiches had gone.'

'Oh.'

It wasn't a problem he'd come across on the Romero private jet, or when he travelled first class, but the roll of her eyes as she told him her tale made him smile.

'Your business is new?' he asked.

'Yes. I've always been into photography, and when I was studying at university, there was a "How to develop a website" module. But…' She glanced up, aware she wasn't being very coherent. 'I didn't finish my degree.'

He nodded.

'Just so you know…'

'I didn't go through your CV, Emily. Sophia recommended you. We want the new website to be fresh and different…to better bring our product to the world,' Alejandro said. 'I suggested we get an outsider in and Sebastián agreed. Sophia showed us your work. I saw how you managed to make that dump of a cottage look quaint.'

Emily bristled at the put-down and wondered what to say—if anything. 'That was my home,' she said.

'Was?' he checked, not appearing even remotely embarrassed.

Possibly he didn't know that the word 'dump' was so offensive? she decided, giving him the benefit of the doubt.

'Yes.' She gave him a tight smile, wishing his question wasn't so pertinent.

This morning she'd left her home of five years, and she'd done so with barely a backward glance. Oh, she'd have to return and properly collect her things, but shouldn't it at least have hurt a little more?

For the first time the conversation stalled and, glancing around, she saw that the *taberna* was starting to empty.

A couple of the waiters were looking over at them.

Some of the patrons too.

Perhaps he noticed the same. 'I'm going to head off,' Alejandro said.

'And me,' Emily responded without thinking, and in rusty Spanish she asked the waitress for the bill for her tapas and wine.

'It's taken care of,' Alejandro told her. 'Dine here whenever you please. The staff will know who you are now. If there's someone new on, just let them know you work here.'

'Thank you.'

It was only as she stood that she felt a little awkward, realising they would be walking out together.

She put her camera over her shoulder and picked up her bag. And it really was awkward, because everyone seemed to want to farewell him as he walked out. As he stopped to talk to a couple, Emily felt it better that she leave him to it rather than stand there.

She left the *taberna* and made her way to the courtyard. She'd been too nervous to really notice it on her way to the *taberna*, but now, with most of the diners gone, she saw its beauty. To one side there were the cellars, but the courtyard itself was entrancing. Trees were delicately lit with fairy lights and laden

with ripe oranges, their fragrance sweet as she passed. There
was a rustic, elegant beauty to the place, and the lightly sanded
ground softened her footsteps as she approached the arched
gates—only to find them locked.

'Damn,' she muttered, wondering if she should go back and
ask one of the bar staff for assistance, and feeling stupid for
getting locked out on her first night.

'You have to go around to the back and sign in with Security after midnight.'

Alejandro had almost caught her up and called to her from
across the courtyard.

'I see.'

'Unless,' he added, 'you're me.'

'Fine,' she said, and clipped off in shoes that were starting to hurt.

'Emily, wait.'

Her awkwardness seemed to mildly amuse him.

'I was teasing. I'm not going to make you walk around.'

He pressed in a code and the gate clicked open. He pro-
ceeded to tell her the numbers as they headed through what
must be his private grounds.

'I won't remember them,' Emily said, although she was
grateful for the reprieve from walking further tonight.

'Why would you forget?'

'Because I'm dreadful with numbers.'

'But there are only four of them!'

He was taller than she'd realised. It felt a little like walking beside the headmaster as he asked her to repeat the code
he'd just told her.

'I've already forgotten,' Emily admitted.

'Seriously?'

'I honestly have.'

They were climbing some steps, beautiful mosaic steps
that led to more gorgeous arched gates, where they would
part company.

He smelt incredible. His cologne was the sort that might make you close your eyes if you inhaled it in the perfume section of a department store. You'd start sniffing, trying to follow the delectable scent, just so you could douse your wrists in luxury for a while. It was the sort where you might have to turn to a complete stranger and ask what on earth they were wearing, because it was surely the most perfect scent in the world.

It was musky, but not heavy.

Citrussy, yet not any kind of citrus she knew.

And so fresh it served as a reminder that she'd been up since five, and on trains and planes, and…

Not so fresh.

How, at five minutes after midnight, did he look as if he were about to head for the office rather than bed?

Apart from the fading smear of lipstick and the heavy growth on his chin…

God, he was a cross between a bandit and the cleanest man she had ever seen.

And just so sexy.

And it was fun—just that—to talk to him, to stand and make idle, silly talk on this, her first night of new adventure. Safe in the knowledge that someone as completely divine as he, was surely not wanting anything of her.

Now she must go.

She would pull the massive key from her tiny bag and take her sore and no doubt swollen feet to bed for the night.

Except he was so nice to speak to…

And he seemed in no rush to go…

'Just use this entrance in future.'

'Okay.' She nodded. 'Thank you.'

'Can you remember the code now?'

'I've had a couple of sherries,' Emily said, but chose not to add that it wasn't the fortified wine making her feel a little dizzy.

She'd never known attraction before—at least nothing so

intense. And she was so down on herself that it didn't enter her head that the feeling might be mutual.

'Come on—try and remember.'

'Four…?' She grimaced as she guessed.

'There's no four.' He gave her a look, a very deep and serious look that made her think, were he a doctor, she'd be terrified of his verdict. But in the periphery of her vision she could see his lips tilt slightly in a smile. And they weren't so pale now…they were a dark and very beautiful pink.

*'Think,'* those gorgeous lips said.

'Five?'

'Jesus!' He laughed. 'You really have no short-term memory.'

'Not when—' She stopped, deciding it would be foolish, at best, to tell him her lack of focus was entirely due to the scent in her nostrils and the absolute concentration it was taking to keep her hands at her sides, rather than…

Rather than what?

She didn't even want to examine that question—not with him so close.

It was a question to ponder later—only he still seemed in no rush to go, and he lounged against the iron gates and carried on talking.

'If you want to take flamenco lessons,' Alejandro said, 'Eva would be a good teacher for you.'

'Lessons?' Emily let out a nervous laugh. 'Gosh, no.'

It had never entered her head. Only Alejandro didn't join in with her smile or her burst of laughter.

It was, she realised, an actual suggestion.

He had no idea what a klutz she was.

'I don't think so.'

'You might like it. And as well as that…'

Alejandro paused. He had been about to say that he would love to see her practising, for Eva brought her pupils over to the courtyard or the *taberna* some evenings…

How he would love to see her ripe body move...

He held back.

This was an odd situation for Alejandro. Not so much the walking up the steps with a beautiful woman he'd met at the *taberna*. More that she would be turning left and he would be turning right, going through the gates to his own residence.

'As well as that...?' Emily checked.

Her blue eyes met his, yet he could not read her, and Alejandro was most unused to that. There was an energy between them—so much so that when he'd seen the staff and patrons looking their way he'd rather abruptly ended the night.

At least, he'd ended it for public consumption.

But now they were alone, and she was unreadable, only a little bold, and there was a certain reticence to her as if she did not know how to conclude the night.

Usually it would be with a kiss.

Usually, with an attraction so palpable, they would be tearing at each other's clothes by now.

But, he reminded himself, she was to be working here, and that might make things messy.

More than that, he still could not quite read those bright blue eyes.

And so he didn't tell her what he'd been about to say and went for the safer option instead. 'It might help you get a feel for the place. Flamenco is a way of life here.'

'Then I'll think about it.' She gave him a smile. 'Goodnight.' She dug in her purse to retrieve the key, then clearly remembered where she was, and felt that she should make some effort. 'Rather, *buenas noches.*'

'Goodnight, Emily,' he responded in English, pushing open the heavy gate. She wasn't sure if it was a little rebuke as to how dreadful her rusty Spanish was, but as she turned to the door he added, *'Que tengas dulces sueños.'*

Emily didn't translate it—she just looked at her shaky hands as she heard the gate close behind him. She walked away and turned the key in the apartment door and let herself in, hearing his footsteps as he walked to his own residence.

It wasn't so much a relief to close the door. It felt more as if she'd achieved an impossible feat.

One more second and she'd possibly have been an English girl behaving badly abroad.

And yet he'd done nothing…said nothing untoward. He'd been utterly polite and nice.

With an edge.

There had been a sharp sensual edge to him that she'd never glimpsed in another, let alone herself.

Taking her shoes off provided no relief—even though it should have, given that her feet had been agony since Heathrow.

Even taking her bra off did not elicit the usual exhalation of pleasure. Her breasts felt as constricted as if she was still wearing it, and her knickers were damp as she slid them off.

She was more aware of her body than she'd ever been.

The bathroom was white, with a huge dome-shaped showerhead that she hurried to stand under. And it was so nice that she didn't even have to dig through her suitcase to find toiletries—they were all there on display, in striking cut glass bottles that she was careful not to drop.

She opened one of the stoppers and took a breath of body wash. But, as decadent and delicious as it was, the scent wasn't his.

Emily washed quickly and wrapped herself in a very soft towel. And then, trying to ignore her thrumming body, she took herself to a very vast bed, with white sheets tucked so tightly in it took her a moment to realise she wasn't under the top one.

*Gosh.*

She'd left the shutters open earlier, and the sound from outside was one of a breezy cool night and a city as close to asleep as the centre of a city ever came. She got up to close them, but then changed her mind and left them. She found the jagged piece of amber resin and placed it by her bedside light. She gazed at it as she lay there, naked in bed for the first time in her life.

*Let me out*, the little butterfly wing seemed to say.

*Not yet*, Emily thought. Because her holiday romance had its allocated slot in six weeks' time… And she doubted it would be with anyone as thrilling or beautiful as Alejandro Romero.

He was probably like that with everyone, Emily warned herself. He no doubt smiled that decadent smile to all and sundry. She thought of the lipstick on the edge of his mouth. Although it had faded by the end of the night, some had remained, as if serving as a warning.

Alejandro had surely just been being polite to a newcomer, Emily decided, confused by the tears suddenly in her eyes. But it was more than a little sad that at the age of twenty-six, without a touch or a kiss, somehow this had been the most wonderful night of her life.

Only as she started to drift off did she allow herself to dwell on his words.

'*Que tengas dulces sueños.*'—'*Have sweet dreams.*'
Emily dared not.

# CHAPTER FOUR

EVEN IN HER very unfamiliar surroundings, Emily woke to a familiar headspace.

Common sense had returned, and all attempts at flights of fancy had been safely battened down.

Her new boss had simply been being perfectly nice.

Selecting a pale grey top to go with a fresh pair of black trousers—more stretchy ones that looked as if they had a belt and pockets but were really just yoga pants in disguise—she dressed, then slipped on some comfortable flats.

After tying her hair back in a low ponytail she was ready to face the day, and slipped out of the apartment with her camera.

It was early, but she wanted to get a feel for the place while it was quiet.

Gosh, it was gorgeous.

She took a couple of shots of the courtyard, and then looked over at a row of archways and saw black barrels, neatly stacked. But really it was the light that caught her attention. She took a few more shots, capturing the morning sun streaming through the high, round, stained glass windows in each archway.

Making her way down past the archways, she saw that there were many of them, and it dawned on her just how immense and magnificent the bodega was.

And then she saw him.

Alejandro.

She had thought he would be in an office, or still sleeping, but he was there, in an archway, leaning over a barrel.

She took a few shots of him.

'Hey!' Alejandro said, straightening up.

'Sorry,' Emily said. 'I was just...' She felt as if she'd been caught staring. 'I wanted some natural shots.'

'Don't be sorry.' He shrugged. 'It's good that you're straight on to it. We want the website up and running as soon as we can. But it has to be right...'

'The light's beautiful in here.'

'And brief,' he said. 'In summer that's important, or it would get far too hot, but by eight the sun has moved on and internal lights come on for the tastings.'

'So, this is where the product is stored...?'

'And aged.' He nodded. 'The barrels are moved...rotated.'

'Is that what you were doing?'

He laughed.

'What's so funny?'

'I would like to say yes, but the truth is I was looking for a lost earring.'

'Oh.'

Last night she had thought he looked ready for work. This morning she saw him when he actually was.

His jaw was clean-shaven, his hair still damp, and for a moment she wished, honestly, that she was the woman whose earring he looked for.

Ridiculous!

She wasn't out of practice—she'd never even got as far as practising.

'Hola!'

Emily turned and saw the elusive Sophia, elegant in white. She felt fat and frumpy and just so unglamorous.

'I am so sorry about yesterday. My ankles...' Sophia turned to Alejandro. 'What are you doing in the bodega?' she asked him. 'I was going to give Emily a tour—I certainly didn't expect you to.' She turned to Emily. 'I really am sorry I wasn't there to greet you. But I've been ordered to rest, so you only have me for today.' She rolled her eyes. 'I have the most brilliant nanny, but unfortunately she can't do my bedrest for me.'

'You have a son?' Emily checked, but she knew because she'd seen pictures of him on social media. 'Pedro?'

'That's right—this little one is my second.' Sophia said, affectionately touching her bump. 'Pedro is going to be so jealous…'

'If you're going to talk babies,' Alejandro cut in, 'I am out of here. Sophia, can you see that Emily has a laptop and a phone?'

'I have my own…'

'Perhaps,' he said, 'but for your work here…' He looked over to Sophia. 'I'll leave it to you to explain.'

'Of course.' Sophia nodded. 'Actually, I'll go and get the laptop and files now. Perhaps we can have breakfast out here, Emily?'

'Sure.'

Sophia clipped off, in heels that defied her advanced pregnancy, but surprisingly for Emily, despite his clear declaration just a moment ago that he was leaving, Alejandro didn't.

'How are you?' he asked.

'Very well, thank you,' she replied rather formally. 'I enjoyed the tasting.'

'That's good,' he responded.

All the ease of last night seemed to have left them, and to Emily it felt like proof that she'd simply misread things. She felt embarrassed at the speed of her attraction to the first good-looking man to pay her attention—like some over-eager fangirl.

Only that wasn't quite true.

There had been good-looking guests at the B&B—though admittedly not as divine as Alejandro. And in her time at university she'd started to socialise and had even been chatted up a few times…

It was her reaction to *him* that bewildered her.

Desperate for something to say, she cast her gaze around and caught a glint of light between two heavy barrels.

'There it is.'

'What?'

'The earring,' she said, getting down on the sandy floor to retrieve it, relieved to have something to do rather than standing there awkwardly.

Only possibly it wasn't her best angle as, bottom in the air, she stretched her arm between the barrels.

'Got it...'

He offered his hand to help her up, but Emily chose to lean on one of the barrels. She looked at the gorgeous chandelier earring made of diamonds for a moment, and then looked back at him.

He said nothing, just held out a hand for the earring, and she dropped it into his palm, trying to avoid contact.

'Thank you,' he said, and pocketed it. His voice was gravelly, and he cleared his throat and looked straight at her. 'What are we going to do, Emily?' he asked.

She was back in the path of his chocolate gaze and it simply melted her.

'I don't know,' she responded.

It was barely seven in the morning and she felt as turned on as she had last night, as full of desire as she had last night, but with one difference...

It was a very mutual desire.

Perhaps she only recognised it in him because she'd never seen it in another until now—pure, naked lust, aimed in her direction.

Nothing was said, their bodies did not touch, and there was no word she could think of to define the odd silence that filled the still space.

'Come here,' he said.

She took a step towards him and his gorgeous scent drew her another step closer.

* * *

'I wish I'd kissed you last night,' he said. 'I couldn't read you, though.'

And that was rare for Alejandro. He could feel their desire, he had seen she was turned on and felt the sensual swirl of the air, yet her eyes were darting and nervous, as if she was scared of something as nice as kissing.

Light fell on her face from the stained-glass window. 'You're gorgeous.'

'I'm really not,' Emily said.

'Oh, you really are.' He seemed to think about her words for a moment. 'Why would you say that?'

'Say what?'

'Why would you put yourself down? I gave you a compliment.'

She didn't know how to accept one, though. There really hadn't been many.

'You're gorgeous,' he repeated.

'Thank you,' she said, her cheeks flaming, and then she added, 'So are you.'

'Thank you,' he said. 'For the record, I never get involved with anyone at work…'

'Liar…' She smiled.

'No!' He shook his head, but then must have reconsidered that statement. 'Oh, Sophia and I were an item ages ago, long before she worked for me.'

Oh, God! He was so worldly, and he was so confident, and everything she was not.

'But tonight,' Alejandro said, 'perhaps we…?'

She could take it no more. She raised herself onto tiptoe and placed her lips on his, just for a second, for one tiny taste.

'Hey!'

He pulled back and she stood there, mortified by her own boldness and appalled at how she had misread things. But as she turned to flee, she felt his hands still on her hips, and it took her a second to register that he was smiling.

'I was going to say,' he said, 'that tonight perhaps we could meet and address things.'

It was not said in chastisement, because his tongue had bobbed out and tasted the place where her lips had been. 'However, I can't let you go after that...'

He lowered his head and his mouth came down on hers. Then he prised her lips open with his tongue.

It was a kiss she had hoped existed.

A kiss so thorough that she moaned into his mouth.

A kiss that just blocked out the sun and made the floor feel absent—as if she were floating.

This was how a kiss should be. She knew it because she'd found out how it felt to crave and to be craved.

His hands pressed into her bottom. His palms were hot through the fabric, and then decisive as he pulled her into his groin. The length and hardness of him pressed into her soft stomach felt indecent. Deliciously indecent and something she ached to explore.

His mouth moved to her neck and she was panting, a little dizzy as his hands slipped under her thin top.

There wasn't time to suck in her stomach—there wasn't even any thought that she ought to suck in her stomach. His hands were giving her flesh a light tickle on their way up to the underside of her breast...

'I love your breasts,' he said into her neck. 'I am going to love your breasts.'

And Emily loved his words, for they promised there would be more of this later.

He stroked her nipples through the lace of her bra and his lips were softer now, gliding back down, and she was grateful for his control. Especially when she heard the distant sound of footsteps, hating the sound of them, and they both pulled back.

For the first time in her life Emily had to make herself decent, pulling down her top. Even if it had been only a kiss, it was her first real one.

She felt as if they might have had sex against the barrels. As if, without his control, they jolly well could have.

'*Discreción...*' he warned, as if this was all new to him too.

'Still here?' Sophia said to Alejandro, and then she looked down and gave Emily a rather startled look.

Emily soon saw why—there was sawdust on her knees.

'Emily just found Mariana's earring...' said Alejandro.

'Oh!' Sophia said and then laughed as if at her own private joke—because *as if* the very shy and awkward Emily would be on her knees with Alejandro! 'Just as well. Mariana has just texted me, insisting that it be found.'

'See that she gets it.'

He handed the earring to Sophia, who replied in Spanish with a smirk, 'You have a very demanding fiancée, Alejandro.'

Unfortunately for Emily, she understood what had just been said.

Fiancée?

He was *engaged*!

Emily was still reeling from their kiss, and was now appalled by this new revelation—not that Sophia noticed.

'Breakfast?' she suggested.

'Of course,' Emily said, unable to look at Alejandro, her lips pinching together as they walked out to a courtyard table.

Just before Alejandro headed off Sophia told him she would take Emily to the vineyards that afternoon.

'I'll take her,' he said. 'You've already done enough by coming in this morning. You really need to get those feet up.'

'I know. They're like balloons.'

They really were not, Emily thought as she and Sophia took a seat at the table. What on earth would Alejandro say if he saw her feet, still swollen from the flight yesterday?

And then she smarted. No, he would not be seeing hers.

The courtyard was the perfect place to take breakfast,

scented with the Seville orange trees, which were ripe with lush fruit, but Emily was too upset by what she'd just heard to really appreciate the gorgeous surroundings.

Sophia ordered hot chocolate and churros, and Emily said she would like the same.

She was frantically trying to turn her mind to work as Sophia went through the new phone and laptop with her, and explained that all her work must take place on these devices. The images she took inside the bodega over the next six weeks all belonged to the Romeros—they were dealing with liquid gold after all.

'Any new programs you need just speak with IT, but it's better for now that it's all on here.'

'Sure.'

The chocolate was thick and sweet and felt almost *necessary*—like hot sugary tea after a shock.

And Emily *was* shocked.

Not just that Alejandro was engaged to another woman, more at her own reckless behaviour. This was the biggest career break of her life, and yet there she'd been wrapped around Alejandro.

Sure, she wanted fun and romance—but after her six-week tenure, not twelve hours after landing.

And yet even if it would never be repeated, and should never have taken place, she did not know how to regret it, for it felt as if she'd glimpsed bliss.

'How is the accommodation?' Sophia asked as more hot chocolate was served.

'Wonderful!' Emily nodded. 'Although I admit, I was worried I was going to be sharing with the housekeeper...'

'God, we wouldn't do that to you! It's always vacant. Alejandro prefers that his staff live out. And it's just as well that they do—they would need to bleach their eyes otherwise.' Perhaps she saw Emily's frown. 'He has many lovers,' she explained.

'My mistake…' Emily did her best to sound casual '…but I thought you just said he was engaged.'

'Not formally engaged.' She rolled her eyes and made a wavering gesture with her hand. 'They're very on-off. He does what he chooses while Mariana waits impatiently in the wings. Or should I say soars overhead like a vulture, waiting for it to go wrong—as it invariably does…'

She pulled up a map onscreen that showed Emily the sherry triangle and the vineyards she would be going to visit today. A lot of the vineyards seemed to be the property of the Romeros.

'The Romeros want that part…' Sophia pointed to another area of the map. 'That's Mariana's family's land. When she and Alejandro marry the bodegas will merge.'

Emily's heart forced her to at least make an attempt at hope. '*If* they marry.'

'Oh, they'll marry,' Sophia said, with a certainty that made Emily's newly kissed lips pinch in tension. 'Both the families want it, and in fairness Mariana is probably the only person who could put up with one of the Romero brothers.'

'I see…'

'They're great to work for, though,' Sophia said. 'You just have to think product, product, product. Have you managed to do any research?'

'Not really,' Emily admitted. 'I tried, but the old website is down and I kept coming up with Maria de Luca…'

'Maria's their mother…' Sophia tapped away on the laptop that would soon be Emily's. 'Technically.'

'Technically?'

'She left José, their father.' She waved her hand in the air. 'Long ago…as soon as Carmen was born. She's a couple of years younger than me…so twenty-five years ago or more.' She leant forward and lowered her voice. 'But now Maria has decided to start visiting José…' She made a money gesture with her hands. 'No doubt she's trying to ensure that her name is in the will and her image remains on the bottle.'

'The woman on the label is their mother?' Emily checked, surprised that Alejandro hadn't mentioned it last night.

'*Sí.*' Sophia nodded. 'Maria's a very famous flamenco dancer—not just in Spain but internationally. Although she won't be attending the festival here! Believe me, she would get the cold shoulder. I'm only telling you this so when you read about who she is for yourself you don't decide to do a section on the website on her. It wouldn't go down well.'

Emily was very relieved to have the warning, because, knowing now that the gorgeous woman on the bottle was actually a legend in her own right, of *course* she would have gone down that road.

'Last year they started working on the rebranding. José wanted every trace of Maria gone, and of course Sebastián and Carmen agreed.'

'What about Alejandro?'

'He wanted her image to remain, but was outvoted,' she said. 'But then José got ill and suddenly changed his mind. Sebastián and Carmen want the new branding to go ahead, but it's Alejandro who has the deciding vote now.'

'So I'm to make no mention of her?' Emily frowned, because it seemed a rather large thing to leave out.

'I honestly don't know,' Sophia admitted. 'Sebastián is in Madrid at the moment, and then he's off to New York. He would rip her off every label if he could.' She shrugged, but more in exasperation than indifference. 'Just tread gently, and don't go planning anything on the website around her.'

'Thanks for the heads-up,' Emily said, and she sincerely meant it.

'You'll be fine. You'll be mainly dealing with Alejandro, and he doesn't let emotions get in the way…' She moved on to other matters. 'Most of the staff speak a little English, or at least enough to get by…'

'That's good.'

'But Alejandro says do your work in English, then we'll ar-

range translation. Just…' She paused. 'The other website design company we looked at was so…' She raised her hands in
an exasperated gesture. 'No original ideas. So staid and boring…' She smiled. 'And the Romeros are not.'

Emily had rather worked that out for herself!

'If Sebastián closes this deal in NYC it will be huge. He
wants the new website up as soon as possible. But Alejandro
is more insistent on you taking the time to get it right…'

'What about the sister?'

'Carmen has very little to do with the bodega. She practically lives in the family stables.'

It was a very busy morning for Emily. She was shown the IT office, and she met the staff she'd be working with, and despite the
ancient surroundings and furnishings it was all very high-tech.

She also found out, when they went for second breakfast—
*second breakfast!*—that lunch was generally taken around
three p.m., and that it was very normal in Spain to work
through till eight.

'You're going to need every hour,' Sophia warned.

'I am,' Emily agreed.

At first six weeks had seemed plenty of time, but there was
so much to take in and find out.

And to avoid!

'The brothers' offices are at the top,' Sophia said, as they
stood at the bottom of a very grand staircase. 'But I for one
am not up to climbing four flights of stairs.'

'There's no elevator?'

'No. And really there's no need to go up there. Most meetings
are held in the courtyard or online, as the brothers are rarely here.
Sebastián spends a lot of time in Madrid, and Alejandro is all
over the place—often in Seville.' She looked up. 'Here he is now.'

Indeed he was—coming down the stairs and carrying his
jacket. He looked busy, and as if a trip to the vineyards was
the last thing he needed right now.

\* \* \*

'I'm fine to take Emily,' Sophia told him in Spanish.

'It's okay,' he said. 'I do appreciate you coming in. But go home. I can take it from here.'

Of course Alejandro didn't add that he *wanted* to take it from here.

He knew that Emily deserved some sort of an explanation.

Actually, so did he. Alejandro had been doing a little research of his own, and had taken a closer look at the website for the bed and breakfast she ran…

It would seem Emily Jacobs might have a few secrets of her own!

# CHAPTER FIVE

'Do you need to collect anything?' Alejandro asked.

'My tripod and such...'

'Sure.' He nodded. 'Sophia, could you have Jorge bring my car?'

'Don't you want him to drive?' Sophia checked, but Alejandro shook his head.

'No need.'

Jorge helped Emily with her equipment, and as he loaded it into the boot Emily got into the passenger side. Alejandro sat, engine idling, strumming his fingers on the steering wheel. It was a very low car—so much so that she was actually pleased with her sensible trousers.

'Thanks for this,' Emily said as they pulled out of the bodega. 'Though I'd have been happy to go and explore by myself.'

'You know about sherry production, then?' he said, and glanced over as Emily fought not to curl her lip. 'It's not a leisure trip.'

'Of course not.'

He manoeuvred the silver car easily through the traffic, telling her it was mainly one-way.

'How was Sophia?' he asked.

'Very helpful,' Emily responded, wishing he would address what had been said earlier, but he did not.

Instead, as they left the city behind them, he glanced over. 'Is this what you look like when you're sulking?'

She didn't answer straight away, but pulled the sun visor down and looked at her pale, pinched reflection in the mirror. 'This is what I look like most of the time.' It was an honest answer, and she closed the shade and went back to looking out of the window. But then she did tell him how she was feeling. 'I would never have kissed you if I'd known you were engaged to someone else.'

'No, you wouldn't have, would you?' he said, glancing over and getting a view of the back of her head.

They drove through rolling hills filled with bare vines and instead of telling her about the different grapes, and pointing out the Romero territories, for once Alejandro was unsure what to say.

'Emily…' he began.

'Yes?' she responded, without looking at him, and after a couple more moments of silence he pulled over.

'Emily,' he said again, and now she looked at him.

He looked at her blue eyes and saw the sparkle of tears in them. They were not unexpected, he thought, when perhaps they should be?

It moved him in an unexpected way. It moved him that this nice, shy, funny, awkward woman did not want to have kissed a man who was engaged to someone else, and he could not fault that.

He could tease her, though.

'It was just a kiss.'

'That should never have taken place.'

She made it sound as if they'd spent a month locked away having torrid sex, rather than sharing a slow morning kiss.

Yet her reaction endeared her to him, and as she went to open the car door Alejandro realised he'd better stop teasing, and caught her arm.

'I was joking.'

She put her bottom back on the seat and he leant over and closed the car door.

'I don't often joke,' he said. 'Perhaps because I'm not very good at it.' He looked at her burning cheeks. 'It was a lovely kiss and you have nothing to feel guilty about.'

He paused for a second.

'If I tell you something, can I ask that it goes no further?'

Emily's eyes darted. Should she say no? It was surely too soon for secrets? She was only just emerging from layers of lies. But then she looked back to his gaze and could see that this very suave man was undecided, almost tentative, possibly as confused as she.

And so she nodded.

'It's complicated,' he said.

'Please—just be honest.'

'Mariana and I broke up at Christmas.'

'No…' She was so sick of being lied to that she was braver than she thought she could be. She put a hand up to his clean-shaven jaw and with her finger brushed the exact spot where the lipstick had been last night. 'So it wasn't Mariana's lipstick you were wearing last night?'

'It was.' He nodded. 'For the last six weeks I've tried to keep up the pretence—because just after Christmas we found out that my father is very ill. He wants our marriage to take place before he dies. But I just can't keep up the pretence any longer.'

'Why start it in the first place?'

'I didn't start it—I was practically born into it. It's all about old legacies and promises. The land belonging to Mariana's family is relatively small, but it is rich and productive and has long been fought over. If another buyer came in, or another bodega merged with it…' He shrugged. 'My family have long since wanted that land. Mariana's father and mine came to an agreement, and it's something we've grown up with. The golden couple in the golden sherry triangle. But I just came to realise that it wasn't for me. I don't want marriage. I'm not even a man to date long-term…'

'I had already worked that out,' Emily said. 'But don't lie, please.'

'I won't. If you're looking for a relationship, don't look to me.'

She realised he was actually being breathtakingly honest.

Alejandro started the car's engine and indicated to pull out, but before he did he asked a question of his own. 'What about *your* fiancé?'

'Touché…' Emily begrudgingly smiled. 'How do you know about Gordon?'

'I looked you up.'

Late last night—or rather early that morning—his curiosity had been piqued. Something that rarely happened. It had taken him ages to find Emily—her business was very new.

He'd seen a lovely family-run business, the happy couple, their smiles for the cameras… But Alejandro had noticed how the man's arm was held so awkwardly around Emily, and the tension in her features…

He'd also realised that her dreadful hair hadn't been caused by some recent ghastly slip of the hairdresser's scissors—she'd worn it like that for years.

He glanced over at her curls when she remained silent.

'We broke up three months ago,' she finally admitted.

'Good,' he said.

'Most people offer their commiserations.'

'Good for them.' Alejandro shrugged. 'So, you owned a business together?'

'No…' Emily swallowed. 'It was his mother's business. She died a few months ago. He broke things off shortly after.'

'Why?'

She sucked in her breath at his question.

'Well, I need to know,' Alejandro said. 'If I'm in the running to be your rebound guy, I have to know what issues to work on.'

He'd brought a reluctant smile to her lips, but it was fleeting.

'Couldn't you afford to buy him out?' he asked.

'It was only his.'

'Emily...' he said in reproach. 'Don't tell me you didn't get your name on a contract...'

'I didn't.'

He tutted.

'I didn't want a messy break-up. You know how hard these things are.'

'No.' He shook his head and said what few people would. 'Breaking up doesn't have to be hard. I do it all the time...' He smiled at her. 'I mean, I do it a lot!'

'I'm sure sometimes it hurts more than most.'

'No.' He would not be swayed. 'I used to say it to my parents when they fought: why do you have to make things so complicated? You love to be with the other? Stay. You don't love to be with the other? Then go. Why do you have to make all this drama between you?'

'Did they fight a lot?'

'A *lot*,' he agreed. 'My mother is a very flamenco talented dancer. Maria de Luca.'

'I don't really know much about flamenco...'

He liked their slow conversation...a few kilometres, a few words, a stretch of silence as they both thought over what the other had said.

'You're unacquainted with it,' he said. 'Is that the right word?'

'Maybe...'

She felt unacquainted with so many things.

'I'd like to see the equestrian school in Jerez,' she told him. 'I'd never heard about the dancing horses before.'

'My sister Carmen is into all that.' He nodded. 'I'll set up a meeting with her.'

A few more kilometres passed. He hadn't driven with such gentle company in as long as he could remember.

'Do you have brothers or sisters?' Alejandro asked.

'No.' Emily shook her head. 'But I have a friend, Anna, and I consider her to be a sister. We grew up together...'

'What about your parents?'

'They're both dead.'

He looked over at her and on this occasion he did commiserate. 'I'm sorry.'

'Thank you.'

'Recently?'

'Not really. My mother died during my final year at university—that's why I dropped out. My father had dementia. He died three years ago...'

'You dropped out to care for him?'

'Yes.'

'That must have been difficult.' He glanced over again. 'Or am I saying the wrong thing?'

'No, it *was* very difficult,' she admitted. 'I still don't know if it was the right thing to do. My mother asked me not to let him go into care, and I felt I had to keep that promise, but...'

'I get it,' he said. 'Well, not exactly. But my father is...' He stared ahead as he drove. 'As I told you, he's not well.'

'I'm very sorry.'

'Well, there's life in him yet, and he too is trying to push for...' He waved his hand in frustration at the limits of his English. 'I can talk business in English, but...' He thought for a moment. 'He uses emotion.' Alejandro glanced over at Emily. 'Did Sophia tell you about the rebranding?'

'She mentioned something...' Emily said.

'Well, you'll know that my father now wants my mother's picture to remain on our label.'

'I'm sure whatever you choose will be right.'

He smiled to himself as she shifted a little in her seat, clearly choosing her words carefully.

God, she was sweet. The least confrontational person he'd ever met. So much so, that she pressed a random button, perhaps in the hope of winding down the window, just for something to do rather than discuss the verboten subject of his mother.

'Why are you putting the child locks on?' he teased, and she laughed.

'Caught!'

She was nervous—he could tell. 'Sophia told you to stay away from it?'

She nodded. 'But I don't see how I can. I want a website that pleases everyone. Your father included…'

'Let me discuss it with my brother and sister.'

'Of course.'

Alejandro was used to playing hardball, and he liked her gentle take on things. He'd never spoken so easily to another person, or listened so carefully…

'Are you proud of your mother?' she asked.

'Yes,' he said. His response was immediate, and surprised even himself—he'd never been allowed to admit being proud of his mother to anyone. Emily was the first person in for ever who had referred to his mother's talent. 'I used to go backstage with her and I could hear the cheers. She is incredibly talented.'

'I'd love to have learned to dance.'

'You didn't?'

'I started ballet, but…'

'But?'

'I hated it.' She sighed at the memory. 'One of the other girls called me fat…'

'*Were* you fat?'

'A bit.'

'We call fat kids cute here…' he said. 'My sister was very "cute",' he said, and made her laugh. 'Now she's a brilliant equestrian.' He slowed the car down. 'This is our family residence.'

She looked at a huge gated property and saw, in the distance, a sprawling hacienda. 'That's your home?'

'It was. See the stables? That's where Carmen spends most of her time.'

'She lives here with your father?'

'Yes,' Alejandro said. 'When she's not practising in the arena here, she's at the equestrian school. It's a kind of horse ballet…' he said, in an attempt to describe it.

'Dressage?'

'A form of it, but really quite incredible. It's a big part of life here in Jerez. Carmen could ride before she could walk.'

'She didn't take up flamenco?'

'God, no, she hates it.'

And for years so had he. But last night, watching Emily's rapt expression, he had found his pleasure in it starting to return…

'What was it like having a famous mother?'

When he didn't answer Emily corrected herself.

'Of course she'd have just been your mum…'

'Oh, no,' he said. 'She was the star at home, believe me. Always she wanted to be on tour or performing. My father was jealous—he wanted her to be at home more. Instead, we had nannies. And every time she came home there was another argument. So, of course, she stopped coming home…'

Alejandro had surprised Emily. She'd expected bitterness—but, no, he seemed to see both sides.

'If your fiancé had asked you to stop working…'

'Oh, he never would have—he *loved* me working,' Emily said, and that made them both laugh. Then she was serious. 'So long as it was in *his* business.'

'You know, you could probably contest his ownership of it. I mean if you were together all these years you could argue you had a verbal contract…'

'No.' Emily shook her head. 'I mean, I know I could fight it—but what's the point? Lesson well and truly learnt. I'll never get involved with someone who has a family business again…'

She halted, aware of what she'd just said, but Alejandro just laughed at her discomfort.

'Good,' he said. 'Because I don't do involved relationships.' Then he was serious too. 'You say he liked you working?'

'Yes, but he'd never have supported me in my own venture.'

'That's sad.'

'Is it?'

'Yes,' Alejandro said. 'I've seen the results of that first-hand. If my father had gone and watched my mother, travelled with her…'

'Well, he did have three children.'

'We'd have been raised by nannies either way.' He looked over to her. 'Like I said before, break-ups don't have to be hard. People just make them so.'

'I think it depends on if you're the one doing the breaking up—'

'No,' he cut in. 'Why not just agree from the start that it goes nowhere? Enjoy each other for however long and then walk away without regret?'

Alejandro had made it sound like an invitation…as if he was inviting himself on her adventure.

They drove in silence but the words hung between them and she played them over and over, wondering if by some chance he'd been talking about them.

He made it sound so easy…so uncomplicated.

Could it be?

# CHAPTER SIX

THE BARE VINES seemed endless, and the sun was low in the late-afternoon sky as they pulled in at a vineyard.

'In summer this is busy,' said Alejandro. 'But now we have just select groups—fine dining for suppliers and exporters, weddings and such...'

He took her up to the function room, where they spoke with the head chef, who seemed a little startled to see Alejandro.

'It's fine,' he said, 'we're not here to eat. I'm just showing Emily around. She's designing the new website. Here we hold weddings, and the annual Romero ball,' he told her.

'I've heard about that.'

'It's stunning when it's lit up for the evening.'

'I'd love to see it.'

'Would you?'

She nodded.

'We're only open for lunches at the moment,' the chef explained. 'Perhaps come back at the weekend?'

They sorted out times, then headed down to the ground floor, where there were just a few staff around. They all smiled at Alejandro and nodded to Emily, as she stood taking frantic notes and the odd photo.

'This is Carlos,' he said, introducing her to one of the staff. 'I'll leave Emily with you for a moment,' he told him. 'Carlos is the person to ask for all historical details and the family tree...'

Carlos was indeed knowledgeable, and took her to the vast

presses where the grapes were crushed. The walls were lined with images of days gone by, when it had been done by foot. She looked at the photos of men pushing the grapes barefoot.

'It was a celebration,' Carlos explained. 'One basket per man…one bottle of sherry for a basket.' He took her outside. 'This is where the chickens used to be kept.'

'A lot of chickens,' Emily said.

Alejandro returned then and took over.

'They used to use egg whites to clarify the sherry,' he told her, and Emily honestly considered recording him, because she could barely keep up with her notes.

Still, it might be better not to, as his voice was so utterly delicious. She'd end up being lost in a daydream rather than getting on with her work.

'It's so beautiful here,' she said as they walked through the vineyards.

The wind was biting, and it was the first time she'd been cold since arriving in Jerez. Only it felt nice being cold with him…

'The staff have all gone.'

'How do you know?'

'Carlos always leaves last…' He pointed to a motorbike threading its way through the hills.

He turned her to face him and she felt relief to be alone with him.

'We'll head back soon,' he said. 'But first…'

And he resumed the kiss almost where they had left it that morning, but with even deeper feeling now.

Alejandro had never held anyone so soft before. He could not get enough of her shapely body.

The bite of the wind was soon forgotten, and even more so when they sank down onto the ground.

'We're going to have to dust each other off,' Alejandro said, his hand slipping inside her top and, with no chance of being disturbed now, unhooking her bra.

'Not here…' she whispered, all the while kissing him back.

'Of course not,' he said, stroking her breast as she lay back beneath the bliss of him. 'I'm taking you home to bed…'

And somewhere during that journey she knew she would have to tell him her truth.

He was half on top of her, lifting her top so that her breast was exposed to the cool evening air, and she bit on her lip as he held her breast and took it in his mouth.

'I told you I would love your breasts.'

She loved his detailed exploration.

He was bruising her with his mouth, she was certain of it, but she was impatient for more, and his busy tongue meant that his hand was free to slip down.

'Alejandro…'

She closed her eyes as his fingers slipped further, to where she was slick and warm, and she knew she had to tell him that she'd never done even a tenth of this before.

And it was at that moment Emily found out the true temptation of sex—because his finger seemed to meet her epicentre.

'Shh…' he said, silencing her faint protests that she had something to tell him. 'Just relax…'

'I want to…'

'Then do.'

The sky was purple and pink and fringed with orange, and his mouth was back on her tender breast as his fingers stroked her, not so slowly now.

'God…'

He could feel her trembling, and the little choking sounds she made had his stomach tightening.

She was fighting with herself, Alejandro realised, and assumed it was some kind of girly guilt after the awful Gordon that was holding her back.

'Do you want me to stop?'

'No, never stop…'

They were just kissing, just touching, but he seemed to be aching for her intimate touch too, because he took her hand and she felt him hard beneath her palm. It excited her—ridiculously so.

He was taking her to a place that she had only ever glimpsed…that no reluctant bland kiss from Gordon had ever taken her to.

He kissed her tense mouth, coaxing her to relax with both his hand and his tongue, and he was so turned on himself, so completely turned on, that he made one straightforward request.

'Take it out,' he said, his voice hoarse. He was so turned on at the feel of her bottom lifting and her thighs tightening on his hand. 'Or I'm going to climax.'

Her hands went for his belt and he closed his eyes in frustration, because he was right on the edge. So he took over. Taking himself out so that he was over her hip. Then his hand returned to the slipperiest, sweetest place.

He had brought her out here for a kiss, but had somehow hurtled back to his teenage years and forbidden gropes among the vines, and he had never enjoyed it more.

The lights went on then. The whole winery lit up and her eyes opened in shock.

He smothered her anguished cry.

'I arranged it,' he told her. 'Don't worry, it's just us here…'

It wasn't just the lights…it was the pressure of his fingers as they buried themselves in her that had caused her to cry out when the lights had come on.

She reached for him, dared to touch him, surprised by the

soft skin and the steel beneath. The feel of his wet tip on her palm spread a delicious warmth through her, and finally she was caving in rather than fighting…

The sight of her clenched jaw and compressed lips, the sounds she made, brought Alejandro a pleasure so pure that if he'd been able to tear his hand away he'd have stroked out his own climax. But instead he leant up on his elbow, feeling the last flickers or her orgasm, and watching with pleasure as her parted lips spread into a smile that felt as if it was only for him.

'Nice?' he asked as her smile faded.

'So nice…'

He rolled on top of her and his erection lay between them. He looked down at her. 'I only brought you out here to see the lights.'

'Please!'

'I'm serious.' He smiled. 'A kiss, maybe, but…' He was rocking a little, staring down at her. The feel of her skin was bliss. 'I thought I was past sex outdoors… But maybe I'm not,' he said.

He wanted more of her secret smile, but her knees had come up enough so that she gripped him loosely, and now she leant up on her elbows.

'Not here,' Emily said again. His fingers had hurt enough for her to know she could not get away without telling him.

If only she knew how she'd have happily used her mouth, or her hand, because she could feel not just his erection but his whole body, taut and turned on. A little as she had felt in the seconds before her first orgasm…drawn towards pure pleasure.

He moved back and his erection sprang free. As he moved to get off her it brushed at her most intimate core, and he held the base as if it was some heat-seeking missile as it nudged her entrance.

She was still raw from coming, and yet so desperate for more.

'Alejandro, I've never…'

'I know,' he said. 'We'll go home.'

He rolled off and was unabashed as he lay on his back and tried to tuck his erection into black silk boxers.

She pulled up her knickers and trousers.

'I've never orgasmed before…' she said.

He turned his head and looked at her.

'I've never done anything…'

'What are you talking about?'

'I've never slept with anyone…'

'What?' He frowned. 'But you lived with your fiancé…'

'We had separate bedrooms.' She wanted to run away, but there really wasn't any point, given they were miles from anywhere and he was the one with the car. 'He said it was for religious reasons, and I accepted that.'

'Look I'm a good Catholic boy, well-lapsed, and it never stopped me…' Then he stopped joking. 'Are you serious?'

'Yes, but it doesn't have to change things. I mean, just because I've never…'

'You're telling me that you're a virgin?'

'Please don't make it sound like an ailment…'

'No.' He shook his head. 'No, it's more a…'

He tried to think of a more suitable word, but where Alejandro was concerned possibly she'd chosen right.

'Emily, it changes a lot of things. Look, I want you, but I don't want…' How best to say it? 'I think if you've waited this long, why throw it away on someone who…?' He was trying to be honest. 'It makes sense now.'

'What does?'

'We were so hot for each other last night…we should have ended up in bed.'

'So, you'd have been fine if it had just been a pick-up in a bar?'

'What's wrong with that?'

'Everything.'

'See?' he said gently. 'You do want more.'

* * *

'I'd want more than one night,' she admitted, surprising herself with how, even on such a personal topic, she found it easy to be honest with him. 'Gosh, can't I have a little romance with my sex, please? I'm not asking for life...'

'Emily...' He looked into her eyes and with clear regret shook his head. 'I don't do romance.'

She would have liked to refute that, because as he helped her up they stood under the lights that he'd arranged to be turned on just for her. And under the starry Jerez night, he was kind...

It was the most romance she had ever known.

It was a horrible walk back to the car.

There, he dusted them off. He even kept one of those lint rollers in the car.

'Do you keep one handy for all the times you take virgins out into the Romero vineyards?' she asked.

He didn't laugh at her joke—just brushed himself down and very neatly did up his tie.

Then there was the long journey home.

Not unpleasant...not tense.

They just talked about work, and the odd cloud formation, and how there were more nails in professional dancers' flamenco shoes than the cheaper ones.

An exchange of information, really, rather than conversation.

Or conversation, rather than talking.

'Thanks for the tour,' Emily said, and got out of the car, after he'd stopped at the front of the bodega.

But of course Alejandro didn't have to do things like go and park his car, so he got out too, and gave his keys to the security officer, and soon caught up with her as she punched in the code to his residence.

'You remembered,' he said.

'I did.'

She walked ahead of him on the steps, and took out the

massive key as she did so. This time there was no lounging at the gates by Alejandro—just a brief goodnight.

Then, 'Emily?' he said as she turned the key.

'What?' she responded rather rudely, without turning around.

Because if she faced him then she might start crying. She could still feel their attraction, and it felt unfair that Alejandro wanted her, yet refused to give in to that want.

'I'm a bastard where women are concerned,' he said.

'I had heard.'

And she wished—how she wished—that he was just a little bit more of a bastard.

And would take her to bed.

She entered her apartment alone and sat in the dark on her sofa, wondering how long she might remain unwanted.

The glimpse of sex he'd shown her tonight had far from sated her…it had just made her more desirous, if that were possible.

Only it wasn't just sex she wanted to discover now.

She wanted *him*.

Well, no more!

A sound had her moving to the balcony. She saw a group of women, crossing the road, walking together and laughing, clapping as they walked.

A couple of other women were calling to them and they turned. Emily looked to where they had come from, and it appeared to be a bar or a café. But then her eyes were drawn to the lit rooms above.

A dance school.

She thought of what Alejandro had said about taking lessons. Her!

He was a nice bastard…

She niggled him. Not at his conscience, because he was certain he'd done the right thing by her, but she just niggled him in a way no one else ever had.

Their attraction had been instant and undeniable, but it was more than that. He'd enjoyed last night. All the things that were so normal…the sherry-tasting, the *taberna*—had been made special.

The music, which he usually kept as background noise in his mind, had come forward. She'd made him laugh, and he didn't do much of that.

He hated it that he'd rejected her—especially given what she'd told him about her ex. Yet at the same time he knew his own reputation.

And a kind and gentle twenty-six-year-old virgin did not need his casual ways.

He loathed closeness.

Intimacy.

Drama and emotion.

Sex was just sex. He never mixed up the two…

And a holiday romance? Not a chance.

# CHAPTER SEVEN

ALEJANDRO ENTERED EMILY'S temporary office, which over-looked the courtyard, the next morning.

'Are you okay?' he asked.

'Of course.'

Actually, she was all frazzled, and feeling frumpy in fresh black trousers and a navy top. And, yes, she knew the two didn't go together, but she'd thought they were both black when she'd dressed.

'Well, apart from the fact that Spanish water hates me.' She ran a finger through her curls, which had gone frothy at the ends, like cotton wool balls. 'What's the Spanish for hair conditioner?'

'*Acondicionador de cabello.*' Alejandro smiled. 'Just go to a salon…there's an excellent one in the *plaza*, or you can go to Calle Larga…'

'No need for that,' Emily said. 'I do my own hair.'

Alejandro, possibly wisely, chose not to comment. He knew she was just making small talk and trying to steer things back to normal between them.

The trouble was, things had *never* been normal between them.

Bad hair day or not, he was still strongly attracted to her, and he hated it that he'd made things so awkward.

'I'm trying to do the right thing,' he said, and took a seat on the edge of the desk. 'I *know* I'm doing the right thing.'

\* \* \*

'Good for you,' Emily snapped, surprised at her own cheek, but she fervently disagreed.

She could think of nothing better than Alejandro being her first lover. Still, she wouldn't be telling him that, so she mustered her pride.

'It's fine, I'm over not having sex with you.' She gave a tight smile. 'I think I seem to go for men who don't want me.'

'Don't say that.'

'I'm joking,' Emily said. 'Sort of.'

She turned the conversation in the direction of work. It was the reason she was here, after all, and she did admire him for coming down and checking in on her.

'I really do need to know if I can mention your mother...'

'Leave it for now,' he said. 'Just work around it.'

'I'll do my best.' Emily nodded. 'I think I've got an idea about the website design. Do you have a moment?'

'Sure.'

'I found this photo...' She pulled up an image on her screen and he came and stood behind her. It was an image of a man rolling one of the beautiful old barrels, taken probably some fifty or so years ago.

'It's from the old website...' he said.

'I know that,' she responded, a little indignantly. 'But look.' She pulled up the image she'd taken of Alejandro yesterday morning, when he hadn't known she was there.

It was almost the same image.

Except with a modern take.

In the photograph, Alejandro's phone was sticking out of his back pocket, and his black trousers and white shirt were far more fitted than the clothes worn by the man in the old photograph. And with his hair and his designer stubble...? God, a model might have been hired for a week and this shot would never have looked better.

'That's really good.'

'Thank you,' Emily said, wondering if he was admiring her work or himself…but it didn't matter.

'I thought if we ran with some timeless images…how some things change but others stay the same…'

'I like it,' he said. 'Yes, I think it's just fresh enough without trying too hard.'

'I won't mention in the caption that you were looking for a diamond earring…'

'No.'

He looked at her then, wincing a little when he saw her red eyes, knowing he'd embarrassed and hurt her when it was the very last thing he'd wanted to do.

'Are you sure you're okay?' he asked.

'I will be.' She gave him a tight smile. 'Don't worry, Alejandro, I'm sure you're not that unique.'

She saw his eyes narrow a little, but he did not rise to the provocative threat, just shrugged one shoulder and had the gall to wish her well.

For the rest of her first week she saw him just a little, here and there.

His office was several flights up, so there was no bumping into each other in the corridors. And despite their living next door to each other their paths only crossed once, in the early hours of morning as she lay on the ground in the courtyard.

She'd headed out to catch the sunrise, and before that she wanted to attempt to capture the moon as it drifted over the empty vines that knotted and weaved their way above the courtyard.

'Heavy night?' Alejandro asked, standing over her.

She had heard his footsteps but refused to acknowledge them. Now he stood looking down at her and making a dry joke, as if he'd found her passed out drunk in the courtyard.

'No,' she said, looking up and resisting saying that the heavy night had clearly been his.

She'd fallen into bed at ten, whereas Alejandro was clearly just getting home from a club, or a casino, or wherever his chosen venue for decadence had been that night. He was unshaven and dressed in a dark suit, his tie undone. Yet he looked so utterly perfect he somehow evoked the image of a movie star from decades ago.

She wasn't embarrassed to be caught lying down in an attempt to capture the perfect shot—simply grateful that she wasn't facing him in the small hours with some glamorous beauty on his arm.

'What are you doing, Emily?'

'I think these vines will be a beautiful border or background for the website. I'm done now...' She moved to get up, and when he offered his hand to help her stand, unthinkingly she took it.

*Thinkingly* their fingers remained laced together...like the vines she had just captured.

'Are you going back to bed now?' he asked, and she was confused by the slightly suggestive tone to his voice. Confused that he could so coldly reject her and still so easily turn her on.

'No.' Emily removed her hand from his. 'I'm actually heading off to the vineyards. I thought I'd try for a sunrise shot.'

'Sounds good.' His voice was husky and he cleared his throat. 'I'm sure it will look amazing...'

'I hope so,' Emily said, and walked over to the steps, where all her equipment was stacked, waiting for her driver to arrive.

He watched as she packed up her beloved camera.

For Alejandro it had been a long night, moving from private club to private party in Seville—one of the hottest spots in Europe for night-life.

It had just not felt like it last night.

Now he knew why.

It was Emily's curves he wanted, her wild blonde curls in

his fingers, and to know again the passion that smouldered untapped just beneath her uptight surface.

'Let me help you...' he offered, though really it was just to prolong their encounter.

But she refused his offer.

'No, thank you,' she responded with a tart edge—it clearly wasn't his chivalry she wanted.

He was trying to be the sensible one, but he was starting to wonder why he was bothering when it seemed neither of them really wanted him to be.

Emily most certainly didn't.

She sat bundled in a blanket in the middle of the vineyard and watched the sky turn a pale gold. It was rather a pale sunrise, compared to the violets and pinks of the sunset she'd witnessed before.

But she'd been with Alejandro then, Emily thought, and he made everything more beautiful, more vivid, somehow.

She kept telling herself to let it go. Only she was stuck in a loop, thinking of all the things he'd said that had made her laugh. His little teases and his easy acceptance of her...his sensual kisses and how he'd made her feel incredible when she was in his arms...

*Enough!* Emily decided as she packed up her equipment.

She was moving on from Alejandro Romero.

And that started today.

Flamenco Workshop... Flamenco for Beginners...

Alejandro had been right. It was everywhere. The shops even had flamenco shoes in baskets at the front, in red, purple, black... Turning them over, she saw there were nails banged into the heels and tips. Flamenco dresses ranged from a couple of euros up into the thousands.

Gosh, it was all so beautiful. There were even flamenco outfits for sale in the supermarkets.

It really was a way of life here.

And she wanted to taste it for herself.

If coming to Jerez was the bravest thing she had done in her life, then walking up the stone stairs and entering the doors of Eva's flamenco studio came a very close second.

Emily was one burning blush as she stood there in front of the very glamorous Eva, who was clearly on her lunch break. She was lying on a chaise longue, eating a sliced-up apple, but she smiled warmly as Emily entered.

*'Hola...'*

'I saw you perform on Sunday night,' Emily said in faltering Spanish. 'And I heard there were flamenco lessons... I was wondering if you do individual classes.' She couldn't bear the thought of dancing in a group—imagining she'd make an utter fool of herself in front of the locals. 'I mean, I'm...'

*'Claro que sí!'*—*'Of course!'* The woman smiled. 'But it is more enjoyable, as well as cheaper, to be in a group. This is my busy time, though, and unfortunately I am booked up.'

'That's fine,' Emily said. 'Alejandro just mentioned...'

'Alejandro sent you!' Eva exclaimed, and clearly that changed everything. 'Then of course I can make room for you.'

Her blush would not fade but Emily smiled at Eva's kind eyes.

'Come through. I'll show you around.'

The studio was mirrored, with wooden floors and silk shawls hanging over dividers, and rows of flamenco shoes all neatly placed in a corner.

'I really have no idea about flamenco,' Emily admitted.

'That is why you will take a beginners' class. I have a group booking at two, so we have some time now. Perhaps...?'

Emily was about to point out that she had to go back at work, but then thought that, in a way, this *was* work.

'I haven't got any shoes...'

'Soon,' Eva said. 'Wait until you have had a couple of lessons before you spend your money. The first lesson is free...'

She tapped her fingers into her palm and that incredible, precise sound was made again.

'That clapping...'

'It is called *palmas*,' Eva told her, tapping three fingers and then moving her hand so that she cupped one palm. Emily heard how the sound changed. 'You try now.'

For almost an hour Emily stayed there, standing in front of a mirror, seeing for herself just how little sense of rhythm she had, but the time flew by.

'Come again tomorrow at this time,' Eva said.

'I don't want to take up your lunch break...'

'You say you have only five weeks here!' Eva pointed out. 'We can do some footwork—you can borrow some shoes, and if you enjoy it then maybe you can get your own, but speak to me first. And Emily!' she called as she left. 'Think about the group workshops. If you want to cram some more lessons in it's a good way to do so, and they are always fun.'

*Fun*, Emily thought as she dashed back to work. Fun was something that had been missing for far too long from her life.

Yet here in Jerez she was starting to discover it.

She was going out, doing new things, kissing new guys... Well, just the one! But she was finally doing all the things she never had.

After a lifetime of attempting to please people, she was finally taking the time to work out what pleased *her*. It was liberating.

'Alejandro is looking for you,' said Andrés, one of the IT workers, when she returned to the office.

'Good for him,' Emily said, perhaps a little cheekily, but Andrés's English didn't quite stretch to sarcasm, and he gave her a smile and went back to his screen.

'Good for me?' a deep voice said, and Emily swung around.

He looked stunning, with no traces of last night's excesses evident.

'Why is spending the last hour trying to get you online for a meeting with Sebastián good for me?'

'I meant...' As Emily took a seat and took a breath, she was a little stunned by her own cheek, and realised she'd come back from her first dance class on a little bit of a high. 'It means...'

'I know exactly what it means, Emily.'

His gorgeous eyes were a little narrowed, as if he was trying to work out the slight change in her, the subtle shift. She knew her outfit was the usual mix of muted shades and practical lines. Her hair was tied up high on her head and was its usual chaotic self. She wore no make-up, but that was usual.

And yet Emily felt a certain defiance as she met his eyes and smiled. 'I'm sorry, Alejandro, I wasn't aware we'd scheduled a meeting.'

'We hadn't,' he conceded. 'That is why I tried to call you.'

She reached into her bag and pulled out her work phone. Sure enough, there were a couple of missed calls from him. It would seem she'd been too busy dancing and discovering *palmas* to hear her phone.

'So you did.' She dropped her bag back in her phone. 'Well, I'm back from lunch now.'

'Excellent,' he said tartly. 'Then can we please get on?'

'Of course.' Emily moved to stand. 'Should I come up to your office?'

'It's an online meeting, Emily. We hardly need to be seated together. There should be an invitation in your inbox.'

Indeed there was.

Emily put on her headphones and logged in, and for a sliver of time she thought the haughty face looking back at her was Alejandro, but quickly she realised it was Sebastián.

*'Buenas días,'* Emily said.

'Good afternoon,' he responded.

Manhattan was stretched out behind him, but neither of these brothers needed a stunning backdrop, Emily thought, as Alejandro appeared. They might be in the same building, but the view behind Alejandro was like a postcard shot of Jerez. She could see ancient buildings and church spires…the vista from his office was simply to die for.

'Finally,' said Alejandro, by way of greeting. 'Okay, Emily's been here for—'

'Just over a week,' Emily answered for him.

'I just wanted to touch base,' Sebastián said. 'See if you have everything you need and if there are any questions.'

'I have a few.' Emily nodded. 'I'm very keen to meet with Carmen. I'd like to mention her love of the dancing horses and perhaps get some photos of her.'

'That can easily be arranged.' Sebastián nodded. 'Alejandro, have you spoken to Carmen about the new website?'

'Probably not…' Alejandro shrugged. 'I'll give her a call.'

It was at that moment when Emily realised that what was a huge venture for her was just a blip on the radar for the Romeros. They simply wanted it done—their product showcased with a new and refreshing take on things. Certainly they weren't waking up, as she was, to be gripped by a city that was so vibrant it literally danced before your eyes. Nor were they falling asleep wondering how to best capture the image of endless vines and the way they laced across the rolling hills.

That was her job. And, if she wanted to do it well then there were some questions she needed to ask, no matter how awkward they might be.

'I've got a couple of questions about the label, and also your father's biography.'

'You have explained the complexities to Emily?' Sebastián asked his brother.

'Not fully.'

They spoke in Spanish amongst themselves for a couple of minutes, and Emily started to understand that her questions were about the things the brothers were having trouble agreeing on themselves.

They didn't discuss it deeply, but it was clear to her that many an argument had taken place on this very subject.

'Okay…' Sebastián finally addressed Emily. 'For some time we've been considering changing our label. We're working with an artist to produce a watercolour. She's using the same colour themes as the original image, so when we change—'

'*If* we change,' Alejandro interjected.

Emily looked from brother to brother and could almost feel the simmering tension between them.

Sebastián was the oldest, and perhaps thought he wielded more power, but Alejandro, seemingly more laid-back, used his strength quietly. Both were forces to be reckoned with.

Emily sat still and, possibly because she was in Spain, thought of bulls and the old saying about two bulls in one paddock.

Both these men were powerful, both natural leaders, and in this case it would seem they had opposing views.

'At this stage we would really prefer that you focus on the product,' Sebastián said.

'Maria de Luca is *on* the product, though,' Emily attempted, looking from brother to brother. Both faces were determinedly impassive, but she knew Alejandro better and could see that his full lips were pinched tight. 'I don't need to go into detail, or anything, but,' she said, very simply, 'would it help if I discussed this with your father? Find out what *he* wants—?'

'What would help,' Sebastián cut in, 'is for you to work to the brief you've been given.'

'Whoa!' Alejandro said, when usually he would not have done.

But watching his brother dismiss Emily's concerns had provoked him—angered him, even. He did not usually allow anyone to get under his skin, particularly when it was a member of his family—*especially* when it was a member of his family—but he knew how hard it would have been for Emily to ask the question she just had.

'Emily is correct,' Alejandro said. 'This needs to be addressed—preferably before the website goes live. And José would like Maria to be mentioned.'

'Thankfully,' Sebastián put in, 'it is not his decision.'

'No,' Alejandro said. 'It is mine.' He looked at the screen. 'Could you excuse us, please, Emily?'

'Of course.'

'I hope to answer your questions soon.'

They both waited until she was gone.

'We don't discuss internal matters with outsiders,' Sebastián clipped.

'Which is why I asked her to leave,' Alejandro said. 'José wants Maria to stay on the label and for her to be mentioned in his bio.'

'He didn't a few weeks ago—he wanted every trace of her gone!'

'He didn't know he was ill then,' Alejandro responded. 'And it has become my decision—because you and Carmen want her erased, while our father wants her to remain.'

'And what do *you* want?' Sebastián glared at his brother. 'To defend her as you did when we were children? To speak nicely about a woman who walked out on her husband and three children so she could pursue her *art*?'

'Flamenco is an art,' Alejandro said.

He had once loved it, but in more recent years, as he'd realised the damage it had caused to his family, that love had become twisted into first resentment and later indifference.

Watching Eva the other night had brought back some of his love for the art. Seeing Emily, a shy woman who had been ready to leave, remain seated, held utterly spellbound, had awoken some of his own dormant thrill for the ancient art.

It was in his blood, after all.

And it wasn't flamenco that had caused their agony.

It was Maria de Luca, the ice queen herself, who had seen to that.

'Why?' Sebastián asked his brother. 'Why would you support her? Surely we need to move on from her? She had no trouble moving on from us.'

'It's nothing to do with defending her,' Alejandro said. 'It is about our father and respecting his wishes.'

'They change week by week, month by month…'

'I'm aware of that,' Alejandro said, 'and that is why I'm refusing to be rushed into a decision. However, I do need to let Emily know what to do for the website.'

'She can wait,' Sebastián said dismissively. 'Now, while I have you, I spoke to José this morning. He suggests a May wedding…'

*'Felicidades!'* Alejandro responded, giving his congratulations.

'What?'

'I didn't realise you were even engaged.'

'I'm talking about *your* wedding.'

'Then don't,' Alejandro said—and exited the meeting.

He headed down to the offices and knocked on the door of IT while at the same time walking in.

'Hey,' he said to Andrés, and then walked over to Emily, who was working away at her desk.

'Sorry about that…' he said.

'About what?' She looked up. 'Alejandro, I knew going into that meeting that I'd be raising a difficult topic.'

He perched on the edge of her desk, right beside where she sat, and looked at her rather than the work she was doing.

She tried not to notice.

There was nothing *to* notice, of course.

Everyone else simply carried on working, presumably more used to his presence than she. Yet she could smell that gorgeous cologne…and was rather too aware of his thighs just inches from her hands. More than that, she knew she was blushing and awkward now. She'd arrived back from her first flamenco lesson so exhilarated and bold, but her newfound confidence had soon faded.

'Emily?'

There was a note to his voice that had her stomach folding in on itself, but his rejection still stung, and so she carried on typing as she gave a curt, 'Yes?'

'Can you stop?'

He put his hand over hers and removed it from the keyboard. She refused to acknowledge the effect his touch had, just looked up and somehow managed to meet his eyes.

'Sorry.' She put her hands in her lap and gave him her full attention. 'What did you want to discuss?'

'I can't give you an answer to your question.'

'That's fine,' Emily responded. 'I'll do two versions dealing with the label and your father's bio.'

'That would be best.'

'One more thing,' she said as he moved to go. 'Is there a photo of all five of you? Only I've been through the archives—'

'There's no photo of the five of us.'

'I thought there might be one at the family home. I'm happy to look myself if you just point me in the right direction.'

'There are no photos of the five of us. Maria put on a bit of weight when she was pregnant with Carmen and didn't want to be photographed until she'd recovered her figure.'

'Oh...' Emily said, trying to pretend that what he'd said was completely fine instead of entirely messed up. 'It was just an idea.'

'I would leave that one well alone, too. There really aren't many happy family photos... Maria always liked to be centre stage.'

'Good to know,' she said, and then thought of earlier, when she'd said, *Good for him*, with that sarcastic edge. 'I wasn't being facetious that time. I really do mean it's good to know...'

And it was good to know a little more about him...although of course that wasn't what she was trying to convey.

'I might have started planning a family page or something like that...'

'Well, I've saved you some time.'

'You have.'

'So, you *were* being facetious before?'

'A bit...' she admitted, and watched the way his face was changed by the ghost of a smile.

Aside from the fact that he was incredibly beautiful, there was something about him that moved her. She could see the tension around his eyes and mouth dissolving, just with that small shift of his sensual lips.

They were in an office, with others present, and nothing untoward had happened at all, because Andrés came over, and chatted with Alejandro about cyber land for a moment, and how the sherry was performing on some blockchain.

It was all gobbledegook to Emily, and yet she wished—how she wished—that they would carry on talking for ages, simply because it was so nice to have him here.

'Right,' Alejandro said, as Andrés headed back to his desk. 'I'll let you get on. Two versions...'

'Yes.'

He nodded, and looked at her with brown eyes that seemed to want to say something else...eyes that were dangerous to her self-control.

Eyes that were so dangerous that as she came home from work Emily didn't fully close the front door...

He might see it was open and knock, she thought, knowing she was being pathetic, but somehow letting her desperation override her.

She attempted to be casual and put on the television—some Spanish soap opera, all glittering eyes and jewels, and people so beautiful she felt pale and unsophisticated in comparison.

She poured a glass of wine and then tried to coax the last of her hair serum from the container and do what she could with her wild curls.

*Oh, hi*... she'd say casually when he knocked and came in, as he had today at the office.

She'd been so sure there was more he'd have said if there hadn't been others around. There was so much still unsaid and undone.

She heard the main gates buzz, and then the sound of his footsteps on the mosaic steps. She held her breath as he climbed the stairs, then halted.

She took a sip of wine but didn't swallow it. Instead her face crumpled as she heard his gates open. It was rather clear that Alejandro Romero had walked right on by and would not be accepting her unvoiced offer to drop in.

Perhaps she should go over there?

What the hell...?

Emily stood up and told herself to have some pride, reminding herself of the talking-to she'd given herself just that morning—sitting watching the sunrise on the very spot where he'd rejected her, telling herself it was time to move on.

She turned off the television angrily—not that the television noticed. And then she picked up her key and before she could talk herself out of it locked the door behind her and determinedly took the stairs.

'Emily!' Eva greeted her warmly. 'You decided to join us.'

'I did.'


Thank heaven for group classes.

She'd been seconds from disaster.

She stood in front of the mirror and picked up the edge of a borrowed shawl, and knew that night she'd been seconds away from making a complete fool of herself and going to him.

*'Quinta!'* Eva said, clapping her hands to gain their attention, and then she raised her hands gracefully in the air. 'Fifth position, Emily. Concentrate.'

Emily loved the group workshop, even if she was dreadful at it—she attended daily when her schedule allowed, and certainly nightly when the Alejandro urge hit.

She borrowed from Eva's selection of flamenco shoes, though rather guiltily she intended to splurge and buy some expensive professional ones, even if they would only serve as a souvenir of her time here. On Saturday she'd been to a flea market at Mercadillo José Ignacio, a pleasant walk from the city centre, and had bought a practice skirt and top. She took these lessons seriously, and even had her own piece of wood to practise on at home.

A heel strike was a *tacón*.

Using the sole of her foot, *planton*.

And *golpe* meant she struck the floor with the whole of her foot.

Eva was a hard taskmaster.

'Come on, Emily, we only have four more weeks. You are like a tree that refuses to bend.'

She always singled Emily out but, given the limited time span, Emily tried to accept the criticism rather than burst into tears and run, as she sometimes felt like doing.

'Be provocative, Emily,' Eva told her now, in the one-to-one class she'd squeezed into her day.

What was the point of being provocative? Emily thought. She'd practically thrown herself at him.

'Emily, *move*,' Eva urged.

'I am,' Emily said, trying to inject some sass into her hips. But Eva was right. She was like a lump of wood that refused to bend to any wind.

Oh, but she tried.

'Tonight, *jaleo*…' Eva said, as Emily slipped off her practice skirt, changed her shoes and took a gulp of water at the end of her class.

'What's that?'

'Hellraising!' Eva smiled. 'Dress up and I shall see you here at eight.'

'If I finish work in time.'

She often didn't, Emily thought, as she made her way back from her midday flamenco class to work, with a tiny detour to the Plaza Santiago to buy a gorgeous handbag she had seen for Anna.

It was the softest leather, and although Emily would never spend that much on a bag for herself, it was perfect for a busy single mum who juggled work and childcare.

As well as that, there wasn't going to be much more time for lingering in the shops. She was pulling twelve-hour days at work, and often continued until late at night. Two weeks were already gone and she still hadn't got the shots she wanted—nor had she spoken with Carmen and seen the horses.

Everyone in the office looked at her sideways when she did dash off, but no one ever asked where she was going—and anyway, she had her answer ready: she was learning more about the local culture.

Oh, and Emily loved it.

As she walked through Plaza de Santiago she checked her phone. But, no, work hadn't called. There was just a missed call from Anna, so she quickly buzzed her back.

'How is it?' asked Anna.

'Incredible,' Emily admitted, taking a second to pause and take in the fountain, the cafés and churches, still unable to believe she was actually here. 'I'm going to get Willow a flamenco dress.'

'Please don't!' Anna said.

'Seriously, they're gorgeous. How is she doing?'

'Another ear infection…' Anna sighed. 'Tell me what you're up to. She loves hearing about it.'

'Well, I still haven't seen the dancing horses, but tell her I'm working on it. Honestly, Anna, there's so much to see and take in, but I'm working on a few ideas and starting to get a feel for it for now. Alejandro said not to rush.'

'Alejandro?'

'He's one of the brothers.'

Emily's face was on fire. She wanted to confide in her friend, but just didn't know what she could possibly say. Alejandro's reaction to her virginity hadn't exactly been inspiring. And so, instead of talking about anything deeply personal she chatted about her dance classes and how she was going to do an online course with Eva when she returned home.

'Flamenco?' Anna checked, as if her rather staid and sensible friend had gone completely mad.

'It is *life*!' Emily said dramatically, as the Jerez people did, and was laughing as she ended the call.

And then she looked up at the church and frowned when she saw the spire.

*Oh, my goodness!*

Was that a nest?

'Hey…'

It was Alejandro, looking amazing in a charcoal-grey suit and eating a bag of potato crisps. But for once she was able to play it cool, so focussed on the church spire was she.

She turned, but only briefly. Her focus was on the church, or rather the spire above it, and she was grateful for the intriguing distraction. 'Is that a nest?'

'For sure.' He looked up too. 'It's a stork's nest.'

'It's huge!'

'They need to be.'

'Look!' she squealed as a face popped up. 'There's one in there. Oh, I wish I'd brought my camera.'

'They're everywhere.' He smiled. 'In most church spires. They come from Africa across the Strait of Gibraltar. It means spring is here…'

Alejandro looked for a moment at Emily rather than up at the spire. She was squinting into the bright midday sun, and looking rushed and breathless, yet still she'd stopped to admire the nest.

'He's waiting for his mate, getting the nest ready.'

'They're monogamous, aren't they?'

'No.' Alejandro was quick to break any fantasy she held. 'That's just a myth.'

'Surely not? I'm sure I read that they mate for life.'

'Then you read wrong—or it was a fairy tale.' He thought for a moment. 'I believe they stay faithful while their mate is alive...'

'Oh...'

'They're good while it lasts,' Alejandro said, and poured some of his crisps on his palm.

He offered her one, but Emily declined and watched him as he chose the biggest one for himself.

'Why are you out here eating crisps?' she asked.

'I love them. But if I call down to the kitchen for crisps they put them in a dish and all the salt falls off.'

'What are you talking about...the salt falls off?'

'They don't taste as good.' He looked back up at the nest. 'Also, these storks you think are so cute kill the weakest of their chicks.'

'No!' She put her hands over her ears. 'That's horrible.' Though he had made her laugh. 'Why would you tell me that?'

'To see you cringe.' He smiled, and then looked back up at the nest. 'Though I stand corrected...both are there.'

'Which one's the female?'

'I have no clue,' he admitted. 'How are you doing?'

'Well—I hope. The website's coming on, and everyone's being really helpful.'

'I meant how are *you* doing?'

'Fine!' She bristled, wishing she could say it with more conviction...wishing her hurt wasn't so raw and visible.

Gordon's breaking up with her had hurt way less than Alejandro's rejection.

His eyes moved to her latest purchase. 'That's a nice bag.'

'It's not for me,' Emily said quickly, embarrassed by the extravagance of her purchase. 'I bought it for my friend.'

'Well, it would suit you.' He looked at her face and she knew she was blushing. 'You deserve nice things.'

'I have nice things,' Emily said. 'Actually, I've seen a tripod…' He stared back at her with unblinking velvet-brown eyes. 'It's so light, and it folds up to practically nothing.'

He frowned—not a frown as such, but the skin around his eyes crinkled a little.

'That's for business,' he said. 'I meant something nice for *you*.'

'I love my work.'

'It's no longer a hobby, though,' he pointed out, his slight frown remaining and his eyes steadfastly upon her, as if assessing her reaction as he spoke. 'Eva says you're enjoying the flamenco classes?'

'She told you I've been taking them?'

'Yes, she said you are very…' He thought for a moment. 'English.'

'What does that mean?'

'Very formal, and not brilliant at being expressive.'

She gaped, feeling appalled. 'She's not allowed to tell you that!'

'Hey, I didn't know there was a flamenco code of confidentiality.' He seemed to be laughing at her embarrassment. 'Anyway, I've heard you practising.'

'You can hear me? I thought those walls were thick enough to block any noise out.'

'They are…' He frowned again, probably at her embarrassment. 'I just hear when I pass your door.'

'So you know how out of time I am?'

'Don't be too hard on yourself.'

'I know I'm not going to master it in six weeks—well, four weeks now. We've got *jaleo* tonight…'

'*Ole!*'

'I'm dreading it,' she admitted. 'I just can't…'

'What?'

'I don't know… I just feel so awkward.' She told her one of Eva's suggestions. 'Eva says I'm to wear red lipstick for my next class.'

'Why?' He frowned again.

'She thinks it might make me smile more.'

'But you're always smiling,' he said. 'You have a beautiful smile.'

'I don't…' She shook her head, because she knew she wasn't being self-effacing. 'Eva's right. I don't readily smile.'

She stopped then. Her explanation was causing more questions as his words started to sink in. All her life she'd been told to smile more, that she was too serious—she'd even joked with Willow that she'd been born with a serious face. Yet with Alejandro she smiled easily. It was as if he'd freed her lips— not just to smile but to speak more easily.

'I think you see a slightly more smiley version of me than everybody else,' she told him.

'Do I?'

She nodded. 'I'd better get some lipstick, I guess.'

Alejandro said nothing. In truth, he was a little shaken by what she had just said.

Just a couple of days ago Eva had thanked him for recommending Señorita Seria to come and see her.

'Who?' Alejandro had asked.

'The English girl…we call her Señorita Seria…'

*Miss Serious.*

And he remembered how, after one of their online meetings, when Emily had gone, Sebastián had rolled his eyes and spoken about their sullen new website designer…

Sullen? Alejandro would never have described her as such.

If she went missing and he was the last person to see her, he'd tell the police about her blue eyes and bright smile. How her untamed curls had a life of their own, and how she argued over storks in a nest, how she made him laugh and smile...

It almost killed Alejandro to hear her practising.

Last night, as he'd made his way up the stairs, he'd heard her. He'd stood there for a moment, trying not to picture her, tempted to knock, but instead he'd made his way through the gates to the safe silence of heavy brick walls.

Here he was, insisting she'd be better off without him, when it would seem that she neither wanted nor needed his care or concern.

He was coming around to the idea that maybe she *could* take the part-time nature of his affection....

Emily fascinated him. She was gentle and she was shy, and yet there was a strength to her he admired immensely. She had no family—a concept he could barely grasp—and she made her own way...taking dance lessons in a foreign country, kissing him amongst the vines, fighting to be brave...

He tried to catch her eyes, but she was glancing at the time.

'I'd better get back,' she said. 'If I'm to have any hope of making it to *jaleo* tonight.'

'Have fun,' Alejandro said. 'You should enjoy your time here.'

'I intend to,' Emily said, and with a brief wave and smile she headed back towards the bodega, wishing any brief conversation with Alejandro didn't affect her so. And wishing that seeing the storks' nest, or her dance class, or even *jaleo* tonight might prove to be the highlight of her day, rather than her few minutes alone with him.

*Don't worry, Alejandro*, she thought to herself, *I shall enjoy my time here.*

She was determined to.

A little *too* determined, perhaps.

# CHAPTER EIGHT

'OKAY!' EVA CLAPPED her hands and forced the chattering to stop. 'Tonight we are going to go over to the courtyard at Bodega Romero...'

'Romero?' Emily frowned. 'But I work there.'

She had followed Eva's instructions and indeed dressed up for tonight. She was wearing the pink practice skirt with violet flowers that she had bought at the thrift market, and had added the violet top that had come with it. She'd never intended to wear it—the low-cut top showed way too much cleavage—but she was really trying to give the classes her all. She was also wearing a borrowed pair of red flamenco shoes, and to top things off had tied a big silk rose in her hair.

Though she hadn't gone out and bought the recommended red lipstick, Emily had thought she was well and truly ready for hellraising—but only in the safety of Eva's studio!

'I thought tonight was *jaleo*?'

'It is.' Eva nodded. 'The restaurant is closed on a Monday, so we can make noise there...'

Emily inwardly groaned. There was no way she was going to get up on stage in front of her colleagues—especially if one of them happened to be Alejandro.

'Is *jaleo* always held at Romero?' Emily asked.

'Pretty much.' Eva nodded.

*Bastard,* Emily thought. He'd known all along. He could

have at least warned her. Well, there was no way she was getting up on that stage.

Eva must have seen her gritting her jaw. 'Just sit and watch if you are too timid to join in, Emily,' she said. 'Now, can you please carry the shawls? Stella, can you bring the castanets?'

Thankfully, having trooped through Plaza de Santiago and arrived at the bodega, she saw no sign of Alejandro, but even so there was no way she was joining in.

She sat at the courtyard bar as the rest of the class took to the stage. People were drinking, idly watching the assembled dancers. Emily simply didn't know how to get up and just dance as the others did.

There was a lot of stamping of male feet as the dancers took to the stage, and Emily baulked at even the thought of the final hurdle. Or rather the stairs to the stage.

'Maybe later,' she mumbled to herself.

*'Gracias,'* she said to the barman, who knew her by now, of course, and smiled when she ordered a diet cola.

'Why aren't you dancing?' he asked.

'Soon!' Emily said, and then offered by way of explanation, 'I've only just finished work.'

*'Hola.'*

She heard a male voice, but knew without turning her head that it wasn't Alejandro.

'You're not dancing?' the man asked.

'No.' Emily flashed a polite smile. 'Perhaps later.'

'Would you like another drink?'

'No, thank you,' Emily said.

Not that it stopped him from trying to make conversation.

His name was Fernando and, if she was being completely honest, a couple of weeks ago she'd have been both thrilled and embarrassed to be chatted up by this man. Her rock-bottom ego would have glowed as red as her cheeks at Fernando's skilled flirting.

Now, though, she felt numb.

Just utterly numb as he moved his stool a little closer and told her how gorgeous her outfit was.

'I love to see a woman dressed in bright colours…'

Emily looked down at her hastily put-together outfit. It was just so not her—and neither was sitting on a bar stool next to a stranger.

It had felt so easy when she'd sat in the *taberna* with Alejandro. So simple to make her way to his table and simply enjoy the night.

Now all she felt was a little less numb and possibly a little bit sad…

And then the man she really wanted to flirt with unexpectedly walked in, and her ego glowed a little at the thought that she wasn't sitting alone at the bar.

Alejandro was carrying a large, flat white box under his arm and walking briskly towards his residence, not wanting to get waylaid in conversation. But then, out of the corner of his eye, he saw blonde curls and glanced over. His reaction was purely mental, but it felt so physical it was like a punch low in the guts as he saw Emily's pretty face turn to her admirer.

What the hell…?

It was none of his business, though he'd been about to make it so.

He tossed the box down on to a table and gestured to the bar staff for a drink.

They were startled into attention, unused to the boss taking an aperitif in the courtyard, particularly during a dance lesson. Usually he'd be punching out two headache tablets from a blister pack on his way past, rather than taking a seat.

Not tonight.

'*Gracias,*' he said to the barman as his drink was placed down, but though he was polite his eyes never left Emily and her new *friend*.

She was leaning forward to catch whatever it was he'd just

said, and Señorita Seria seemed to have discovered how to laugh, because she kept throwing her head back and laughing, when Alejandro knew that Fernando wasn't in the least funny.

Now she was swirling her straw in her glass, just blatantly flirting...

He could take it no more and walked over.

'Emily?' She felt Alejandro tap her shoulder. 'Do you have a minute?'

'I'm actually at a dance class.'

She could see his dark eyes glinting and knew this was not about business.

'Well, you're not exactly dancing,' Alejandro said tartly. 'It will just take a few moments of your precious time.'

She turned to look at him, about to point out that it was after-hours, but one glance at his black expression had her biting her lip.

'Excuse me a moment,' she said to the very vain Fernando, who was looking into the bar mirror and smoothing his hair as she slid down from her stool.

She went to follow Alejandro to his table, but instead of taking his seat he picked up a box and gestured towards the gates to his residence.

'In private.'

He smiled a black mirthless smile, and she watched his tense fingers type in the code, but once the gates had closed behind him all attempts at niceties subsided.

'What the hell are you doing?' he demanded.

'I don't know what you're talking about.'

'Don't give me that.' He was not mincing his words. 'You and Fernando were practically on top of each other.'

'We were talking,' Emily said. 'It's nice to talk with some-one who's actually attracted to me.'

'Fernando's a player.'

'Well, that's not your concern—you've made that very clear.'

'Are you so determined to lose your virginity?' He took her arm, as if trying to shake some sense into her, as direct and as blunt as ever. 'Just for the sake of it?'

'Go to hell!'

He did not go to hell, though.

As she wrenched open the gates to return to the courtyard he followed her out. And when she took her seat back at the bar he took his own at the table.

*Arrogant idiot,* Emily thought.

'What did he want?' Fernando asked.

'Just work stuff.'

'Another drink?' offered Fernando.

'No, thank you.'

'A dance then…?' he said, and put his hand over hers.

Emily knew she was playing a dangerous game. She didn't want Fernando at all.

'No, thank you.' Emily gave him a tight smile and got down from the stool a little awkwardly.

God, she felt pathetic. She turned, ready to meet Alejandro's glare, but saw that he had got bored with her stupid game and gone.

'Emily…'

Eva, too, was possibly trying to save her from Fernando, and was calling her to join the dancers on the stage. But instead she turned to speak with her.

'I think I'm going to call it a night.'

*'Perdón?'*

'I'm going to go up.'

'Oh,' Eva said, and did not try to dissuade her, but got back to the rest of the class.

Emily wanted to hide, completely embarrassed by her own actions. She was so out of her depth when it came to men, or relationships.

A few tears spilled down her cheeks as she hurriedly made her way towards her apartment. She went to open up her front door, and then turned and looked at the gate behind her—the entrance to Alejandro's residence—and knew he deserved an apology.

But did she dare?

Oh, she wasn't going to his door out of temptation, or to throw herself at him—thankfully she had got over that…

Really, it didn't take a mirror to tell her she wasn't looking her best, with her face red from crying and her mismatched outfit and the silk flower in her hair.

She just wanted to thank him for looking out for her and to say sorry…

Alejandro had poured himself a drink and was fighting with himself not to go back down to the courtyard and wrench Emily away from that creep, and at the same time telling himself it was not his place to do so.

As Emily had just pointed out, she was not his concern.

Then he heard the tentative knock on his door and opened it. And what he saw further exacerbated the recent thaw of his usually cold and emotionless heart. Emily was shaking in her attempt to suppress tears…so much so, the silk rose was almost falling out of her hair. Her face was flushed and she couldn't look at him.

It was he who spoke first. 'Emily, I apologise.'

'For what?'

'I overreacted. You have every right to…' He rolled his hand, but couldn't bring himself to say *flirt with whoever you want* without sounding bitter. 'But Fernando's a player, Emily.'

'Alejandro, I was just… I was trying to make you jealous.'

'That's not very sensible,' he said gently.

'I know.'

And he could have lectured her, but who the hell was he to scold her?

'It worked.'

* * *

She looked up, embarrassed, but so grateful that rather than being scathing he was being nice. With Alejandro she had always been honest, and she was being honest now.

'But don't do that again,' he warned. 'It might not end so well next time.'

'I know.' She took a breath. 'I am sorry.'

'Forget it,' he said.

'Thank you for warning me,' she said.

And she really wasn't here for anything more than that, so, taking her wounded pride, Emily turned from his door.

'Hey, Emily?'

'What?' She looked back over her shoulder.

'Why don't you come in and flirt with me?'

Still she didn't turn around, and she remained honest. 'Because you don't want me, and it hurts too much.'

'Stop it!' he said. 'You know that's not true.'

He left the door open and went inside, entirely giving Emily the option whether to leave or go in.

She stepped inside, not into a hallway, but into a dark, sensual space.

His residence was stunning.

Male, sexy, vast...

And unlike in her little apartment there were no sounds coming up from the street or the courtyard.

The walls were white, hung with ancient hangings and a few musical instruments, as well as a lot of art. Random sculptures were dotted about the place. The place was like a very stylish and muted Aladdin's cave—or rather a grown-up Aladdin's cave. Because rather than garish jewels, everywhere she looked there was a subtle treasure...a chest, a piece of art...a guitar...

The room also contained a pair of low leather couches and she perched on the edge of one as he offered her a drink.

'A gin and tonic,' Emily said, as his hand hovered over the black Romero sherry bottle.

'I'd have to call down to the bar for that.'

'A brandy, then,' Emily said. 'Or cognac.'

He poured her a generous measure of cognac and she took it silently and stared at it for a very long time, not really knowing what to say. Then she plucked at the awful skirt that had felt so right for fun in the studio, but was not her outfit of choice when sitting in the home of this very sophisticated man.

Then he spoke.

'You make me smile, too,' he said suddenly.

Emily looked up from the depths of her gloom, wondering if she'd missed something he said.

Possibly he saw her confusion.

'I was thinking about it after we met at lunchtime. I didn't get it that Eva said you needed help to smile, or...' He took a breath. 'Emily, from the day I met you, you've always smiled.'

'I'm actually quite serious,' Emily said. 'When I'm not frantically on the pull with Fernando...'

'See?' Alejandro said.

And she looked up and saw that he smiled. It had never occurred to her that it might be rare for him too.

'I want you to have an amazing time while you're here, and I'd love to spend time with you, but you have to understand I am not into relationships. Believe me, if you want more than bed then I am not your man.'

'You are, though...' She shivered. That had come out sounding too needy. 'I mean, I want bed,' she admitted. 'With you.'

'I don't want tears at the end,' Alejandro said. 'I told you... ending things doesn't have to be complicated.'

'I know. I've just got this...' Still she was able to be truthful. 'I didn't know how a kiss should be until I kissed you. I have a past. I've seemingly lived with someone...been engaged. And yet I feel like I've got a millstone around my neck...'

'A millstone?'

'A weight on my shoulders,' she said, trying to explain something so intensely personal to the man with those dark, knowing eyes. He made her articulate things… 'I don't want to be a virgin. It makes me seem…' She looked at him. 'It put *you* off.'

'No,' he said. 'It caused me to hesitate.'

'Please don't lie when I'm being so honest.'

'Okay,' he said, and gave her the truth. 'It did put me off. I was already a little hesitant, given we're working together, and with all that's going on in my private life…'

'Your fiancée?'

'We were never formally engaged—but, yes. I didn't want to stir gossip. I wanted you, though. And then you told me that you'd never slept with anyone and it felt too much. I thought that if you'd waited this long then you should be very sure—'

'Do you know what?' she interrupted, and looked right at him. 'I like you.'

It was the bravest she had ever been. Braver than flying to Jerez or walking into a flamenco studio. Braver than coming to his door to admit she'd been foolish. Just brave.

'I have an awful lot of hang-ups, and sometimes I forget them when I'm with you. Maybe I like the fact that we can go nowhere. That I can talk openly to you.'

Even with her face on fire, even cringing with embarrassment, Emily could not think of anyone else she could have had this conversation with.

'I don't want it to be a big deal—except it is. I don't want to be a virgin and have some guy telling me that if I've waited this long then I ought to be "very sure…" as if I don't know my own mind.'

'Hey…' He winced at his own choice of words. 'I just said that—'

'Well, don't say it again. Because I am sure. I want you—physically, at least. It doesn't mean I'm going to fall in love with you. I know you're not interested in long-term. I just want to make love with someone I want.'

'Fine,' Alejandro said. 'I won't warn you again. I've already told you I'm a bastard.'

'I want to be like the storks,' Emily said.

'God, no.' He shook his head. 'I looked it up. They are monogamous for the life of their mate…'

'I meant,' Emily said, 'I don't want there to be anyone else for as long as we last.'

'That's my rule too.'

Finally some common ground.

'And I have another rule,' Alejandro said. 'We have to be discreet.'

'What do you mean?'

'I don't want anyone finding out about us.'

Her eyes narrowed. She was not quite sure as to his reason.

'Emily, I don't bring my entire life to work.'

'You *have* broken things off with Mariana?' she checked.

'Yes. I'd just reminded her that we were over on the night we met,' he told her, and then asked a question of his own. 'If you know I'm that much of a player, what are you doing here?'

Emily gave a tight shrug.

She wasn't feeling quite so bold now. She'd liked it better out in the vineyards, when it had just happened so easily. Now she felt a little as if she were in the doctor's waiting room, and that at any moment she'd be called in.

God, she was so jumpy, but trying not to show it, Emily thought, as he came and took a seat on the sofa beside her.

'Why didn't you dance tonight?' he asked. 'Aside from…'

He didn't want to say Fernando's name, Emily realised.

'How come you didn't get up on the stage?'

'Because I would have looked ridiculous.'

'Why? You were looking forward to *jaleo*.'

'Yes. When I thought it was going to be held in the studio.' She shook her head. 'I'm really not very good at dancing. Eva says I'm like a tree that won't bend.'

'Maybe this will help… I've got you a present.'

'What?' She frowned. 'Why?'

'Like I said, I was thinking about you today.'

She realised the white box he had been carrying was actually for her.

'Open it,' he said.

She peeled open the edge and then pulled back handfuls of tissue paper. Atop some layers of red fabric was a pair of black leather flamenco shoes. Turning them over, she saw that the nails were already banged in. These were serious shoes… more beautiful than she would have ever chosen for herself.

'Alejandro, they're for a professional.'

'They make an amazing noise.'

'But how did you know my size?'

'Eva can be discreet when required.'

'You told her!'

'I said I wanted to get you some shoes and asked which ones you practised in.' He shrugged. 'I said you were trying to find out more about flamenco for the website.'

'Do you think she believed you?'

'I don't know about that. I just know she would never say anything.'

She could not quite contemplate that Alejandro had left her looking at the church spire and gone to Eva, and then gone shopping with her in mind.

'Why would you do this?' she asked.

'Why not?' He sounded bemused. 'I wanted to get you something nice. You deserve it. Maybe I wanted to treat the strongest woman I know.'

'Please…' She rolled her eyes. 'Don't go too over the top.'

'But you are. I cannot imagine living my life without family. Yet you do.'

'Alejandro, for years I hid behind a man who didn't want me.'

'Yet here you are, taking dance classes in a foreign country…starting your own business. Emily, I thought my mother was strong, but she always had her parents behind her, or my father, or a lover.'

She'd never been called strong before. It was almost laughable, and yet his eyes were serious.

She looked at the box of gifts. There was also a gold tube of lipstick, and beneath the shoes something in a sheer, silky fabric that intrigued her…

'What's this?'

'It's a flamenco dress,' he said. 'Modern flamenco,' he added.

'I've never seen one like this.'

'They are not in most stores,' he said. 'It's not something you'd wear to the studio.'

'Then where?'

She touched the silk as if it were hot coals, sharply pulling her hand back.

'You want to dance? Dance for *me*, then.'

She stared at him.

'Go on.'

'I can't wear this,' she said, holding up the very sheer dress. 'I'll look ridiculous.'

'Why do you say that?' He was impatient. 'You don't need to have a degree in flamenco to wear it…you don't have to reach some high standard. Go and get changed…tonight we make our own *jaleo*.'

'Do you play the guitar?'

'Good God, no.'

He smiled and, standing, took out a vinyl record. As she stood there, the sounds of a guitar and a *cajón* filled the room.

'You can use my bedroom to change.'

He said it so casually…as if her going to his bedroom to get changed was normal.

'Straight down the hall.'

The hall was long, the huge wooden doors at the end were already open, and she clipped towards them, hearing the tinny metal sounds her borrowed shoes were making on the tiles.

The room was softly lit and the low bed was dressed in

white. The scent of his cologne hung in the air, and it felt oddly like an unwanted reprieve to be in here without him.

If he really wanted her, wouldn't it be *his* hands undressing her?

She looked at the bed and it terrified her, but then she looked into the mirror and that worried her even more.

She stood there, alone in his bedroom, in front of a full-length mirror, and decided that anything she put on now would surely be an improvement on this.

Her purple practice skirt and plunging top looked as if she'd been raiding the dress-up box at some amateur theatre club. The flower in her hair had fallen down and now hung from one curl. She peeled off her clothes and looked at her underwear, which was by far too sensible for the new dress.

She pulled the dress over her head, absolutely certain that it would never stretch enough and could never fit…yet the liquid silky fabric meshed to her body like a second skin.

The neckline was far too low for her to wear her T-shirt bra beneath it. And her awful knickers did nothing for the clinging fabric.

She slid them off, but the fabric now clung to her bare stomach, so she took down the sleeves and removed her bra.

Then she slid the arms of the dress back on.

She was fully dressed, but her nipples were thick and the fabric so sheer she could see her tummy button. Somehow it clung and yet it smoothed, making her breasts and stomach look shapely. It hugged her bottom and thighs.

Sitting on the edge of the bed, she lifted the skirt as she slid on her shoes and saw that, even though it clung, there was yard after yard of fabric in the dress.

God, it was too sexy by far, Emily thought as, with her new shoes on, she looked in the mirror.

Now she looked as if she'd raided the costume box of some upmarket opera house.

*Tonight, Carmen will be played by Emily*, she thought, laughing to herself and retying her silk flower.

She turned around and saw that the back of the dress was so low it revealed most of her spine, then she spun back to the mirror.

Her red cheeks looked as if she'd been slapped and they stung in her pale face.

She took out the lipstick and painted her mouth red, and then she walked out.

The shoes sounded fabulous, the metal nails ringing out with each step she took, and there was no chancing of pausing or taking tentative steps because she knew that he'd hear her.

She was one burning blush as she entered his lounge.

His tie and jacket were off and he had changed into boots rather than the shoes he'd had on before.

And he was watching her in a way she had never been looked at in her life.

'Come closer,' he said, and turned on a side light.

She wished he hadn't, because she'd felt a little less exposed in the semi-darkness.

Now shadows fell, and she could see his expression as he looked at her hair and her neck. He stared at her breasts for so long that they ached, and she wanted to touch them. He gazed at her stomach, and she wanted to suck it in, but it was way too late for that.

'You look incredible…'

'Stop.'

'How do you feel?'

'Somewhere between a fraud and amazing.' She was shaking, but with excitement, and the dress was somehow cool on her inflamed skin.

'Lift the hem of the dress.'

'I haven't got any knickers on.'

He laughed, a low sexy laugh, and then corrected her assumption. 'I meant lift it at one side.'

'Oh.'

'I'm not asking you to flash me.'

She started to giggle. To relax just a touch.

She leaned forward and with her right hand lifted the hem of her dress. It unfurled as she held her arm out to one side.

'Higher,' he said, and she held it up high.

The fabric lifted as if with miles to spare. The dress really was incredible. She ached to look down, but remembered her classes and kept her chin up.

'Dance for me, *señorita*.'

He struck the floor with his foot and then clapped—or, as she now knew, gave a *palma*. One, two, three, *palmas* that shot arrows of lust to her stomach. And then he followed that with cupped *palmas* as his foot struck the floor again.

She struck back with her heel. Then her toe, then her sole. Then she gave a *palma* back at him and moved her hips. And then he smiled appreciatively and she *did* know how to dance, it would seem. But perhaps there was no one else in the world she could do this in front of.

Not even Eva.

She moved her hips and walked forward, and then she lifted the dress and swayed with it, and, God, she might not be sexy, but he made her feel it.

He was stamping one foot and that made her move faster. The rolling sound of the guitar and the *cajón* made her feel a little frenzied. It was accompanied by the sound of men singing and cheering, and she could see he was turned on.

He stood up and she danced a little dance around him.

'I feel stup—'

'Shut up and be sexy,' he told her.

And then made her quiet with his mouth; with hot wet kisses as still she moved to the music.

His lithe body barely moved, but each motion, each stamp of his foot or clap of his hand, spun her, so that she continued to dance around him.

His hand slid to her waist and it felt hot through the fabric. They were just dancing bodies, loose but close, and then he caught her in his arms so that her back was to him, and she stood breathless as he kissed her neck.

His mouth was on her flickering pulse, his tongue on her flesh had her pressing into him, and she closed her eyes at the bliss of his lips on her neck and his hand on her breasts.

'Not so wooden…' he said, and turned her as easily as if the floor was revolving beneath her.

He kissed her hard on the mouth, the music still playing, their hips still swaying. Then he removed his belt as his tongue chased hers, and she opened up his shirt with desperate fingers.

His skin, his torso, was so incredible that she had to see it, and she explored his arms, his shoulders, his chest and toned stomach and he made her dizzy with lust.

He had moved the fabric of the dress so that her breasts spilled out, and now they were locked in mutual admiration as they resumed kissing, their naked chests pressed together.

'I thought,' he admitted as he kissed her down on to the couch, 'that I would have to drag you from the bedroom.'

'I told you…' Emily gazed up at him. 'I want you.'

Perhaps her confidence was the new sexy…? Or was it just the absolute desire in her eyes? Because, with Emily, he thought he might have veered from his more practised moves. But hearing her wanton voice, feeling the way she licked at his ear as her hands slid over his torso, Alejandro was in uncharted territory.

But not quite.

He was kissing her breasts, lifting the skirt of her dress, as he recalled they had been here before. Last time they had been in the vineyard, where they'd been just utterly lost to each other.

Now they were warm, and sexed up, and there was nothing to stop them.

'Christ…' he said, lowering his head, licking down her neck and bare chest.

He slid her arms out of the dress so that she was naked from the waist up. And then so practised and skilled were his fingers that he moved the garment down her hips, as if he were unpeeling her, exposing her.

Now all she wore were her shoes…her gorgeous, beautiful new shoes. And as she lifted one foot up to admire them he saw the shining pinkness of her, and held her leg higher and placed it on his shoulder.

Her hand shot out to cover herself but he caught it. She licked her lips a little nervously, but then bravely lifted the other leg.

'I was going to take you to bed,' he said, stroking her. 'But instead I am on my knees…'

He lowered his head and licked up her thigh. He nipped at the tender skin so that she writhed, and then she stopped fighting as his mouth found her centre.

He was so slow and so thorough and so noisy in his pleasure that she thought she might die. She lay rocked by the waves that swept through her, trying to resist them.

'Go with it,' he told her.

'I can't,' she admitted.

Because no matter how delicious the feeling of his mouth on her body, she could not give in to it while knowing there was more to come.

His erection was huge, and perhaps he saw the trepidation in her eyes, because he knelt up and they touched it together…

'Don't stop,' she begged. 'I never knew…'

'God…' he moaned.

'Please…' she said.

His mouth felt amazing…her only regret was that it was only she who was weak.

'You're so hot…' His naked torso came up to hers. 'We're going to bed. Condoms…?'

'I'm on the pill.'

'Emily,' he warned, 'you don't have unprotected sex with a man you picked up from a *taberna*.'

He was kneeling up...rubbing her breasts and batting her thigh with his erection.

'It's *you*, though...' Her voice sounded breathy and wanton...she didn't want to move from this heavy bliss. 'You're not dangerous.'

She should have heard the warning in her own words. But she could not have done this with another man—not even her fiancé, had he wanted her. With Alejandro it felt normal to be kissing with reckless passion and to be desperate for the feel of the other's skin.

She could only have been like this with him, and they were both too far gone to dwell on anything other than the other.

The record had stopped and the needle was making little scratching noises. He could hear her ragged breathing as she looked down to where he stroked himself.

She was glistening wet, from desire and his tongue. The scent of her turned on was heady, and the taste of her had driven him wild. He could not resist a feel of her. In truth, he wanted to gauge her pain and her pleasure, but he wasn't all gentleman—he wanted to feel her too.

'I'm going to so lecture you later,' he said.

But for now...

He eased in a little way and watched her pale thighs tremble, heard her little moan as he inched in further.

'Please...'

It wasn't the pain Emily was terrified of—more that he might stop.

'Shh...'

His finger stroked her and then slipped inside, as if he were toying with that idea, but then he came up and kissed her.

His kisses were like oxygen, just completely necessary, and it was Emily who turned her head as he nudged in deeper than he had before.

It hurt, and she tried to hold on to her moan.

'Oh, God…' She turned her face away and screwed her eyes closed.

'Emily!'

He called her name and she faced him. With one hand he caressed her face as the other held his thick length. It was the most delicious moment of her life to date.

They were staring at each other as he drove in, making a breathless sound as he tore through the barrier of resistance, and she sobbed—but it was a moan of both pain and desire.

'Oh, Alejandro…' She was clinging to his back, feeling the silky skin and taut muscles beneath, and her eyes closed as she tried to acclimatise to the feel of him inside her.

He started to move, slow thrusts that made tears squeeze from her eyes, and her teeth bit into her lip as she arched at the new sensations. She did not know how to move, but she knew he did not require her expertise—she had none. So she gave in to his.

He took her leg and pushed it back, then did the same with the other, and she cried out as he drove in deeper. It felt as if she were being swallowed, or buried, as if she were being consumed…

'There…' she said, although what 'there' meant she did not know. She knew just that this was everything she wanted.

'Alej…' She had never shortened his name until now, but she was dropping syllables with her every inhibition, pleading with him for more of whatever this magic was.

He was moving deeper, and faster, and she realised just how controlled he was only when he let go a little.

His thrusts were building…he was holding her thighs open and watching them…and then he put his forearms either side of her head and took her fast.

'Ah…'

The last syllables fell away. Emily could not have shouted his name if she'd tried, because her jaw was tense.

She was twisting, but not moving, because his body had her pinned, and she gave in to the pleasure—just succumbed. His sudden shout, the way he stilled and then came deep within her, was a sensation overload, and she cried out again. Not in pain, nor regret, just in the release he gave her.

'It's okay…'

She didn't mind her tears. They seemed normal when her every emotion felt as if it had been leeched from her.

'Hey…' he said, scooping her up and finally taking her to his bed.

It didn't intimidate her now.

# CHAPTER NINE

EMILY WAS FALLING in love.

But determinedly not with Alejandro.

She would not allow herself to do that because it wasn't a part of their deal, so instead she told herself that it was the city and its surroundings that so deeply appealed.

She was falling in love with the food and the buzzing atmosphere, the spontaneous singing and dancing that broke out not just in the *peñas*, but as people walked in the street.

And as well as all that there were her dance lessons.

*'Alfojar!'* Eva would repeatedly tell her. *Relax, loosen...*

And over and over she was told to smile. She was told to be sexy, told to be angry. Eva would pat herself under her own chin and Emily would raise her head higher. Or Eva would draw a swift semi-circle near her own lips and that would tell Emily to smile.

'Chin up!' Eva said. 'And smile. Show how you are feeling. You are happy, yes…?'

'Yes!' she answered instantly.

Two weeks with Alejandro and she was the happiest she had ever been. She felt adored, wanted and, yes…happy.

'Then show it,' Eva said. 'We have just two weeks left.'

Her smile faltered then, but Emily quickly snapped it back, determined to keep to her side of the deal. A holiday romance was what she had wanted. Breaking up didn't have to be complicated, Alejandro had said, and she'd told him with certainty that she could handle a short-term relationship.

'You are confident,' Eva said.

'Yes…' Emily said, and she heard the waver in her voice.

'Emily?' Eva checked, and made a gesture with her hand beneath her own chin, which told Emily to raise hers even higher. 'Better,' Eva said. 'You are confident, yes?'

'Yes,' she responded more firmly, and raised her chin a fraction higher.

And, indeed, she did feel more confident.

Flamenco was such an expressive dance, and somehow it made her more able to show her emotions, to examine her own feelings, even when she was away from the dance studio.

'Can I ask you a question?' she asked Alejandro that very night, as they lay in his gorgeous bed. 'Without you thinking I'm being all needy. I'm just curious, honestly…'

'Ask.'

'Why are you so closed off to relationships?'

'I don't want to rely on any one person.' He thought for a moment, then said, 'I don't think you can ever really rely on another person. You might think you can, but…' He turned his head on the pillow and looked at her. 'Look at you and your fiancé.'

'That was never love.' It was odd, but with Alejandro she could be honest—even with herself. 'I can see now that Gordon never loved me.'

'Did you love him?'

He asked the question lightly, in a way that said she didn't have to answer, but for Emily it brought a moment of self-examination as she thought back to their early days.

'No,' she admitted. 'I didn't know it, of course, but looking back I think I was so cooped up with caring for my dad that I just longed for the weekend and our nights out. I thought I loved Gordon when he was there for me after my father died, but…' She took a breath. 'No, I didn't love him.'

'Yet you stayed?'

'I did.' Emily nodded, scarcely able to believe that she'd set the bar to her happiness so low. 'It sounds weak, but after losing my parents I felt lost. He was always kind...'

'I'm not criticising,' Alejandro said. 'In fact, I can see why people might choose the safer option. It's a lot better than the rollercoaster of my parents' marriage.' He shook his head. 'How can you say you love someone when they cause you nothing but pain?'

'You mean your parents?'

'I would come home from school, or wherever, and they would be in the middle of a row. My father would be shouting and my mother would be throwing her clothes into her case. Sebastián would be angry... Carmen crying.' He screwed up his nose in distaste. 'I haven't thought of that in ages.'

'What about you?'

'I wanted to go on tour with her.' He gave a tight smile. 'She would say, "Next time, Alejandro." And then she'd point at me.' He did the same to Emily, pointing his finger in a warning gesture. 'And she would say, "Don't you cry, now."'

'Did you?'

'No.' He shook his head. 'I didn't want to add to it all. There was just too much drama and emotion. I never wanted that. I can remember telling my father to just stop...let her leave without a row...' He rolled his eyes. 'It was no wonder she didn't want to come back.'

Their nights were intimate and sexy. Discretion ruled the day, though. A feat far more easily achieved by Alejandro.

Emily's heart just leaped whenever she saw him, and it took all her restraint to give him only a vague wave if their paths crossed. And she kept forgetting—so much so that now, as he stared impassively at her bright smile on his computer screen, she wondered if her camera was on.

Rather quickly she worked out why his face was so bland when Sebastián's face dropped into the screen.

'Emile...' Sebastián said.

'Emily,' she corrected him nervously, and then smiled that bright smile. But it was a false one now, just so he wouldn't get a hint that she'd been smiling for his younger brother.

'We've had a first look at the new website,' he went on.

They approved of her work, it would seem, although Alejandro was definitely more effusive in the bedroom than during this, a business meeting, and Sebastián warned her that it wasn't a tourist guide to Jerez they wanted, and told her to focus more closely on the product.

'There's a photo shoot in the courtyard this afternoon?' Alejandro checked, and Emily realised that he was giving her a little prompt.

'Yes.' Emily nodded. 'All the courtyard images that are on the website now are placeholders. I'll be sure that the product is more prominent. Also, some of the images of the vineyards are being replaced with views from inside the restaurant. Ideally, I'd like a couple of images of you...'

'There are plenty.'

Sebastián was actually being helpful, perhaps because time was starting to race and she was still relying heavily on archive photos, because apart from Alejandro none of the family was particularly available.

'Actually, if you speak with the manager of the *taberna* he should have some old shots we were going to use for last year's summer festival.'

'I'll do that.' She took a breath. 'I was hoping to speak with Carmen about some images of her with the dancing horses...'

'Alejandro should have taken care of that,' said Sebastián.

He hadn't, though.

Despite a couple of prompts from Emily to meet his sister, a meeting had never materialised.

Now Alejandro gave his reasons. 'Carmen's not feeling particularly sociable at the moment.'

Sebastián rolled his eyes. 'I get it. But remind her the new website goes live in ten days.'

'Sure.' Alejandro nodded, then addressed Emily. 'Anything else?'

'They were my main questions.'

'Then if you can log out?' Alejandro responded. 'I would like to speak with Sebastián. Thank you for joining us.'

She'd been dismissed a little too harshly.

And Alejandro knew it.

He was trying not to show that there was anything going on with her to his brother, who knew him better than most. It was for the same reason he was avoiding introducing her to Carmen.

There was an electricity between himself and Emily that was hard to understand, let alone explain.

She lit him up.

There had been comments already about their first night in the *taberna*, sharing sherry and doing a tasting. It was something he had done many times; he hadn't considered it might draw attention. Yet people had noticed.

And they had noticed, too, how he'd intervened when she'd been being chatted up by Fernando.

So now he was attempting to halt them from becoming the talk of Jerez—and not just out of respect to Mariana. He was trying to shield Emily from the drama that would erupt if it was found out that they were seeing each other.

By keeping things secret he was trying to protect their increasingly diminishing days, and yet he knew Emily was getting irritated with being tucked away. She had asked him the other day if he was ashamed to be seen with her, and it had been so far off the mark that Alejandro had actually laughed.

'Why haven't you taken her to see Carmen?' Sebastián asked now.

'Because I have more on my mind than the new website and dancing ponies.' Alejandro shrugged and moved the subject back to Sebastián's stay in the States. 'How are the talks?'

'I'm headed to California tomorrow. Then back here to NYC in a couple of weeks. It would be great to have the new website by then… Or at least have them put up the old one.'

'No.' Alejandro would not be swayed. 'They've all seen the old one. This will launch by the due date.'

'Why are you so stubborn on this?'

It was because of the links to Mariana's family on the old site. The sherries the two companies shared, with more planned in the future. A personal future that had been designed with only the business in mind and one Alejandro didn't now want.

He buzzed his PA. 'Can you get Carmen to join us please?'

It took a while, but she came online and Alejandro told his siblings of his decision as far as the label went.

'I agree with Padre—we keep the original photo for the label.'

Maria de Luca's image would remain the face of the Romero sherry.

'I am also prepared to insist that she be included on the new website.'

'Why?' Sebastián demanded.

'Because our mother is a part of the Romero history—her first performance was here at the *taberna*.'

He had looked at both versions of Emily's work on this, and what he had seen had blown him away.

'You cannot tell our father's story by erasing our mother from the website. Although, of course, if that is what he wants I would stand by his choice.'

'Alejandro…' His older brother's face was as dark as thunder. 'The change was agreed months ago. *He* was the one who demanded it.'

'And then he found out how sick he is and changed his

mind,' Alejandro pointed out. 'He wants to ensure Maria is taken care of.'

'I want her gone!' Carmen, his younger sister, sobbed.

But he would not allow her tears to move him, even if, out of all the siblings, Carmen had reason to hate their mother the most.

'It's all right for you—you were always her favourite,' his sister told him.

'Please…' He dismissed the notion. 'Anyway, it's not about us. It's about respecting our father's wishes. At the end of the day, it's a photograph on a bottle and a proper mention on the website—why would you let that bother you?'

'It's not just that. She's visiting him…she's at the hospital all the time, sneaking in after we've gone.'

'So what if she is?' Alejandro said. 'He loves her. What do you want to do—put guards on the door?'

'She's after his money.'

'Please,' Alejandro said again, once more dismissing the notion. 'She is one of Spain's most famous flamenco dancers. She has sell-out international tours even in her fifties…'

'You really believe she loves him?' Carmen snarled.

'Not for a moment—but it's what he wants to believe.'

'You know we'll just change it once he's gone,' Sebastián said. 'It will be two to one then.'

'Perhaps.' Alejandro stared at his older brother. 'But I haven't written him off as dead yet. Anyway, it's up to you if you want to disrespect his wishes.'

'Speaking of our father's wishes,' Sebastián said, 'what is happening with your wedding? We need a date…'

He spoke as if it were still a given—for both his and Mariana's family. The fact that they would one day marry had long been considered as such.

Alejandro didn't answer directly. 'I'm going to visit Padre this afternoon,' he informed his siblings. 'I'll tell him my decision about the label, and I also want to speak with his surgeon.'

Alejandro wanted to see his father for himself.

It was late afternoon when his plane landed in Madrid, and early evening by the time he'd spoken with the specialist before seeing his father.

'I don't want more surgery,' José said, and all Alejandro could think was how frail he looked.

But he did not address him as if he were—instead he chose to be blunt.

'Then do you want me to look at hospice care?' Alejandro asked. 'Because that is what all the specialists have said is the alternative. For the treatment to have any chance you need surgery…' He took a breath. 'Padre,' Alejandro said to this most difficult man, 'why are you not fighting?'

'I am,' he said.

'I have told Sebastián and Carmen that you have my vote for keeping Maria on the label, and I also agree she should be mentioned on the new website.'

'What did they say?'

'They are not best pleased.' Alejandro shrugged. 'But while you are still here there is little they can do. You can tell Maria the good news when she visits tonight…we all know she's here all the time.'

'Hmm…' His father let out a soft laugh. 'You don't approve?'

'It's not for me to approve.'

'She is talking of cancelling her summer tour to be with me.'

'So she'll take time off now you're dying? Are you worried she might not do it if you have a year or two left rather than months?'

'You sound like Sebastián.'

'No,' Alejandro said. 'Have you discussed surgery with her?'

It was a cruel question, perhaps, but had not been cruelly asked.

'No, I try to keep things light. She's seen enough of my moods.'

'Jesus…' Alejandro let out a soft laugh. His parents' relationship was toxic at best, fatal at worst—but then he had always known that. And so he sat on the bed and held his father's hand.

'I love her too much,' José said.

'No...' Alejandro shook his head, and looked around the luxurious private suite.

His father had everything he needed—Maria talking about cancelling her tour and visiting him. Sebastián and Carmen might hate her, but to Alejandro his father was as guilty in the breakdown of the marriage as she, and his summing up was an honest one.

'You would just do anything to keep her.'

'Alejandro, I want to make sure that the people I love are all taken care of.'

'I get that.'

'I think your wedding should take place sooner rather than later—' he started, but Alejandro cut in.

'I'm not marrying Mariana, Padre.'

'What are you talking about?'

'I shall support your business decisions, but you cannot dictate who and when I marry.'

'No! I have been patient, but it's time. I need to go to my grave knowing the future of the bodega is secure. And for that to happen—'

'Save the deathbed speeches,' Alejandro said. 'If you have the surgery there might be no need for them.' He would not be manipulated. 'I'm not going to marry on your command.'

Alejandro's voice halted as a rather too unfamiliar face peered around the door.

'Alejandro...' His mother gave a tight smile when she saw him. 'I didn't know you were here.'

'Since when do you ever know my plans?' He picked up his laptop and started to pack up.

'Don't rush off because of me, Alejandro.' She smiled at him.

'I have to fly back tonight.' Often he would stay on in Madrid, but on this night, after this exhausting day, he simply wanted to be at home.

'Alejandro has voted,' José told her. 'Your beautiful face shall stay on our label.'

'You voted for me?' Maria looked over to Alejandro and smiled in delight. 'You have always stood up for me.'

'I'm just respecting my father's wishes.'

'Not all of them,' said José. 'Alejandro, I'm asking you to reconsider. Take some time to think.'

'I don't want to reconsider,' Alejandro said. 'And I don't need time to think. I mean it, Padre. I have your back when it comes to the business, but just stay the hell out of my private life.'

The thought of home, with Emily, was tempting, and Alejandro flew through the late evening to be with her, rather than staying in a hotel.

Emily heard the soft knock on her door at what she guessed was around midnight. She lay there, trying not to be pathetic and jump out of bed just to greet him. He'd want her to go to his place, because her bed was too small for his frame.

It wasn't just because of his earlier cool treatment of her that she lay there. She'd actually felt a little ill after work… had just come home and gone to bed.

She was hurting, and she was worried she was going to get needy and mess up her side of the no-strings interlude to which they'd agreed.

He didn't knock twice.

And it should have come as a relief—except it did not.

She'd heard his PA book him a flight to Madrid and guessed he must be visiting his father.

Had there been bad news?

Hating herself for being so weak, she climbed out of bed and pulled on the rather tatty robe that he teased her about. Taking the key, she locked up.

He'd taught her the private code for his door, so she was able to slip in.

'Sorry about earlier,' he said as she entered his apartment. 'I just didn't want Sebastián getting wind of us.'

She didn't know what to say to that, so she said nothing.

'I went to visit my father,' he went on.

'I heard your PA calling the pilot to take you to Madrid. How is he?'

'At his manipulative best.'

And possibly so was his son. Because he peeled off his clothes and climbed into the vast wooden bed that had seen so much passion in recent weeks.

She wanted to be in his bed—that was why she'd come to him tonight. A little too easily, perhaps, but the damage to her pride was worth it.

Because he took her in a way he never had before.

He took her slowly, and held her arms above her head just to watch her orgasm.

'Alej…'

She was coming apart, and he was taking her as she did so, deeply kissing her, then pausing to softly kiss her eyes. And all the time he drove into her. Then he knelt up and held her hips as he took her to the limit, and the groan he let out as he achieved his own climax had her calling out as she orgasmed again more deeply than she ever had.

It was sex like she had never known existed.

Emily lay there in the dark, staring into the night and feeling Alejandro asleep, spooned into her, his arm over hers, his hand on her breast. And she didn't know any other way to describe the sex they'd just had.

It felt as if they had just made love.

# CHAPTER TEN

'HEY!' ALEJANDRO SMILED as Emily came up the stairs carrying a large box. 'What the hell is that?'

'A flamenco doll,' Emily said, laughing as she opened up the door to her little apartment. 'I got it for Willow.'

'Your goddaughter?'

'Yes.'

He picked up the large boxed toy as she put it down and peered at the gaudy doll. She was dressed in a green frothy lace dress and her nails were painted red. There were plastic gold hoops in her ears.

'She's a bit creepy,' Alejandro said.

'Willow's four,' Emily said, by way of explanation. 'She'll love it. I've also bought her a dress to match.'

Emily had bought a lot of things for her goddaughter. Little sweets, a fridge magnet… It surprised him.

After all she was here working, not on holiday.

'Where are you going?' she asked. 'You're looking very smart.'

'I have a business lunch in Seville.'

'It's the weekend,' Emily said and he heard the slight strain to her tone.

It was her last weekend.

Her suitcase was out, and he hated the sight of it.

Usually it was tucked away in her wardrobe, but now and then she dragged it out, and he'd found it brought back too many memories.

Black memories that seemed to be becoming more vivid with each passing day.

His mother angrily throwing clothes in a suitcase as his father ripped them out.

Or the less eventful times…just coming downstairs in the morning and seeing the cases lined up, knowing that she was leaving again.

'I can come with you,' he remembered saying. 'I'll sit quietly.'

He'd often gone backstage, but as his mother's star had risen so too had the distances she travelled, and the number of after-parties and the demands of the tour.

'Not this time,' she would say. 'Next time, maybe?'

He'd sit quietly on the stairs, wishing his brother, who was five years older, would stop scowling, or his father would stop shouting, or the baby stop screaming…

'You're a good boy, Alejandro,' she'd say, as if in warning, and he'd halt the threatening tears and carry her handbag to the car.

Aside from staff, he'd been the only one to stand at the drive and wave her off. Smiling and waving while never knowing when or even if she'd be back.

He'd learned to turn his emotions off like a tap.

Yet he'd never mastered turning them back on.

He looked over to Emily, who gave him such a bright smile he was almost tempted to look over his shoulder to see who'd come in. But he knew that smile she wore only for him.

'Do you want to come with me to Seville?' he asked.

'To a business lunch?'

'No.' He pulled her towards him. 'That would not be very businesslike, but we could stay there for the night? Have dinner somewhere nice?'

There were nice places here in Jerez—beautiful, romantic places—yet he didn't take her to them, and not for the first time Emily found she had to bite her tongue.

She was growing tired of this endless discretion.

'You could go shopping,' he suggested, and named a very exclusive fashion house. 'I have an account there...'

'I can afford my own clothes, thank you!'

'Get your hair done, then,' he said.

It wasn't the first time he'd suggested it, and she knew he must have seen her expression.

'Or stay in bed...order champagne, or cake, or whatever. I thought most women loved to shop?'

'I don't.' Emily frowned. 'At least I don't think so.'

'I hate it,' he admitted, 'but I go there a couple of times a year and they make it as painless as possible. I'm just giving you options. It's up to you. But if you do want to come then we need to leave very soon.'

Emily wanted to go—and not just because she'd love to see Seville. It was simply the prospect of spending more time with Alejandro along with the prospect of a romantic night away.

Even if Alejandro insisted he didn't do romance, sometimes it felt exactly what this was.

'I'd love to come,' Emily admitted.

'Get ready then.' He glanced at her suitcase. 'You'll just need an overnight bag.'

Emily packed in a matter of moments. Her wardrobe was starting to fill with colour, but as she flung in a rather nice red top she'd purchased she paused and caught sight of herself in the wardrobe mirror. Despite her wishing he'd take her somewhere nice here, even if he offered she had nothing suitable to wear.

God, maybe she did need a wardrobe update.

Or was it that he was embarrassed to be seen out with her?

'Hey!' He was waiting in the car to take her out for their unexpected adventure, and smiled when she got in. 'I just have to drop into the equestrian school. I need to leave some brochures for Carmen.'

'Can I meet her?' Emily said. 'I still haven't taken any photos of her.'

'You found some, though.'

'Yes, but I'd love to speak to her, and I do want to see the equestrian school.'

'Another day,' Alejandro said. 'I'm just dropping these off. We don't have time to stop.'

There never was time to stop, but instead of dwelling on the elusive Carmen, she told him her news.

'I've got two new clients,' Emily said. 'Well, one's paid a deposit.'

'That's great. You're building their websites?'

'Yes.'

'What sort of businesses are they?'

'A sports centre in the North of England.' Well, it was an indoor bowling centre…and the other was an MOT and tyre replacement franchise. 'And I've got a craft beer company who've made a couple of enquiries.'

'That's great.'

'I don't know how I'm going to pretend to like beer.'

'Were you pretending about the sherry?'

'You'll never know!'

He smiled at her teasing as they pulled in at the equestrian school. 'I'd know,' he said, and gave her a quick kiss before heading into the building.

She waited in the car, but the place was simply too beautiful to ignore and soon she climbed out, looking at the glorious mustard-yellow and white building, itching to go inside and find out more about the famous dancing horses.

Gosh, there was so much to explore and to see…six weeks was never going to be enough time. She doubted a full year would be enough.

It was her time with Alejandro that had especially raced by, though.

'Couldn't resist,' Emily said, and he smiled as he walked towards her and saw she was taking photos. And, no, she couldn't resist. As he approached her she took some shots of him.

God, he was beautiful.

He continued to walk towards her, his suit in the bright sun almost like liquid on his long limbs. And then he made her laugh, because he took off his jacket and threw it over one shoulder, then gave her a look, as if he were strutting down the catwalk.

'Work it, baby...' she said, and that made him laugh too. He pouted his lips and strutted, and she laughed so much she possibly took more photos of the ground and the sky than of him.

'Alejandro...'

A woman, who could only be Carmen, was calling him. She had the same beautiful bone structure and the same effortless grace as she ran to catch up with her brother.

'What are you here for?'

'Carmen...'

His laughter quickly dropped away, Emily noticed.

'I've just dropped off some brochures, as I told you I would.'

'So why not stop by and say hello?' she asked in Spanish.

'Because I have to be in Seville by midday.'

Carmen was slender, dressed in jodhpurs and a black T-shirt and boots. Though tiny, her stance was confident and her dark eyes suspicious, and her question as she glanced over towards Emily was direct.

'*Quién es ella?*' Carmen asked—'*Who is she?*'

'This is Emily,' Alejandro said in English. 'Emily, this is my sister Carmen...'

'*Buenos días,*' Emily said.

The greeting wasn't returned.

'Emily is doing the new website.'

'*Just* the new website?' Carmen said. 'Or one of the Romero brothers too?'

'Hey...' Alejandro warned his sister, but it didn't stop Carmen.

'Does Mariana know?' she asked, again in Spanish.

'Don't even go there, Carmen,' he told her.

'Clearly she doesn't know, if you're heading to Seville. Isn't that where you hide all your lovers?'

'No one's hiding.'

'Why do people have to lie?' Carmen sobbed, and then turned on her heel and ran off.

Alejandro stood there, shaking his head. Then he turned and must have seen Emily's stricken face.

'Did you understand all that?' he asked.

'I think so.' She felt a little sick, in fact. 'Am I being hidden?'

'Don't be ridiculous,' he snapped, and they got back in the car and drove in silence.

Alejandro could feel the tension in Emily and he addressed it. 'You think I'm hiding you because I'm still seeing Mariana. But I told you right at the start we'd broken up. I confided in you.'

She stared ahead but didn't respond.

'Say it—whatever it is you're thinking. Because if you don't fight your corner, Emily, then no one else will...'

She clearly did not know how to, though.

'So we drive in silence.' He shrugged.

Fast too.

She pulled down the sun visor and tried to ready herself for the hotel in Seville. To make matters worse there was a shiny red bump on her chin—when she'd stopped getting spots by the time she was sixteen.

She could see the signs for Seville now, and suddenly not only had she been invited to address the situation, she wanted to. She was so tired of ignoring her own insecurities.

'Have you told Mariana that it's over?'

'As I've already told you—yes. I told her in December,

and then I told her to make it public the very night that you and I met.'

'But she hasn't?'

'Not to my knowledge.'

'And you haven't told your brother or your sister?'

'I'm thirty-one years old. I don't need their advice or their take on things. I have been quite busy, in fact, since the so-called break-up...' He glanced over. 'Why do you think I'm lying?'

'Because I *do* feel hidden.' She screwed her eyes closed. 'We don't go out together...'

'We've been together for three weeks,' Alejandro said. 'And we've spent all our time in bed.' He looked over at her. 'Do you want us to make out at work?'

'No!'

Emily was unused to a row.

Or rather she was unused to a row with passion.

'I feel...' She didn't know what to say—or rather knew that if she did say anything it would be too much.

She was crazy about him. She was trying to tell herself it was just fun, a little holiday romance, only she craved more.

And if he was cheating on Mariana then at least she could end it, start to hate him, rather than feeling this wave of emotion that had been building since the second they had met. Emotion she was trying to contain, to push down.

Because she wanted him all the time. She wanted to know about his father, his family, his sister... She wanted more involvement than he did.

'You feel...?' he invited as they entered the city of Seville.

Its stunning architecture would have taken her breath away on any other day, but she saw it now through tear-filled eyes, turning her head so as to not let him see.

He drove expertly through the heavy traffic, with her his tense, silent partner... Finally, she spoke. 'I feel like a secret.'

'We agreed to keep things discreet.'

'No, you told me that was how it would be,' Emily said, the floodgates opening and a lifetime of insecurities finally being given voice. 'Are you ashamed to be seen with me?'

'Where the hell did *that* come from?' He looked genuinely perplexed.

'You're the most demonstrative man I've ever met, but only when we're in private.' Emily was as close to shouting as she had ever come. She so badly wanted to believe him, but knew she was being fed lies. 'You don't want a relationship—I get that. You couldn't have made it any clearer. And now you're suggesting I buy a new wardrobe.'

'Because you so often say you have nothing to wear.'

'And you want me to get my hair cut.'

'Every morning you complain about your hair. You told me you cut it yourself. I thought it might feel nice?'

'Hair salons are a waste of money.'

They were pulling into a hotel forecourt. Doormen were leaping forward, whistles were blowing as Alejandro's car came to a halt. And so too did her heart as she choked out a question.

'Are you embarrassed to be seen with me?'

'Emily...'

'Am I not sophisticated enough?'

She didn't await his answer.

As the doorman opened the passenger side Emily leaped out.

For a full moment he sat there, gripping the steering wheel, stunned at their row. He'd never cared enough to row before, and he never invited drama in.

Alejandro was appalled, too, that in trying to shield Emily from the wrath of both his and Mariana's family if their affair was exposed he'd made her feel like some grubby secret.

He looked up to where she stood, delving in her bag for a

tissue, apologising and stepping out of the way as some arrogant hotel guests brushed past.

Alejandro would have liked to get out and tap her on the shoulder, correct her on one vital point...

It was Emily who was embarrassed by herself, Emily who apologised if another person stepped on her shadow. Emily who would rather buy gifts for others than spend anything on herself. And, for all there was much to address from her outburst—Mariana, his family, work—it was the evidence of her insecurities that had shaken him the most.

And those were the first things he would address.

*His* way, though.

There was no checking in required at the opulent hotel—they knew him well—but as they took the ancient elevator to his suite there was an explosive energy between them.

The elevator pinged. Emily didn't even look at the suite they stepped directly into—just stood there as Alejandro dismissed the butler.

'You don't come near me when we're out and I don't get why,' she said suddenly.

'You want to know why?'

Oh, he was going to come near her now.

'Because I have recently broken up with someone. And even if there was no love there, there was respect. Do you think it would be fair for her to hear that we're together?'

Emily caught her breath.

'Do you think it would be kind for us to be seen dancing in the *taberna*...' he pulled her in '...like this? Pressing in to each other?' He lifted her hair and deeply kissed her neck, touched her as he wanted to all the time. *All the time.* 'If you think I'm a cheat you're wrong about that, and if you think I'm ashamed or embarrassed by you, then you might as well go. Because that means you don't know me at all.' He looked right at her. 'I think you're beautiful.'

'You're just saying that.'

'Why would I just say that? I want you all the time.' He watched her rapid blink, and the pinch of her lips as she fought his compliments. 'I don't want others to find out because I want to protect you for what little time we have.'

'Protect me from what?'

'If my family thought you were the reason for Mariana and I breaking up you would be hated.' He looked at her. 'And you don't deserve to be.'

'Hated?' she checked.

'At the very least you would be blamed. I'm trying to protect you. Protect *us*,' he elaborated. 'We have a week left, and I don't want my family or Mariana's to spoil a single moment of our time.'

'Why would they spoil it?'

'My father still wants to see a marriage between Mariana and me—even more so since he fell ill. I've told him it won't be happening. I just don't want him, or anyone, to think you're the reason why it isn't going ahead.'

'So *why* isn't it going ahead?' Emily asked. 'I mean, if the land and the business are so important, and you don't care for love…'

He was knotting his tie, and as his hand paused on the heavy silk he hoped she didn't notice that he faltered.

He met Emily's eyes in the mirror and answered her question honestly. 'I couldn't promise that I'd remain faithful for the rest of my life.'

Alejandro watched Emily blink, and her lips pinch in distaste at his response, and he wanted to amend his answer—*I couldn't promise Mariana that I'd be faithful for the rest of my life. But I could promise you…*

It was as if the mirror had cracked before his eyes—the mental correction was completely at odds with his usual thinking. And absolutely not what they had agreed.

'That's a very good reason not to marry,' she said.

'Yes.'

He turned from the mirror and looked at Emily.

She hid herself from the world, but not from him. She was like a star, glinting and starting to brighten in a night sky, and he wanted her to soar.

Alejandro wanted more for her than barely formed promises he didn't believe in nor know how to keep. He wanted her to take her newly discovered self from his bedroom out into the world. For her to know she could stand up for herself and fight her corner. To know, as he had the day they met, that she was beautiful, talented and funny.

'Emily, I have kept things quiet because of the reaction of my family and Mariana's. Not because of you.'

She nodded, but he could still see the shadow of doubt in her eyes and knew he had to do more to convince her. So he turned back to the mirror and pulled his hair forward.

'You know what? You're right.'

'About what?'

Emily was trying to keep her voice steady and hide her disappointment at his response, reminding herself that he'd said from the start he didn't do long-term relationships.

'About cutting your own hair. A professional salon is not just a waste of money,' Alejandro said. 'It's a waste of time. Every two weeks I have to sit in that chair getting this trimmed. It's due now.'

She tried to drag her mind from fidelity to hair, from his family's wrath to the business lunch he was getting ready to attend…

'You look fine,' she said, when in reality he looked perfect, with his dark suit, his silver tie, and his hair that didn't look as if it was due a cut. But then that thick, glossy hair was always superbly styled, his sideburns neatly trimmed. Of course there was some serious grooming going on.

And then she saw him pulling a few strands of hair down

and delving in his toiletry bag. He took out some small nail scissors.

'What are you doing, Alejandro?'

'I told you—I'm due for a trim…' He took a chunk of black silky hair, right at the front.

He was teasing…she was sure.

*Oh, no!*

'Stop it!'

'Why?' He hacked into his fringe and she watched open-mouthed as several inches of black hair fell to the floor. 'See?' he said. 'Nothing to it.'

'Alejandro!'

'What?' He frowned. 'Don't you like it?'

'It's…'

It was dreadful. More than that, she couldn't believe he would do that just to make a point. And as he stood there, still impossibly beautiful, to her utter surprise Emily found she'd started to laugh, and so had he.

'You cannot go out like that.'

'Why not?' he demanded.

'Let me fix it.' She reached for the scissors but his hand closed over hers.

'Oh, no,' he said. 'I've seen your handiwork. Anyway, if my hair is so awful that you don't want to be seen with me tonight, then we can get room service.'

'Don't be ridiculous…' Emily's voice trailed off as she re-alised what she had just said—it was *ridiculous* to suggest that she wouldn't want to be seen with him because of his hair.

'Get it?' he said, and lifted her chin so that she looked into those beautiful eyes.

Finally she nodded.

'I think you're beautiful,' he said. 'I just wish we were in agreement.'

'I feel guilty,' she admitted in truth. 'I feel guilty spend-ing money.'

'Spend mine, then.' He smiled and kissed her briefly, hard on the mouth. 'I'll see you after this lunch,' Alejandro said. 'Although it might go on for a while.'

'Sure…' As he picked up the swipe card and went to go, she halted him with a statement. 'Alejandro, I don't care if your family hate me.'

'I do,' he said. 'My family don't always play nice.'

He left her then.

Only Emily no longer felt as if she was being hidden.

She dug into her handbag and took out the amber seal. She held it between her fingers and up to the light, looking at the little trapped butterfly wing. She thought of Alejandro, chopping off his beautiful hair just to make a point to her. She thought of their row, and the way she'd voiced her fears and been listened to when she had.

Emily almost expected the amber resin to crack and the little wing to fly off.

She felt a little more free…

Seville really was incredible—she could easily see why Alejandro chose to spend a lot of time here. The architecture was stunning, and she visited the cathedral and then walked through a park. The scent of orange blossom was heavy in the air and it was, despite everything she'd heard, just a bit too sickly-sweet for her taste.

And then she found herself back at the hotel and in the hair salon, rather hoping she'd be told there were no appointments. But she was soon sitting in a seat with a black cape around her shoulders.

'Just a little,' she said, on constant repeat, but she was suitably ignored as layers were added to her hair.

She almost didn't care. She just closed her eyes and told herself she could not be in love with a man who didn't feel capable of being faithful to his wife.

*Just enjoy the time you have*, she kept telling herself.

And, despite feeling teary, she *was* enjoying herself. Every second of their time was to be treasured, because even their row had been a revelation—she could say what she was thinking, fight her corner, state her case. She simply couldn't imagine doing so with another man.

'Señorita?'

She opened her eyes, surprised by her own reflection. Her hair was still the same length, yet now it fell in ringlets, and the cotton wool ends had gone.

The style brought out natural highlights and, even if it was fiercely expensive, apart from her camera she knew it was the best money she had ever spent.

She felt braver, somehow. And, given she'd hardly ever spent money on clothes, she walked into the boutique he'd recommended.

'Señorita...'

She had a feeling Alejandro might have alerted them to expect her, because they were so ridiculously nice.

She was offered champagne, which she declined, and opinions and gentle suggestions, some of which she accepted.

There was a gorgeous red dress that felt like too much, and a pale lilac one that washed her out.

'I don't know what colours suit me,' Emily admitted. 'I tend to wear grey and black.' She knew that made her sound boring. 'And navy,' she added.

'What colour do you like best?'

'Brown,' she answered without thinking, just imagining Alejandro's eyes. 'But that's not a colour. I suppose I need bright...'

'No, no! Wear what you love!'

As it turned out, chocolate-brown *was* a colour.

The dress was very simple, with a scoop neck and bias cut, and it fell to the knee and made her curves look curvy rather than... Well, rather than making her want to hide them.

Was this what love did? Emily wondered.

It was her first true acknowledgement that she'd been deluding herself.

She was crazy about Alejandro.

Head over heels in love with him.

She knew then why she'd almost shouted in anger before… why she'd been shaking as she'd confronted him.

Because she was angry with herself.

It was she who was lying in this relationship.

She who was breaking their rules.

Emily utterly and completely loved him.

And it would ruin their last days if he knew.

She went a little wild…bought the shoes that matched the dress and a small handbag too.

'Thank you,' she said, as she took out her credit card, and saw the assistant's slight frown.

Ah, so Alejandro had indeed called ahead.

But no. She didn't need him to buy her clothes. She had just needed a nudge to do so, and she knew that never, ever would she be in this position again.

Never, ever would she walk through Seville on a bright spring day, knowing she would be with Alejandro tonight.

Never, ever would she turn down an itty-bitty lane and peer into an antiques shop window, stare at the cover of a flamenco record leaning on an old gramophone. Instead of showing a colourful female dancer, it was the shadowy silhouette of a man by an open fire.

It could almost be Alejandro, Emily thought.

It wasn't, of course—the vinyl was far too old for that. But it was enough to propel her into the shop.

'Excepcional…' the owner told her, letting her know it was rare, but it wasn't that, nor even the gorgeous cover, that had her entranced.

As she looked at the track list she was sure there was a

version of the song they had danced to on the night they had first made love.

It was too much, Emily thought, putting the record down. Though for once it wasn't the cost she was wrestling with, but the gesture. It was too romantic, she told herself, and she thanked the owner and moved to walk out.

Anyway, Alejandro had a huge record collection, and he could afford anything…

But she wanted to give him a gift.

Something from her.

To him.

She turned around.

*'Me gustaría comprar esto.' 'I'd like to buy this.'*

No, never again would she be walking along the balcony of a Moorish palace, excited by her purchase, wondering about his reaction, feeling like an Arabian princess who would be with her prince tonight. Looking up at the mosaic tiling and soaring arches, and then down to the maze of plants beneath…

And wondering how not to cry.

How to get through the upcoming days and somehow hide the love she'd just acknowledged—but only to herself.

She was nervous as she crossed the hotel foyer. Worried that her silent admission might be blazing in her eyes. And there he was, shaking hands with his lunch date, so she held back, not wanting to disturb them.

But he looked over—and then looked again.

'Good God!' He gave her a smile as he came over. 'I just had to give myself a quick talking-to. I saw this gorgeous blonde smiling at me and had to remind myself that you were upstairs and I'd promised you a month of commitment.'

'You did.' She started to laugh.

'Then I realised it was you…' He ran a hand down the silky curls and toyed with them. 'You!' He looked at her. 'I think we're good for each other. Because *you* are smoking hot and *I've* just nailed a deal I've been chasing for two years.'

'Seriously?'

'Yes,' he said as they made their way up to their suite. 'He's usually terrible at small talk, but he asked what had happened to my hair…' His mouth came down to hers. 'I told him I'd tried to cut it myself. Talk about opening the floodgates… Apparently he shaved his eyebrows off when he was ten…'

She was laughing as he took out the swipe card and they went into the suite where they'd previously rowed. Although she put down most of her bags, she held on to one.

'I got you this.'

'What is it?'

'Just a…' She felt nervous, unsure if it was too little for a billionaire, or too much for a brief romance as he pulled the record from its wrapping. 'I saw it and I thought of you. You've probably already got it…'

'No…' He was reading the back of the cover. 'We danced to this.'

'Yes.' She gave a slightly nervous laugh as he turned the record over in his hands. 'He looks like you,' she said. 'Well, a bit. I just saw it…'

For once, Alejandro did not know what to say.

She'd floored him.

On a day that had clearly been about her she had stopped and thought of him.

He thought of the doll for her goddaughter, the handbag for her friend and how she stopped in the midst of a busy day and thought of others.

It meant more than he dared admit.

'Thank you,' he said, worried that if he said more he might say too much.

Emily was watching him as he put the record down, as if trying to gauge his reaction.

He took her face in his hands and looked at her, and then ran his fingers through her curls.

He looked at all the changes—not so much the make-up and the hair, but the fact that she'd gone and done it. Then he turned her around so that she faced the mirror, and he slowly, carefully, removed the dress and placed it over a chair.

She stood in rather disappointing underwear, considering her transformation, but he didn't care about that at all.

'Stay there.'

Emily stood, watching him move behind her and feeling his fingers as he unhooked her bra. She watched her breasts drop a little, and then his hands peeled down her knickers.

'Alejandro…'

She turned her head, aching for his mouth, or at least his touch, but he was undressing now, placing his clothes on the chair, and then he came and stood behind her again.

She watched him toy with her breasts, rolling the nipples into indecent lengths, and then he moved his hands down, and she watched him stroke her.

'Face me,' he said, and she did so.

She looked at the dark hair on his chest and his mahogany nipples and she kissed one, feeling it salty on her lips. He smelt of cologne, and now he was pulling her into him, wanting to lift her.

'I want to watch us…' he said, but she refused to scale that magnificent body and instead dropped to her knees.

'Watch this…' she said.

It was the first time she'd taken him in her mouth because, despite the fact he'd tasted every inch of her, there were still things she hadn't tried.

And this was one.

She'd felt too naïve before, too gauche to attempt it, but now she knew she wasn't being judged, that it was just sheer pleasure they gave to each other.

'God…' he moaned as she kissed up his dark length and came to the tip.

He was tall, so he hooked the chair with his foot and brushed off all the lovely folded clothes, letting her sit down.

'Hold it,' he said, lifting her glossy curls so he could see her hands and her face and her lips around his length. He guided her hand for a moment, and then he stopped and sank into the pleasure of her untutored mouth working him.

He started to thrust and then attempted not to.

She pulled her head back and looked at him, all gleaming and wet from her mouth, and then she took him in her mouth again, a little more boldly. Her bottom was lifting off the seat as he started to thrust. Her own sex was hot as she took him more deeply than she'd ever thought she'd dare.

He was brushing her hair from her face, tucking it behind her ear, tender with his hands. And he was no longer watching in the mirror, just tending to her as she tended to him.

'Emily...'

His voice held a warning, and she could feel him swelling in her mouth, and then he shouted a breathless shout, and she tasted him for the first time, stunned at the pleasure of this intimacy, taut and on the edge of coming herself as she looked up at him, so glad for these moments.

'Come here,' he told her.

He pulled her up and took her to bed, and they lay silent together, wrapped in their own thoughts but not sharing them.

She knew it might be a little dangerous to do that.

# CHAPTER ELEVEN

IT WASN'T JUST the brilliant sex, or the walking hand in hand to the restaurant, it was the long slow dinner, where the waiter kept having to come back because neither was ready to order.

'You look incredible.'

Alejandro took Emily's hand in the candlelight. The white tablecloth was dotted with little gold foil stars and, feeling his hand over hers, she felt the happiest she ever had.

'And with that curly hair you won't have to get it done again for ages.'

'How do you know that?'

'I'm not sure…' He shrugged. 'Perhaps I read it.'

'Or one of your lovers told you?'

'God, no, they're always at the hair salon,' he said. 'Not you, though?'

He sounded curious, rather than scathing, enough that she shook her head and told him how her mother had always cut her hair.

'She made all my clothes too.'

'Seriously?'

'She was very talented at sewing and knitting.' She felt a surge of tears, out of place on such a gorgeous night, but his hand simply held hers and he allowed her to speak on. 'I don't think my teenage self appreciated that at the time.'

'You wanted high fashion?'

'Yes,' Emily admitted. 'But now I feel so dreadful for all

the times I sulked when she made me yet another jumper...'
She gave a shrill laugh. 'She made me a pair of jeans once.
They were awful, and I told her so.' He held her hand tighter.
'I'd give anything to have a pair of her hand-made jeans or
one of her jumpers now.'

'It sounds as if you had incredible parents.'

'I did,' Emily agreed. 'I just didn't always appreciate it at
the time.'

'Emily...' He sounded both practical and kind. 'You just
wanted to fit in.'

She nodded, thinking of how she'd been teased, growing
up, about her clothes, her hair... And how she'd always wanted
to protect her mother.

'I feel guilty.' She reached into her new handbag, but of
course there were no tissues, so she had to dab her eyes with
the heavy serviette and she felt him watching. 'I don't expect
you to get it.'

'You don't think I know about guilt?'

'I didn't mean it like that.' She looked over at him. 'You
feel guilty too?'

He nodded, and told her that things were strained with his
siblings. 'We've been arguing,' he admitted.

'Since you came down on your father's side about the label
and Maria in his bio?'

'No, since my father grew ill.'

He poured wine for himself and held the bottle up for her,
but Emily declined. She just wanted to hear about him.

'The three of us are so different, but we have always been.'
Putting down the bottle, he laced his fingers and gripped his
hands together. 'We are tight-knit. At least we were—now
we argue.'

'About...?'

'My mother visiting my father...getting more medical opinions. I was taking Carmen some brochures for a hospice...'

'Alejandro…' Her face fell. 'I didn't realise it had come to that.'

'It hasn't,' he said. 'Although if he doesn't have surgery, it soon shall. Carmen and I are trying to jolt him into action.' He gave a thin smile. 'We all used to get on better, but since my father fell ill we seem to argue over everything.'

'That's good,' Emily said.

He frowned at her words. 'Good?'

'I wish I'd had siblings—especially when my father was so ill and confused. I would have loved someone to argue a point with me. I just felt so responsible—that every decision was mine and mine alone.'

'I hadn't thought of it like that.'

'At least you all want the best for him—you just have different views as to what that is. Still, it sounds as if the choices are his.'

'Yes.' He nodded. 'He's not confused or anything.'

Then he told her something she already knew, but she felt very privileged to hear it from him.

'My mother has started to visit him in the hospital. Sebastián and Carmen think it's just for his money.'

'Do you?'

'No.' He dismissed the notion out of hand. 'I pointed out to them that she is still on tour, even in her late fifties… I know she's extremely comfortable.' He thought for a long moment. 'She is also incredibly vain, and likes having her photo on the Romero product.'

'Yet she never took his name?' Emily frowned. 'Or is de Luca a stage name?'

'No, it's different here. Wives don't take their husband's name, but the children take both their parents'… My full name is Alejandro Romero de Luca.'

'Did you drop your mother's name because of the divorce?'

'No.' He was clearly trying to explain the complicated system to Emily, who hadn't grown up with it. 'You are addressed by your paternal surname, so I am Señor Romero. Given the business side of things, for me it is more prominent.'

'Oh…' She hadn't known that. 'So Sebastián and Carmen are Romero de Luca too?'

'*Sí.*' He nodded.

'But what happens when you have children?'

'Never.' He shuddered at the very thought, and certainly didn't explain further. So much so, she thought, that rather than enlighten her as to the surname of his hypothetical babies, he called for the dessert menu.

'I can't decide…' Emily admitted.

'I already have,' Alejandro told her. '*Tocino de Cielo.* It is like your crème caramel—you remember how I told you sherry was clarified with egg white?'

'I think so…' Emily nodded, because it was rather difficult to remember anything when she was locked in his gaze.

'Well, they used to give the unused egg yolks to the local nuns, and they came up with this dessert. It's very traditional in these parts…'

'Nuns made this?'

'They still do. We could go to Acros de la Frontera on the way home, and if you like it we can stop at the convent and get more.'

It really was the most delicious dessert—as well as the most gorgeous night.

When it ended she scooped up the little gold stars from the table and put them in a pouch in her bag.

'For Willow?' he said.

'Yes.' She nodded, except she knew she might have to keep these little gold stars for herself, along with the amber resin from the sherry bottle.

Only she didn't want them to be mere memories…an amber and gold shrine kept to remind her of him.

He took her to Plaza de España and they strolled across the bridges and stood by the water fountain. It was stunning, with ceramic-tiled bridges and even seats, all blues and yellows. For once Emily was glad not to have her camera with her. Oh, she'd come back and take photos, but on this night it was just so nice to walk hand in hand and take it all in.

It was only when they were walking back to the hotel that she felt him tense. His stride slowed for a brief second, but he said nothing and carried on walking, though she quickly saw why.

There was a poster—one of many pasted onto the wall. But Maria de Luca certainly stood out. She was so stunning and beguiling that Emily couldn't pretend not to have seen it—in fact she herself had already slowed down.

'Your mother's performing here?'

'No, I think that's an old poster.'

They wandered over to read it, but Emily was right. His mother was performing this weekend in Seville. It was a chance, the poster read, to see her before she headed off on an international tour.

Alejandro looked at his mother, smiling for any passing stranger, or for patrons who were willing to drop a couple of hundred euros to see her perform.

Maria de Luca.

Loved, revered and adored.

Just rarely at home.

And when she had been she'd simply been filling time before she went away again.

'She never bought us gifts when she went away,' he said.

'I'm sure she was busy...'

'Come off it, Emily—you're working twelve-hour days, and putting in extra at night. You're cramming in dance lessons, sleeping with me...' He refused to make excuses for his mother. 'You're only Willow's godmother, yet you still make the time to call her, to bring back gifts, you think of her.'

'Yes...'

'And you thought of me today.'

'Of course,' she said. 'It might only be a holiday romance, but you'll always be my first lover, Alejandro.'

Her words brought him little comfort, though.

First? This night he wanted to amend her words, to kiss her against the wall and correct her, tell Emily that he would be her *only* lover.

Who was he to hold her back, though?

# CHAPTER TWELVE

THE WEBSITE LOOKED INCREDIBLE.

The photo she had taken of Alejandro that first morning was the site's main image and her favourite.

They hadn't even kissed then, Emily thought as she sat at her desk in this her final week working for the Romeros.

It felt too soon to be leaving.

So much so that she'd secretly considered forgoing her bonus just to delay things. But then, Emily had told herself, she'd actually be paying for the pleasure of more time with him.

No.

Anyway, she doubted Alejandro would appreciate it.

Things had been a little strained between them since their dinner on Saturday night, in a way she couldn't quite define.

Yes, they'd made love, and on the Sunday he'd driven her to Acros de la Frontera, where they'd bought more of the sweet dessert they'd enjoyed from the nuns, but she'd fallen asleep on the car ride home.

He'd woken her as they'd approached Jerez and asked if she was looking forward to going home, and she'd looked at the city, spread before them, and felt a little ill at the thought of leaving…

Or had she simply been car sick?

She'd taken a drink from her water bottle and looked at the cathedral and the *alcázars*, the ancient buildings and the streets she loved to wander…

How did she tell a man who wanted no strings that this place felt like home?

How did she tell a man who didn't believe in love that she had fallen in love with him on sight?

Emily knew now that she had lied from the start.

It had always been love.

But instead of telling him that she'd told him how excited she was to return home. To see Willow and Anna and face the new challenges that awaited her, and how she was already sorting out dates with the trye replacement company.

'Tyres?' he'd said, and she hadn't been able to define his tone.

A little derogatory?

Or had he just been bewildered?

She wasn't sure.

'It will be brilliant,' Emily had told him, taking another sip of water as she thought of all that rubber and oil and tried to be upbeat. 'You know, I thought sherry was an old ladies' drink before I came to Jerez,' she'd said brightly. 'I'm sure that tyres…'

She'd given in then, unable to face the fact that her time here was almost done. Wondering if she should admit she'd given herself two weeks' leave at the end of this trip. Unsure if he'd welcome the news.

And so rather than feign delays, Emily had just got on with her work.

Yet there were so many memories on the website. The written pages were lined with pictures of the intricate laced vines in the courtyard that she'd taken while lying down.

She forced herself to click past that page. To turn her attention to an image of José and Maria on their wedding day, the gorgeous couple dancing in the courtyard. There was also a beautiful, previously unseen image of Maria, performing flamenco in the *taberna*.

Even without Carmen's input Emily had found a photograph of her on a gorgeous black Andalusian horse, riding through the vineyards. Sebastián though, was proving harder. There were no smiling faces where he was concerned, nor casual shots that she could easily find.

But today, at the eleventh hour, Emily had come across one. He was on the rooftop terrace, with the sun setting behind him, the church spire in the background, and he was toasting a stunning woman. Both were holding up sherry glasses, and even the bottle had the label facing the right way.

Emily was almost shaking when she found the perfect shot. It was just a couple of days before the website went live.

She called Alejandro's office.

'I've found a photo of Sebastián…' She described it. 'It has everything.'

'God, no,' he said, almost instantly. 'Just forget you even saw that.'

'But it has the bottle, the sherry, the sunset and the spire…'

'That is him and Isabel.'

'Isabel?' Emily frowned. She'd never heard that name, and there was a bitter note to Alejandro's tone. 'Who's she?'

'Sebastián's reluctant ex. That was taken when they had just got engaged. It all fell apart a couple of weeks later.'

'Why?'

But Alejandro wasn't about to enlighten her. 'Seriously, Emily,' he warned, 'don't even go there.'

Emily sighed. 'Okay. There is another one of him on the same photo shoot. It's just Sebastián, with his back to the wall. He's holding a glass, but it doesn't show the bottle… He looks incredible.'

It was almost as good. Actually, it was just as good, as the amber sherry reflected the sunset and glinted like liquid gold.

'Can I use that?' she asked.

'Send a copy over to me and I'll discuss it with him.' He sounded distracted. 'I'm meeting with him soon. I'll see what he says.'

Emily did so, and then spent a good couple of hours with

her translator, who was, thankfully, pedantic. She could see now why Alejandro had insisted that she write in English, because the translator managed to convey things she could not.

'*Sobremesa,*' he said now. 'Sitting with family and friends after a heavy meal, just relaxing and talking.'

'Perfect.'

It was so exciting, seeing her photos come to life with the words beside them. And who knew that *concuño* or *concuña* meant the spouse of an in-law, which helped so much to shorten the descriptions on ancient family photos.

Romero tradition and history went way back. It was something that she pondered on as she made her way to her lunchtime dance class. It was to be followed by another one to one with Eva, as she was trying to cram in as many as she could before she left Jerez.

Before she left…

She felt the days peeling away, as if the wind had caught the paper of a calendar and was simply blowing their time away.

As she waited for the group class to conclude Emily eyed the wall chart and tried to see if there were any more classes she could take, and when her private class commenced she asked Eva about it.

'I have my male class,' Eva said. 'Okay, now footwork…' She was clearly able to keep two conversations going at the same time. 'You are welcome to join in.'

'I don't think so.' Emily's confidence had indeed come on, but she wasn't ready to take a lesson in front of a group of men. Still, it was interesting to think of men taking classes.

'Faster!' Eva said. '*Tacón, tacón, tacón, golpe*! Put some anger into it…'

Emily tried, but even after weeks of faithful practice, and lots of expert tuition by Alejandro, Emily simply couldn't get her body to express itself in the way she wanted. Oh, it was improving, but she still felt like a wooden doll compared to the other women.

'Did you teach Alejandro?' Emily asked, taking a quick drink of water. It was hard doing footwork and holding a shawl.

'Teach?' Eva laughed. 'Well, I suppose you could call it that...' She saw Emily's frown in the mirror. 'Oh, you mean flamenco...' She gave her a smile. 'No, I never taught him that.'

Emily's face was as bright as the practice skirt she wore. Even her arms were blushing as she raised them when Eva did. Then the teacher struck the floor with her full foot and Emily started to *palma*...

'Come on, now, Emily.'

Emily met Eva's eyes and gave in with light palmas and matched her foot strike. It felt good to stamp.

To stamp for her jealousy and at the *ick* factor that here was another of Alejandro's lovers, and he clearly remained friendly with her.

Would he with her?

The question was immaterial, Emily quickly realised—very soon she wouldn't be here.

They were down to their final days...

Actually, as Alejandro was just finding out, they were down to their final hour.

'How is Padre?' Sebastián asked after their father at the beginning of their online meeting.

Alejandro could hear the strain in his older brother's voice. Usually they spoke first about work, and got that out of the way before addressing family matters, but their father's health was the first topic Sebastián raised.

'He's much the same as when you left,' Alejandro informed him. 'He's still refusing surgery, but I think he's starting to understand that is his only choice.'

'So why are we looking at hospices?'

Alejandro turned his pen up and down on his desk, annoyed. He'd trusted Carmen not to discuss this with their brother until they could meet face to face.

'Exactly as I said,' Alejandro responded evenly. 'I'm trying to get him to see that surgery is his only real choice. Carmen shouldn't have said anything to you.'

'Why not?' Sebastián snapped. 'I told you that I want to be kept informed.'

'You are.'

'Well, it doesn't feel like it from this end. I'm flying home—you can take over the talks here.'

'Why?' Alejandro demanded. 'I've told you…there is no real change.' He pressed his lips together rather than tell Sebastián he was overreacting. 'If there was anything serious I would have called you.'

'I just know that I need to see him,' Sebastián said. 'I can't sleep.'

'What time is it there?'

'Three in the morning.'

Alejandro took a breath, surprised at his brother's sudden sentimentality.

'All this talk of hospices,' Sebastián said. 'It wasn't even on the agenda when I left—'

'Sebastián, listen,' Alejandro cut in. 'It isn't on the agenda now…' He halted, realising that he was being selfish.

Usually he'd have hopped on a flight to New York without a second thought. But he and Emily were down to mere days, and Alejandro wanted all of them. Then he thought of what Emily had said—about how she wished she'd had a brother or sister to lean on—and knew that perhaps it was time to be that person.

'Of course,' Alejandro said. 'I'll organise my flight now.'

'Thanks.'

Alejandro had always kept things incredibly professional at work. So much so that when he buzzed down and asked her to come up to his office, Emily truly thought it must be about the website.

She hadn't actually ever been in his office.

There had been no need.

The Romeros really did keep themselves private, even if they both worked and lived on the premises.

His office was on the top floor, and it was quite a climb to get there.

'Wow!' Emily said, looking more at the gorgeous view than at the office itself. It was a bright blue morning in Jerez, and it was on full display up here. 'Is this all yours?' she asked, casting her eyes around.

'It is. Sebastián has the south wing.'

'You've had your hair cut.' She smiled, looking at his closely cropped hair and itching to run her hand through it, but refraining.

'I have,' Alejandro said.

He decided to deal with business first—or perhaps he was just putting off telling her about New York?

'I just spoke with him about the shot and he's fine with you using that image of him. He asks that you don't use any pictures that have Isabel in them.'

'Of course...'

'How's it all going?'

'It's coming together. The translator's been brilliant, and the IT guys are just checking the links. It will be ready to go live on Friday.'

'Great.'

With business out of the way, he still could not quite bring himself to tell her, and decided instead to delay, just so he could see her smile.

He stood up from his desk and beckoned her to come over.

'We're at work,' she said.

'I'm not summoning you up here for sex,' he said, opening up the latches on the window.

* * *

She frowned as she walked towards it, but then she saw that there was a view of the church spire, almost on the same level.

'There have been arrivals…' He pointed to the nest.

'When?'

'I only noticed them this morning, but I'd say they're a few days old…'

'I can't see…'

'Wait until she moves.'

They stood watching, waiting for the stork to move, and his fresh citrussy fragrance was strong.

'Did you spill your cologne?' she teased.

'No—why?'

'Just…' She shrugged, and then stopped talking as finally there was movement in the nest. 'Oh, my…'

There were three not-so-tiny chicks that she could see, and as she counted them it was with a smile. She stood there, feeling privileged to watch.

'You have the best office view, Señor Romero. I'd get nothing at all done if I worked up here…'

Alejandro briefly closed his eyes. 'No, it is I who would get nothing done if you worked up here…' he said.

He was tempted to turn her to face him, to share a deep kiss, but knew he had to tell her the real reason he'd asked her to come up.

'Emily, Sebastián just called…' He knew she'd hear the more serious edge to his voice. 'I have to go to New York.'

'When?'

'This morning. Now. He wants to see our father for himself. All these discussions about a hospice have unsettled him, so I'm going to take over the talks there.'

'I see.'

She nodded, and he told himself that this shouldn't come

as a surprise. From the start she'd known that the brothers were often away.

'How long will you be gone?' she asked.

'I don't know,' he admitted. 'Emily...' He was rarely hesitant, but he wanted to ask her to stay on, knowing he had no real right to do so.

As they stood there, staring out of the window, Emily watched one of the adult storks leave the nest and soar and knew she somehow had to leave just as gracefully.

Leaving Jerez was never going to be easy—Emily had known that for some time. But leaving Alejandro was an entirely separate agony she'd refused to address. Somehow she'd convinced herself that she'd know how to deal with it when it happened...that it was a future problem that she shouldn't dwell on.

But now the future had unexpectedly arrived.

She took a deep breath and the heady scent of orange blossom wafted in on the breeze and filled her nostrils, tickling the back of her throat. Emily licked her lips, a little wave of dread washing over her at all she would soon leave behind.

No, not dread.

She felt nauseous.

Again!

It had happened a couple of times in recent days, Emily thought, running a worried hand over her chin and feeling a fresh crop of pimples... She'd blamed them on his scratchy jaw, or the water...or...

'I'll know more once I'm there.'

Alejandro carried on talking, and thankfully her back was still to him, so he wouldn't see the look of panic that flitted across her features.

It was that paella from the market making her nauseous, surely. Only it had been as fresh as the breeze, and she knew it.

Perhaps she was simply lovesick, Emily thought as she stood

there, battling the wave of nausea and frantically trying to recall when her last period had been.

She was on the pill, for goodness' sake.

Only she had been a little lazy in the times she took it, given
she was only on it for the convenience of regular periods rather
than protection or pregnancy prevention.

Oh, God, she'd been the one to refuse a condom that first
time. She'd been more careful since, but that first night…

He'd wanted to be careful…whereas she'd simply wanted
*him*.

Please, please, may she not have made things complicated.

Breaking up didn't have to be complicated. Alejandro had
said that from the very start.

'You don't have to rush off…' Alejandro said, and though her
back was to him he watched her shoulders stiffen and the way
she gripped the window ledge.

He assumed it was to do with the conversation taking
place—that his hinting that she stay on a little longer fell outside the boundaries they had so carefully put in place.

'I mean, the website is close to completion, and it's good
that offers are starting to come in for you, but you can surely
have a break between…' He halted, because for a brief second he could almost hear his father arguing with his mother.

*'You don't need to go on tour so quickly, surely?'*

Or, *'I know it's a good offer, but it's not as if we need the
money…'*

All the reasons his father had used on his mother to keep
her from leaving, to try and hold her back…

Four weeks into a relationship, was he starting to do the
same?

'As I said, I'll know more once I get to NYC…'

'Of course.'

'Are you okay?'

'I'm fine.'

'Only you seem distracted.'

'No.' She turned and faced him. 'I ought to get back to my office…the translator wants to go through some things again.'

He caught her wrist as she went to walk out. 'Don't I even get a farewell kiss?' he asked, looking into her suddenly guarded blue eyes and completely unable to read her.

'Of course.' She kissed him lightly, briefly. 'Have a safe flight.'

'Emily?'

'What?' she snapped. 'Do you want me on my knees under your desk, or pleading with you not to leave?' She shook her head. 'I thought you didn't like drama and emotion.'

So had he.

'We always knew this was ending,' Emily said.

'We did.'

'So you don't get to demand tears when it does.'

He would never quite know her, Alejandro realised as he watched her stalk out. He hopped on international flights without a thought, he was used to leaving with little notice, he didn't want tears over open suitcases.

He'd had a gutful of that growing up.

But he hadn't expected that he'd feel shut down by the sudden removal of her smile. That the end of them would be so…

Well, by his own standards this ending was perfect.

Emily Jacobs had given him everything he wanted: four weeks of passion and an easy parting.

# CHAPTER THIRTEEN

BY SECOND BREAKFAST he had left the bodega. And now his plane would be well and truly in the sky, Emily knew as she stood in a pharmacy.

While her Spanish had vastly improved, she'd still had to look up the words for a home pregnancy test, but she had been sensible enough to dig out her own phone from the depths of her bag.

*Prueba de embarazo.*

She bought the kit and stuffed it down in the bottom of her bag, and then carried on with her long working day, sitting with the translator and the IT guys until late into the night.

Finally, she headed back to her apartment, listening to the music coming from the *taberna* and looking at the couples who dined in the courtyard.

Emily hated going up the stairs and knowing that there wasn't a chance of him being there.

More than that she hated the way they'd parted—how horrible she'd been when in truth she'd been panicking and scared.

She was oddly calm now, as she stepped into the apartment.

Alejandro was right—the flamenco doll was a little bit creepy, and she seemed to stare at Emily as she crossed the room.

'You'll give Willow nightmares,' Emily said aloud, turning her around to face the wall and sitting on the couch.

Above all else, she was missing him. Wishing he was somehow here, to tell her to get on with it, to just get up off the couch and do what she had to and find out.

Even though she'd braced herself for it, the two pink strips on the indicator still came as a shock: *Positivia*.

So she used the second test and checked again, but of course the answer hadn't changed: *Positivia*.

Oh, why hadn't she been more careful?

Her heart felt as if it were racing.

Alejandro could not have made it any clearer that he wanted short term, and she'd gone into this hoping for nothing more than a holiday romance...

No. Emily had to be a little more honest.

She might have arrived in Spain hoping for a holiday romance, but she'd been kidding herself that she could achieve that with Alejandro.

Her feelings for him had exceeded anything she could have anticipated right from the very start.

God, she'd made such a mess of things.

She could imagine Mariana's scorn, or the rolling of his sister's eyes, and Sebastián... But it wasn't their reaction that daunted her.

It was Alejandro's.

Alejandro was usually brilliant at switching off all feelings. But he'd arrived in New York to unexpected snow and a dinner to host, when all he wanted to do was close his eyes and think.

There really wasn't time.

With six hours tagged unexpectedly onto his day, by the time he fell into bed all he knew was that it might be better to leave calling Emily to when his head was clearer, tomorrow.

It was no clearer, even after he called.

'Hey,' he said. 'How are things?'

'Fine,' Emily said, in a voice that told him someone else was present. 'I'm just doing some last-minute updates.'

He waited while she excused herself from whoever she was with and felt a pang of guilt for keeping things so discreet that she hadn't even acknowledged his name when she'd answered the phone call.

'Sorry about that,' Emily said. 'Carmen's here.'

'Carmen?'

'She brought in some photos,' Emily explained. 'I'm just going through her bio and things.'

'She's changed her tune,' Alejandro said.

'Yes,' Emily agreed. 'She's being really helpful. Although…'

'Although…?' Alejandro pushed, and wished she felt able to state the obvious—that it was a bit too close to the deadline for Carmen to dump work on Emily, or for her sudden involvement. 'Although…?' he repeated, more gently.

'I'm just busy,' Emily said, clearly refusing to bitch about his family, and he adored her for that. 'How's New York?'

'Cold,' he said, and looked at the snow swirling outside the window of his penthouse suite, wondering how at the age of thirty-one for the first time he felt homesick.

*Her* sick?

'Emily,' Alejandro said. 'I don't like how we ended things.'

'No…'

'We can do better than that, surely?'

She said nothing in response, but he thought he heard her swallow.

'What are we going to do?'

He asked her the question he had asked on the first morning they'd kissed. What were they to do with this attraction, this ache, this desire and perpetual want?

Did he ask to upend her life?

Or did he upend his?

It was a bewildering landscape and like nothing he knew.

Or possibly he had once known—but his parents were such a poor example that he didn't want to draw on them.

Yet, here he was, doing just that.

*How do you ask someone you love to stay?*

*How do you let someone you love leave?*

Then she gave her response. 'You said it didn't have to be complicated.'

'I didn't know you were a virgin then.' He smiled as she gave a strangled laugh. 'And you hadn't danced for me then, *señorita*.'

There was a stretch of silence, but it was the nicest silence he'd ever known. Not a word was required for them to go back and live that night again.

It was a shared silence, he in his luxurious hotel suite and Emily, he guessed, outside the office thousands of miles away.

Then the silence was broken as Carmen called Emily by the wrong name.

'Emile!' Carmen said.

*Emily,* he wanted to say.

'Tell her to wait...'

But of course she wouldn't do that.

'I'd better go.'

'I'll call you tonight.'

'We're having a pre-launch party this evening,' Emily said.

'Since when?'

'Carmen suggested it and managed to get Sebastián to agree. It will be nice for the IT guys...they've been brilliant—' Her voice was cut off as he heard his sister's impatient tone again.

'Emile?'

He gritted his jaw.

'I really do have to go.'

'*Do* you?'

He said it too harshly, still unused to switching those turned-off emotions back on, but his question was a loaded one—and it was not just about ending the phone call.

Work was not enough to distract him.

And, in the city that never slept, when usually he'd be taking his guests to a smart private club, Alejandro found himself back in his suite.

Unable to sleep.

The website wasn't yet live, but he logged in and looked

at it. Emily's work was incredible. And then he saw pictures coming in on Carmen's social media, of the pre-launch party on the rooftop, the church spire in the background, the sun setting the sky on fire, and he felt more homesick than he had ever thought he was capable of being.

No, it was *her* sick—because she was wearing that grey top she had worn the night they'd first met.

Emily was smiling for the camera, but he could tell she'd been crying. And he felt a little mean that this insight pleased him because he hoped her tears were for him.

In the small hours—way before sunrise—it dawned on him that in trying to protect her from the backlash if he and Mariana's family found out about them, he might well have damaged her.

God, he had never ached to speak with another person more in his life.

Alejandro really wasn't one for making emotional phone calls, but he managed to convince himself he had a good reason to call—after all the website was going live today, and it would look childish if he didn't call to congratulate her.

He couldn't get through.

So he called his long-suffering PA, but she couldn't get through to Emily either.

His suite was warm, but he felt a chill of foreboding as he recalled his own words.

*'My family don't always play nice...'*

Yet Carmen was being...nice.

And Sebastián too, agreeing to a sudden pre-launch party.

While celebrations were commonplace at the bodega, he didn't understand his brother signing off on it, or his sister suggesting it, when they were so worried about their father...

Alejandro called his brother. 'Hey,' he said, 'how's Padre?'

'Doing well.'

'Put him on.'

'He's asleep.'

'Or is that me?' Alejandro checked. 'Am I the one asleep at the wheel? You're not in Madrid, are you…?'

'Since when did I have to check in with you?' Sebastián responded, and hung up.

Alejandro knew then that his hunch was right—he should have protected Emily better.

His father would have told Carmen that he had declined to marry Mariana, and Carmen would have told Sebastián about Emily.

Sebastián had never really been worried about their father moving to a hospice—it had all been a ruse to get Alejandro away.

Carmen dropping in with photos and being nice to Emily…?

Sebastián, whose mind was always on business, suddenly desperate to get home…?

Alejandro had known that he needed to protect Emily. That if word got out about them it would not be received well.

He called Reception at the office and asked to speak to Emily Jacobs.

'I don't believe she's in this morning,' came the reply.

'Of course she's in!' Alejandro was trying to keep himself from shouting. 'Okay, can you put me through to the house-keeper's apartment.'

There was a long silence.

'I'm sorry.' The receptionist finally buzzed in. 'There's no one picking up.'

He thought of her half-packed suitcase and their unfinished conversations…

Emily had left Jerez.

Alejandro was certain.

But it didn't change how he felt.

Alejandro wanted her smile, and her voice, and the way they were sometimes silent but still together in peace.

He wanted to be there when her star soared.

He wanted her for the long-term.

With Emily he would readily commit to being faithful.

It was love…

Emily wore her chocolate-brown dress for the launch. She'd make an effort for her final day of work, even though she was exhausted.

Last night's pre-launch party had gone on for ever.

All she'd wanted to do was escape and call Alejandro, resume their conversation. But Carmen had confided in her about a recent break-up, and Emily simply hadn't known how to excuse herself.

She'd sat in the courtyard with her teary new friend, drinking hot chocolate until two a.m., before falling into bed and a dreamless sleep.

Now it was eight a.m. on Friday morning and Emily had found out that she loved Alejandro more than she was terrified of telling him about the baby. Because, as she crossed the courtyard, for a fleeting second her heart soared.

She honestly thought Alejandro had returned.

The charcoal-grey suit, the thick black hair…

But Alejandro had had his hair cut, she remembered, and even before he turned around, she'd quickly worked out that it was Sebastián.

'Emile.' He smiled and shook her hand. 'It's all up and running?'

'Yes.' She couldn't be bothered to correct him about her name.

'It's looking great.'

'Thank you.'

'Could we speak in my office?'

'Of course. Now?'

'No rush—although I do have a lot on. And if you can bring your laptop? I want to check a few things.'

'Sure.'

He was Romero sexy, but with a more savage look, and

his air was far more formal that Alejandro's had ever been. If anything, he was aloof.

'In your own time,' he said.

She took from that that he meant now!

Of course he was four flights up too, and by the time Emily got there he was sitting at a large desk on his computer, looking at the new website.

'The website looks excellent,' he said. 'I admit, I was cautious about commissioning an outsider, but I have to say it's worked well. As well as that, you came in on time…'

'Thank you, but there's just a few tweaks. I want to go up to the vineyard and get some images now that there are fruits on the vines.'

'There's no need for that. It's all just updates and minor things from here, and IT can sort all that out.'

'Of course.'

She chewed her lip. Was that it? She felt a slight flutter of panic as it dawned on her that this was officially her last day. Sebastián was here to wrap things up, thanking her for her work.

'I'm pleased I got back in time to thank you personally. My father is impressed too.'

'That's great,' Emily said, and then cast around to fill the silence. 'I was going to stay for the horse festival. It sounds so interesting…'

'Did you manage to get accommodation?' He sounded mildly surprised by her intention. 'It's usually booked out long in advance.'

'N-no,' Emily stammered, embarrassed. Her gorgeous apartment was clearly off the table.

Well, what had she expected? A holiday with free accommodation while she hung around waiting for Alejandro to return?

'I might look into finding a B&B…'

'Well, good luck with that,' he said, clearly meaning that

she'd need it. 'All our accommodation is booked a year in advance for this particular festival.'

He was clearly not about to step in as her private travel consultant.

This really was it.

Of course it was!

Her contract expired today.

She'd allowed herself a couple of weeks' holiday, so her flight out from Madrid wasn't booked for a couple more weeks. More to the point, had she not been involved with Alejandro then her luggage and equipment would already be packed.

'Again, we're thrilled with your work, and we will certainly be happy to recommend your business.' Sebastián gave a tight smile. 'Now, just a few minor details… You have a company computer and phone…?'

'I do.'

She had to hand in her phone and laptop right there and then. It was the normal thing to do, but it felt as if they were being removed by force.

Her services were no longer required.

She made her way to her apartment, to think, but was met there by a rather harried-looking maid.

'There you are!' she greeted Emily. 'The new guest is waiting to check in!'

She had fifteen minutes to pack up her equipment and all the things she'd accumulated in her time in Jerez.

Emily went to say goodbye to the IT guys, but they were all busy and barely looked up to say goodbye.

Her welcome hadn't exactly been a warm one, Emily reminded herself as she came out to the courtyard. It had been a driver and a brief note from Sophia, suggesting she dine in the *taberna*.

But then she'd met Alejandro and everything had changed. He wasn't here now, though, and without him she felt like an unwelcome guest at the bodega—one who had outstayed her welcome.

Even walking into the *taberna* felt a little daunting. Guessing she had no access now to the Romero table, she waited to be seated and was shown to the same small table where she'd sat on her first night.

She ordered coffee and a *tocino de cielo*, and as she cracked the caramelised crust with her spoon a waitress came over and rather pointedly put the bill down on the table.

No more free meals for her!

It wasn't that she minded paying, more that she was cross with Sebastián—not just for removing her, but for all the minor details that would be left out on the website. She'd wanted to picture this dessert, and to write about the nuns...there was so much more she'd wanted to do.

Or was it simply that she couldn't bear that it was over between her and Alejandro?

She ordered a glass of salted grapefruit juice, but it made her feel a little sick, so she asked the waitress for some water.

The waitress actually rolled her eyes, and Emily knew she was dragging things out.

She simply didn't know how to leave.

The worst thing was that without the company phone she didn't have Alejandro's number and couldn't call him. With her laptop handed over too, all channels of communication were gone.

Aside from the pregnancy and all things complicated, Emily wanted to say goodbye properly, and of all the regrets she had there was a ridiculous one—that she hadn't run her fingers through his short hair on the morning they'd parted.

'Emily...'

She looked up at the husky sound of a woman's voice, and although they'd never met she recognised her immediately.

'Mariana.'

'Oh, you know who I am?' Mariana said, as if surprised to be recognised.

'Of course.' She gave a tight smile. 'I've spent the past six weeks going through the Romero family's photos.'

As well as that she recognised the dangling diamond earrings she wore. But of course she didn't mention that as the rather ravishing Mariana took a seat.

She had glossy black hair cut in a jagged bob. Her eyes were a vivid green, and she oozed nothing but confidence.

'I saw the new website,' Mariana said. 'It's impressive.'

'Thank you.'

'I remember saying to Alejandro that an outsider might give a fresh perspective.'

'Did you, now?' Emily said, trying to keep the sarcastic edge from her voice. She did not do sarcasm well, but that wasn't quite the way Alejandro had relayed it—he hadn't sneered when he'd said 'outsider', nor had he made her feel unwelcome with his gaze.

'Of course we have to attract the tourists...' She looked at Emily. 'Have you enjoyed your time in Jerez?'

'Very much.'

'I hear Alejandro has been an excellent tour guide...' She laughed at Emily's clear discomfort. 'Now, don't go getting all flustered.'

'I'm not.'

'But you are!' Mariana gave a low laugh. 'Emily, I know what's been going on. We all do. And I know how charming he can be...' She gave Emily a sympathetic smile, as if she were some poor, deluded fool to think that Alejandro would actually care for her. 'Alejandro might wander, but he always returns. It's been the same for as long as I can remember— especially at the end of the summer, when the tourists are gone... Of course, that was when we were younger. Now he has more sophisticated tastes...' She looked down at Emily's attire. 'At least most of the time.'

'Are you always this charming?' Emily asked, surprised at her own sarcasm and unable to believe her own boldness.

But even at her pluckiest, Emily was no match for Mariana.

'Go home, Emily—it's getting a little awkward now.'

'Awkward?'

'Embarrassing,' Mariana corrected herself, and then added, 'For you. No one likes to see someone make a fool of themselves.'

Emily didn't blush—rather she paled. Was that what everyone thought of her?

Mariana confirmed that it was.

'Seeing your puppy dog eyes following him around... Alejandro, he found it cute at first. But now he would rather do his brother's work in New York than be here, the place where he loves...'

Emily thought back to their first drive. How he had said that love only complicated things...that breaking up shouldn't be hard to do.

Yet here she was, clinging on.

Well, no more.

Homeless and pregnant was an exaggeration, but as she dragged her case through the *plaza* it wasn't far from how she felt.

The wheels of her case clacked over the cobblestones and it sounded like women walking and doing *palmas*, so close to the sound she loved, and so she went to drop in and bid farewell to Eva.

But, looking up to the studio, she saw she was mid-class.

Everything was just carrying on.

She sat on the edge of the fountain, trying to work out what to do. Whether to stay and try and find accommodation, or just head back to England...

*'Fight your corner, Emily...'* Alejandro had said.

She didn't want to fight her corner, though. She didn't want to plead her case, or ask if it was true that he was avoiding her.

If it was true, and he *was* avoiding her, then how did she tell him she was having his baby?

She reached into her bag to pull out her phone and call for a taxi. Perhaps her head would clear by the time she got to Madrid…

*No!*

She was tired of living like a frightened mouse.

What she didn't want to live with was regret.

Emily already regretted the way they'd parted, and she knew that the passage of time would only make things worse.

She dragged her case back to the bodega, unsure whether she was being completely pathetic or dreadfully brave, just knowing it couldn't end like this.

She was halted by Security.

'I'm sorry. Access is for staff only.'

'I am staff,' Emily said—she had been contracted until five p.m.

But it would seem that when the Romeros closed ranks and wanted you gone, you were gone.

'If you could watch my luggage for me.'

'*Señorita!*'

The guard called her back, but she was already clipping her way across the courtyard and through to the main building. Instead of taking the stairs to Alejandro's office, she headed for Sebastián's.

'*Señorita.*'

There was another guard, and he'd been clearly warned to stop her, but although that would once have terrified her, it actually reassured her.

They wanted her gone! But the Alejandro she knew would not hide in New York hoping she'd leave. If they were over, he'd have told her so.

She knew that about him, at least.

'*Señorita!*' the guard shouted.

'I need to speak with Sebastián,' Emily said, her heels ringing out as she took the stairs, wondering if she was about to be tackled, terrified she might be risking the baby.

But then she heard Sebastián's voice.

'It's fine.' He stood calmly at the top of the stairs, peering down and making her feel more dishevelled and inconvenient than ever. 'Come up, Miss Jacobs.'

Emily did so—slowly. Not really knowing what to say or do once she got there...just knowing she wasn't ready to leave.

Knowing, more importantly, that Alejandro would never subject her to this.

Sebastián's office looked out across the *plaza*. It was incredibly imposing, with an iron staircase in the centre, which Emily knew led to the rooftop terrace where those romantic images of him had been taken.

The smiling man in those photos was not the one she faced now.

'What can I do for you?' he asked.

'I have some things I'd like to discuss with Alejandro.' She took a breath to steady her voice. 'Is it possible to have his contact number?'

'No.' He was blunt.

'Well, is it possible that you can contact him and give him mine?'

'I'm sure Sophia has all your details. I'll ask her to pass them on. But right now I believe she's a little busy giving birth.'

'Can you call him for me, please?'

'Emily.' He came around the desk. 'I'm sure if Alejandro wants to contact you, then he will.'

'Well, I am not leaving Jerez until I've spoken to him.' Her voice was starting to rise.

'You are making a fool of yourself.'

'No!' Emily retorted. '*You* are being incredibly rude!'

There were tears in her eyes, but not of embarrassment, more of frustration.

'Your brother has manners, and as well as that he has guts, and if he wanted me gone then he'd have said so himself. If you don't give me his number then I'll—'

She never got to finish.

'You bastard!'

It was Alejandro, crashing through the door. An Alejandro she almost didn't recognise, because he was angry and menacing as he sped across the room.

'All this crap about wanting to see our father for yourself...'

He was furious, and for a moment she thought he was going to land a punch on his older brother, but instead they stood, two angry bulls facing each other.

Alejandro was no longer the reasonable one!

'Emily, go and wait in my residence...'

Alejandro didn't turn and look at her—he was still staring his brother down.

'Assuming my brother didn't change the code to that too. Go!' he said, still facing Sebastián.

Only when her footsteps had faded did he speak again.

'What the hell are you doing?'

'Taking care of business,' Sebastián said. 'You know our father's wishes.'

'He also wishes that his wife would come back to him. He wishes his cancer was gone without him having to make a decision about surgery. I am not marrying Mariana just because it suits his business plan!'

'It's been arranged since for ever.'

'It's been arranged since before I could talk,' Alejandro said. 'You all just assume that I'll marry her...that I'll stay because I was born into it.'

'What are you talking about?'

'I'm not sure I even want to be here,' Alejandro said. 'I don't know that I want to spend the rest of my career fighting against you and Carmen as you erase our mother from the brand.'

'You're not going to quit—'

'I wouldn't have to. I could just go and pursue my own interests like Carmen does,' Alejandro said, and raised a warning finger to his brother. 'Don't you ever mess in my private life again.'

'I'm trying to stop you from making a stupid decision.'

'Oh, and marrying someone I don't love is a better one?'

'You think you *love* Emily?'

Alejandro chose not to answer or correct him.

He would not be telling Sebastián that he knew for certain that he loved her.

Someone else deserved to hear that first…

She was sitting on the sofa where they had first made love, but jumped up when Alejandro pushed the door open and walked in.

'Well done,' he said, 'for standing up to him.'

He smiled when he thought of the words he had overheard as he'd raced up the stairs.

'I don't think many people would dare speak to him like that…especially in his own office…'

'I'm not scared of Sebastián,' Emily said—because she honestly wasn't.

She was more scared of Alejandro's reaction when she told him her news—when he found out that their holiday romance had turned into something rather more permanent.

'What did Sebastián say to get you to leave?' he asked.

'Not much. He just thanked me for my work and got me to return my computer and phone. I didn't even have time to write down your contact details…' She shot him a look. 'When your family close ranks they really do it in style.'

'They do.'

'Then I found a maid waiting to service my apartment for a

new guest. And then I was told you were in New York, avoiding me.'

'Who said that?'

'I don't want to tell you…'

'You have to.'

'Mariana. I went over to the *taberna*, to work out what to do, and she came and took a seat at my table and told me a few home-truths.'

'Mariana truths, you mean.'

'Perhaps… She said that it was getting embarrassing, me following you around like a puppy. That you needed someone strong. That you were incapable of being faithful.'

'No.' He shook his head. 'I am always faithful. It is long-term commitment I am incapable of—or thought I was.'

He took a breath, and as they had been on the night they had met his lips were pale, his eyes more serious than she had ever known them.

'Emily…' He looked right into her eyes. 'I told Mariana we were over in December, and since then they've all been worried. Usually we get back together, but I was serious when I ended it this time. I didn't know what I wanted, but I did know that it wasn't a convenient marriage. I wasn't just hiding you to keep Mariana happy. I was trying to hide how happy you made me…'

Emily frowned.

'The second Carmen saw us together she must have known this was something different.'

'How?'

'I was always a miserable bastard. Not depressed, or anything, but I don't strut and play models, as Carmen saw me doing.'

Emily smiled at the memory, and could see how it had been then that everything had started to go wrong.

'She must have called Sebastián straight away,' Alejandro explained. 'That's why I was suddenly needed in NYC. It had nothing to do with him being worried about my father, and everything to do with keeping us apart.'

'Why?' she asked. 'What could that possibly achieve?'

'Nothing.' He shook his head. 'Of course Sebastián thought that in a few days I'd be over you, because that's how his mind works, but I would have come to England, or...' He looked at her. 'Or you'd have gone to our hotel in Seville.'

'I couldn't afford a night in that hotel—let alone to stay there and wait things out.'

'Then I'd have called Sophia for your number. Nothing he could have done would have kept us apart.'

He sounded so sure—a little like she'd felt as she'd brushed past Security and demanded an audience with Sebastián.

It was her secret that might ruin things, though.

They were too new to this, surely?

Too fragile for such news so soon in their relationship.

But his mouth was on hers and, rather then tell him, she sank into his kiss. Allowing his mouth to smother the pain of the past few hours and his tongue to chase away any doubts as to their future.

And even if she *was* avoiding the truth, at least she got to feel his shorter hair beneath her fingers, and feel the anger she had witnessed with his brother turn into passion.

They were, for the most part, still dressed. It was naked passion that pushed up her gorgeous dress and unzipped him. Desperate, necessary sex. And he moaned as if he needed it every bit as much as she.

He made her frantic, yet as he thrust into her he made this moment the only one that mattered. And Emily knew she was a liar, because she closed her eyes as she was taken on the sofa, just allowing herself the bliss of being made love to by Alejandro before she told him.

'Alejandro!'

She wasn't trying to tell him her truth. She just said his

name as she orgasmed with alarming haste, and then closed her eyes as he followed.

They were breathless.

Joined.

Sated.

The closest they had been.

And yet she averted her eyes as he stared down at her, unsure as to his reaction when she told him her news, not wanting this moment to change.

He kissed her, then slowly stood and tidied himself. And as Emily sat up she watched him walk over to the record player and select the album she had bought for him.

She didn't want him being romantic when she had something so important to tell him, and yet it wasn't her words that changed the moment… It was Alejandro who rocked her world.

'Marry me?'

'Marry you?' She started visibly, and hauled her mind from babies to weddings.

'Yes, will you marry me? Emily, I know you have your career, and I swear I won't be like my father and hold you back. I've told Sebastián that I'm willing to pull out of the company if he tries to mess with me again. We could start our own bodega with my share of the land…'

'Stop!' She had a sudden image of her and Alejandro in a little hacienda, surrounded by vines, but then she shook her head, because she would never keep him from his family.

'I can't stop,' Alejandro said. 'Because I cannot stop loving you. So, whatever it takes…'

'Alejandro, please…' She made herself say it. 'I'm pregnant.'

She looked to him for a reaction, but he gave none.

'I *am* on the pill, but I must have messed up the times, or not been careful enough. I only used it to be regular in my periods…'

'Shh,' he said. 'We were both there.'

'And I know you don't want children—'

'It's more that I've never considered it a possibility for me…'
He looked at her. 'Is that why you came back? Is that what you
wanted to discuss with me?'

'Yes.'

She saw the dart of doubt in his eyes, as if he thought the
only reason she had fought to see him was because of the baby,
and it dawned on her that the very experienced Alejandro was
as new to love and babies as she herself was. Maybe it was
time to simply tell the truth and share this journey together.

'No. I came back because I didn't think we were ready to
end just yet.'

He stared back at her.

'I came back because I wanted to tell you to your face that
I'm…' she took a breath '… I'm not ready to give up on us.'
She admitted her truth, although she covered her eyes as she
did it. 'I love you. I have since the night we met. I've been
lying all along.'

He smiled, unseen, and looked at the shyest, yet somehow
the bravest woman he knew, and could only guess how hard
it must have been for her.

Not just facing Sebastián and Mariana, but finding out she
was pregnant in a foreign country, by a man who… Well, he
wasn't exactly husband material. Or rather he hadn't been husband material until he'd lain there on a lonely New York City
night wanting simply to come home.

'Thank you,' he said, removing her hand from her eyes.
'For not giving up on us.'

He was too used to a mother who had angrily packed her
cases at the first sign of a row, who had put her art and her
career first, before everything, as well as a father and brother
who always put business first.

'I know it's all too soon…' she said.

'No.' He shook his head. 'It's quick, and yet I love the
thought of having a baby with you.'

And then he smiled a slow smile and answered the question he hadn't before. 'Romero Jacobs.'

'Sorry?'

He told her how her baby—their baby—would be named. 'It will be called Baby Romero Jacobs.'

'Oh!' That brought tears to her eyes.

'Why does that make you cry?'

'My father was always upset that I was the last Jacobs.'

'Oh, no,' Alejandro said, and ran his hand over her plump stomach, where their tiny baby grew inside. 'There are going to be many more...'

'Stop!' Emily laughed. 'We haven't even had one!'

But her protests were deliciously muffled by his kiss and his nicest words yet.

'We've barely even started...'

# EPILOGUE

'THERE ARE RUMOURS…'

Sebastián knew he would happily end this marriage before it had started, even as they stood in the vestry, waiting to take their places for the wedding.

'A lot of talk going around—'

'I don't address rumours,' Alejandro interrupted. 'And usually neither do you.'

'I'm your brother, and if you're feeling pressure to marry because Emily is pregnant then know that—'

'Save the speech for the party,' Alejandro cut in.

He knew his brother had every reason to be mistrusting, but his caution wasn't required, and Alejandro would tell him exactly that.

'Can't you just be happy for me?' He glared at his brother. 'If you can't paint on a smile, then Carmen can be my *padrino…*' He gave a mirthless laugh. 'Then again, she is as suspicious of love as you. Listen, within an hour I will marry the woman I love. If you can't see that then it is *your* issue—don't make it mine.'

He could understand his brother's wariness—and in truth, if it were the other way around, then Alejandro might have doubts of his own.

Alejandro looked over to his brother. 'Just try…'

'Very well.'

But Sebastián rarely conceded, and as they headed out of the vestry to the church he halted his younger brother.

'Alejandro, I want nothing but the best for you.'

'Today, that is exactly what I am getting.'

'Then I wish you well.'

'Thank you.'

Their mother was arriving. Late to the church, as she'd no doubt planned. For there was no such thing as a discreet entrance for Maria de Luca.

She wore a silver silk dress and a high *peineta*—a traditional Spanish comb with an intricate white veil.

*'Dame pan y dime tonto...'* Sebastián muttered, and Alejandro actually smiled at the old saying.

It translated as *Give me bread and call me a fool*, but the real meaning was *I don't care what you think as long as I get what I want*.

It fitted their mother perfectly.

Maria did not blush or appear in any way awkward as she glided down the aisle and kissed a very tense Carmen—then affectionally kissed their father and took her seat by his side.

He'd had surgery the very night Alejandro and Emily had gone to his hospital suite to inform him they were engaged.

'We all know how Maria loves to upstage a bride...' he'd told him, as he'd kissed the top of Emily's head. 'Not that she'll be able to on this occasion.' Then he'd looked right at his father. 'It is something to look forward to, yes?'

José had frowned. This was not what he had intended for his middle child, nor the future of the business, and he had begun telling Alejandro so when Maria had walked in on them.

'Leave them alone,' Maria had said. 'I have never seen my son so happy.'

'You've not exactly been around to do so,' Alejandro had pointed out, but he'd been pleased to have his mother's support, for once.

'How long till the wedding?' Maria had asked.

'Four weeks.'

'Is that long enough for you to recover from surgery?' Maria had said to José. 'Or will the happy couple have to drop by the hospice?'

'*Madre...*' Alejandro had warned.

But, used to his wife's rather dark humour, surprisingly José had laughed. A wedding! Now that *was* something to look forward to.

'You can tell them,' Emily had said then, and Alejandro had gone over and sat on the bed, grateful to be able give his father their news.

'This is to go no further,' he warned, 'but Emily and I are expecting a baby in November.'

He'd watched his father start to cry, and Maria, who was the least maternal person he knew, had embraced his future bride.

A wedding and a baby!

There really were a lot of reasons for José to try and live...

Emily's *dama de honor* was, of course, Anna.

Little Willow had been unable to fly, because of her ears, but Anna's parents had come around somewhat, at least where their granddaughter was concerned, and she was spending her first weekend with them.

She'd come online now, and squealed when she saw Emily in her wedding dress.

'It's so pretty!'

'Thank you.'

It was pretty, and feminine, and actually quite bold for Emily, in the softest shade of magnolia. There were shoestring shoulder straps, and the fitted bodice hugged her curves and then flared into a gorgeous lace skirt, which would be perfect for dancing the night away!

'The flowers in your hair are so cute,' Willow said, as Emily lowered her head so that her goddaughter could see the delicate orange blossom tied through her hair. And when she looked at the screen Willow complimented her on one more thing. 'You're smiling.'

'I am.'

Despite her nerves, Emily smiled more readily these days although nerves caught up with her now, as they waited to head out of the boutique hotel where she had readied herself for the big day.

It was the *dama de honor*'s job to ensure that the bride and groom did not set eyes on each other until the bride's arrival at the church, and Anna was taking it seriously.

'You have to be late…'

'He'll surely be there by now.'

'Perhaps, but I have to be certain…'

Finally, Sebastián called and said they were safely in the church.

*'Gracias,'* Anna said, and rolled her eyes at Sebastián's sparse tones. 'He makes it sound as if the hearse has arrived.'

'I don't think I'm a very popular choice,' Emily sighed.

'Do you care?' Anna asked.

'I do,' Emily admitted. 'This is going to be my home, after all. Still, I'm happier than I ever thought I could be, whether they like it or not.'

They walked together beneath the arched orange trees and down the lane to the square.

The storks were flying high above the Jerez church spire and she smiled when she saw them, and remembered standing gazing up at them with Alejandro.

She'd felt so raw that day, so unsure of the world, and yet that night he'd taken her to bed.

Today they'd declared their love.

In front of a rather cold congregation…

Inside the church every head turned, and for a second she wanted to turn and flee. Alejandro had a lot of exes—Sophia, Mariana and Eva, to name but a few—and it was all so nerve-racking that she felt like the most hated bride in Jerez.

*Oh, turn around, Alejandro*, she thought.

But then her soon-to-be mother-in-law caught her gaze.

Well, how could she not? Maria de Luca was no fading beauty, and she looked Emily right in the eye and caught her by surprise, for she was making a slight motion of her hand, as Eva would—one that told Emily to lift her head high—and then she made another gesture that told her to smile.

And that was what Emily loved about flamenco.

It gave her the passion and confidence to express herself, or to hide herself and then appear brave.

It taught her to look someone in the eye and frown or smile, and to talk freely with her eyes. And that was how she faced her groom as he relented and turned.

Confident and smiling, she walked up the aisle. It wasn't that he made her so. More that she was ready now to *be* so... As if, that first night in Jerez, he had encouraged her true self to emerge with his dark eyes.

'I've waited for you for a very long time,' Alejandro said as she joined him.

'I'm only ten minutes late.'

'No...' He made things clearer. 'I didn't know it, but I feel as if I've been waiting for today my entire life.'

'And me,' Emily admitted, as his hands closed around her trembling ones.

She had longed for a family, been desperate to fit in, to be less shy...

Now, thanks to love, all her wishes had come true.

* * * * *

# RETURNING FOR HIS RUTHLESS REVENGE

LOUISE FULLER

MILLS & BOON

Thanks to Vic and Awo.

If you hadn't stuck with me on the last book,
I would never have got to write this one.

# CHAPTER ONE

'Good morning, Ms Cavendish. Did you have a good holiday?'

Without breaking her stride, Dove Cavendish turned towards the young paralegal who had interrupted her thoughts and her progress across the foyer of Cavendish and Cox and forced her lips into the shape of a small, careless smile.

'I did, yes. Thank you, Mollie.'

'You picked a good week to take off. There was another tube strike on Wednesday and loads of us didn't get into work until halfway through the morning.' Mollie hesitated. 'Oh, and we've got a new client. Did you hear? I mean, about Mr—?'

Before she could say his name, Dove cut her off with a swift, emphatic nod. 'I did, yes,' she repeated. It was all her numb mind could come up with.

A shiver ran down her spine and her cheeks felt hot, but she knew her expression would not betray her. Growing up as the Band-Aid baby of her parents' failing marriage, she had learned early on to keep her thoughts to herself and concentrate on defusing conflict. It was one of the reasons she was so good at her job as a corporate lawyer. Even today, when her carefully rebuilt world had been knocked off its orbit, nobody would ever guess what she was really thinking. What she had been thinking since her boss, Alistair Cox, had called her at home last night.

She had just returned from a long overdue and much-needed week away, and had been in the middle of emptying her bag. It hadn't been a long conversation, and truthfully she'd barely heard most of what Alistair had been saying, but after he'd hung up she hadn't had the strength to finish unpacking. This morning her suitcase was still on the floor in her bedroom, gaping open as if, like her, it was still in shock at his bombshell revelation.

Gabriel Silva had hired Cavendish and Cox to handle his latest acquisition. M&A.

She stopped in front of the lift.

*Gabriel Silva.*

The name pulsed inside her head in time with her heartbeat as she watched the numbers light up.

At thirty years old, he was a legend in the corporate world—an apex predator in an ocean filled with hunters…killers. Ruthless, relentless, never tiring, he pursued his prey remorselessly and in doing so had built one of the most successful businesses in the world from scratch.

But it wasn't his business reputation that was making a silent scream of panic rise up inside her. Six years ago, Gabriel Silva had broken off their relationship and broken her heart. Actually, he had shattered it into a thousand pieces. And he hadn't simply broken up with her. Her father, Oscar, had offered him money to disappear from her life and Gabriel had accepted his offer, pocketing the cash and walking away without so much as a word of explanation or apology.

*And now he was back.*

Her throat tightened. People said that time was a great healer: they were wrong. Hearing Alistair say his name last night had been like a serrated blade slicing through her skin. The pain of his rejection was as raw and as agonising just as if it had happened yesterday.

'It's pretty exciting, isn't it?' Mollie looked over at her, her brown eyes wide with undisguised awe. 'I Googled him this morning and he's like the real deal.'

*No, he isn't*, Dove thought, her heart lurching forward as the lift doors opened. There was nothing real about Gabriel Silva.

Everything—every word, every smile, every touch—had been fake. All of it carefully staged to look like the real thing so that she would take the bait. And she had. Despite knowing that 'love' was a hoax, a bow to prettify something essentially pragmatic and transactional, she had allowed herself to be reeled in.

And, like every other gullible woman who had fallen for a pair of blue eyes and a brain-melting smile, she had paid the price. Or rather her father had. And that hurt the most. Not just that Gabriel had never loved her, but that her love for him had been transformed into currency in some horrible, distorted alchemy.

There was only one positive in the whole sorry mess. Knowing how everyone would react to her dating a man whose father was an electrician, she and Gabriel had kept their relationship secret. No one other than her father had known the truth, and Oscar had died a month after Gabriel left—not of a broken heart but a diseased one. So her humiliation had been hers alone.

As much as she'd wanted to confide in her mother,

she hadn't. Not when she'd known how devastated Olivia would be.

She knew the story of her parents' marriage back to front and inside out. Officially, it had been the love story of their generation. Beautiful, wealthy American heiress Olivia Morgan and handsome, upper-class Englishman Oscar Cavendish.

But just weeks after exchanging their vows the marriage had been floundering. The bills for Oscar's expensive tastes—including her mother's engagement ring and the honeymoon—had started rolling in. Only Oscar had had no money to pay them. His inheritance was gone, and he'd had no intention of doing anything as menial as working.

It had been the start of a very long and disappointing marriage, and ever since Dove could remember her mother had warned her daughters—particularly her youngest—against making the same mistake. Or maybe it just felt that way because she was the last one at home and there was nobody around to dilute Olivia's fears.

Either way, given her mother's feelings about men without money but with ulterior motives, she had never been able to bear to tell her the truth.

Diverting her thoughts away from that particularly unedifying dead end, Dove leaned back against the wall of the lift as it started to move upwards jerkily. Like everything else in the firm's Grade II listed headquarters in Lincoln's Inn Fields, it needed upgrading, but clients didn't come to Cavendish and Cox for glossy interiors. They came because they wanted a lawyer they could trust implicitly—they came for Alistair Cox.

Her pulse darted. Or that was what they usually came for anyway. But was the same true of Gabriel Silva?

Feeling Mollie's gaze on her face, she blanked her mind to all the possible and equally unnerving answers to Mollie's observation. 'Yes, he is the real deal,' she agreed. 'But I shouldn't get too excited, Mollie. It will be Mr Silva's people we'll be dealing with. Not the man himself.'

Of that she was certain. He would review the data as it was presented to him, and obviously it would be his signature on the dotted line, but he wouldn't be a part of the exhaustive day-to-day process of negotiation and due diligence.

'But *he* must have had the final say.' Mollie smiled up at her shyly. 'Which means we must be the best. Why else would he hire us?'

That question again. Her stomach lurched. *Were* Cavendish and Cox the best? Historically, yes. Nowadays they had rivals for the top spot, but their name still carried weight. Then again, they were a small family firm. Too small and traditional to be a natural fit for a slick, carnivorous outfit like the Silva Group.

*A natural fit.*

Her stomach did a slow somersault as her brain unhelpfully offered up a memory of Gabriel's sun-soaked body moving against hers. They had fitted together like pieces of a puzzle, their hot, damp skin sticking, his hand splayed against her back, her breath scratching in her throat as their bodies arched into one another—

'I'm afraid that's not something you or I can really answer,' Dove said, feeling a rush of relief as the lift shuddered to a halt. Have a good day, Mollie.'

'Ah good—there you are. Don't worry, he's only just arrived.'

She blinked. Alistair was standing slightly to the left of the lift, his reading glasses perched precariously on top of his once blond, now grey hair, a clutch of files in his right hand.

'Who's just arrived?'

Her boss frowned. 'Gabriel Silva, of course.'

For some reason, even though her stomach was in freefall, it wasn't hard to smile and say with apparent sincerity, 'That's wonderful.'

Alistair beamed at her. 'Annabel is getting everything set up. I'm going to go down and meet him.'

She nodded, still smiling madly. She felt as if she was outside of her body, watching herself react. Or rather, not react.

'So I'll see you in the war room.'

Dove felt her smile freeze on her face as a ripple of foreboding snaked down her spine. *'Me?'* Her heart was jumping against her ribs like a trapped bird banging into a window. 'Why do I need to be there?'

'Because Mr Silva has specifically asked for you to be at the meeting. I told you last night. Remember? Seems he met your father once, several years ago, and never forgot the encounter.' Alistair paused, pursing his lips, as if he couldn't quite believe what he was about to say. 'They had a good chat, apparently. About his options for the future.' His mild, grey eyes rested on her face. 'I don't know what Oscar said, but it made quite an impression on our Mr Silva. "Life-changing", he called it.'

Her heart was thudding in her throat. That chat hadn't

just changed her life, it had destroyed it, and now he was threatening to destroy the fragile life she had rebuilt.

*So tell him. Tell Alistair you can't be in the same room as this man. You're like a daughter to him. He won't make you do it.*

But it was too late. Her boss was gone. She stared at the lift doors, feeling sick. This couldn't be happening. Except it was. Gabriel Silva was in the building, and any moment now he would be stepping through those doors.

Muscles tensing, she let her eyes flicker down the corridor to the staircase. She could leave—just go now. Walk out of the building and disappear, just like he had done. Only something inside her baulked at the idea. It wouldn't be disappearing—it would be hiding.

And why should she hide? She had done nothing wrong. And besides, she thought, stomach lurching, if she didn't turn up it would look as if she still cared about him, and she couldn't bear for him to think that was true.

Plus, it wouldn't be fair on Alistair to leave him in the lurch. Picturing the look of confusion on her boss's face as he discovered her absence, she snapped her shoulders back.

It would be fine. If Gabriel had wanted to meet her one on one he could easily have arranged to do so. Just because he was curious about the woman he had left behind, it didn't mean it was some kind of reconciliation. It was a business meeting in the war room. First, though, she needed to apply some war paint...

Five minutes later, her cheeks lightly flushed, hair smoothed into a low ponytail, she walked through the door, her pulse twitching a beat behind the click of her heels.

'Here she is.' Alistair greeted her warmly.

His flushed face was comforting and familiar, and just for a moment she kept looking at him, as if by doing so she could somehow ignore the man standing to his right. But even now, even when she hated him with every fibre, she couldn't resist the pull of the past or the demands of the present. And, lifting her chin, she turned to face Gabriel Silva.

Her pulse stumbled, and for a moment she couldn't move—couldn't feel anything. Her body was as rigid and cold as if it had been frozen. And then pain swept through her, scraping against the scars that should have healed but hadn't. A pain that tore at the protective barriers she had built between herself and the world. And she wanted to turn and run and keep running until she found somewhere she could hide away.

After six desolate years, it was a shock to come face to face with him. She had hoped that time might have punished him for what he'd done. But, as her eyes fixed on his absurdly handsome face, she was forced to admit that he was still the most beautiful man she had ever laid eyes on—and the most masculine. Thick dark hair that looked black in the moonlight, a curving, sensual mouth, and those mesmerising, unyielding blue, blue eyes.

Lifting a hand to the single-strand pearl choker at her throat, she breathed in shakily.

And then there was his body—

Her throat was suddenly impossibly dry. She had never seen him in a suit before, and she very much wished she hadn't now. Because she doubted she would ever forget it. There was something about the severity of its cut that softened his fierce beauty and made a knot of something hot and tight pulse in her belly.

Something that should have perished at the same time he turned their 'relationship' into a financial transaction.

Despair and frustration punched her in the gut. She didn't want to feel like this. She shouldn't be feeling like this. Gabriel Silva was a cold-blooded chancer, and the only reason she was even deigning to meet him was Alistair, the man standing beside him.

Stepping forward, Gabriel held out his hand and she stood there, her heart lurching against her ribs. Now, even though it hurt to look at him, it was impossible to turn away.

'Ms Cavendish.'

He was smiling, and suddenly she couldn't seem to breathe, because the Gabriel she had fallen in love with had rarely smiled. When he had it had been miraculous—like the 'fire rainbows' they had seen above Dorset on one of their secret weekends away together. Only this smile was something entirely different. It was calculated, disposable, and purely for Alistair's benefit.

She knew that the moment their gazes met and his eyes slammed into hers with such force that she almost lost her balance.

On the days when she thought she might choke on her sadness she would imagine this moment. Imagine how she would deliver a cool, cutting critique of his character. Instead, she said quietly, 'Mr Silva.'

Reaching out, she took his outstretched hand, intending simply to shake it briefly. But as their palms brushed she felt a jolt of heat, sharp and stinging, like the lick of a flame. His eyes locked with hers and his hand momentarily tightened.

'So this is the family firm,' he said softly, finally loosening his grip. 'Although I understand from Alistair that your father didn't work here?'

'No.' She flexed her fingers, trying to look calm and unaffected. Trying to forget that jolt of heat. Trying not to let her brain linger on how simply shaking hands with him could make her feel so on edge and exposed. 'He thought he lacked the talent for business,' she said stiffly.

In truth, Oscar Cavendish had been smart, and ruthless enough to have reached the top in whatever profession he chose. But he had been lazy and self-indulgent and, unlike Alistair, instead of working at the law firm founded jointly by their great-great-great-grandfathers— or working at all, for that matter—he'd preferred to live off the dividends from his shares in the business.

'And yet he was instrumental in kick-starting *my* career.'

Her heart thudded painfully as he held her gaze.

'Without his input I would never have been able to make that first investment.'

*Input.*

The word tasted like ash in her mouth. That was one way of describing it. But it was a little opaque, imprecise...misleading, even. Most people—herself and Alistair, for example—would call it a bribe, although no doubt Oscar had called it something less vulgar. An inducement, perhaps. Either way, Gabriel had accepted the money. He had been paid to break her heart.

*Are you proud of yourself? Of what you did?*

A part of her wanted to beat her fists against his chest

and scream bitter, accusatory questions at him. Only that would take them back to the past, and she didn't want to go there. She didn't want to scrape a wound that was still weeping and sore. She just wanted to get this over with, and then get as far away from him as soon as possible.

'Well, thank you for sharing that with me.'

She didn't like the way he was looking at her. It made her feel like a rabbit caught in the headlights of an oncoming car. But this time she wasn't going to let him flatten her.

She had met him, and looked him in the eye, and now she was done.

Straightening her slim shoulders, she lifted her chin. 'I'll let you two get down to business.'

'Of course, of course…' Oblivious to the current of tension swimming around the room, Alistair nodded enthusiastically. 'That's why we're all here.'

Actually, it wasn't, Gabriel thought shifting back in his seat, his lowered gaze fixed on Dove's delicate profile. He was here for one reason and one reason only: revenge. The acquisition of Fairlight Holdings was necessary only to achieve that goal.

The woman standing in front of him also had a part to play. Not that she knew that yet. But no matter. Revenge was a dish best eaten cold, so why not drag things out for just a little longer? Make sure everything was nice and chilled. A couple of minutes would make no difference in the scheme of things. In fact, he was going to enjoy every moment of making her squirm. It was the least she deserved after the way she had treated him.

Remembering the expression on Oscar's smoothly,

handsome face as he apologised for his daughter's 'change of heart', he felt his back tensed against the chair.

What heart? Dove Cavendish didn't have one. She was a living, breathing Snow Queen, with ice in her veins, and even now the memory of that conversation with her father burned him—almost as much as her beauty dazzled him.

She was still beautiful.

More than beautiful, he corrected himself reluctantly. She could be a mythical goddess, with her long pale blonde hair and ethereal silvery grey eyes. He had been looking into those same silvery grey eyes when she'd told him she loved him.

Was it any wonder he had been smitten?

He felt something flicker across his skin, and he recognised the hot lick of shame. Later, he had questioned his intelligence and his sanity in believing what Dove had said to him as she lay in his arms. But back then, blinded, foolish, senseless with love, it hadn't been until Oscar Cavendish turned up at the hotel with his 'proposal' that he'd understood how naive, not to say stupid, he had been to think she wanted anything more than a summer fling.

Now, though, it appeared that *she* was the naive one.

Swallowing the bitter taste that rose in the back of his throat, Gabriel turned towards Alistair Cox. 'And I'm very much looking forward to Cavendish and Cox helping me achieve my goal.'

The older man gestured towards the Herman Miller chairs tucked around the large conference table. 'Then let's get started. Thank you, Dove—'

'Oh, Ms Cavendish doesn't need to go.' He glanced over to where Dove stood, poised to leave, her body turned away from him so that he could see the silhouetted curve of her breasts against her blouse. 'We're all friends here.'

Something flashed in those molten silver eyes, just as they'd used to when they'd made love and he wondered if they still did. And, if so, with whom? His jaw tensed. The thought of another man holding her close at night, touching her, pressing his body against hers, made him see every shade of red.

He steadied his breathing. Once upon a time he'd thought they were friends, lovers. Soulmates, too. Not now. This was not some sort of reconciliation. He didn't want or need to be her friend. In fact, enemies could be just as useful and committed as friends—given the right incentive.

Fortunately, he knew exactly which buttons to press to ensure Dove Cavendish's compliance.

'And besides, my interest in acquiring Fairlight Holdings will soon be made public,' he said softly.

'Fairlight Holdings?' Alistair Cox frowned. 'I knew old Angus Balfour. He made some good investments in the mid-nineties' property rebound, but they made a mistake, in my opinion, when they failed to extend beyond the residential market.'

Gabriel held his gaze. There was a steeliness behind the older man's soft grey eyes, and a first-class brain. Despite his genial demeanour, Alistair Cox was clearly not just some clueless beneficiary playing at the family firm. So how had he ended up getting in such a mess?

Not that it mattered to him. Nothing mattered to him except getting even with the two women who had so callously upended his life. His mother, Fenella Ogilvy, and the woman standing opposite him, who was doing her best to pretend she wasn't there. Or more likely that he wasn't. But this time he wasn't going anywhere. This time he was the one with all the power—and most importantly the money.

Alistair Cox smiled at him pleasantly. 'Which is why I would advise choosing a company with a broader portfolio that covers commercial units as well. I know of a couple that would be interested—'

'Maybe another time,' Gabriel said neutrally.

The older man lifted off his glasses and began polishing them on the cuff of his jumper. 'Might I ask why you're so interested in Fairlight?'

Gabriel stared at Cox impassively, the anger he had held tightly inside for so long tearing at him.

His interest in this acquisition had nothing to do with business. His empire had started just five years ago, with a stake in the social media app Trill, and it had grown, hydra-headed, into a diverse portfolio that included a cryptocurrency exchange, a slow-food restaurant chain, several media outlets, and most recently some commercial real estate in New York.

Unlike his father, Luis, he hadn't had a vocation. His business had grown organically. But he liked picking up other people's businesses and refining them. Acquisitions had clear goals and they were profitable.

Only that wasn't why he wanted Fairlight Holdings.

The reason for that was simple.

Fenella Ogilvy, his birth mother—the woman who had rejected him at birth—was 'old' Angus Balfour's daughter. She wasn't actively involved in the business—she had a career as a successful TV presenter—but she had shares, as did her two children, and currently her son, the son upon whom she had bestowed her father's name was acting as interim CEO following his grandfather's death sixteen months ago. In short, Fairlight was an old family firm, much like Cavendish and Cox. He had worked on enough acquisitions to know how sentimental people could be about such businesses. And how much it hurt for them to lose control of them...

But Fenella Ogilvy was no businesswoman, and her son was out of his depth. She wanted out, and that made her vulnerable. And he fully intended to take advantage of that vulnerability. He was going to do to her what she had done to him. He was going to take her need and her weakness and turn it against her. Make her trade her family's business, her family's past and future, for cash.

And then he would shut it down. Erase it for ever as she had tried to erase him.

Glancing over at Dove's carefully composed face, he gritted his teeth. But he wasn't about to share the real reason with anyone.

He shrugged. 'I'm interested in anything that can make me money, Alistair.'

Beside him, Dove flinched. Or perhaps it was a trick of the light, he thought a moment later, glancing over at her pale, composed face. Before he could make up his mind, there was a knock on the door, and he watched as Cox's PA stepped into the room, smiling apologetically.

'I'm terribly sorry to interrupt, Mr Silva—' she looked over at her boss '—I have a call for Mr Cox.'

'Can't it wait, Annabel?' Alistair Cox frowned. 'We were just about to start—'

Gabriel held up his hands. 'Please don't refuse on my

account,' he said smoothly. 'Ms Cavendish can keep me company—if that's all right with her, of course?'

There was a small, pulsing silence, like a held breath. 'Of course,' she said finally.

Her face was impassive but, watching her small, swift nod, he felt a rush of satisfaction.

'That's sorted, then. No, really,' he added as Alistair started to protest again. 'It's not often that I get the opportunity to mix business with pleasure, so you'll be doing me a favour, Alistair.' He glanced over to the bottles of still and sparkling water on the table. 'Perhaps we might have some coffee—'

As the door closed the room fell silent, and just like that they were alone.

His heart was suddenly hammering inside his chest. *So this was it.* He had imagined this moment so many times inside his head. Had thought of all the clever, caustic things he'd say. Only now his mind was blank.

Stalling, he moved past her, taking his time, walking with slow, deliberate steps, sensing her gaze on him. And that—her need to track his progress—calmed him, for it meant that she was feeling this too.

He stopped in front of some portraits, tilting his head to read the small brass plaques beneath them, then turned slowly to where Dove stood motionless, her grey eyes fixed on a point past his shoulder. Not that it mattered, he thought, anger pulsing over his skin. Sooner or later she was going to realise that he wasn't going to disappear this time.

*Not until he'd got what he came for.*

'Beautiful view.' He nodded to the tree-lined cruciform-shaped gardens outside the windows. 'And not just beautiful… Apparently green encourages elevated levels of alertness and vitality.'

Her eyes locked with his. Grey, on the other hand, he thought, was a cloaking colour, designed to hide and obscure. He felt his heart tighten around the shard of ice that had been lodged there ever since Dove had cast him into the wilderness. If only he'd known that six years ago.

She was staring at him in silence, and he waited just as he had waited in that hotel bar. Only this time she was the one who didn't know what was happening. Didn't know that she was about to be chewed up and spat out. But she would…soon enough.

'What are you doing here, Gabriel?' Her voice was husky, but it was hearing her say his name that made his breathing jerk.

'I've told you what I'm doing,' he said softly. Up close, he could see the dilation of her pupils and the flecks of gold in her irises and, unable to resist the cool fury in her eyes, he took a step closer. 'I'm buying Fairlight Holdings.'

Their eyes met. 'And what? You just randomly picked Cavendish and Cox to act on your behalf?'

*No*, he thought. There had been nothing random about it. It had been a deliberate choice. It had to be that particular law firm.

He stared down at her as the silence between them lengthened. Her cheeks were flushed and the morning sun looked like glitter in her hair. His breath stalled, his groin hardening as he remembered how it had felt to tangle his fingers through its silken weight, to wrap it around her throat and draw back her head to meet his mouth—

Redirecting his thoughts to the matter in hand, he

shrugged. 'I was told that Cavendish and Cox were meticulous, diligent and reliable.' He glanced pointedly around the empty war room and frowned. 'But I'm starting to wonder if I was upsold—'

Her chin jutted forward, just as if she was wanting to be kissed, but her eyes were the colour of storm clouds and he could practically see lightning forking across the irises.

'Alistair is the best corporate lawyer in London.'

He had never heard her speak with such vehemence before, and he didn't like the tightness in his chest that it provoked. Maybe that was why he couldn't quite keep the taunting inflection from his voice when he said, 'I could almost believe you mean that—which is surprising, given that loyalty isn't one of your strong points. What, I wonder, did the estimable Alistair Cox do to earn such devotion?'

'He doesn't lie.' She took a step backwards. 'I want you to leave.'

The pulse at the base of her throat was leaping against the pale skin and he felt something pinch inside him, but he shook his head slowly. 'That's not going to happen.'

'Then I'll leave.' Her voice was faint, but firm, in the vast, sunlit room, and he could hear the anger rippling underneath the clipped consonants.

Hear it and feel it in all the wrong places.

His teeth on edge, his eyes held hers. She wasn't going anywhere. And yet part of him—a very specific part—almost wanted her to walk away, so he could see her move again on those teetering red-soled heels that added another four inches to her memorably endless legs. Watch her hips sway in the fitted blue pencil skirt that skimmed her delicate curves.

As she made to move past him he stepped in front of her. 'That's not going to happen either.'

She glared at him, her glossy blonde ponytail quivering like a cat's tail. 'You know, this whole big-shot, ruthless tycoon schtick is starting to wear a little thin. I don't take orders from you.'

*You will*, he thought, feeling his body respond to the challenge in her words and the small upward tilt of her chin.

Holding her gaze, he shrugged. 'Your surname might be above the door, Ms Cavendish, but you're just a cog in a wheel.'

There was a second of absolute silence.

'And you're an imposter.'

She sounded as if she had been running. Or been winded.

'And one of these days the whole world is going to realise that. Because you might have money now, Mr Silva, but you don't have class.'

The disdain in her voice snatched at his already fraying temper, but he was grateful. This was the real Dove Cavendish. And he needed to see the snobbish, careless woman who hid behind that beautiful, serene mask.

'And *you* don't have a choice.'

He felt suddenly calmer than he had in weeks. This was it. The moment he had been waiting for. He wanted to see the dawning recognition in those grey eyes that the trap had been sprung and there was no escape.

'You see, six years ago I made a mistake. I thought our relationship had run its course. But I was wrong. I've realised now that you and I have unfinished business. Can you see where this is going, Dove?' He kept his eyes on her face, wanting, needing to enjoy every quiver of shock, every shudder of understanding. 'I think you can. You always were smart.'

Now she was shaking her head. 'I am *not* working for you.'

'You already are.' Watching two streaks of colour wing along her cheeks, he felt a sharp sting of satisfaction. 'As of this moment, you are in charge of managing the Fairlight acquisition.'

# CHAPTER TWO

He delivered this statement almost casually, but his words hit her like a wrecking ball. In charge of the Fairlight acquisition?

Dove stared at Gabriel in stunned silence.

She couldn't feel her face, but her body was so tense she felt as if she might suddenly snap and fly apart into a million pieces. What was he talking about? Had he completely lost his mind? How could he think that she would work for him after what he'd done to her? After the hurt he'd inflicted?

On her way to the war room she had told herself that seeing him again was just something to be endured, and then ended as soon as was legitimately possible. That for some reason—most likely curiosity—Gabriel Silva wanted to see the woman he had conned and cast aside. And after the shock and panic had worn off a part of her had almost welcomed the encounter. She wanted to show him she hadn't crumbled, that she was managing just fine without him.

But it had only been meant to last a moment. She wasn't supposed to become part of his work with Cavendish and Cox.

She pressed her nails into her palms. Surely he wasn't being serious.

'This is some kind of joke, right?' Heart hammering, she searched his face, but Gabriel wasn't laughing or smiling. He was simply staring at her steadily, calmly, like a chess player who knew that the endgame had been reached.

Finally he shook his head slowly, his piercing blue gaze never leaving her face. 'I never joke about business.'

And now her heart felt as if it was going to burst through her ribs. A fresh shudder of panic raced through her. 'But you can't seriously expect me to work for you,' she said slowly.

'Why not?' He tilted his head up and a shaft of sunlight carved a shadow across his profile.

*Why not?* His words spun slowly inside her head like a car skidding on black ice. How could he even ask that question? Had he forgotten everything that had happened between them? The lies. The betrayal. The pain.

*Her pain—not his.*

She felt her stomach lurch. For him, it had only ever been for show. And yet even now, six years after she'd discovered the truth, it was still so hard for her to believe that all of it—the way his eyes had softened when he'd looked at her, the catch in his breath as he'd kissed her throat—had been a lie. It had felt so real at the time. And it had been real for her—achingly, agonisingly real.

But she had too much pride to raise that with him. And what would be the point? He didn't love her. He never had. So there was absolutely no way she was going to hint at how she had loved him.

There was a knock at the door and Becky, one of the office juniors, stepped into the room. She was holding a tray, and Dove saw the delicate Wedgwood china cups and saucers that were Alistair's favourite, and almost certainly irreplaceable. But she suspected that wasn't why Becky's hands were shaking.

'Thank you, Becky.'

'Mr Cox said to let you know that he'll be along shortly.' Becky's cheeks were flushed, and she sounded slightly breathless—as if she was about to faint. Which meant that she had also Googled Gabriel Silva earlier, and was now stunned to discover that his face matched the impossible flawless perfection of his online image.

Dove gritted her teeth as Becky put down the tray.

*Be careful what you wish for*, she wanted to shout at the younger woman. *Looks aren't everything.*

With those blue eyes and high, hard cheekbones, he might resemble an angel, but he was cruel and dangerous and utterly without conscience. And, yes, she knew that was probably true of a lot of their clients, but this was personal.

To her, anyway.

As the door closed, she turned to face him. 'Don't do that,' she snapped. 'Don't pretend you don't understand what I'm talking about.' Six years ago she might have been like a puppet on a string, blithely dancing to her doom, but that young woman didn't exist any more. 'You know exactly why I can't work for you.'

She stumbled over the words. But then she shouldn't even be having this conversation. After a normal break-up most people wanted to avoid their exes at all costs. But theirs had not been a normal break-up. Or a normal relationship, she thought, her heart twisting with misery.

Her pulse quivering in her throat, she watched as he pulled out one of the chairs and sat down, stretching out his legs just as if he owned the building and this was *his* war room. Except wars required armies, and this was just the two of them, locked in combat like gladiators trading blows.

She tensed as his eyes flicked up to her accusing face.

'I take it you're referring to our history?' he said softly.

*History.* Her breathing jerked and, lifting a hand protectively to her throat, she felt her pulse pound against her fingers. It was such a soft, vague term for something that had been so deliberately brutal.

She gave a humourless laugh. 'You're damn right I am.'

'What happened—happened.' In the sunlight, his handsome face was suddenly as harsh and unyielding as a statue. 'It's in the past, and I'm willing to leave it there.'

For a moment Dove couldn't breathe. *He* was willing to leave what happened between them in the past?

It was almost impossible to stop herself from grabbing him by the perfectly tailored lapels of his suit, hauling him to his feet and shaking him hard. Did he not know how much she had loved him? Or care about the pain he had caused? Her wide grey eyes fixed on his face as his careless indifference clawed at her throat.

Of course not. And that was why it was so simple for him to forget what hadn't happened.

It wasn't for her.

Stomach in freefall, she silently replayed the years that had passed. Years spent trying to come to terms with the reality of their brief one-sided relationship. Working every night until her head ached and her vision blurred, and then working out at the gym, pounding the treadmill until she was too exhausted to think or remember or, most important of all, feel. Because that was the only way she could carry on.

*By not feeling.*

None of which would be relevant to Gabriel because he didn't have feelings. Nor did he care about other people's feelings either. As she knew only too well, all he cared about was money.

Outside, the sun was rising higher in the sky, and for a moment she watched its slow ascent, grateful for the reminder that not everything was subject to the will of Gabriel Silva. Then, lifting her chin, she returned his gaze full-on.

'Well, I can't,' she said stiffly. 'So I'm afraid you'll have to ask someone else to manage your acquisition.'

There was a long, heavy silence. Around her the huge meeting room seemed to shrink and grow airless, so that it was suddenly difficult to breathe.

'I didn't *ask* you to work for me,' he replied, and her stomach curled at the clipped ferocity in his voice. 'I told you it was going to happen.'

She shook her head—more to clear it than out of defiance—and he lifted his chin, looking past her in that way of his that already felt too familiar, as if her opinions and wishes were irrelevant to him. Which, she realised with a thump of panic, they clearly were.

'You know, this is all going to be so much harder if you fight me every step of the way. And there's really no point.'

She felt the hairs stand up on the nape of her neck as his brilliant blue eyes fixed on her face.

'You *will* end up working for me.'

She stared over to where he sat—no, lounged in his chair, like some bored potentate who was regretting his decision to grant an audience to one of his minions. He had unbuttoned his jacket and she could see the outline of contoured muscle pressing against his shirt. It was a tantalising hint of what lay beneath.

Not that she needed reminding. She knew exactly what he looked like beneath that crisp, tailored cotton.

A beat of heat danced across her skin. A heat and an awareness, a hunger, she hadn't felt in a long, long time. As if her body was waking from a deep sleep. Only how could that be true? How could she feel anything for this man other than loathing?

'Why are you doing this?' she asked hoarsely, batting those questions to the dark outer reaches of her mind.

His startlingly blue eyes lifted to hers, and the coolness there was such a contrast to her own fraught feelings that she had to clench her hands tightly to stop herself reaching down and hurling the fine bone china cups at his head.

'For the same reason I do everything,' he said, getting to his feet with the leopard-like grace that characterised every moment he made.

'Because I can.'

She couldn't breathe for a moment. Was that what had happened six years ago? Had he taken her father's money simply because it had been offered? Or had he been angling for that all along? It was on the tip of her tongue to ask him. But she didn't want to talk about the past with this cold-eyed stranger.

She licked her lips. 'That's not an answer.'

His eyes homed in on her mouth like a heat-seeking missile tracking its target and she felt the tension throb between them. But then, just as swiftly, he turned away without replying.

Watching him walk across a room six years ago, she had fallen in love with him. Now, though, she stared in appalled fascination as he sauntered slowly round the table. Her eyes fixed to the dark jacket that stretched endlessly across his back and she felt a tic of heat pulse across her skin. Once upon a time she had loved to slide her fingers over the smooth muscles of his shoulders, guiding his movements, her breath staccato in her throat as he drove into her—

Heat bloomed inside her as a blurry montage of their entwined bodies wove through her head…

'So this is him? The guy you're related to?'

Blinking, she glanced over to where Gabriel was standing in front of the gilt-framed portrait of Arthur Cavendish.

She nodded. 'He's my great-great-great-grandfather.'

'Handy. To have a ready-made corporate law firm in the family.' He turned and stared at her, long and hard, a muscle working in his stubble-covered jaw. 'Although I seem to remember you telling me on more than one occasion that you would never work at Cavendish and Cox.' His mouth slanted into a smile that was more of a baring of teeth. 'But perhaps you didn't mean what you said.'

Resentment surged through her, and anger—a hot, sweeping anger such as she had never felt in her life before, so that she wasn't even sure it *was* anger. 'We both said things we didn't mean, Gabriel.' Her eyes met his, grey clashing with the blue. 'And you weren't the only one who made a mistake.'

He didn't like that. She saw the flare of male pride and arrogance in his eyes. But she didn't care. Even if it was too little, too late, she wanted him to hurt—wanted to hurt him as he had hurt her…was still hurting her.

'So now we both know where we stand, why don't you stop with the games—?'

'You think this is a *game*?'

His dark brows snapped together and she took an immediate, defensive step back, her hand rising instinctively in front of her body as he made his way back around the table.

'You think this is a game?' he repeated as he stopped in front of her.

She forced herself to hold her ground.

'I don't know what this is, but I do know that if it was up to me I'd tell you exactly what you could do with your acquisition.'

'Then it's fortunate for all your colleagues that it's Alistair who's in charge of Cavendish and Cox and not you.' His blue gaze held steady and the tension in her stomach wound tighter. 'In case it's passed you by, he's running a business—not a charity. So I doubt he'll be turning away wealthy clients any time soon.'

'But that's where you're wrong.'

She took a step closer, pushing her hand against the solid wall of his chest to emphasise her point. It was harder than she remembered, and warm through his shirt.

'Alistair's not just a lawyer. He's a man of principle. He cares about the way things get done, the way people behave, because he knows that there's more to business than making money. Not that I'd expect a man like you to understand that.'

'And what kind of man is that, Ms Cavendish?'

He leaned into her hand and the touch of him, at once familiar and forbidden, scorched her fingers. She jerked them away.

'A ruthless, amoral, cold-blooded one.'

She flung the words at him, wishing they were sticks or stones, or better still rocks, but instead of hitting their target they seemed to lose their force, like waves hitting a breakwater. And, gazing up, she saw something in his eyes that made her spine tense.

'You forgot successful. But you're working here, so I can understand why *that* word might have been dropped from your vocabulary.'

How dare he say that? Angry words bubbled up in her throat. Maybe the firm was no longer the legal powerhouse it had once been, but it was still a solid, reputable business.

'Cavendish and Cox have been in existence for nearly two hundred years,' she snapped. 'I'd call that pretty successful.'

Watching his mouth twist, she felt her stomach clench. So many smiles, each one different and infinitely more disturbing than the last. This one was doing something strange to the air, making it quiver as if a storm was approaching.

Or maybe the storm was already here, she thought as he stared down at her, his blue gaze glittering in the sunlight, bright and sharp like tempered steel.

'And yet word on the street is that Cavendish and Cox is going under.'

For a few half-seconds she had that same sensation as earlier, as if she was floating outside her own body. Whatever she had been expecting him to say, it hadn't been that.

Her heart thumped hard inside her chest as she remembered the conversation she'd overheard in a bar. It had been several months ago now. A couple of lawyers from a rival firm had been discussing office space, and one of them had said he had heard that the Cavendish and Cox building was going on the market.

In a panic, she had confronted Alistair, but he'd been unperturbed, almost amused.

'It's just gossip. Honestly, I've lost count of the number of times that this place has supposedly been up for sale.' He had patted her arm reassuringly. 'Things get a little sticky sometimes, but we always get through it, Dove.'

And she had believed him. Selfishly, she'd wanted to believe him—because she couldn't face thinking about what it would mean if he was wrong. She couldn't deal with yet another loss.

But what if he *was* wrong?

A shiver of panic scuttled down her spine.

What if Alistair had lied to her?

Fighting for calm, fighting for control, trying desperately to hold on to her anger and keep the panic at bay, she met Gabriel's gaze. 'I don't know what stone you were under when you heard that particular rumour, but you're mistaken,' she said crisply, as if she wasn't the least bit shaken. 'Everything is fine.'

His face was impassive, but the sudden glint in his eyes sent a dizzying drumroll of adrenaline pounding through her veins.

'Maybe it is,' he agreed, but there was a taunting softness to his voice that made her shiver inside.

'That's the trouble with rumours. Once they're out there…' his gaze shifted momentarily to the tree-lined square outside the window '…they get a life of their own. All it would take would be one high-profile, wealthy client to walk away or perhaps express his concerns—

privately, of course—to some of his other equally high-profile and wealthy friends and all of this—' his eyes snapped back to her face '—would come tumbling down like a house of cards.'

The air thumped out of her lungs and she felt her face drain of colour. The room was suddenly silent. Outside in the street even the traffic stilled, as if he had cast a spell over the whole of Lincoln's Inn Fields.

'You wouldn't—'

He must be bluffing.

But she knew from the tiny pause before he answered that he wasn't.

In fact, she was certain he would have no compunction in making good on his threat, and it was all too easy in that moment to remember why, and how much, she hated him.

He looked at her assessingly. 'I wouldn't want to. And I won't have to. Just so long as we're on the same page.'

'And what page is that?'

'Now who's playing games?' he said softly. But his face was hard like polished bronze.

Stiffening her shoulders, she forced her gaze up to his. 'I'm not. I just don't understand why you would want me to work for you.'

'Isn't that obvious?'

The question was accompanied by a careless, deliberately provocative lift of his broad shoulders. 'This acquisition is particularly important to me, so it's vital that I have someone managing it who is as invested as I am. I need someone whose commitment to making it happen matches mine. You're that person.'

She gave a trembling ghost of a laugh. 'You think *I'm* that person?'

Her heart was racing, and the dampness of her hands had nothing to do with the warm morning sunshine filling the room. This was insane. *He* was insane—he must be if he thought that was possible.

Her chin jerked upwards. 'The only thing I'm invested in, Gabriel, is never having to see you again.'

He looked at her, his gaze impassive. 'So you don't mind if Alistair loses the business? The business founded by your great-great-great-grandfather. You don't care about his legacy? Or about all the people who will lose their jobs?'

The challenge in his voice danced lightly over her skin, making her insides prickle with anger—and something softer and more treacherous.

'Of course I do.'

He shrugged almost lazily. 'Then I've no doubt you will do the very best job you can for me. Because if you don't I will ruin this business. I will drive it into the ground.'

Tears stung her eyes and she blinked them away. She wanted to scream and keep on screaming. At him, and at a world that allowed a man like him to become powerful. Only his words had sucked all the air from her lungs.

'This is how you do business, is it?' she said finally. 'By issuing threats, bullying people, blackmailing them?'

'I do whatever needs to be done to get what I want,' he said, and it was the softness in his voice that made her understand just how ruthless he was.

She glared at him. 'You know, I wish I could say this was a revelation—a hitherto unforeseen glimpse into your character—but frankly it doesn't surprise me at all—'

She broke off, hating herself for becoming so emotional, for letting him get under her skin. Hating him for coming back and tearing down another set of illusions—that she was getting on with her life. In reality she had simply been ignoring a huge, jagged wound…pretending it was healed.

He took a step closer, and every single nerve-ending in her body jerked into life as she breathed in the masculine scent that had been tormenting her ever since she'd walked into the war room.

'This isn't business, Dove.'

His voice rolled through her, fierce and dark and compelling. Or perhaps it was the sound of her name in his mouth as his gaze held her captive.

'This is personal.'

She stared up at him, panic stampeding through her veins, her muscles clenching, tightening hard around the hollow at the bottom of her stomach. Earlier, she had been wrong. He had changed. Now he didn't have to hide who he was any more. He didn't need to pretend or play games. Now he was a man who openly pursued what he wanted. A man not used to failing.

But he was going to fail this time. Because there was no way she was going to work for him. Not without a fight.

'Like I said earlier, we have history.'

Her train of thought snapped in two as images of that 'history' popped into her head. It had been frenzied. *She* had been frenzied. Frantic. Out of control. And strong and hungry and demanding in a way she wasn't in life. Gabriel had released a side to her she hadn't known existed. His kiss had stirred her, his touch unravelled her, and her body had ached at his absence—

*It still did.*

Her pulse quivered. Because he had left her. In exchange for money. And that was what she needed to focus on and remember. Not this strange, shimmering weave of tension between them that made her heart pound high up in her throat and her body shake inside.

'We had a relationship. We were going to elope. Then my father offered you money to walk away, and you took the money and walked. So, in fact, we don't just have a *history*, Gabriel. What we have is a conflict of interests.'

He was shaking his head, certainty etched into the contoured arcs and planes of his gorgeous face. 'There's no conflict. You want Cavendish and Cox to be around for another two hundred years, and I want that too. All you have to do to make that happen is manage one small acquisition for me.'

*And look into his beautiful lying eyes every day and relive the pain and misery of his deceit.*

She didn't have a choice. But she tried again.

'Any acquisition is a complex process.' She kept her voice calm and professional. 'As you know, there are multiple steps. At Cavendish and Cox, we believe that communication at each stage of the process is the most important factor in achieving the optimum outcome for our clients.'

His fine dark brows arched. 'So it says on the website. What's your point?'

'How do you expect us to do that?' The slow burn of his gaze made her feel light-headed. Knots were forming in her belly. 'You and I...we don't communicate. On any level. We never did.'

There was a long pause, and the knots inside her tightened as he stood studying her. His blue eyes were so intent it was like being held in a tractor beam. He was so close she could see the ring of darker blue around his irises and the minute constriction of the pupils. Feel the heat and energy and intent humming beneath his immaculate suit.

'I'd have to disagree,' he said finally, breaking the taut silence.

His bright and intensely blue eyes rested on her face, reaching into her, seeing more than she wanted him to see, seeing far too much.

'You see, as I remember it, you and I…we communicated extremely productively,' he said smoothly, but with that same edgy undercurrent that made her head feel light and her nerve-endings judder like telephone wires in a high wind. 'On one level,' he added.

She felt heat spill over her skin, and suddenly her breath was hot and tangled in her throat and she tensed, remembering. Glancing up at his face, she knew from the tension in his jaw that he was remembering it too.

'That was a long time ago.' Her voice sounded scratchy.

Even though it might look like a retreat, she knew that someone as smart as she was supposed to be would have moved out of reach of that tractor beam gaze by now. But it was impossible to stop her own eyes from lingering on his beautiful face and his lush, curving mouth. Impossible not to imagine how that mouth would feel against hers.

He reached out and touched her hair lightly, his thumb brushing against her cheek. 'And yet it feels like only yesterday.'

Heart clattering in her throat, she stared up at him, blindsided by that admission. The sudden roughness in his voice holding her captive just as surely as if he had grasped her wrists, the truth of his words acting like a brake on her anger and panic, so that suddenly her body was incapable of doing anything sensible or sane.

Like pushing his hand away.

Or turning and walking as fast as she could out of the room.

The air quivered, pressing in on them like a force field, and then, before she could chivvy her brain into some kind of response, he bent his head and covered her mouth with his own, just as he'd used to.

Just as if the last six years had never happened.

Just as if she was still his.

The air left her body. Everything stopped, and grew silent. All thought. All awareness. All the barriers she had created. All of it dissolved and there was only the melting heat of his mouth and their banked hunger for one another sweeping through her like the most potent drug.

Around her the room was spinning, blurring the walls into a smear of blue and gold, and instead of sunlight she could see a million stars. Her breath caught as his fingers slid around her waist to the indentation at the small of her back, his thumbs skimming her ribcage, burning her skin through the silk of her blouse. And then she was reaching for the hard, smooth muscles of his shoulders, pulling him closer, flickers of heat skating down her limbs as his lips found the hollow at the base of her throat.

She wanted him so badly she could hardly bear it. Wanted to pull off his clothes, then hers, and press her naked body against his. He must be feeling the same way. Her belly clenched as the tips of his fingers slid over the bare skin of her collarbone and—

A ripple of conversation swelled in the corridor outside and they broke apart as if stung. She stumbled backwards on her heels, gripping the edge of the table, heat pooling in her pelvis, heart running wild.

Gabriel was staring down at her, breathing unsteadily, his eyes blazing. It was some consolation to see that he looked as floored as she felt—but not much.

'We shouldn't have done that,' she said hoarsely. She could hardly string the words into a sentence. Her brain felt dislocated, and she was struggling to pull herself together and catch up with what had just happened. 'Anyone could have walked in.'

There was a tiny shift in the air and something crossed his face—a dark flicker of emotion she couldn't place. And then he was back in control, straightening his cuffs, fixing his gaze on hers, narrowed and so intensely blue it felt like a high tide rushing over her.

'We were lucky.' His mouth curved into a vicious flick. 'But don't worry—I'm not planning on telling anyone. You won't have to pay me to disappear again. Not that you could afford to.'

She stared at him dazedly. Coming so close on the heels of that brief, feverish moment of intimacy, the cool hostility in his voice was as shocking as if he'd slammed a door in her face.

'We can't do this. I can't work for you—'

'Too bad,' he said flatly. 'Life demands sacrifices, Dove. And not even you would be so selfish as to bring down the family business just to spare your ego.'

Her heartbeat was fluttering high in her throat.

But she hadn't been selfish. She hadn't done anything...

'I am so sorry.'

Her head snapped round. Alistair was striding back into the war room, his face flushed with apology. 'I thought I'd be gone five minutes at most.'

She watched Gabriel swing round to face him. 'It's perfectly all right, Alistair. Ms Cavendish has kept me thoroughly entertained. And what's more she has agreed to manage the Fairlight acquisition for me. That is, of course, assuming you can spare her?'

'I can, indeed.' Alistair beamed at her proudly. 'Dove is a very talented lawyer. I can guarantee that you will be impressed by the quality of her work and her dedication.'

'I don't doubt it.'

She felt something complicated happening to her breathing as Gabriel's eyes locked on hers, cool, taunting, daring her to speak, to call his bluff.

'I'll get my people to sort out the paperwork, and we can start prepping on Monday.'

'Wonderful.'

Alistair rubbed his hands together and, sensing his relief, Dove felt a rush of guilt. It wouldn't be obvious to just anyone, but she could see the legacy of fine worry lines fanning out from his mild grey eyes.

Now, though, he was as excited and eager as a child on its birthday. 'I hear the views from your offices are magnificent,' he said to Gabriel.

Dove managed to make a smile appear on her face as Alistair turned to share his excitement. She knew the Silva Group had recently moved into London's latest exclusive high-rise development. A multi-tiered white tower known colloquially as the 'Wedding Cake'. She felt a trickle of relief wash through her, picturing the gleaming open-plan offices. At least there, surrounded by his attentive staff, there would be little opportunity for them to be alone.

'You must come and visit, Alistair. But…' Gabriel paused, and she looked up at him uneasily. 'We won't be working out of the office. You see, when I greenlight an acquisition I prefer to work from *The Argentum*. My yacht,' he added, his eyes on hers. 'She's moored off the Côte d'Azur.'

Her throat was suddenly so tight that it ached to breathe.

Beside her, Alistair was looking even more delighted. 'And you call that working?'

Gabriel inclined his head. 'I know it sounds a little crazy, but it actually works very well. Aside from privacy issues, on shore there are distractions, temptations. Out at sea, everyone stays focused. It's perfect, really.'

The sunlight was behind him now and she couldn't see his expression, just the faint gleam of his eyes. But, staring up at him, Dove felt a warm, slippery panic rising up from her stomach.

Sailing around the Mediterranean while working would be most people's idea of a dream job. Only how was she supposed to stay focused, stay *sane*, when it was clear, after what had happened this morning, that the most distracting temptation for her would not be on shore but on the yacht?

# CHAPTER THREE

GABRIEL STRODE OUT into Lincoln's Inn Fields, his blue eyes narrowing. Not at the unusually bright London sunshine but at his complete and utter lack of self-control.

What had he been thinking? Dove Cavendish was the woman who had scorned and then humiliated him. She had taken his heart and trampled on it in her red-soled heels, and yet all it took was one touch and he had forgotten his anger, his thirst for revenge. Had anyone asked him he would have struggled to tell them his name...

His jaw clenched tight, and for a few quivering seconds he could almost feel her body pressed against his as intensely as if it was reality.

Frustration in every sense of the word burned through him.

He had broken his first rule of business. He had let himself get distracted.

But it wasn't as if he had bumped into her randomly in the foyer of some hotel. This day had been long coming. It had taken six long years for everything to fall into place so that he could finally confront Dove Cavendish on her home turf. He had planned it all out, scripted each word, fully intending to cut her down to size, to make her feel as small and powerless as she'd made him feel all those years ago.

Instead, he had behaved like some stupid, oversexed teenage boy.

Holding her in his arms, feeling the fever-heat of her skin beneath that silky blouse, had made time lose its shape so that the past had overlapped the present. In those few devastating seconds when Dove had melted against him it had been as if ten thousand years of evolution had reversed in the blink of an eye. He had no longer been Gabriel Silva, billionaire CEO, whose suits cost the same amount as a small family car. He had been just a man. A primitive man driven by mind-melting impulses and unconscious need.

And that wasn't all. Shaken by his sudden loss of control, and the sweet, wild lightness of Dove's response, he had suggested that she fly out to join him on *The Argentum*—even though, up until that moment, he had been intending simply to keep her dangling in London.

He swore under his breath, then lifted his hand with the mix of carelessness and authority that was now as instinctive to him as breathing, watching as a sleek, dark limousine with tinted windows pulled up alongside the kerb.

Inside the car, the air was cool. Jaw clenching, he sank back against the pale leather upholstery.

It hadn't always been the case. Making money was the easy part—but being rich took surprisingly long to master. Because being rich was about more than just having a lot of money. And he had a *lot* of money. More than he could have ever imagined, growing up in his parents' two-bedroomed terraced house in Swindon.

Some of the tension in his shoulders loosened, as it always did when he thought about his mother and father. Luis and Laura Silva might not have had much money, but they had given him everything a son could want or need. They had supported and guided him and had faith in him. Most of all they'd loved him—unconditionally.

Once upon a time, when he had been younger and more trusting, he had believed Dove loved him like that too. He knew better now.

He pressed the heel of his hand against his forehead, then closed his eyes, seeing again the look of panic on her face as they broke apart. For her, it had never been a relationship. It had been just a summer fling. Maybe she'd liked it that he'd been nothing like any of the men in her circle, with their floppy fringes, striped shirts and loud, braying voices. That summer, when he'd worked as a waiter for an events company, he'd had his fill of them. He had thought Dove had too. It was certainly what she'd implied.

But what had he really known about her?

His eyes snapped open.

Nothing, that was what.

More incredibly still, he hadn't cared. The first time he'd laid eyes on Dove, he'd wanted her. Wanted her more than he had ever wanted anything or anyone. Wanted her so badly that it had hurt to breathe.

He had been working since the start of the summer. Sometimes in the kitchens, scraping food from pots and pans, loading plates and cutlery into the dishwashers. Other times he'd been required 'front-of-house' to wait at tables. All of it had been dull, repetitive, exhausting work, but he'd needed money—he'd always needed money then. And he had still been smarting from what had happened a year earlier. Work had taken his mind off the pain. And the guilt.

*And the shame.*

The shame of failing. Failing to be wanted, welcomed, embraced. Not once but twice.

Truthfully, he'd been a mess—only then Dove had walked into his marquee. Dazzling, flawless, untouchable. With her gleaming pearl-blonde hair streaming down her back and those soft kissable lips parted in an extraordinarily sweet smile that had spread like nitrous oxide through his limbs.

And she had been so much more than the sum of her parts. She'd been smart—book-smart—but also curious about the world beyond hers. And her voice… She'd had a beautiful voice…soft and precise and hypnotic.

Just like the touch of her fingers, he thought, his pulse quickening.

His own fingers bit into the leather upholstery. He had been so certain she was the one. And, fresh from Fenella Ogilvy's brutal rejection, he had been hungry to be seen, recognised. To be wanted, heard, needed…

Instead, for the second time in his life, he had been paid to disappear. He'd become yet another dirty little secret to be buried. And he had felt not just rejected but buried alive.

His gaze drifted to the window, to where a woman with a blonde ponytail was jogging along the pavement. His pulse accelerated, as if to keep pace with her stride. He hadn't felt as if he was buried alive back in that war room. On the contrary, his need for her had been like a roar of flame and lava beneath his skin.

Remembering Dove's face, the restless heat in her eyes

and the flushed cheeks, he felt his groin tighten. He swore softly, yanked his tie loose from his neck and tossed it across the back seat, wishing he could tear off the rest of his clothes.

*Or go back and tear off hers.*

His whole body tensed, and before he could stop himself, he was picturing a naked Dove, splayed out on the oversized table in the war room, blonde hair spilling over her pale shoulders, mouth parted—

Groaning, he smacked his head back against the padded upholstery—and then he caught sight of his driver's eyes in the rear-view mirror and checked himself.

*That wasn't going to happen.*

It was true he had lost control earlier, but that was understandable. Seeing her again had been a shock, and that shock had momentarily swept aside everything. Erasing their history as if it had never happened. Changing his priorities so that in those few febrile seconds he had effectively been a blank slate.

Put like that, was it any surprise that some kind of muscle memory had kicked in?

He tapped on the glass behind his driver's head. 'Take me back to the hotel.'

Kissing her had been inevitable—necessary. Cathartic, in a way. But it would be different next time.

Feeling calmer, he sank back in his seat. Everything was still on track. And now he was just one very long, very cold shower away from purging Dove Cavendish from his body for ever.

As the sleek white helicopter rose up into the sky, hovering momentarily like a seagull riding a thermal air current, Dove felt her stomach flip. This was it. After nearly a week of pretending this might never happen, she was now just minutes away from seeing Gabriel again.

Living with him.

Working for him.

It was five days since he had waltzed back into her life and effectively shaken it like a snow globe. Now, to all appearances, everything was settled and calm again. The letter of engagement had been signed and Alistair was humming to himself as he walked the corridors.

She leaned her head back against the seat.

But beneath her pale skin chaos reigned.

Twisting slightly, she gazed down. Beneath her, the legendary Château Saint-Honoré was shrinking, turning into a dolls'-house-sized palace beside the glittering Mediterranean. A syncopated beat of panic and anger drummed across her skin as she watched the coastline disappear. If it had been anyone else footing the bill she would have enjoyed staying at the Saint-Honoré. The hotel was eye-poppingly opulent, sun-soaked, *soignée*— a one-of-a-kind testament to Riviera grandeur, harking back to a time when European aristocrats and Hollywood film stars had wintered by the famous pool with its dramatic black and white tiles.

But she suspected that the lavishness of her accommodation had simply been Gabriel's way of reminding her yet again that he was calling the shots.

Her hand tightened around the leather armrest.

First, she had been invited to his offices at the 'Wedding Cake', to meet with his team—including his intimidatingly polished and articulate chief operating officer, Carrie Naylor. Then there had been a chauffeur-driven limousine that had appeared like Cinderella's carriage to ferry her to the airport, where a sleek, snub-nosed private jet had sat waiting for her on the Tarmac to take her to the most exclusive hotel in the French Riviera.

And now she was in a helicopter, flying to *The Argentum*.

All thanks to the 'generosity' of Gabriel Silva.

The only consolation was that the man himself had been conspicuously absent. Apparently *'unwinding in Paris'*.

She sucked in a breath. Carrie had let that slip. And it shouldn't have mattered. It shouldn't have hurt. Only it did.

Everything hurt. Seeing him again. Having him back in her life but *not* back in her life. He was a stranger, and yet he knew things about her that no one else knew. So much had happened between them—only everything she'd felt had been false. For Gabriel it had all been just a game. And now she was going to have to work with him.

Her shoulders stiffened against the cool leather. When Dove was a child, her mother had used to read her the Greek myths. Some she'd loved, like the tale of the Golden Apple, but the one she'd hated was the story of Theseus and the Minotaur. Only it hadn't been the monster that had scared her, but the labyrinth. She hadn't been able to bear to imagine how it would feel to be trapped in the darkness, blundering into one dead end after another.

She didn't need to imagine it now.

Ever since Gabriel had left the office she had been trapped in a labyrinth of his making. She had tried repeatedly, and unsuccessfully, to find a loophole—she was a lawyer, after all. But unless she was willing to call his bluff there was no way out.

And she couldn't do that. She couldn't risk doing something that might harm Alistair. Or the fifty or so people who worked at Cavendish and Cox. And then, of course, there was Olivia. Refusing to work for Gabriel would have meant telling Alistair the truth about Gabriel and Oscar, and then her mother would have found out everything—because that was how it worked. One moment of transparency would lead inevitably to another, like flowers bursting into bloom in spring.

After all this time, could she really just casually drop that kind of grenade in her mother's lap? It would serve no purpose except to upset her, and Olivia was finally in a good place.

'Not long now, Ms Cavendish.'

Her chin jerked up. The helicopter's co-pilot had turned to face her, smiling reassuringly.

'We should see *The Argentum* in around ten minutes.' His eyes dropped to where her hand was clamped around the armrest. 'Would you like me to play some music through the speakers? Some of our more nervous passengers have found it helpful not to hear the sound of the rotors.'

She smiled stiffly. 'Thank you.'

Moments later, soft piano music filled the cabin and, uncurling her fingers, she rested her hands in her lap. She wasn't a nervous flyer. But there was no need to tell a perfect stranger the truth. That the real reason for her nervousness was sitting on *The Argentum*.

All six foot four of him.

Nothing short of a medicated coma was going to make this terrible edgy feeling disappear. Not when she could still feel the imprint of his lips against hers.

She felt a sharp warning twist through her stomach, like seasickness, just as if she was already standing on the deck of the yacht. But in her mind she was back there in the war room, replaying the moment when Gabriel had kissed her.

It shouldn't have happened—she had been right about that. But being right with hindsight didn't change the facts. He had kissed her, and she had let him. Worse, she had kissed him back.

*Why had she done that?*

There was no making sense of it. But that hadn't stopped her from asking herself that question roughly every ten minutes since Gabriel had sauntered out of the Cavendish and Cox building five days ago. The only difference was that this time it was asked to the accompaniment of Chopin's *Prelude Op 28 No 15*.

And she still didn't have an answer—or at least not one that didn't make her want to jump out of the helicopter and into the sea below.

Glancing out of the window, she felt her heart start to beat arrhythmically. But it was too late even for that now.

Beneath her, a glossy white yacht rose out of the shimmering sheet of water like a displaced iceberg. Stomach churning, she pressed her hands together in her lap to hide how badly they were shaking. Back at the hotel, she'd thought Gabriel had deliberately already taken the yacht out to sea for some Machiavellian reason designed to put her in her place. But now she saw there could be only few marinas that would be able to take a boat of that size.

'She's beautiful, isn't she?'

Turning her gaze, she saw that both pilots were gazing down at *The Argentum* with undisguised admiration.

'And not just beautiful,' the co-pilot added. 'That bow can cut through Arctic ice.'

'That's amazing.' Dove smiled automatically. It was the kind of detail Alistair would have loved, and she felt a sharp pang, picturing his excitement when she told him.

The helicopter began to descend, just as she had known it would, and ten minutes later she was stepping onto the sleek white deck, panic punching through her like a jackhammer. She was half expecting Gabriel to meet her—not out of courtesy, but simply to gloat. Instead, a short, bright-eyed man wearing navy trousers and a white polo shirt greeted her with a firm, dry handshake. In his other hand he was holding a tablet.

'Welcome on board *The Argentum*, Ms Cavendish. I'm Peter Reid, the chief steward. Did you have a good flight?'

'Yes, thank you. It was very...' she searched for an adjective '...smooth.'

'That's what we aim for.' Lifting the tablet, he typed something, then swiped across the screen. 'Just updating the manifest,' he murmured. 'Now, if you would like to come this way, Mr Silva is waiting for you in the lounge.'

She followed him through the boat, the sound of her heartbeat swallowing up his voice intermittently so that she only caught occasional snatches of sentences.

'...sixty-member crew...twenty thousand square feet of living space...encased in bomb-proof glass...fingerprint security system...twenty-four thousand horsepower diesel engines.'

It sounded more like a floating high-security prison than a boat, she thought, panic swelling in her throat.

As they stopped in front of a door, the steward turned

and smiled. 'We can outrun almost anything on the high seas—including pirates. Although that's not something we have to worry about in this region.'

He knocked briskly on the door, and without waiting for a reply opened it.

Dove stepped reluctantly into the room. Frankly, the idea of coming face to face with a pirate was not nearly as unsettling as the sight of the man standing on the other side of the room with his back to her, gazing out to sea.

Only this time it was going to be different, she told herself firmly. There would be no sliding back in time, no picking over the bones of the past. She would be cool, calm and professional.

But as Gabriel turned slowly to face her, her heart lurched like a scuttled ship.

Five days ago, when this moment had been simply a concept, she had thought that it would be easier seeing him the second time. She'd been wrong. If anything, she was having to fight a quivering, betraying flush as he walked towards her, shockingly beautiful in dark suit trousers and a pale blue shirt.

'So, you made it, then?'

As he stopped in front of her she forced her eyes up to meet his, and for a moment she thought she saw a flicker of admiration or respect. But then it was gone, and he was gesturing towards one of the large cream Barcelona chairs that were grouped around a delicate scallop-edged eau-de-nil wool rug.

She took a furtive glance around the room. It was cool and modern and minimal, with sculptural lighting, one vast Cy Twombly canvas in muted shades and ocean views on three sides. It was nothing like the war room at Cavendish and Cox but, judging by the edgy, pulsing tension filling the room, it was still a battleground, she thought, tucking her legs to one side as she sat down.

'I wondered whether you might send someone else in your place.'

His voice was cool, taunting, silky-smooth, and she couldn't tell if the tightness in her chest was anger or foreboding or confusion. Because she *hadn't* sent her father to find him all those years ago. It had been Oscar's idea to challenge Gabriel—to test his intentions. She didn't know to this day how he had found out about their relationship—it hadn't seemed to matter much in the scheme of things. And, really, what did it matter now what Gabriel had mistakenly thought all those years ago? It was a detail. It wasn't something vast and life-changing…like lying to someone about being in love.

She squared her shoulders. 'I'm not like you, Gabriel. Once I've committed to something I don't change my mind.'

'Nice try.' His tone matched hers, but it was layered with a dark edge that made her legs tremble. 'But we both know the only reason you're here is because you're scared of calling my bluff.'

She swallowed, her hand reaching up to touch the pearls at her throat. Was this how it was going to be? Death by a thousand cuts. Every word, every glance, a fresh blow to parry or contain.

*I can't go through with this*, she thought, misery gnawing at her insides.

But she knew she would; It was what she'd been trained to do—both as a lawyer and as the daughter of Oscar and Olivia Cavendish.

'I'm not scared of you.'

Oddly enough, she wasn't. Not now that she was here and the danger of him making good on his threat had receded. Mostly she was scared of herself. Or rather she was scared of her body's strange, ungovernable response to his.

As if to prove the point, she felt her gaze drift towards him, drawn irresistibly by the triangle of light gold skin that was visible between the open collar of his shirt.

*Stop it*, she told herself. *It was only one kiss.*

But even as she shoved the memory aside she felt it prickle beneath her skin.

He raised one, smooth, dark eyebrow. 'Let me guess… This is where you tell me all about how you've worked with far more demanding and difficult clients than me.'

'Actually, I don't see you as a client,' she said crisply, her pulse flicking back and forth like a flame in a draught. 'To me, you're just a bully. A rich man without scruples. A man who uses his wealth and power to get what he wants.'

His pupils flared, turning his blue eyes into dark, fathomless pools. For a moment he didn't reply. He just let the silence and the tension build between them, swallowing up the air so that she thought she might never breathe again.

'Not *everything* I want,' he said finally. 'Or have you forgotten what happened in the war room?'

This time the silence was shorter—like a caught breath. Pulse stumbling, she stared back at him, her skin growing hotter and tighter as his gaze meandered slowly over her puffed-sleeve blouse and pencil skirt down to her towering nude court shoes, and her mind replaying the burning heat of his mouth and the hardness of his body against his.

No, she hadn't forgotten—and she suspected that Gabriel knew that. And then his gaze dropped to her mouth, as though he too was reliving those frantic moments when his lips had fused with hers, and she felt heat bloom high in her pelvis, just as if he had reached out and touched her there.

She swallowed…shifted.

It would be so easy to lean in and clasp that beautiful face in her hands, to press her mouth to his and slide her fingers through his silky dark hair and pull him closer, then closer still, until there was no daylight between them. And then his hands would start to move with unimaginable freedom over her body, owning her, claiming her, making her ache inside—

She balled her hands as heat rushed through her and, shaken by this new evidence of her weakness, she dragged her gaze away.

'I haven't forgotten it yet. But from memory it shouldn't take me long,' she said quickly. *Too quickly.*

She could tell from the dark gleam in his blue eyes that he didn't believe her. But then she couldn't blame him for that. She didn't believe herself. Suddenly she felt dizzy, the thought that this was her life now, for however long it took to get the acquisition over the line, making her head spin.

He stared at her for a long, level moment, considering her, weighing up his response. 'Gets under your skin, doesn't it?' he said at last, breaking the taut silence. 'That you still want me.'

A tiny, quivering flicker of heat skated down her spine and she felt her breathing wobble.

She gazed up at him, her throat impossibly dry, feeling the blueness of his eyes like a touch or a caress. He had a wonderful sense of touch…light, but precise. Sometimes before, when they'd been in the car or walking down the street, he would reach over and stroke the nape of her neck, and she would feel it all the way through, just as if she was melting…

Her cheeks were on fire, and she knew that her face must be red, but she would be damned if she was going to agree with him.

'What gets under my skin stopped being your concern a long time ago, Gabriel, so I suggest we put that behind us,' she said crisply. 'After all, you're paying me to work, and I wouldn't want to waste your money. I know it's all that matters to you.'

The air between them seemed to thicken and he stared at her, a muscle pulsing in his jaw, his gaze narrowing on hers in a way that made her breath stop in her throat. Finally, he gave one of those infinitesimally tiny shrugs that made a vortex of emotion rise and swell inside her.

'What else is there?'

Dove blinked. There was no reason that statement should hurt as much as it did, but she couldn't stop a shiver of misery seeping over her skin. And once again, it was as easy to hate him as it was tempting to hurl insults at his handsome head. But, reminding herself of her decision not to discuss the past, she changed the subject.

'So, what happens next?'

She felt his gaze sweep over her.

'We start developing strategy tomorrow, after breakfast. My people have already compiled a detailed history of Fairlight Holdings—the financials, customer base, et cetera, et cetera… There's a paper copy in your suite. Get acquainted with it.'

She nodded, grateful for the reminder of why she was there. If she could just keep that fact at the front of her mind, and banish all the other stuff, then maybe she would get through this unscathed.

'The rest of the afternoon is yours to do with as you wish.' He paused, his blue gaze resting on her face. 'And tonight it will be just the two of us dining.'

*Just the two of us.*

Heart pounding fiercely, she stared at him.

*Dinner. Alone with Gabriel.*

The words whispered inside her and she curled her fingers into the palms of her hands to steady herself, her mind shying away from an image of the two of them seated beneath a canopy of stars.

'What do you mean, just the two of us?' she said stiffly. 'I thought your team was here.'

It was happening again—that feeling that she was watching things from outside her body, almost as if she was watching a movie with an actor and actress playing herself and Gabriel. She forced air into her lungs.

'Then you thought wrong.' He gave her a razor-edged smile. 'They arrive tomorrow. So, like I said, it will just be the two of us tonight.'

Blood was pounding in her ears. 'I'm really not very hungry.'

It was hard enough being here with him now. But she didn't want to spend any more time with him than was necessary. She certainly didn't want to spend an entire evening with him alone—not after what had happened in

London. It would be too close to what they'd once had in the past, when eating together had often been foreplay.

'Marco is a two-star Michelin chef. I'm sure he can conjure up something to tempt you.'

'I'm sure he can—but I don't want to eat dinner with you.' She was shaking her head. Her voice was shaking too, with panic and anger, and she knew she was revealing too much—revealing things she should be trying to keep hidden. But she couldn't seem to help herself.

For a moment Gabriel didn't respond. He just stood there, with the sunshine pouring over his shoulders so that he looked like his celestial namesake. But then the warmth and the light faded and he took a step towards her, and instantly that shimmering thread between them she had been trying hard to ignore pulled tight.

'I don't care.'

His tone more than the words themselves made her flinch. It was so hard and unsympathetic and gut-wrenchingly remote that she felt as if he was talking to her from a script.

'How charming.' She held his gaze as if she wasn't the least bit shaken. 'First threats and now a complete lack of empathy. No wonder you have to blackmail people to work for you.'

He took another step, and now his lean, muscular body was dangerously close to hers.

'I don't know how things are done at Cavendish and Cox, Dove. Maybe your surname means that people go easy on you. But let me be clear about how you and I are going to work—how *this* is going to work.'

His eyes on hers were steady and cool, like deep ocean water…the kind that never felt the warmth of the sun's rays.

'I don't have the time or the patience for theatrics. So if I say you're eating dinner with me, all you need to ask is what time and where? It's eight p.m., by the way, on the owner's deck. The stewards will show you where to go.' He paused, then, 'A word of caution, Dove—of warning, even. I would advise against any pointless displays of temper or defiance. The stakes are too high.'

She watched mutely as he turned and walked back to the window.

'Oh, and shut the door on your way out.'

# CHAPTER FOUR

ONCE IN HER SUITE, Dove sank down into a chair. There was a jug of iced water on the table beside her, and she poured a glass and drank it quickly.

She was used to confrontation…to conflict. Her parents' marriage had not just been unhappy, it had been a war zone. Rows had punctuated every day, with the shelling starting over the breakfast table and often continuing long into the night.

They'd both wanted to leave, but Olivia had sunk her inheritance into the Cavendish estate and Oscar had been too lazy to divorce and so they'd stayed married—unhappily, bitterly married. And it had been up to Dove to negotiate the ceasefires between them and act as go-between.

In other words, this wasn't the first time she'd had to grit her teeth and try to stay calm, neutral, unaffected…

Glancing down at her shaking hands, she breathed out unsteadily. Only she didn't feel unaffected. She felt exhausted in the same way that a soldier returning from the trenches must feel. Felt relief, paired with the stifled horror of knowing that at some point in the not too near future she was going to have to go back and face the enemy again.

*Only what kind of enemy made you want to lean in closer and touch, caress, kiss...?*

She was just trying to think of an answer that wouldn't make her sound mad or foolish or both when her mobile rang. Her bags had been brought to her room and it took her a moment to fish out her phone. She glanced at the screen. It was her mum.

'Hi, Mum—what's up?'

'Nothing, darling. I just wanted to check that you'd got there all right.'

Dove sat down on the bed, toeing off her heels. 'I messaged you yesterday.'

'Yes—to say you were at the hotel. But you said you were flying out to the yacht today and I hadn't heard anything. And I've never liked helicopters. Look at what happened to poor Roddy Conroy.'

'That was a hang-glider, Mum, not a helicopter.'

There was a second of silence and then her mother's laugh filled her ear. 'Oh, yes, that's right—it was.'

Dove laughed too then. It had been a long time since she'd heard Olivia sound upset, but she still got a buzz from hearing the happiness in her mother's voice.

Picturing her father's handsome, petulant face, she felt a pang of guilt. She'd loved both her parents, but her father had often been hard to like. When he could be bothered, Oscar had a great deal of charm, but in private that charm had rarely been visible. Scratch the surface and that beautiful glitter had revealed base metal.

Nobody knew that better than her mother, and the idea of her daughter losing her heart to a man like Oscar was what Olivia dreaded most.

It was why Dove had chosen to keep secret her short, harrowing relationship with Gabriel.

More importantly, it was why she had lied to Gabriel about her parents.

He hadn't talked much about his family, but there had been a softness in his voice when he had, and he had shown her some photos on his phone. She'd been able to tell by their easy body language that his family dynamic was the polar opposite of hers.

She'd felt ashamed and scared. How could she possibly have explained to him her parents' fraught marriage or her own role as referee-cum-counsellor? So she had lied. Just a small white lie at the beginning. But after that she hadn't known how to backtrack to the truth. In the end, it hadn't mattered anyway.

'Everything's fine,' she said soothingly now.

And it wasn't quite a lie, she thought, glancing round her beautiful, understated cabin, with its dazzling, uninterrupted view of the Mediterranean.

'It certainly is.' Her mother's light voice danced with excitement. 'Alistair is just thrilled. So tell me, darling, what's he like, this Gabriel Silva…?'

The question bumped around Dove's head long after her mother had hung up.

Picturing Gabriel's arresting face, she tightened her fingers around the cold glass. Whatever she had expected in London, this was a million times worse. It would be easier if they just hated one another. And sometimes she did hate Gabriel. But at other times she could feel her body reaching out to his, and she knew that he was feeling it too—that knife-edged need that had somehow survived the terrible implosion of their relationship.

It made no sense. But then it wasn't supposed to. Sexual attraction wasn't a science. You couldn't apply logic to it. It supplanted reason, analysis and argument. Her mouth twisted. Apparently, it overrode pain and betrayal too.

Only so what if it did?

Maybe her body's response to him—that alarming, shimmering reaction that swamped her whenever he was near—was impossible to change. But she could change the way she reacted to those feelings. Even if this was personal—and it was—she could make it about business, about the acquisition.

If she wanted to survive this—survive *him*, Gabriel Silva, again—that was what she was going to have to do.

And she would survive, she told herself firmly.

This was a long way from the worst place she had been. A long way from the dark place she'd been in six years ago. So even though his beauty made her catch her breath, she would pretend it didn't. She would pretend as Gabriel had pretended.

After all, how hard could it be?

Gazing across the dazzling indigo sea that was one shade lighter than his eyes, Gabriel felt his pulse slow. He knew the science of 'blue space', but for him there was more to it than just the generic restorative powers of the colour of the water or the sound of the waves. Out here, away from the rigidity of the land, there were no boundaries or barriers. Just an endless vista of blue, stretching unhindered to the horizon and beyond.

Maybe that was why someone like him found it so calming. Having doors shut in your face was not something you forgot.

*Or forgave.*

He looked away to where a reddish sun was slowly slipping beneath the line of the horizon. After Dove's rejection he'd took a flight to America alone, wanting, *needing* to go somewhere no one would know his past or see his pain.

And it had worked. Living among strangers, he had found his humiliation and misery was invisible to most people. Only his parents and siblings had sensed the change in him. His father, ever the romantic, had put it down to *saudade*—a potent word used by the Portuguese to describe an impossible to translate mix of melancholy and longing. His mother had just thought he was homesick.

But home had not been the solution. In fact, even just thinking about England had made all his symptoms worse. It was work that had helped. Just having a routine, a focus.

But a part of him had never forgotten or forgiven the two women who had rejected him so coolly, so brutally, and six months ago it had been work that had offered up a way for him to avenge himself on both Fenella Ogilvy and Dove Cavendish.

He glanced down at his watch. It was already eight o'clock, but he made no effort to move. He had no qualms about keeping Dove waiting. Why should he? Six years ago she had happily left him sitting in that hotel bar for two hours.

His chest felt suddenly too tight for his ribs. He could still remember the sidelong glances of the bar staff as he'd checked his phone for messages, and then the slow, creeping shift from excitement into apprehension, then panic, and finally shock when Oscar Cavendish had strolled towards him, looking as out of place in the shabby hotel as a Rolls Royce in a scrapyard.

It had been almost a carbon copy of what had happened a year earlier with Fenella Ogilvy, his biological mother. Different hotel bar. Different smiling emissary. But the same conversation. The same mix of politeness and pity. And, of course, a financial incentive for him to disappear for ever.

Only despite all of that—or maybe because of it—he had been as shocked and hurt as the first time it happened. Devastated, in fact. Because Fenella had only ever been a name, whereas he'd thought he knew Dove.

*He did now.*

He took one last look at the sea and then stepped back into his luxurious suite.

Dove was waiting for him on deck, and even though he knew it was petty, seeing her standing there made him feel immensely satisfied. He glanced over to where she stood, facing the Mediterranean. He couldn't help wishing she had defied him, and he realised that the prospect of sparring with her excited him...made him feel more alive than he had in years.

Why that should be the case was beyond his comprehension. It was certainly not something he had anticipated back in New York, when all of this had been theoretical.

But since then he had summoned her to *The Argentum* and now he was dining with her alone. He hadn't planned that either.

'Good evening, Mr Silva.'

'Good evening, Hélène.'

The stewardess stepped forward, smiling, and as he greeted her, Dove turned towards him.

He felt the air snap to attention. He hadn't told her to do so but she had changed for dinner, into a simple grey sleeveless wrap dress. It was the kind of dress that would make most women fade into the background. But on Dove the silky fabric shimmered like a mountain stream in moonlight.

He stared at her in silence, his gaze skimming over her light curves, his body twitching with a hunger that had nothing to do with the food his chef Marco was preparing at the end of the deck by the teppanyaki grill.

Taken individually, her delicate features were mathematically perfect. But as a whole the effect was breathtaking. Add in the pearl-blonde hair and she was as flawless and untouchable as a goddess. His breath felt suddenly hot and heavy in his throat as his brain reminded him where to kiss her neck, so that her eyes would flutter shut and she would stir restlessly against him, blindly seeking more contact—

'Would you like an aperitif, Mr Silva?'

He turned towards Hélène. 'No, I think we'll sit down. Ms Cavendish, will you join me?'

Dove gave him a smile that could only be described as glacial and nodded. 'Of course.'

Settling into the chair at right angles to her, he watched her reach for a water glass. 'Would you like wine?'

'No, thank you.'

'How is your suite?' he asked softly. 'I hope everything is to your satisfaction?'

Her grey eyes lifted to meet his. 'It is—thank you.'

Her voice was soft and cool, like newly fallen snow, but

the way she was sitting told a different story. Every line of her body suggested tension and distance, almost as if she was behind glass, and he knew that she was counting down the seconds until she could leave.

He stared across the table, his teeth suddenly on edge, a tic of irritation pulsing down his spine. Earlier, when she tried to get out of eating with him, he had reacted instinctively, harshly, wanting and needing to demonstrate to her that *he* was in charge this time.

So instead of skulking in her room she was here, sitting at his table, being faultlessly polite.

Only strangely he hated that more.

*But why?*

His heart thumped against his ribs, but before he had a chance to think too deeply about how to answer that, or why the question even needed to be asked, the stewardess reappeared.

'Today, we have a starter of broad bean, rocket and pecorino cheese salad with a champagne vinaigrette,' she said, carefully sliding plates onto the table. 'Enjoy.'

'Thank you.'

As Dove looked up at the stewardess her face softened, the guarded tension leaving her eyes, and she smiled a smile so genuine, so warm, and of such irresistible sweetness, that for a moment he just stared, transfixed.

And then, remembering the cool, careful smile she had directed at him, he felt as if he had been kicked by a horse. He stared at her in silence, momentarily off-balance, unsure of what to do with the feeling of envy rolling through him. It didn't matter how Dove smiled at him—he knew that. And yet, inexplicably, he wanted her to smile at him like she'd used to.

As if he was everything to her.

Not just a man who used his wealth and power to get what he wanted.

That feeling was another of those things he hadn't anticipated back in New York. But then, back in New York everything had seemed cut and dried, black and white. His eyes locked with hers. *Not grey.*

'So why did you change your mind?' he asked.

Her chin jerked up. 'About what?'

He leaned forward to pick up his glass and caught a whisper of her light floral perfume. 'You wanted to become a barrister. What changed?'

She bit into her lip and then stopped, shrugged. 'I grew up. To be a barrister you need to enjoy arguing your point. You have to get a buzz out of confrontation. And I've had—'

Now she broke off, glancing away to the fragile paper moon that had replaced the setting sun.

'What I'm trying to say is that I worked out that the kind of law I like—the part I enjoy—is the problem-solving, the attention to detail, the academic rigour that goes into crafting an acquisition.'

*Crafting.* His pulse twitched. Interesting... And certainly not a term you'd find in the average corporate lawyer's word cloud. Should he be surprised, though? Dove had always been a whole lot more than just a pretty face...

Eventually they were drinking coffee, and the stewards had retired to the crew's lounge.

He'd been on other yachts where the crew would be held in limbo at the edges of the deck for hours, stifling yawns while the guests partied on until dawn and then slept in until midday. But he could still remember what it had felt like, waiting endless hours for his shift to end, and it was one of the promises he'd made to himself as his career took off. To treat the people at the bottom with humanity and respect.

Of course, if he needed anything all he had to do was wave his hand across the screen of his phone and one of the stewards would reappear.

He picked up his cup. He'd been pretty sure Dove would refuse coffee, had she been given the choice, but the stewards had brought it out automatically and they had moved to sit on one of the deep modular sofas. Actually, he was sitting. She was standing, feigning interest in the distant lights of another yacht.

Or perhaps she was looking at the stars. They were particularly bright tonight, and Venus was also making an appearance in the night sky.

And on deck too, he thought, his gaze locking on to where Dive was braced against the railing.

Instead of a ponytail her hair was twisted at the nape of her neck with some kind of ornamental stick, and a gentle breeze was catching the loose tendrils that had escaped. In the moonlight, the pearls around her throat gleamed like stars that had fallen to earth. She looked even more like a mythological goddess than before.

She turned to face him. 'I read the report,' she said.

He stared at her blankly. *What report?*

As if that question was written in block capitals across his face, she frowned. 'You suggested I get acquainted with it. So I did.' Her eyes found his reluctantly. 'Whoever compiled it should be congratulated. They did a good job.'

He got to his feet and walked slowly towards her, taking his time. 'That's good to know.' He stopped in front of her, his eyes snagging on the pulse-point hammering beneath the pearl choker. 'I mean, what would be the point of blackmailing them into working for me if I don't get results?' he said softly.

There was a silence. Above them, the dark sky quivered.

A flush of pink was colouring her cheeks. 'I shouldn't have said that.'

He heard the catch in her voice.

'I know it's not true. I've met your staff, and they don't have a bad word to say about you.'

'You sound surprised.'

He studied her profile. From this angle, he could see the knot of hair at the nape of her neck, and suddenly he had to fight against an urge to reach out and pull it loose.

'Can you blame me?' Her eyes met his. 'After all, we both know the only reason I'm here is because I'm scared of calling your bluff.'

A pulse of heat danced across his skin. Hearing his own words in her mouth felt oddly intimate—distractingly so. There was a hollow, hungry feeling in his stomach, and for a moment it was difficult to get his thoughts in order.

'But you're not scared of me, are you?' he said finally.

Her eyes widened, the pupils flaring like twin stars imploding, and they stared at one another in silence for one long, shattering moment. He could feel his pulse leaping against the light cotton of his shirt and the deck felt unsteady beneath his feet, almost as if it were tilting.

She ducked away from his gaze. Glancing down, he saw that there were goose bumps on her bare arms.

'Are you cold?' Without waiting for a reply, he slid off his jacket and draped it around her shoulders. 'Here.'

I'm fine. I don't need your jacket.' Frowning, she tried to wriggle free of its weight.

His fingers bit into the lapels, pulling it tighter. 'And yet you're trembling.'

'So are you,' she said hoarsely, her hands coming up to grip his arms.

And with shock, he realised he was.

He stared down into her pale upturned face. He could feel the sea breeze through his shirt, but that wasn't why he was shaking. It was her. And he wasn't just shaking. His whole body was throbbing with a desire he had never experienced before.

But even as he was accepting the truth of that thought Dove leaned in and kissed him.

It was nothing like the kiss in London. That had been hard and urgent, with their anger and frustration and the pull of the past combusting with the oxygen in the room to create a sharp flare of light and heat.

This was slower, more tentative. Almost like a first kiss. That stop-start, slow-slow, quick-quick-slow fox-trot of new lovers.

And she tasted so good. Her mouth was hot and sweet and soft, and the lush curve of her lips fitted into his exactly like the pieces of a jigsaw. Holding his breath, he pulled her closer, kissing her back, gently teasing her lips apart with his tongue, pushing, probing, tasting her excitement, her hunger.

He heard her take a quick breath, like a gasp, almost as if she was drowning, and then she was swaying forward, her slender body pressing into the wall of his chest. He let go of the jacket and cupped her face with his hands, angling her head for a better fit. He deepened the kiss, back and forth, deeper and deeper, losing himself in the raggedness of her breath and the feel of her fingers biting into his arms.

It was as if all the jagged edges between them had softened. Everything was smooth and easy. And he was nothing but a man. A man who knew the rhythm of her body…the beat of her heart. All of her was close and warm—and his.

Letting his mouth slip down the pale arc of her throat, he felt his body grow harder as she moaned softly. And then her hands were in his hair, tangling, tightening, holding him captive, pulling him closer so that he almost lost his footing.

His heart running wild, he nudged her back towards the sofa, his knee between her thighs, and lowered her onto the cushions, his mouth still fused with hers, his hands moving beneath her body, lifting her closer, pressing her soft belly against the hardness of his erection.

Her dress had fallen away from her shoulder and he kissed the skin there, breathing in the scent of her beneath the perfume. Then he traced a path with his tongue to the soft mound of her breast, tugging the lacy bra aside to suck the stiff peak of her nipple into his mouth.

As she swallowed, deep in her throat, tiny shivers of fire and need darted over his skin and he groaned softly, lifting his face and moving lower to kiss the soft skin of her stomach, then lower still…

She arched against him, moving frantically and pulling at his shirt, her mouth seeking his blindly. And then he felt her hand press against the outline of his erection, and he was arching against her, his breath jerking. Her fingers were pulling at his waistband and, pulse quickening, he reached to help her, his hunger rolling through him like wildfire. He was close to losing control...

*'And you know how easy it is to lose one's head in the heat of the moment.'* Oscar's voice was soft inside his head. *'Things got out of hand. It wasn't intentional. She's mortified.'*

His body stilled, muscles tensing, and he shook his head as if that might expel Oscar's malicious drawl. But he could still hear it, whispering at the margins of his mind, like a prompter in the wings.

*'Things got out of hand... She's mortified.'*

'What is it?'

Dove was gazing up at him, her grey eyes huge and dazed, her mouth pinkly swollen from his feverish kisses.

'Gabriel?'

Gritting his teeth, ignoring the huskiness in her voice and the protests of his body, he peeled himself away from the treacherous heat of her skin and got to his feet.

Breathing shakily, Dove stared at him in confusion. Her head was swimming, her body pulsing uncontrollably, her skin burning from the heat of his touch.

But Gabriel was no longer touching her.

He was standing with his back to her, and that in itself should have been a red flag.

But she wasn't thinking straight. Glancing down at her dishevelled state, she felt her shoulders stiffen. Actually, her brain hadn't been involved at all.

'We should call it a night.'

She stared at his back, felt his words bouncing into

one another inside her head, as random and ridiculous as bumper cars at a funfair.

'Call it a night…?' she echoed.

As he turned to face her, her skin jumped as if he'd touched her.

'We start early tomorrow, and as this acquisition is so important to both of us it would be better if there are no distractions.'

Around her the sea and sky seemed to have merged, so that it felt as if she was surrounded by a never-ending darkness that was keeping everything else at bay.

'And that's what this was? A distraction.'

But how could that be true? It wasn't possible to kiss someone like that—as if the world was about to end—and then just lose interest and walk away. Her heart felt as if it was in a vice. What was she talking about? She knew it was possible, and true, because Gabriel had done exactly that six years ago.

And now she had allowed him to do it all over again.

The realisation pierced her, slicing so deeply she felt as if she might double up.

'After what happened in London it was clear to me that we both had something we needed to work out of our systems…' He paused, and his blue gaze rested on her face, cool and distant as the exosphere. 'And now we have. So, yes, this was a distraction. A necessary one. Because now we can concentrate on the job in hand. That's what matters here.'

'That's what matters…' she repeated slowly, trying to square his words, the remoteness in his voice and the rigidity in his spine with the hot-mouthed lover of moments earlier.

He stared down at her. 'I'm not saying it wasn't enjoyable in the short term. But that's the point of a distraction. It's not the main event. It doesn't matter enough to last. I would have thought you of all people could understand that. Try not to take it personally, Dove. It's just business. It always was—although maybe you didn't understand that.'

She surged to her feet, swaying slightly as she clutched her dress around her trembling body. This was the man who had broken her heart all those years ago. The man who had ruthlessly blackmailed her into working for him to punish her for revealing his worst self to the world.

'You're contradicting yourself, Gabriel. You're the one who said this was personal.'

Her face felt hot, and she was acutely conscious of how she must look, with her hair spilling onto her shoulders and her dress gaping at the front, but she was too angry to care. Too shocked and horrified by how close she had come to letting her hunger take her back to the past.

'But I guess that's how you live with yourself, isn't it?' she said. 'By twisting and distorting things to fit your purpose—'

'I didn't twist anything.' His face was like stone, the high, flat cheekbones a cliff face of contempt, and his words were like hard little chips of rock. 'You just don't like having to accept responsibility for your behaviour.'

They were facing each other, their bodies straining, their anger circling them, pushing them closer like a fang-toothed creature.

'*My* behaviour?' She said the word slowly, not quite able to believe what she was hearing. Her lungs felt as if they were on fire. 'I'm not the guilty party here, Gabriel.'

'Why? Because you sent your snobbish father to do your dirty work? You're such a hypocrite.'

'And you're a fraud.'

'At least I own my mistakes.'

'If by "mistake" you mean our relationship, then you didn't own anything. You sneaked away like the coward you are.'

'Except I'm not the one who sent Daddy to make my excuses.'

'I didn't send anyone!' she snapped.

He was shaking his head. 'Sent. Asked. Coaxed. What's the difference? You're just trying to shift the blame.'

'I know exactly who's to blame.' The injustice of his words clawed at her soul. '*You* took a bribe. *You* took my father's money.'

'And what? You think you were worth more?'

His voice scraped over her skin like a serrated knife and she heard her breath escape in a tiny, ragged gasp. Suddenly she felt as if she might throw up. A flare of anger exploded inside her, white and hot and so bright it could have lit up the night sky.

'I could ask you the same question. After all, you're the one who got paid off, Gabriel—not me. You're the one who put a value on our relationship and your part in it.'

His expression didn't alter, but when he spoke she could hear the rage in his voice, feel it rolling towards her in waves.

'But I didn't have a part in it—did I, Dove?'

Their eyes met—hers shocked, his blazing with fury, and a pain that took her breath and her anger away. But before she had a chance to respond, a chance to ask him what he meant, he turned and walked swiftly off the deck.

Heart pounding, she stared after him. Her head felt as if it had been punched. After the sound and fury of moments earlier the deck felt preternaturally quiet and still, like a stage after the curtain had fallen and everyone had left the theatre.

Everyone but her.

She was still there…alone, abandoned, again.

Her legs started to shake uncontrollably and she sank down onto the sofa. Beside her, his jacket lay discarded against the cushions, and she had to fight an urge to pick it up and hold it close.

Beyond the pale wood the sea was dark and smooth. A black mirror that swallowed up ships and secrets. Including, she realised with a jolt of misery, those of the man who had just stormed off the deck.

# CHAPTER FIVE

'COFFEE?'

'Thanks, Chris.'

Looking up from her laptop, Dove smiled as she took the cup from the lanky analyst. She liked Chris. He was polite, helpful, disciplined and focused. Like everyone on the Silva team he was good at his job. But, as in all well-run businesses, the staff took their lead from the top—and Gabriel was a remarkable boss.

Glancing over to where he was talking on the phone, at the edge of the room, his profile carving a pure gold line against the background of glittering blue, she felt her stomach knot. She had been working on the acquisition for five days now, but it had become obvious to her after less than five minutes why Gabriel Silva had achieved such stratospheric success.

He was not just smart, but also clear-minded. He made everything seem simple, at the same time acknowledging the shifts and fluctuations that would inevitably complicate the process. In the same way, he knew what he wanted from every member of his team.

Her cheeks felt warm.

One thing was clear. His staff didn't need to be blackmailed into working for him. In fact, it was quite likely that they would have worked for him for free.

None of the seven women and five men sitting around the huge lacquered white table had a bad word to say about their boss and most of them had a lot of good—offering up stories, unprompted, of how Gabriel had supported and empowered them in some way.

And she believed them. Even to a critical observer like herself it was obvious that he encouraged his staff to be independent, self-motivated, and to take pride in what they did. And it worked. The entire team was as invested in this acquisition as he was.

All except her.

She hadn't shared her confusion, but privately she was surprised by Gabriel's determination to acquire Fairlight Holdings. It just didn't seem to match the pattern of his other acquisitions. But then if she could understand what drove Gabriel Silva to behave as he did, she wouldn't be sitting here…

'So, are there any other updates?' Gabriel was leaning forward now, over his laptop, typing something on the keyboard. He stepped back, his blue eyes scanning the room like a Roman emperor looking over the senate house.

She shifted in her seat so that she was shielded from his gaze by her neighbour.

'No? Then let's break for ten minutes.'

They all worked long hours, and sometimes at quiet points in the day she would notice him staring out to sea intently. At first, she'd thought he was just looking at the view. But there was always a tension in his body…almost as if he was looking for something. Something that wasn't there or that was just beyond the horizon.

In those moments she caught a glimpse of the serious young man she'd met six years ago. But then the next moment she would look again and see a stranger. A beautiful, intense stranger. Someone she had loved but never really known.

But was that even possible? To love someone and yet not know anything about them?

Apparently so—because what had she really known about Gabriel aside from his name and the fact that he was a waiter?

They had talked cautiously at first, in the way that all couples did at the beginning of a relationship. But they'd been young, and the air had been warm and honeyed, and most of that long hot summer had been spent in bed. They'd touched, slept, watched TV and each other, lying there and listening to the sound of each other's breathing.

*And they'd had sex.*

Teasing sex. Tender sex. Fierce sex, tearing at each other's clothes. Sex that had left them both clinging to one another as if they were drowning.

Her pulse fluttered. And last night they would have had sex on the deck if Gabriel hadn't stopped them.

Picking up her coffee with a hand that shook slightly, she took a sip. 'Ouch!' She jerked the cup away from her mouth. It was scalding hot.

'Are you okay?' Chris was leaning forward, his forehead creasing in concern.

'It's fine.' She smiled reassuringly. 'It's my own fault. I normally add milk, but I forgot.'

As she pressed her finger against her top lip she felt a

cool shiver shoot down her spine and, glancing up, felt her insides tighten. Gabriel was watching her, his body taut and still like a stalking leopard, his blue eyes fixed on her mouth. Her heart thudded hard as he lifted his gaze, and for a moment they stared at each other across the room. Then abruptly he turned away to talk to Carrie Naylor.

His glance had been brief—a few seconds at most— but it had felt as intimate and tangible as a caress.

Breath snarling in her throat, she stared at his back, wishing she could shut her eyes and shut him out. But she knew from the last four restless nights that it wouldn't matter if she did. Asleep or awake, eyes open or shut, in daylight or darkness, she could always see Gabriel.

Even if she couldn't touch him.

Her fingers twitched against the keys of her laptop and she slid her hands into her lap, pressing them between her knees as if she didn't trust them. *Because she didn't.* She was like an addict. She might have spent six years sober, but when Gabriel had kissed her in London she'd been no more able to stop at one kiss than an alcoholic could stop at one drink.

Keeping her gaze fixed on the screen, she thought *again* about what had happened that night they'd been alone on deck. It had been reckless. Stupid. Dangerous. And yet despite being all those things it had felt like coming home.

There must be something wrong with her head—something wrong with *her*—to think that way after what he'd said to her, the way he'd acted. He had been cold, and cruel, and yet it wasn't his cruelty or his fury that was imprinted on her brain. It was that look on his face and the words he'd flung at her in response to the accusations she'd made about the part he'd played in their relationship.

*'But I didn't have a part in it—did I, Dove?'*

Her stomach tightened. When she wasn't replaying their heated on-deck encounter, she kept on trying unsuccessfully to untangle the meaning of those words as they rolled around inside her head.

But they still made absolutely no sense.

And it would probably stay that way.

It wasn't as if she could ask him, she thought, glancing furtively to where he was now once more talking on the phone.

They hadn't been alone since that night on the deck. Gabriel's team had arrived early the following morning, and from that moment onwards there had been no opportunity to talk—much less kiss.

Breathing out a little unsteadily, she pressed her finger harder against her lip, replaying those endless seconds when the world had stopped moving,

'I thought this might help.'

She blinked. Chris was back.

'I got you some ice.' He held out a glass.

'Actually, applying ice to a burn is the worst thing you can do.'

A lean hand plucked the glass from her fingers and, her heart thumping in her chest, she looked up to find Gabriel standing beside her.

Every nerve in her body snapped onto high alert. Panic was snaking through her body—and something else... something that made her feel jittery and irritable.

'I know it feels logical, but it can cause further damage to the skin. Something to do with shutting off the capillaries too forcefully, I believe,' he said, in that quiet way of his that made her stomach knot. 'The best treatment is a cool compress.' He turned towards the analyst. 'Chris, could you go and ask one of the stewards to sort that out asap? Any of them will be able to help.'

In the moment of silence following the analyst's departure his eyes found hers. She knew it shouldn't move her the way it did, like flame and chaos beneath her skin, but what should and shouldn't happen rarely seemed to be relevant where Gabriel was concerned.

'You didn't need to do that. It's really not a big deal,' she said stiffly, keeping her gaze firmly away from the man taking up too much space beside her.

'I'm afraid that's not your decision to make, Ms Cavendish.' His voice wrapped around her skin, as cool as the compress he'd suggested. 'You're on my yacht, so I'm responsible for your wellbeing. I wouldn't want Alistair thinking I don't take care of his people.'

Gabriel's people were all around them—typing, talking, taking notes—but it didn't matter. She could feel her body reacting just as if it were the two of them alone, her skin tingling and growing tighter, hotter.

The goosebumps of the other night had returned. She wanted to cover her arms, conceal her response, but that would only draw attention to the thing she was trying to hide. If only she could snatch the glass from his hand and upend the ice over her head and her overheated body.

Instead, she gave him a small, tight smile and said, with a briskness she'd perfected over the last five days, 'I'm sure Chris can look after me.' Still smiling stiffly, she glanced pointedly to the other end of the room, where the stewards had appeared with trays of freshly baked pastries. 'Don't let me keep you—'

She let the sentence teeter and balance in the space between them, but he didn't move away. He just stood there, staring down at her in that edgy, nerve-jangling, quiet way of his.

'You work hard,' he said finally.

It wasn't what she was expecting him to say, but it was business, not personal, she told herself. And yet the glitter in his eyes didn't feel impersonal.

By now most of the team had gravitated towards the burnished pastries at the end of the room and she refocused her gaze, away from Gabriel's distracting face to where the Mediterranean sparkled in the midday sun. Only that was like looking straight into his glittering blue eyes...

'Did you think I wouldn't? I'm not that petty,' she said, answering her own question.

She *was* working hard—but not because of the threats he'd made back in London, if that was what he was implying. For her, there was something intensely satisfying about helping a complex, multi-tiered business acquire another.

Lifting her chin, she looked past his shoulder at the door, wishing she was on the other side of it. And that it was locked and barred and guarded by a couple of large, unfriendly dogs.

'And, just for the record, my work ethic has nothing to do with your "incentive" either. Believe it or not, you're not the most difficult or demanding client I've ever worked for.'

For a moment Gabriel didn't reply. She tried to pretend that his silence didn't get to her, but eventually she couldn't help herself, and she looked up to find him watching her intently, as if she was a puzzle he was trying to work out.

'I don't know whether to be disappointed or flattered.'

That remark was accompanied by a small, crooked smile that made a flicker of heat fan out low in her pelvis.

Their eyes locked. 'I should stick with disappointed,' she said, her arm curved across her stomach to press against the ache that still lingered there from when Gabriel had kissed her five days ago. 'That way you won't have to go out of your comfort zone.'

There was a beat of silence. His face was unreadable, but his blue gaze seemed to tear into her.

'I wasn't the one who was disappointed,' he replied.

She stared at him, struggling to breathe, as if his cryptic words had displaced all the air in the room. That was the second, or maybe the third time he had insinuated that *she* was the guilty party in their relationship.

'You know, if you have something to say—'

'Here we are.'

Chris was back again. This time, he was holding a compress and a bowl of presumably cool water.

'Sorry I took so long. I got confused on the way back and went left instead of right.' Frowning, he glanced up at his boss. 'Sorry, did I interrupt something?'

Gabriel shook his head, his gaze beating down on her like a wave breaking. 'Not at all. Ms Cavendish and I are finished.'

It was lunchtime. Pushing his fork into the carefully arranged Cobb salad on his plate, Gabriel speared another piece of chicken. It was perfectly cooked, but he wasn't hungry.

Understandably, he thought, tilting back his head to gaze up at a melting yellow sun. But, much as he longed to do so, he knew he couldn't blame the heat of the day for his lack of appetite. Or for the tension that was making his body feel as if it might fly apart at any moment.

At the other end of the table he heard Dove laugh and his head turned without permission, drawn irresistibly to the sound, and to the pale curve of her throat.

Not that he needed to look to know where she was. For the last five days he had been devastatingly aware of her exact position in any room, and his neck and shoulders ached with the effort of not looking at her.

He gritted his teeth.

And his body ached with the effort of not crossing the room and finishing what she had started on the deck five days ago. Fortunately the constant presence of one or other member of his team had acted as an unwitting chaperone, so that his feverish imaginings had stayed in his imagination.

But even though he had kept his distance he couldn't avoid Dove completely, and whichever way he turned it felt as if she was always there, poised and polished, with her pale blonde hair smoothly knotted at the nape of her neck.

Turn left and she was leaning forward to look at some paperwork, her bottom pushing against the fabric of one of those snug-fitting pencil skirts that seemed designed to make him unravel.

Turn right and she was biting into the soft pink cushion of her lower lip as she talked on the phone.

Occasionally, when required to do so, she would meet his gaze, with a cool, defensive light in her grey eyes.

Glancing down the table, he felt his stomach twist. And now she was laughing with someone other than him, her eyes dancing with light and delight.

It made him want to punch something.

His jaw was so tight it felt as if it had been wired together. He had made himself wait so long to get to this moment of reckoning, but things weren't going quite how he'd imagined they would.

Forcing Dove to work for him, taking her out of her comfort zone, was supposed to punish her—but instead he felt as if he was the one being punished. And, rather than confirming that she was a heartless bitch who had used and then discarded him, he kept seeing her pale, stunned face as she'd tried to cover her body.

Putting down his fork, he gave up pretending to eat and picked up his water glass instead. Although frankly he would rather it was wine. Or better still whisky. Then at least he could numb his senses and dull the ache of need.

But why was he putting himself through this? He had made his point in bringing her here. There was no need to extend this torture any more. He could dismiss her as she had dismissed him. Although, unlike Dove and Fenella, he would do it in person.

Thinking about Fenella made his stomach knot. When he'd found out that she was looking to sell the family firm, it seemed like fate. Finally a chance to do something concrete that would make it impossible for her to ignore him. With the added bonus of his being able to pay her off.

It was a convoluted way to prove a point, and it certainly wasn't good business—Alistair Cox had been right about that. There were many other, better property companies. But that was part of it. He wanted to show her that she had been wrong to give him away. That unlike the son she had kept, he was a business leader who had so much money he could afford to waste it in acquiring her precious family firm. The family that *he* had no part of.

But first he would deal with Dove.

He waited until lunch was over and his team were back around the table.

'Before we begin, I want to thank everyone for their hard work. As usual, your focus and dedication has been outstanding. Please know that it is recognised and greatly appreciated.'

He paused. Now that the moment was here, he felt an uncharacteristic flicker of doubt.

*And that was why he needed to end this now,* he thought irritably. Dove did something to him that no one else did. She made him feel things, want things. She confused him…

Remembering how her body had curved against his, he felt his groin harden. But she wasn't just making him unravel physically. He was so tense right now, and he'd reached for her because she was still the only person alive who could soothe him. Only that had angered him, and that was why he'd lost his temper with her. Said things that he should have kept hidden. And since that night more things, more feelings, had kept slipping out.

He was like a wound seeping blood. And he couldn't risk haemorrhaging any more ugly, sordid truths about himself. Certainly not to Dove.

'We now have several valuation models for the target

company, and sufficient information to enable us to construct a reasonable offer, so today will be our last day here together. We'll wrap things up tonight and start back again on Monday morning in London. Sorry, people,'

There were a few groans, followed by applause. Then several members of his team came over to him, and it was a couple of minutes before he could look over to where Dove was sitting.

She was staring down at her laptop, but as if sensing his gaze she looked up at him, and he felt his pulse stumble.

He had expected her to look relieved, but instead her grey eyes were the colour of storm clouds.

Leaning back against the lounger, Gabriel gazed out to sea. It was only nine o'clock and the sun was starting to rise through the clear blue sky. The day was just beginning.

Normally there would be a background hum of people talking and laughing as they opened laptops and shuffled papers. But not this morning. This morning there was no sound aside from the gentle slap of water against the boat. He was alone. The day was his. He could change out of his work clothes and take a dip in the pool, laze in the sun, maybe finish that book he'd started six months ago. He could have a drink—a cocktail, perhaps. A Last Word might be apt...particularly if he got the stewards to go heavy on the gin.

His team had left after an early breakfast.

And Dove had gone with them.

His jaw tightened. She had shaken his hand before she'd left and said goodbye in that careful, precise way of hers. Remembering the cool touch of her fingers, he felt his throat tighten. It had all been very polite, very civilised. Maybe that was why he felt so dissatisfied now. So thwarted.

Swearing softly, he got to his feet and stalked to the other side of the deck—only to remember as he got there that he was standing where Dove had reached up and kissed him. For a second the air around him seemed to ripple and, his heart beating out of time, he scowled down at the smooth teak.

Did events imprint themselves on buildings? He closed his eyes. Could wood and brick retain some memory of the heat and intensity of human encounters?

He breathed in deeply, then tensed. He could almost smell her scent…that teasing light mix of summertime and sweet peas. His eyes snapped open and he blinked into the sunlight. And now he was seeing her. Holding his breath, he gazed across the deck at the blurred shape of a woman. Except, of course, it wasn't her. It was just a mirage. An illusion caused by the refraction of light off the gleaming polished deck.

The shape moved and everything inside him slid sideways, almost as if the yacht had run aground. But it wasn't *The Argentum* that had run aground. It was him.

And the woman standing on the other side of the deck wasn't a mirage.

Something swift and sharp scudded across his skin and he watched in stunned, silent disbelief, his mind groping for some kind of explanation, as Dove Cavendish walked slowly towards him.

She had changed clothes. The clinging pencil skirt and soft blouse were gone. Instead she was wearing denim shorts and one of those blue and white striped matelot tops, and her hair was tied loosely at the nape of her neck.

His hands flexed by his sides as she stopped about a yard away. She looked nervous, but defiant—and shatteringly beautiful.

None of which helped explain why she was still on board his yacht...

His head was starting to spin and he realised that he was still holding his breath. He let it out carefully and, hoping that he looked more composed than he felt, he said softly, 'What the hell are you doing here?'

That was a good question, Dove thought as she felt her stomach drop to her feet. One to which she should probably have a ready-made answer. But earlier, when she'd been sneaking back to her cabin, she hadn't given much thought as to what she would say when she finally confronted Gabriel. She'd been too busy worrying that she would get caught.

There had been no plan. It had been a spur-of-the-moment decision—the kind her mother had warned her about. The kind she knew led to heartbreak and despair. So of course she had ignored the warnings.

Now, though, she wished she had come prepared. It was hard to breathe, much less string a sentence together, when he was standing there with the fading sun's rays caressing his beautiful face like a lover. And he did look particularly beautiful. Beautiful and formidable...

But she couldn't say for sure whether it was his beauty or his severity that was making her pulse dance a tarantella across her skin.

'We have things to sort out…things we need to talk about—'

'Such dedication,' he said, cutting her off. 'But I think it can wait until Monday, don't you?'

She took a deep breath. 'It's not about the acquisition.'

'Then there's nothing to talk about,' he said, in that soft, lethal way of his that made her want to dive into the Mediterranean. And made her body shiver in response.

Tilting her chin, she met his gaze. 'How can you say that after what happened the other night?'

His eyes narrowed. 'I'm saying it *because* of the other night.' Shaking his head, he turned. 'Go home, Ms Cavendish.'

Anger rose up like a wave, swallowing her whole. Moving swiftly, she stepped in front of him. 'I am so done with you turning your back on me. Being rich doesn't give you the right to be rude, you know?'

'Actually, it does,' he said softly. 'It pretty much gives you licence to do whatever you damn well like. Like bribing someone to get out of your life, for example.'

She stared at him, her pulse beating so fast she thought she would pass out. 'That's not the same.'

'Of course it isn't.'

'You're twisting things again—'

'No, everything is plumb-straight.' He stared down at her, his face taut. 'Go home, Dove. You have work on Monday—an acquisition to close. That's all that matters here.'

She shook her head. 'Then you're going to have to fire me and get someone else, because I am not leaving this boat until we've had a conversation.'

There: she had a plan, after all. And she would do it. She would chain herself to the ship's wheel if she had to.

There was a tiny snatch of air around them.

'And it's always about what *you* want, isn't it?' His voice was harder and edgier than before. It sounded like bones snapping. 'When to talk. When to end things.'

For a moment she couldn't breathe. His words thudded inside her head in a terrifying drumroll. 'That's not true.' She tried to shake her head, as if that would somehow validate her denial, but her head wouldn't move. 'I didn't end anything. *You* ended us.'

'Is that what you tell yourself? Tell other people?'

'No, it's what happened. My father offered you money and you took it.'

Her pulse jerked as he took a step closer, his blue eyes sharpening on her face.

'And you can't complain about that. Not when you made sure that was all that was on offer.'

Her hand crept up to her throat and she stared at him, mute with shock. She had offered him so much more than that. And he had tossed it aside.

'That had nothing to do with me. My father went to see you because he didn't trust you. He didn't think you were who you said you were.'

Gabriel's face stilled. 'What do you mean?'

'He thought you were a gold-digger. A chancer.' Remembering how she had defended him to her father, she felt her face burn. 'So he went to the hotel to find you. To test you. And you failed.'

She saw his jaw tighten.

'You set me up to fail.'

His tone was still harsh, but now there was a different

note beneath the anger and frustration, almost questioning, as if he was asking her, not telling her.

'Of course I didn't.' Her head was spinning. 'Why would I do that?'

*I loved you*, she finished silently. Hadn't he known that? Hadn't he known how much she'd loved him?

Gabriel was staring past her, almost as if he had forgotten she was there. 'That's what I've been asking myself for six years.'

Her heart was beating slow and heavy, as if it was being squeezed in a fist. Something wasn't right. At the margins of her mind pictures were forming, then blurring too fast for her to follow them.

She took a painful shallow breath, then another. 'Well, you're not the only one with unanswered questions, Gabriel,' she said hoarsely. 'So why don't we answer them once and for all? Why don't we say what has to be said, and then we can get on with our lives? That's what you want, isn't it?'

It was why she was standing there. Why she had stayed on *The Argentum*. But when finally he turned to look at her and nodded, his blue eyes darker than she had ever seen before, she felt no relief—just a shattering sense of sadness.

# CHAPTER SIX

IT WAS THE QUICK, easy rhythm of the stewards' voices, so similar they were almost interchangeable, that grabbed Dove's attention.

Not that she was really reading. The book in her hands was just a prop. Something to stop her from staring at the man sitting on the other side of the cabin or thinking about what she had set in motion. Up until that moment it had certainly helped with the former. The latter, not so much. Pretty much from the moment Gabriel's private jet had taken off in Nice her brain had been preoccupied with all the possible outcomes after it landed.

Her heart beat hard and slow as the stewards walked back up the cabin, smiling politely as they passed. They were friends as well as colleagues—she could tell. That was why they sounded so alike. She had read about it in a magazine at the hairdresser's. It was called phonetic convergence, and it was something that happened between close friends and family. She had it with her mother.

But with Gabriel that mirroring and overlapping had only ever happened with their bodies. When they'd talked he'd been guarded, careful, and there had always been a point in any conversation where he'd checked himself.

*When they'd talked.*

It was ironic that since agreeing to talk to her on the deck of *The Argentum* Gabriel had said approximately twenty words to her. Maybe he thought that the cabin of a plane—even a spacious private jet like this one—was not private enough for the conversation they needed to have.

But then they could have stayed on the yacht.

Turning her head slightly, she gazed down through the oval of glass at the water below. They had been in the air for nearly four hours, en route to Pico, one of the islands of the Azores off the coast of Portugal, where Gabriel owned the Quinta dos Louros—a private estate and vineyard.

She had thought they were going back to London. It had only been when they were taking off that he had told her they were flying to Pico. He'd given her no explanation, and she'd been so stunned that he had agreed to talk that it hadn't occurred to her to argue or cross-examine him. Later, when the burn of adrenalin had faded, she'd concluded that it was just his way of regaining the upper hand and put it to the back of her mind.

Her throat tightened. But now other things were taking centre stage—specifically Gabriel's insistence that it was she who had sent her father to end things on her behalf. The anger and pain on his face was bright and achingly clear in her memory.

Her eyes darted to where he sat, working on his laptop, his long legs taking up every inch of the generous space in front of his seat.

It wasn't the first time Gabriel had accused her of sending her father to end their relationship, but she hadn't given it much thought before. It had felt more like a question of semantics, not fact. He had as good as said so himself.

*'Sent. Asked. Coaxed. What's the difference? You're just trying to shift the blame.'*

They were his words, but they could just as easily apply to her. She'd assumed he was trying to shift the blame—lying to her, and to himself, because he didn't want to associate the billionaire businessman he saw every day in the mirror with the greedy, unscrupulous, self-serving man he had been six years ago.

She felt her heartbeat catch.

But yesterday it had been clear from the unfiltered rawness in his voice and the tense way he'd held his body that Gabriel believed what he was saying. He really did think that it had been her idea. That, in his words, she had sent her 'snobbish father' to do her dirty work.

Only what had she ever done to make him think that she was that kind of person?

Suddenly afraid that he might look over and answer her question, she turned and stared out of the window at the silvery blue water. A drumroll of nervousness hammered across her skin. There had been nothing but ocean for hours. But now she could see shapes appearing in the distance. Vast, jagged outcrops of rock splashed with vivid green, were rising out of the Atlantic like the spine of some huge prehistoric creature. She was looking at the Azores.

The plane landed fifteen minutes later. From the air the archipelago had looked dark, almost menacing, but as she stepped out of the plane into the pale morning light she felt her mouth drop. There was only one word that could describe what she was seeing: epic.

Everywhere was green and lush and humming with sound and life. What wasn't green was black, and towering above the landscape was a mountain crowned in wispy clouds.

'It's called Montanho di Pico, which means mountain peak.'

She jumped as Gabriel's voice cut across her thoughts.

'It's where the island got its name,' he said. 'Although it's more than just a mountain—it's also a volcano.'

*A volcano.*

Her chin jerked up towards the towering peak. Back on the boat, she'd thought they had called a truce. So naturally he'd brought her to an island which could be covered in hot lava at any moment.

'I did wonder why we couldn't just talk on the yacht,' she said, her eyes narrowing on the distant summit. 'Now it's all starting to make more sense. Although I have to say it does feel a little contrived. I mean, we were in the middle of the Mediterranean. You could have just made me walk the plank if you wanted to do away with me.'

There was a small silence. She caught a sharp glint of blue as he turned his head. 'Unfortunately I didn't have one on hand. It was on the list of optional extras, but I chose a submersible and a jet ski instead.'

Their eyes met and the intimacy of years earlier branched out, blossoming effortlessly, just like it had on the deck of *The Argentum.* She felt her heart thud inside her chest and wondered what would happen if she took his hand and told him that she didn't want to talk any more. That there were other things they did better.

And then his eyes flicked away, and she wondered if she was losing her mind.

'Seriously, you don't need to worry. It's what's known

as a quiescent volcano. That means it's not active, but it's still registering seismic activity.'

A bit like the man standing beside her, she thought, remembering that ripple of deep anger beneath the flare of frustration and resentment. Which made her either stupid or unhinged. After all, what kind of person went anywhere near a volcano, quiescent or not?

He guided her towards the stocky off-road vehicle that sat at the edge of the runway. As they walked towards the waiting car his fingers brushed against hers and she felt her skin pop, but if Gabriel noticed he gave no sign.

There was no traffic on the road, and soon they were climbing into the green hills. But it didn't seem to matter how high or in which direction they went, the mountain still cast its vast triangular shadow across them.

For the next twenty minutes she forgot everything but the view from her window. Up close, the landscape looked almost extra-terrestrial, with its rippling outcrops of long-since cooled black magma. Then they swept round a corner and there was a crater-shaped lake, edged with swathes of delicate ferns the colour of parakeets and strange-looking trees with swollen, crepey trunks. She felt her heartbeat accelerate. It was the first time she'd had a sense of what the planet might have looked like before humans had begun to dominate it.

'They're called dragon trees.'

She frowned. 'Is that because their trunks look like dragon's legs?'

'Good guess…'

His eyes rested on her face and she felt the darkness in the pupils shudder all the way through her.

'But I'm afraid the truth is a little more far-fetched—as

is often the case. Supposedly they got their name when Hercules killed the hundred-headed dragon guarding the garden of the Hesperides. Everywhere the blood spilled a dragon tree grew. Or so the myth goes.'

Hearing him speak, she felt that same dark magnetic pull as earlier. It was no wonder she had fallen for him. Fallen for his stories. This was a man who could make a tree sound sexy. And she was here with him, on a clump of volcanic rock, with nothing but hundreds of miles of sea in every direction. And there was nothing she could do about that now.

The road gave a tiny, sharp twist to the left and she felt the car slow. It was too late to do anything. They had arrived.

She stared in silence at the rugged grey stone house in front of her. Oaklands, her childhood home, was beautiful, but like most big country houses in England it was designed to be the jewel in the crown of its parkland setting. This house was different. It looked as if it had been birthed from the land, with the mountain soaring into the clouds behind and in front the wild green curves of vegetation tilting away to the Atlantic.

Inside, the Quinta dos Louros had little in common with Oaklands' chintzy, antique-filled interior. Someone—possibly Gabriel, more likely some expensive designer—had decided to let the scale of the rooms and the light seeping in from the ocean speak for itself, and the result was a masterclass in sophisticated simplicity that was as beautiful and cool as its owner.

His housekeeper was waiting in the hall, and after a quick meet-and-greet—her name was Sara—Gabriel took her on a brief tour of the house, including her bedroom.

Finally, he led her back downstairs into a sitting room the size of a tennis court.

She turned a slow, admiring three-hundred-and-sixty-degree circle. 'It's amazing,' she said truthfully.

Everything felt balanced, calm and comfortable, so that she had the oddest feeling—almost as if she had come home. Although she had never once felt like that walking into Oaklands, she thought with a jolt. There was always an edge inside her whenever she went home—a pulse-skipping apprehension about whether she would find Oscar and Olivia sniping at each other over the dining table or her mother weeping alone in her bedroom.

Just thinking about it made her spine snap to attention. She'd hated everything about those rows. The weave of tension beforehand. The sickly swell as the accusations and counter accusations had started, building to the actual row itself. Mostly pointless. Often vicious. Always exhausting. And then, the worst part of all, the terrible aftermath when all the things that shouldn't have been said lingered in the shadows.

Now, as her eyes flicked to the sunlit corners of the room, she realised that she had no idea how long she had been standing there in silence, and that Gabriel was staring at her, the blue in his gaze bright and sharp in a way that made it hard to breathe.

'Take a seat,' he said finally. 'I've asked Sara to bring us some coffee.'

Gabriel waited until Dove had sat down on one of the pale green linen sofas, then dropped into his favourite armchair—the one which offered up an uninterrupted view of the Atlantic. But today his eyes were resting on

Dove's face, because even an ink-coloured ocean that covered twenty percent of the earth's surface seemed to fade into insignificance beside her pearlescent beauty.

She looked tired and on edge, he thought. A week ago that would have pleased him immensely. But a week was a long time in business—particularly, it turned out, when you were working with the woman who had broken your heart. Long enough for the countless things he had taken for granted to become not quite so cut and dried.

Some, he'd discovered, were simply not true. Having worked alongside her for five days, he knew now that she wasn't the talentless, entitled heiress to the family firm he'd imagined her to be. She was diligent, disciplined, and good at her job. In another lifetime he wouldn't have hesitated to offer her a job with the Silva Group.

But it was the past—their past—that seemed to be shifting before his eyes like the shards of mirror and glass in a kaleidoscope. Only how was that even possible? The past was history. Unchangeable, fixed, immutable.

And yet this morning he'd felt himself waver. Just for a moment he'd let her get inside his head, and for a few half-seconds he had questioned what he knew to be true. Even questioned himself. That was why he had agreed to talk to her—so that he could pin her down, refute every single one of her lies and exorcise her from his blood once and for all.

*Of course, that didn't explain why he'd needed to bring her all the way here.*

Gritting his teeth, he ignored that little voice inside his head, just as he ignored the flicker of heat that danced across his skin every time she walked in or out of a room. Every day he was ignoring more and more. Soon he would be like one of those sightless creatures that lived in the darkness of the Mariana Trench.

Thankfully Sara arrived at that moment, with coffee and some delicate lacy biscuits. After she'd left, closing the door softly, he leaned back in his chair.

*Now what?*

He felt stretched taut. There was no process for this. He had no idea how to start the conversation he wanted to have. Or even if he wanted to have it. It would mean reliving the moment of her rejection by proxy that had sent him spinning into the darkness...

'Why did you choose to buy a house on Pico? Is there some family connection?'

Dove's voice cut through his thoughts and he glanced over to where she was sitting. She was talking about his father. His adoptive father—Luis. But his biological father—the man who had spent a night with Fenella Ogilvy thirty years ago—was a man without a name or a face. Not that he could tell her that. He couldn't tell anyone. But he especially couldn't tell Dove.

'No, not really.' He shook his head. 'My father's family come from Porto. But when I first went out to the States I made friends with some surfers. They were taking a trip to São Jorge and they invited me along.'

He saw her ball her hands into fists. So they had got there in the end. It had been by means of a rather circuitous route, but they were there nonetheless.

'Of course. You went surfing after we broke up.' Her mouth twisted. 'And there I was, worrying that your guilty conscience might be keeping you awake all night. Only how could it? You don't *have* a conscience.' She shook her head. 'You know, I keep thinking about what you said earlier. About *me* setting *you* up to fail. But it was you who set me up. You met me at that party and you thought, *Here's someone I can scam.*'

Wrong, he thought silently, his gaze roaming over her flushed cheeks and that lush pink mouth. When he'd met her at that party, he had thought she was every man's fantasy come to life. And he had wanted her. God, how he had wanted her. He still wanted her now, and he hated that…

'And you didn't think at all,' he said. 'You just took. Because you could.' They were both on the edge of their seats, fists clenched, eyes narrowed. 'Because you were rich and beautiful and bored.'

It was the way she had been brought up, he told himself, remembering Oscar Cavendish's cool, reptilian smile and his arrogant assumption that the world had been set up to satisfy his wishes above all others.

He held her gaze. 'That's how you people operate.'

'Which people?' She was staring at him, her grey eyes wide with confusion and an exhaustion he refused to acknowledge.

'You and your *friends*.' He tossed the word at her as if it was a grenade, and they both jerked to their feet at the same time. 'Those trust-fund babies who went to all those parties. The ones who used to get drunk and smash stuff up, and then just throw money on the table as if that made everything all right. You told me you were different.'

He had thought she *was* different. Gentle and sensitive. And the way she had looked at him then… There had almost been a purity to it.

'I was. I *am*,' she protested shakily.

At some point they had edged closer to one another, drawn by the invisible gravitational pull of desire, and now he could see the faint tremor beneath her skin, the flush across her cheeks. He wanted to touch her so much, and that knowledge made him furious.

'No, you're exactly the same. The only difference is you don't pay with cash,' he snarled.

For a splinter of a second she stared at him in the jagged silence that followed his remark, and then she took an unsteady step backwards.

'And that's the sticking point for you, isn't it? That's why you agreed to this.' A hard flare of anger crossed her face. 'You hate me knowing that you took the money. It makes you feel small. But frankly—and this might come as a shock to you, Gabriel—I don't care about your pride.'

Her face was pale and wide-eyed, but her voice had stopped shaking.

'I care about mine. So I'm going to get my bags, and then I'm getting off this island on the next boat or plane. In fact, I'll swim if I have to.'

She spun round and was gone, moving with a grace that his eyes tracked even in his feverish state, moving so swiftly she was already in her bedroom by the time he caught up with her. As he slammed the door shut behind them she stepped towards him, her eyes blazing.

'What do you think you're doing?'

And now his anger was blazing too—rolling through him high and fast, like a bushfire.

'You think I needed to bring you here to work out that you don't care about my pride? You left me sitting in that hotel bar for nearly four hours,' he said, and it cost him a lot to keep his voice calm, when the muted agony of it was still reverberating inside him. 'Do you know how humiliating that was?'

There was a pulsing silence, broken only by the fractured sound of their breathing.

'You want to talk about humiliation?' She lifted her chin like a boxer entering the ring—a flyweight squaring up to a heavyweight. 'Try coming in second place to a pile of money.'

Fire and fury swirled in her beautiful grey eyes along with something less sharp, something shadowy and frayed that almost undid him.

'You turned our relationship into a financial transaction.'

He stepped forward, his hands closing around the tops of her arms. 'No, you sent your father to do that, Dove.'

'For the last time—I didn't send him to find you and I never asked him to pay you off. I didn't know anything about what he'd done until he came and told me.'

She tried to pull away from him but he tightened his grip, holding her firmly, pressing his fingers into her skin.

'You're lying. How did he find me, then? No one knew about us except you and me.' He felt a sting of shame. 'You didn't want anyone to know. Or are you going to deny that too?'

He could tell from the heavy silence that followed his question that she wasn't, but instead of feeling a warm rush of satisfaction, he felt a dull ache creeping through his chest.

'There was no way your father could have found out where I was waiting unless you told him.'

'I didn't tell him.'

Now she jerked her arms violently, and this time he let her go. Her beautiful face was pale and the shake was back in her voice as she said, 'I don't know how he found out. But I do know that when he offered you money to leave me you took it.'

He stared down at her, his heart hammering against his ribs. She was making it sound so easy, and in some ways it had been. All he'd had to do was say yes. Only it was so much more complicated than that. More than anything he had wanted to throw the money back in Oscar's face, take his rage and his pain and unleash it upon the woman who couldn't even be bothered to reject him in person.

But confronting Dove, making her *feel* what she had done to him, would have meant revealing so much—too much. That was why he had taken the money and walked. Because the hardest thing to do had also been the easiest.

He shook his head. 'That's not how it happened.'

'Then tell me what did happen.'

Remembering the helpless, nightmarish daze of his conversation with Oscar Cavendish, he felt his stomach knot. But he knew they had always been heading to this point. Everything along the way had just been diversions on the road…

The train had been delayed twice. First because of engineering works, then because of a points failure. Gabriel checked his phone again. But he had left plenty of time, so he still had ten minutes to spare before Dove was due to meet him in the hotel bar, and they weren't flying out to the States until this evening.

The dingy hotel wouldn't have been his choice, he

thought as he nodded at the barmaid. But Dove had suggested it, and it would only be for one drink.

He ordered a lager that he knew he was too nervous to drink and forced his breathing to slow. They had agreed to tell their parents after they'd reached California. Part of him would have liked to tell his family now; he knew they were worried about him, and that they would worry less when they met Dove.

Her parents would almost certainly be less enthusiastic about the match. She hadn't said as much, but he'd guessed that was why she wanted to keep their relationship a secret. And he understood secrets.

His phone buzzed and, picking it up, he felt his heart skip a beat as he read the message from Dove.

Running late. Wait for me.

She was never late—but then it wasn't every day you ran off with your lover.

He stared down at the screen, seeing Dove's soft grey eyes, and that extraordinarily sweet smile that made his heart bang like a drum.

It had done more than that. Her smile, her love, had been a balm for the sting of Fenella's rejection. Dove made him feel safe and reckless. He almost wrote back *Until the end of time...* But in the end he settled for a simple X.

'Can I get you another drink?'

The barmaid was hovering by the table.

'Why not?' He held out his glass. 'And a gin and tonic as well, please.'

'Are you meeting someone?' Her face changed just a little.

He nodded. 'She's running a bit late.'

*Just one drink.*

*Running a bit late.*

Throughout the afternoon, as the minutes ticked into first one and then two and then three hours, he remembered those words. He texted her, obviously. Then he called her, but it went straight to voicemail.

His mind was filled with panicky, unfinished thoughts and unanswered questions. All except the one he should have asked. And all the time he knew he should leave, but to do so would be to accept the unthinkable, the unbearable...

After the first hour the bar staff kept their distance, as if rejection and betrayal were some kind of terrible, contagious disease. By the end of the second hour they were actively avoiding looking at him.

At a little under four hours after he had arranged to meet Dove, he looked up and saw a man strolling into the bar as if he owned it. He had a juddering moment of déjà vu, and then the man was walking towards him, his handsome face lit up with triumph.

'You must be Gabriel Silva.' He stopped next to the table. 'I'm Oscar Cavendish, Dove's father. She's fine,' he added, dropping into the seat opposite. 'There's just been a slight change of plan.' His mouth curled into the smile of a pickpocket palming a wallet. 'I'm afraid she won't be joining you.'

Gabriel stared at him, his brain doing cartwheels. The panic of earlier had returned, and now it was pressing in on him like a thick cloud, sliding over his skin, squeezing his throat.

'I don't understand...' Except he did. He knew exactly what was happening because it had happened before.

'Yes, It's all a bit awkward.' Oscar glanced down at the bag by Gabriel's feet. 'She's had a change of heart.'

Gabriel stared at him, felt his own heart lurching against his ribs. He felt as if Oscar Cavendish had scooped out his stomach and dumped it on the table, and he was grateful that he was sitting down because he felt too hollow to stand.

'She feels dreadful...truly dreadful. She honestly never intended it to get this far. And she hates being the bearer of bad news. Always has. That's why I'm here.'

There was a scraping sound as Gabriel pushed back his chair. 'I want to talk to her. I *need* to talk to her.'

The ache in his voice, the intensity of it, made him flinch. He had never felt more exposed...more powerless. More unwanted.

'I know... I know,' Oscar said soothingly. 'But she doesn't want to talk to you, so it would probably be best for everyone if you just stuck to the plan.' He touched Gabriel's bag with the toe of his handmade shoe. 'Look, I know it's upsetting, but you're young. You have your whole life ahead of you. You'll find someone who feels the same way. And in the meantime...'

Reaching into his jacket, he pulled out his phone and slid it across the table.

'Your former boss, Bill, is a great friend of the family. He gave me your bank details.' He tapped the screen. 'Dove wanted you to have a little something by way of compensation, so I took the liberty of transferring some money into your account. With the understanding, of course, that she won't be hearing from you again.'

It was like a meteor strike. Everything crashed and burned around him, just as it had before. The hotel bar imploded, the table and the undrunk drinks turned to ash, and inside his chest, his heart shattered into a million pieces, devastatingly and irrevocably broken...

When he finished speaking the silence in the room was sharp-angled, serrated. Dove was staring at him, her gaze frozen on his face.

'That's not what happened.'

She was shaking her head, her grey eyes pure with shock and denial. Actually, her whole body was shaking. He could see her legs and her arms trembling, as if she was standing in a high storm.

'It's not true. You're lying.'

Her eyes were huge and dark and stunned, as if he had hit her.

'He didn't do that. He didn't say those things. He wouldn't do that.'

He stared at her, his heart pounding. He had dreamed of this moment so often, and in his dreams she'd looked just as crushed and diminished as she did now. In his dreams, he revelled in her misery. But now that it was happening for real he didn't feel satisfaction or triumph. He just felt her shock. Her distress. Her pain. As if it was his.

It rolled through him like a pyroclastic cloud, flattening the memory of that day, swallowing up his need for revenge. And what was there to avenge? She had been telling the truth. She had known nothing about what her father had done that day until now.

'I'm sorry, but I'm not lying. Everything I've told you is the truth.'

Not the whole truth—but there was no time or place in the world for that.

She was still staring at him as if he was a stranger. A dark, menacing stranger with a terrible weapon. And he knew only too well that there was no more terrible weapon than a truth you didn't want to hear.

'You didn't send your father.'

It was a statement of fact, but she shook her head as if he had asked a question. 'I was on my way out of the house…on my way to you—' she swallowed, cleared her throat '—and he was waiting for me. I remember being shocked that he was there, scared that he'd found out about us…' Her voice shook around the word. 'And that he was going to stop me. But he just told me that he had something to show me on his phone.'

She was looking past him now, at the stupidly cheerful sun outside the window.

'I didn't understand what I was looking at, at first, and then I did.' Her face seemed to lose shape, like a flower in the wind. 'He told me that he didn't trust you, so he'd gone to find you and offered you money to leave me. And it was there, in black and white, the transfer to your account.' She shivered. 'I never told him to give you money.'

'I know that now.'

He heard her swallow. 'Why did you take it? Why didn't you call me?'

The air was so still the room felt like a tomb. His heart was a dark thud inside his chest.

'I didn't know about the money. He got the account

details from Bill. And I don't know why I didn't call you. I suppose I didn't feel there was anything to say.'

He had been in shock. After Oscar Cavendish had slithered out of the bar, he'd been shaking so hard it had been another twenty minutes before he could get to his feet.

'Nothing to say?' Her voice had an undertow of misery that made his nails cut into his hands. 'How could you think I would do something like that?'

Easily, he thought. His self-doubt, his fear of rejection…

They'd been like a trail of breadcrumbs, weaving through their relationship, so that the whole time they were together a part of him had been waiting for it to happen…hoping it wouldn't, but fearing it would. That at some point Dove would see whatever was in him that had kept his biological mother from wanting him and loving him.

It had just happened sooner than he'd thought it would.

And it had hurt a whole lot more than he could have imagined.

'I didn't think I had any reason to doubt him. I mean, he was your father…'

She flinched, and it tore at him again that she should feel this confusion about her father.

He cleared his throat. 'I was hurt, and angry. I thought you didn't care and I wanted to show you that I didn't care either.'

It was the truth, but not the whole truth.

'I did care—'

Her voice cracked and he reached out for her, but she stumbled backwards, holding her hands in front of her.

'Just leave me alone!' Tears were slipping down her face.

'I can't leave you like this.' He didn't want to leave her.

She tried to push him away, but he wouldn't budge, and finally she leaned into him and he gathered her against his pounding heart.

'It's okay Shh…it's okay.' He sank down on the edge of the bed, pulling her with him. 'It's okay,' he said again, his hand moving in slow, rhythmic circles until finally her sobs subsided.

'I'm sorry,' she whispered. 'I should have called you… I should have known—'

He slid his hands into her hair and tilted her face to his. 'We both made mistakes.'

He felt a sharp stab of guilt. But only he could have put it right at the time. Obviously Dove was going to believe Oscar. He was her *father*. But he could have—*should* have—questioned Oscar's version. He should have confronted Dove. Demanded an explanation. Had he been a different man…a braver man…he would have done so. Instead, he'd let an old truth swamp love and logic. He'd taken the money and walked away, just as he had done a year earlier.

The hardest choice had also been the easiest.

She shifted against him, her hand pushing into the hard wall of his chest to steady herself, her face lowered. 'It's okay. You can leave. You don't need to stay with me.'

'Is that what you want?' His voice sounded different. Not his own. He knew that he was revealing too much, but he couldn't seem to do anything about it. 'You want me to leave?' he said, over the dark, panicky thud of his heart.

There was a long silence.

He stared down at the top of her head, feeling emotions he couldn't name much less control expanding in all directions.

Moments earlier he had been staggering through the past, dazed and bloodied, hurting and angry. Alone. But somehow they had found their way back to each other, and now the past felt like another world, a distant moon, or a planet far, far away. All that mattered was here and now and the woman in his arms.

As Dove lifted her face to his he could see her pulse beating a wild allegretto against the fragile skin of her throat and he held his breath, knowing that she was feeling it too. And then she was shaking her head, and her soft, 'No…' was lost as he pressed his mouth against hers and kissed her, and everything melted, and there was just his body reaching out to hers…

# CHAPTER SEVEN

GABRIEL TOOK A quick breath like a gasp, his fingers reaching to capture her face. She tasted like melted honey, and for a moment he savoured her softness and her sweetness. His hand tightened in her hair and he pulled her closer, pressing against her soft, pliant body, breathing in the scent of sweet-peas and warm skin.

Everything was white and gold and grey, and somewhere over his shoulder he could hear the sea's endless murmur. She moved closer, reaching up to stroke his face, and he felt her fingertips grazing against the stubble on his jaw, light as butterfly wings, then moving lower to his shoulders. And all the time she was kissing him, angling her mouth against his, her teeth catching his lower lip, nipping, teasing…

His heart running wild, maddened by her touch, wanting more, needing more, he broke the kiss and tipped her onto the bed. Stepping back, he yanked his shirt over his head and tossed it on the floor. His heart was beating inside his head, in time to the thick, urgent pulse of his blood, and he tried to think of the last time he'd felt so out of control.

But then she pulled off her top and wriggled out of her shorts and it was impossible to think. He edged back slightly, the better to admire her small, high breasts in a white cotton bra and the dip of her waist, his body hardening.

She saw it, and her hands reached for him, pressing flat against the outline of his erection, feeling the length and shape of him. He sucked in a breath as a jolt of hunger, hot and sharp like electricity, snaked across his skin, his body stiffening to stone as she unzipped his trousers and freed him.

For a moment he couldn't breathe. His whole body was shivering, as if he was cold, but his skin was on fire. Her fingers curled around the length of him, and then he breathed out jerkily as she leaned forward and he felt the tip of her tongue flick over the blunt head of his erection.

'Ah—' Groaning, he threaded his fingers through her hair, pulling it free so that it spilled over her shoulders like a pale waterfall. She was moving now, dipping lower, licking the shaft, holding him in her mouth...

He swore softly. 'My turn.'

Teeth clenched, he pulled free and nudged her back onto the bed. Breathing unsteadily, he hooked his fingers into her panties and slid them off her body. Her eyes were fixed on his face, narrowed and storm-dark with passion. Leaning forward, he kissed her softly, his thumb shaping her waist and her stomach, moving lower to trace a path through the triangle of white-gold curls.

She rocked towards him, whimpering against his lips, and he slipped his fingers deep inside her, moving them back and forth, feeling her pulse in his hand. Breaking the kiss, he gently parted her legs and crouched over her, breathing in her scent. Her legs were trembling slightly and, sliding his hands under the curve of her bottom, he steadied her, And then he lowered his mouth to the slick heat between her thighs.

Dove arched against his mouth, her fingers digging into his shoulders. Her body was humming like a train track. She could feel the flat of his tongue against the hard nub of her clitoris, feel the muscles inside her clenching as she moved beneath him. The humming inside her was getting louder and louder. She felt soft and ripe and open. Could feel her body coming adrift…

Her fingers flexed against his shoulders. 'I want you inside me…'

He stared at her, his face blunt with the effort of stopping. 'I'll have to go to my room—' he said hoarsely.

'No.' She grabbed his wrist. 'It's fine.'

She pulled him back onto the bed, and his eyes narrowed with a hunger that made her shudder all the way through. He slid her under him, moving against her, his weight on his elbow as he reached down to stroke the head of his erection between her thighs.

Her hands moved to his hips as she felt him push up and she lifted her own hips, felt him push again. And then he was inside her, warm and sleek and hard. He started to move slowly, lifting and lowering like the cresting waves outside, and each time she felt a whisper of liquid heat ripple through her body like a current beneath the water.

It was delicious, and the bliss of it dazzled her.

Her eyelashes fluttered shut and she moaned softly, her hands curving round his arching back, gripping his vertebrae as if she was holding on to the side of a mountain.

He was thrusting deeper now, and harder, then deeper still, and she could feel the heat building inside her, fierce, white-hot, stinging.

Her muscles were tightening now, tensing around him, holding him but not holding him. Flames were dancing inside her eyelids. She was burning, melting, chasing the heat, wanting to escape it, yet wanting to make it go on and on and on, wanting it to last for ever, knowing she would die of pleasure if it did—

She shuddered helplessly, her body spasming, tightening and loosening all at once. His mouth found hers and he groaned her name, his muscles snapping tight as he thrust inside her.

Breathing raggedly, Dove gripped his shoulders to steady herself. Her whole body was trembling like a sapling in a storm. She was aware of everything and conscious of nothing. The clean white walls and the shell-pink curtains fluttering in the breeze. The endless blue outside like a Hockney swimming pool. And beside her, inside her, Gabriel, his shuddering breath hot against her throat, his damp skin sticking to hers, so that it was impossible to tell where she ended and he began.

She felt him shift, move his weight, but she couldn't move. She just lay there, trying to breathe. It took a while, and even then it was all her throbbing body and hammering heart would allow her to do for a long time. She knew that there was only him, and there would only ever be him. And the truth of that scared her, and made her want to hold him close for ever, even though she knew it wasn't possible and that this was the end not a new beginning.

For a few seconds she tried to hold herself apart from him, but then she pressed her face against his shoulder, tears spilling onto her cheeks.

'Don't cry.' He kissed the tears off her face, kissed her eyelids, her forehead, her mouth, with gentle, tender kisses that wrenched at her heart. 'I don't ever want to make you cry.'

'It's not you—'

Obviously that wasn't true. Being here with Gabriel's body inside hers was like standing in a thunderstorm on a hill. Like breathing in raw ozone with electricity crackling through her blood. But with it there was the sadness of a summer lost, of days of sunlight and newly cut grass turned to ash in confusion and doubt and a lack of faith.

And then there was the pain of her father's betrayal. Her throat tightened. Betrayal was surely too strong a word. But why, then, did it feel as if the world had broken apart beneath her feet?

She had no idea what could have motivated Oscar to act like that, or why he had said all that stuff about her having a change of heart. For so long she had believed that he had been trying to protect her. Or perhaps more accurately she had *wanted* to believe that he'd been trying to protect her. But the truth was her relationship with her father had been difficult for as long as she could remember. Sometimes he'd been sweet, but often he'd been cold and distant and impossible to like. And then he'd be funny and charming and she'd forget. It was almost as if he hadn't been able to decide how he felt about her.

Gabriel's arm felt warm and heavy against her body. It made her feel safe, secure in a way she hadn't felt in the longest time. Only she knew that she didn't deserve to feel that way.

Her lungs felt as if they might burst. 'I just wish I could go back in time and do things differently,' she whispered. 'If I'd left earlier... I should have left earlier... I should have—'

'Shh...' He pressed his finger against her lips. 'Don't think about that now.'

Gazing up into his eyes was like diving into cool blue water. It soothed the ache in her throat. Curling her arms around his neck, she let him roll her underneath his body, losing herself in the heat of his kiss. Because even though she knew it wasn't true, it felt as if she was meant for him.

Gazing down at the sleeping woman in his arms, Gabriel felt a jagged weight in his chest. Outside the window the sun was sliding jerkily between clouds, disappearing and then returning to view in time with the beat of his heart.

He had thought he couldn't feel worse than he had that day at the hotel—but then he hadn't truly understood what it felt like to feel someone else's pain.

*To be responsible for that pain.*

And he *was* responsible. He had let his grief and anger and misery at what had happened with Fenella colour his relationship with Dove. It had been like a bruise, a weakness, and the moment Oscar Cavendish had pressed against it, it had cracked apart. Blind with panic and pain, he hadn't seen the truth.

Actually, he hadn't looked. It had been easier to accept what he was told, even though doing so meant thinking the worst of the woman he had loved.

He shifted his body, but the guilt was solid...immovable. And he deserved it. If Dove had been a business he was buying he would never have made any decision without completing due diligence. Every single piece of data would have been sifted and analysed and assessed. And yet he had accepted Oscar's words at face value.

Worse, he had acted on what he'd been told without even the most cursory of conversations. Forcing her to work for him, threatening her—threatening her boss, her colleagues—dragging her on to his yacht to rub her face in his wealth and success.

No wonder she had fought him so hard when he'd confronted her at Cavendish and Cox. She must have been devastated by what happened between them. But he had seen it as just temper—frustration at finally being held to account. He had ignored her distress and blackmailed her into working for him anyway.

And he could never make it up to her.

He couldn't change the past—and he certainly couldn't change himself.

His stomach clenched tight. He was broken in some fundamental way. There was a blankness, a gap inside him—like a missing step in a staircase.

He gazed down at Dove. And yet when her body fused with his he felt complete. In those hectic moments he forgot everything…cared about nothing but the light, delicate touch of her fingers and the hot press of her mouth.

Hunger had stormed through him like a conquering army. His hunger and hers. She'd been like a curling flame in his arms. Everything between them had pulled taut, the white heat of their bodies consuming the pain, and the past, so that there had been nothing but fire and need and the bliss of her being his once again.

\* \* \*

Dove stared up at the waterfall, blinking into the cool spray. She had come across it by accident. It had just appeared out of the lush greenery as she'd made her way from the house.

Waking in Gabriel's arms, she had wanted more than anything to stay pressed against his warm, sleeping body. But she knew there was no purpose to thinking like that.

What had happened had not been a mistake. Nothing that perfect could ever be called that. But it would be an act of reckless self-harm to let it happen again. And she didn't trust herself to be there when he woke up. Didn't trust herself to resist that beautiful golden body...

'There you are.'

She turned, her feet slipping on the wet rocks, and steadied herself. Or rather she regained her balance. Nothing could possibly steady her heartbeat, she thought, gazing up into Gabriel's glittering blue eyes.

'I just thought I'd take a quick look around before I left,' she said quickly, trying to pull her mind back in line.

There was a small pause, and then he nodded. 'Of course. But it would probably be better to have a guide. There are quite a few treacherous paths, and it's easy to get lost and not know where you are.'

She frowned. 'Isn't that what being lost is?'

One corner of his mouth twisted into a smile that kicked up sparks in her all over again, and she was instantly, hopelessly aware of the shimmering blue heat in his eyes and of how close he was standing.

'What I am trying and failing to say is that there's no point using a landmark as a guide if you don't know how it relates to anything else.'

'I see what you mean, yes…' She nodded, but honestly he might have been speaking Portuguese or Mandarin. Her brain didn't seem to be working properly.

'We could walk up to the lake. Or we could head down to the beach. See if we can spot any dolphins.'

'Dolphins?'

He nodded. 'Dolphins, whales, sharks…'

They did see dolphins.

Crouching on an outcrop of rock, Gabriel suddenly pointed out to sea. 'Just there…watch the waves,' he said softly.

Seconds later she saw them. A school of dolphins, ten or twelve maybe, rising and diving in perfect synchronicity, their sleek grey bodies shining in the sunlight as they carved a path through the water with enviable grace.

'Where have they gone?'

Holding up her hand to shield her eyes, Dove squinted into the sunlight, but the dolphins had disappeared from sight, swallowed up by the cresting blue waves.

Gabriel moved beside her. 'Just wait a moment. They'll be back.'

She could feel the vibration of his voice against her shoulder and a flicker of heat skated across her skin. Her palms itched to reach out and touch him again.

'There!'

Her heart skipped and she gasped. A perfect half-sized version of the adult dolphins was leaping effervescently through the water.

'That one's probably just been born. They calve around this time of year.'

She tried to say something, but her chest was churning with a wild joy and a throat-clenching sadness that made speaking impossible.

'Dove…'

Gabriel said her name in that soft, dark way of his, and she felt it ripple through her like warm sunlight. She looked into the sun so that he wouldn't see the tears in her eyes.

*'Vai ficar tudo bem.'*

He'd spoken in Portuguese. She had no idea what he'd said but it didn't matter, because she was lost somewhere between the softness of his voice and the thumping of her heart.

'It's going to be okay,' he translated. His hand closed around her wrists and he turned her to face him. 'I know you said you wanted to go back to London, and if that's what you still want then you can take the jet and leave tonight.'

'But…?' she prompted.

'I thought you might stay for a couple of days.'

His beautiful face, that she'd once loved to kiss from brow to chin and cheek to cheek, was taut, and his blue eyes were fixed on her face.

'I don't want it to end like this. It feels wrong.'

His words touched her skin like warm drops of rain. Could she stay? Should she stay?

She glanced out to the dancing waves. She could no longer see the dolphins, but she knew that even if she never saw them again, she would always be able to see them in her imagination. And in the same way she knew that if she left now she would carry this sense of sadness and unfinished business with her for ever.

But their relationship wasn't the only unfinished business. 'What about the acquisition?'

She felt his hands tighten around wrists. 'It can wait.' He pulled her closer. 'Carrie can handle things for a couple of days.'

Gazing up into his face, she felt her mouth dry. His gaze was even more blue than usual, and it made her feel as if she was drowning.

Her heart was beating out of time. Would she be mad to stay? Her mother would certainly think so if she knew, but she had no intention of telling her.

What would she say? *Oh, hi, Mum. Just to let you know I'm going to spend a few days having sex with an ex I never mentioned before because Dad paid him to leave me alone and he took the money and broke my heart.*

Okay, some of that was not true anymore, but she didn't need to ask her mum if this was a good idea. She knew that danger signs should be flashing red inside her head. Wanting him as she did made her vulnerable, but maybe this was the way to break the spell.

Unbidden, a memory swelled up inside her, hot and bright and as clear as if it was happening now. His fingers tangling in her hair, rough and tender, slow and urgent, tracing the line of her mouth...

*And his mouth...*

She swallowed, heat flooding her body so that her skin was flushed with it. Her breasts were hot and heavy, the nipples pulling tight, and there was a pulse between her thighs. She wanted to kiss his beautiful curving mouth until neither of them could think or breathe. She wanted to tear off his clothes right here and now and lick every inch of his skin. She wanted to pull him inside her and feel him swell and harden, feel him take over her body...

'Okay, then,' she heard herself say. 'I'll stay for a couple of days.'

The next few days were a merry-go-round blur. A head-spinning fever dream of a hunger as deep and endless as the ocean.

It wasn't real. They both knew that.

Maybe that was why it was easy between them—easier than it had been six years ago, when there'd been so many layers of the truth. Now there was just the two of them, in the moment. There was no future, no commitment, no expectation. They lived each minute, each hour.

They ate and drank...walked and swam and slept. And all the time they were touching, stroking, caressing, kissing...revelling in the blissful freedom of being able to slide their hands and mouths over each other's bodies.

And she loved the island. Although it felt like several different islands throughout the day. She loved the smell of the wild mint that grew everywhere. And the way the mountains slid in and out of view between the clouds. She loved the ferns and the moss and the banks of pastel-coloured hydrangeas. Most of all she loved the sea.

Every direction she looked she could see blue—every shade from ink to glass. But there was no blue even in nature that was as beautiful as Gabriel's eyes. And it wasn't just his eyes that set her senses alight.

She glanced up at his face, trying to take everything in—each feature, every tiny shift of expression—wanting to remember. It was what she did every time she looked at him, and she rarely looked away. But still she feared that she would forget something, and the thought almost stopped her heart.

'What are you thinking?' he asked.

He was playing with her hair, running it through his hands, twisting it around his fingers and then unfurling it. Unravelling it.

*Unravelling her more*, she thought, heat blossoming deep inside her.

'Nothing, really,' she lied.

They were in bed. It was two o'clock in the afternoon. The sun was spilling across his naked body and he was so smooth and golden and gloriously male that it hurt to look at him.

'What are *you* thinking about?' she countered as he drew her head back with a tug of his hand, lowering his mouth to the long line of her throat.

'Me? I was just admiring the view,' he said softly, and she felt the softness in his voice gather low in her belly.

His other hand slid over her stomach to caress the curve of her hip and bottom, his light, precise touch sending little ripples of pleasure across her skin. He lifted his head a fraction and, pulse stumbling, she stared at him, wordless and undone, held captive by the mesmerising blue glitter of his gaze, fascinated by the casual intimacy of his touch, as if all of this was just foreplay. And in a way it was…because there would always be another time.

*Until there wasn't.*

But she didn't dare think about that. She couldn't think about the moment when she would have to wake from this dream and return to London.

'I thought maybe we could go and look at the vineyard later,' she said quickly.

Things were getting out of hand. She needed to keep some control.

'Today?' His gaze held hers, steady and unblinking. 'It's a bit late. Why don't we go tomorrow?'

'You said that yesterday.'

'And I'll probably say it again tomorrow.'

His gaze moved over her and he smiled then—one of those hesitant almost-smiles that seemed to flip a switch inside her.

'And the day after that…and the day after that…'

She let him pull her closer. She wanted to be closer. Wanted him inside her again…and again and again—

A beat of need pulsed lightly across her skin. Lying here with him, she could feel her feelings growing reckless.

As if he could read her mind, he said softly, 'We could just stay here.'

'We could,' she agreed.

Her pulse jerked as his fingers tiptoed with excruciating slowness down her belly, coming to a stop at the mound of pale curls. She could see his hunger imprinted on his face, the same hunger that was stamped all the way through her, and she was just trying to arrange her face so that he might not realise just how badly she needed him when his phone rang.

He frowned, then hesitated, dragging his eyes away slowly, and with regret. She watched him reach over and pick up the phone.

Glancing at the screen, his frown tugged at his mouth. 'It's Carrie.'

'Answer it,' she said quickly.

His COO would be uber-keen to prove herself capable of steering the ship in Gabriel's absence, so it must be something important for her to get in touch. As he swiped the screen she slipped away to the bathroom to give him some privacy, grateful for the breathing space.

It was dangerous to let herself think about for ever. Even if her own failed attempt at a relationship could be excused, she had watched her parents' marriage limp on until death had parted them. But they were not unique, and she needed to remember that the next time she started telling herself stories which ended with happy-ever-after.

This was sex—and that was all it could ever be, she told herself as she walked back into the bedroom.

Gabriel was facing the window, but she didn't need to see his face to know that something was wrong. The phone was wedged against his ear, and even though he was no longer naked there was a visible tension in his shoulders.

'It's not up to her. If she's got a problem with it, she needs to talk to her s-son—' As he stumbled over the word, he turned and saw her hovering in the doorway.

'I need to go. Keep me updated.' He rang off and tossed the phone onto the bedside table.

'Is there a problem?' she asked quietly.

Reaching for her bathrobe, she slipped her arms into the sleeves and knotted it around her waist.

'You could say that.' The skin on his face was pulled taut and his voice was stretched even tighter. 'Fenella Ogilvy is kicking off about the name-change.'

Dove stared at him in silence. Name-changes were not unusual in acquisitions. The interim chairman of the company, Fenella Ogilvy's son, Angus, had already agreed to lose the name, but clearly he hadn't squared things with his mother.

'What does she want?'

'It doesn't matter—it's not happening.'

She frowned. 'What's not happening?'

'She wants to meet with me.' His words were clipped and cold. The ease and intimacy between them earlier had evaporated as quickly as the mist around the mountain.

'Okay...' she said slowly. 'It's a family firm. Sometimes shareholders, particularly family members get jumpy about their legacy. You know that. Maybe if she met you—'

'I'm not meeting her. I'm not ready.'

*Not ready?*

She stood in the doorway, staring at him uncertainly. That was just not true. Gabriel was easily the most capable, most informed person on the team. 'I don't understand what you mean by "ready"...' she said slowly.

'You don't need to understand.' His eyes were as hard and flat as his voice. 'You're just a cog in a wheel, remember?'

She flinched—more than she'd meant to. But his harshness was like a blow to the head. Before when he said those same words they had both still been smarting from old betrayals, lashing out, wanting to hurt.

It was supposed to be different now. Together they had worked through the lies and the mistakes of the past to find the truth—their truth. A truth that might not mean they had the same relationship as before, but it wasn't this either. A sniping range where old anger was used like armour-piercing ammunition.

She didn't want this…didn't want to be like Oscar and Olivia…

The thought made her reach out and brace her hand against the doorframe. The old Dove—the Dove who had soothed and conciliated such outbursts—would have counselled calm, but she wasn't the old Dove anymore and, lifting her chin, she said coolly, 'Please don't talk to me like that. It's rude and unnecessary.'

His eyes snapped to her face, the blue choppy with anger and frustration and an emotion she didn't recognise.

'Blunt, not rude. But I agree it was unnecessary. I shouldn't need to remind you that some decisions are above your paygrade.'

Her heart was pounding, but she kept her gaze, deliberate and unflinching. 'I know that. But that still doesn't give you the right to speak to me in that way.'

His eyes locked with hers, his face taut and pale against the shadow of his stubble. 'Why? Because we're having sex?'

'Actually, yes.' Now she was angry. 'I don't just sleep with anyone, Gabriel.' *Make that nobody in the last six years.* 'I'm sleeping with you because I like you and I care about you, even when we're not having sex. I thought you felt the same way. Clearly I was wrong.'

'Clearly.'

There was a brittle, crushing silence.

She stared at him, hurt, angry, disbelieving, her mind jolting against the shock of his words. 'Why are you being like this? What is wrong with you?'

He spun away and walked towards the window. She stared after him, still angry, but something in the set of his shoulders made it impossible for her to just walk away. There was an ache in her chest, and she pressed her hand against it. Seconds earlier she had told him she cared, and if that was true then she couldn't walk away. His anger was defensive. She knew that. He was pushing her away to protect himself. Only from what?

She stared at his back, feeling his anger like an uncut diamond scraping over her skin, and at the same time she realised that there was something else—something bigger than his anger. Something like fear, only not fear. It was a gap in him…a hollow that she badly wanted to fill so that he could be whole.

'You are ready, Gabriel.'

He was shocked. Not at her words, which he couldn't hear above the pounding of his heart, but at her not leaving. He had wanted her to leave—needed her to leave. So that he could go back to blaming her, hating her. And she should hate *him*; he was being cold and cruel. But she was still here, and that was intolerable. Or it should be intolerable. Only it wasn't. It was a relief.

'You are ready,' she said again, and now he heard her. *But he wasn't.*

Blood roaring in his ears, Gabriel stared out at the huge dark peak. He could have stalked over to the other window, that overlooked the sea, but for some reason he was drawn to the mountain. Maybe because, like him, it was the legacy of something intense and unplanned.

Unlike him, it didn't have to think about what that meant…

The idea of meeting Fenella pressed against a bruise inside him that had never healed.

He could feel Dove's gaze on his back and he wanted to tell her that she was right. He *had* been rude, not blunt, and deliberately so. Because she was there, and he was feeling small enough to need to lash out at someone. Only then he would have to explain why he'd needed to lash out, and that would be a slippery slope.

He had kept so much hidden for so long for a reason.

Keeping his gaze fixed on the mountain, he shrugged as if his heart was beating normally. 'It's complicated,' he said.

For a moment she didn't respond, and then she took a step towards him, then another 'So simplify it,' she said. 'If you had to sum up the problem with Fenella in three words, what would you say?'

He turned, opening his mouth to tell her another lie, but then he saw her face. Sunlight was illuminating her features and he could see that she was worried. *About him.* And it was the simplicity of that fact that stunned him into speaking, into telling her the truth.

'She's my mother.'

# CHAPTER EIGHT

IT WAS THE first time he had said those words out loud, and he half expected the world to fall away beneath his feet and that he would slide into the crack. But Dove's grey eyes steadied him.

'My birth mother,' he added, in case she hadn't understood.

But of course she had.

Only she didn't know everything.

She probably thought he was upset at having been given up for adoption. She didn't know that his mother had turned away from him twice.

'I didn't know you were adopted.'

'It never came up.' *Obviously.*

It had been up to him to share that particular truth, but telling someone when you first met would be weird, and if you didn't say anything then it got harder and harder to think of a way to just drop it into the conversation. And anyway it had felt disloyal to Luis and Laura, who were his parents in every way that it was possible to be a parent.

'When did you find out?' she asked.

'That I was adopted?' He frowned. 'I can't remember not knowing. I don't remember my parents sitting me down and telling me on a particular day. They were just always open about it—but in a good way. They made it seem that their adopting me wasn't about solving some horrible mess. It was a way for us to build a family. I think that's why I didn't actually even think about my birth parents for a very long time.'

If only he had kept on feeling that way, then maybe he would never have hurt this beautiful, clear-eyed woman. She could have stayed safe and happy in her beautiful clean world, far away from the mess and turmoil in his head.

'What changed?'

The steadiness in her voice pulled him back, and he felt some of the turmoil ease. He felt again the shock of her being there with him, caring enough to stay there. It was the same shock and gratitude and disbelief that he'd felt the first time she had turned and talked to him.

'We found out that my brother, Tom, was a haemophiliac. It's carried in the female line, and I suppose it made me think about my mother. My biological mother. And the more I thought, the more questions I had. What was she doing now? Did I look like her? Why did she give me up for adoption?'

*And then, later, did she regret giving me up? Would she love me if she was given a second chance?*

'Did you ask your parents about her?'

The directness of Dove's questions surprised him. But then again so much about her surprised him.

'No.' He shook his head. 'They would have helped me…supported me…but I felt bad that I wanted to know. Like I was judging them.' His throat felt scratchy. 'And they don't deserve that. They're good people.'

*Like you*, he thought, glancing over at her, seeing the concern in her grey eyes.

'I didn't do anything about it for a long time, and then, about eighteen months before I met you, I went to an appointment at the hospital with my brother and there was a poster in the waiting room about finding your birth parents. I suppose it felt like fate.'

Her eyes held his. 'So you decided to contact her?'

He nodded. 'It took about six months after I decided to get in touch to do anything about it.

'In the end I sent her a letter. I put my phone number in it.' He paused, remembering how it had felt...the thrill, the fear, the guilt, the hope. 'The agency told me that I needed to be positive, but realistic. Often birth mothers didn't want to be contacted. But she texted me almost immediately, suggesting we meet at a hotel.'

His throat felt so tight it hurt when he swallowed.

'I was nervous, but excited. I bought her flowers. Tulips. I was early, and she was late, but I thought she was probably nervous too.'

He glanced away, staring across the room, seeing again the hotel bar with its scratched dark wood tables and worn armchairs. It had been clean, but shabby, and a long way out of town. He should have known then what she had planned, but he hadn't been thinking straight.

'I was checking my phone when this man walked in. I remember thinking that he was way smarter than everyone else. Wearing a proper suit and polished leather shoes. He seemed to be looking for someone, and I thought he must be having an affair.' He laughed roughly. 'But then he saw me, and he came over and asked if I was James Balfour.'

His pulse jerked as he said the name, and he waited for his heart to steady itself...waited until it was easier to carry on.

'That's the name on my birth certificate,' he said finally.

Dove nodded, which was more than he had managed to do at the time. He'd felt as if he was floating, looking down on himself. Except that he wasn't Gabriel—he was James. A stranger talking to another stranger in an unfamiliar bar.

For weeks afterwards he hadn't been able to look in the mirror in case he saw no reflection. Even the memory of it now was doing something strange to the air, making it hiss like an untuned radio.

'Who was he?'

Dove's voice cut across his thoughts.

'His name was Charles Lambton. He was a lawyer. My mother's lawyer. You see, I'd got it wrong.' He couldn't keep the shake out of his voice. 'She wasn't late. She wasn't coming. In fact, she hadn't even texted me. Lambton had.'

'What did he say?'

This was one of the reasons he had never told anyone about what happened that day. The questions they would ask that he couldn't answer. But it was different with Dove. Her quiet voice helped. Like a hand on his arm, guiding him through a treacherous landscape.

'Not much. It was very civilised, very polite, but we didn't make small talk. He apologised for "the subterfuge", I think he called it, and told me his client had decided against meeting me in person. She thought it would be better to send a trusted third party.'

He had been stunned, unprepared. Around him, the colour had drained from the bar, so that the tulips on the seat beside him had looked overblown and obvious.

'Better in what way?'

His stomach snapped tight. He felt vulnerable, panicky. This was always the worst part to remember—that and the bit that had followed. Usually whenever he got there he couldn't seem to make the room stay still. The first time it had happened at work he'd had to hold on to the desk to stop it moving. Mostly he had a whisky to get past it. Or he went for a run and kept on running until his lungs screamed and his muscles ached more than his chest and it was as if it had never happened.

Only Dove's questions were like a crack in a dam, and the truth was a swell of water pushing against it. It was impossible to hold it back, but somehow that made it easier for his words to flow.

'She had—*has*,' he corrected himself, 'a life. A husband. A daughter. A s-son. He's three years younger than me.' He heard his own voice, the stammer, clumsy and stupid like a child, and he didn't know what hurt more. That she had gone on to have another family so soon after she'd discarded him or that it hadn't made her think about him.

'Oh—and her family has a property company.' He felt his mouth twist into something like a smile, but not, because smiles shouldn't hurt.

'Basically, the gist of it was that she didn't want everything good in her life ruined because of a drunken one night stand on a Portuguese beach.'

In the past, when he'd thought about shining a light into the dark corners of his life, what had stopped him was the certainty that nobody else would want to look. But now the sun was streaming into the room, turning everything gold, and Dove was still there.

He stared at her, feeling lightheaded.

'I was a mistake. A secret, unwanted mistake. And

that's why she gave me up for adoption. So that I would stay a secret. She wasn't looking for a second chance. There was no place for me in her life, and nothing would change.'

It sounded ugly. It *was* ugly. But Dove didn't flinch or look away, as if he too was ugly. Instead, she reached out and took his hand.

He stared down at her soft fingers, feeling not just their softness but their strength, and he took that strength and said, 'Then Charles Lambton took out an envelope and pushed it across the table. He told me that his cilent wanted to give me something to compensate for any distress I might have felt.'

Dove stared at him in silence. Her throat was so tight she could hardly breathe. 'Oh, Gabriel…'

'I thought it would be different. I mean, I can see why having a baby on your own when you were nineteen would be difficult, but she didn't even want to meet me—'

The skin on his face was stretched taut across the bones, and without thinking she stepped forward and slid her arms around him. 'I'm so sorry,' she whispered.

No wonder he had been so devastated when her father had walked into that hotel bar. No wonder he had taken the money and left. It would have felt like *déjà vu*—or rather *déjà vecu*. And now she knew why he hadn't told her any of this before. She knew because telling people things that were hard to hear, to know, to accept, was almost impossible.

She knew because she had spent her life *not* telling people those things.

But he had done it.

Her arms tightened around his body and it was then, holding his body tightly, feeling Gabriel's heart beating against hers, or maybe her heart beating against his, that Dove understood that she loved him. He was in her heart and he had never not been—no matter how much she had tried to forget about him.

For a moment she couldn't do anything but lean into him. She was shaking inside with shock. And yet a part of her had always known. That was why she hadn't called his bluff back in London. And why, before that, she had found it so easy to stay single. For her, there had never been any other man but Gabriel. She just couldn't imagine anyone but him kissing her, touching her, holding her.

Her pulse shivered and her hands trembled against his shoulders. The urge to tell him the truth was overwhelming. But there were other truths in the tense way he held his body.

She looked up into his face, seeing the boy beneath the man. Right from the start she had questioned why he wanted Fairlight Holdings so badly. The business had some plus points, but there were far better investments. None, though, as owned by the family of his birth mother, and that was the reason he was doing all this. To prove himself to Fenella Ogilvy and perhaps finally forge a connection with her.

'That's what this is about, isn't it?' she said softly. 'You want to give her another chance.'

'Another chance?'

He was staring at her, his blue eyes narrow on her face as he stepped back out of her embrace. His mood had changed. The anger was back.

'I don't want to give her another *chance*. I don't want

anything to do with her. When the acquisition is signed off, and her family's business is mine, then I'll send someone to meet her in a hotel of my choosing—just to let her know that everything her family once owned now belongs to *me*. The son she gave up. The son who wasn't good enough.'

Dove held her breath. She had been wrong. The anger had never left him. It was always there...like his shadow. Her stomach knotted and her heart was beating very hard. She knew first-hand the consequences of living with anger and resentment day in and day out. It was corrosive and crushing. Even her father, who had seemed outwardly to thrive on it, had not been a happy man.

The thought of Gabriel turning into her father made her stomach cave in on itself.

'And then what?' she said quietly.

He frowned, his anger still there. 'I walk away and get on with my life.'

Dove stared at him, feeling his words chafing beneath her skin, seeing her own life. The arguments...her father's inexplicable cold anger. Her mother's equally inexplicable refusal to leave, trapped, fused with her father in some baffling mix of money and manners and fear and loathing and helplessness.

She shook her head. 'Walking away isn't closure, Gabriel. We both know that. Because if it was you and I wouldn't be here now, having this conversation.'

'That's different.'

'Is it?'

She bit her lip, hating the tension in his face. The coiled-up pain of his birth mother's rejection was visible in the taut set of his shoulders and the bunching of muscles beneath his shirt. He could barely hold it in. But the acquisition would only be a temporary fix. A Band-Aid, she thought, her stomach knotting around the word.

But a sticking plaster was only for cuts and grazes. It couldn't fix a mother's rejection. Or a doomed marriage.

'I know you're angry, and hurt, and you have every right to be. Your mother was wrong to do what she did—but it was seven years ago. Things are different now. *You're* different now. Maybe if you talk to her...say what you want to say—'

'I tried that once before, remember?'

There was no softness to his beautiful face. He looked like an angel carved of stone...stern, unforgiving, locked in with his anger and misery for eternity.

'And what? You can't try again? Give her a second chance?'

'I don't do second chances.' There was a hard edge to his voice.

She lifted her chin. 'You gave me one.'

'That's different,' he said again.

'But it isn't.'

Her heart was pounding fast, as if she was running, and she wished that she was. But there was nowhere left to run from the truth. His or hers.

'I know it's hard to let go, but believe me—whatever punishment you think you're meting out to Fenella Ogilvy won't be enough,' she said flatly. 'It wasn't enough for my parents. You'll just end up punishing yourself.'

Her ribs tightened as his blazing blue eyes lifted to hers.

'I thought your parents loved one another,' he said.

She felt suddenly fragile. That was what she had told

him all those years ago, out of necessity and fear and shame. But after everything he had told her she couldn't pretend any longer.

'I lied to you. I didn't mean to. I thought I could tell you the truth. But then you showed me that photo of your family at Christmas. You all looked so happy, and your dad was looking at your mum as if they were unconquerable—'

Her throat felt hot and heavy, and she knew that it was full of all the tears she had never cried. For him. For her parents. For herself.

'Nobody I've ever known feels like that—certainly not my parents. Maybe they were in love right at the beginning, but then I think my mother realised that what my father really loved was her inheritance. When she found that out she punished him by keeping him short of money. So he punished her by having countless affairs with her friends.'

Gabriel was staring at her, his beautiful face blank of expression, but she knew how it sounded.

'Where did you fit in?' he asked.

'Me?'

She knew her mouth had moved to curve into a smile, but her voice sounded raw and tight, as if it hurt to speak.

'I was the Band-Aid baby. One last attempt to make things work. And it did for a bit. And then it didn't.'

Her lips were aching now.

'Sometimes they would be okay for a day or two, and then my dad would goad my mum and it would all kick off. My mother would go so far, but Oscar would always go further. *Too* far. And I knew it was my fault. I knew they were only together because of me. So I'd try to head things off. That was my job. To find ways to defuse the tension and smooth things over.'

'Problem-solving…' he said slowly.

Remembering the conversation they'd had on *The Argentum*, about why she had chosen corporate law, she nodded. It was why she lived her life as she had, coolly distant from intimacy and any kind of dependency.

Until Gabriel.

And then she had wanted him so badly, and in wanting him she'd forgotten that she knew nothing of how relationships were meant to work.

'I know I shouldn't have lied, but when you showed me that photo I panicked. I was scared that if I told you the truth—if I told you that my parents had spent their marriage hating one another—you might see things differently. See *us* differently. So you're right. I did lie to you. I lied because you made me want the thing that scared me most of all.'

*Love, and the possibility of love everlasting.*

Lying in his bed, with his arms wrapped around her and sunlight and birdsong filling the room, for the first time she'd had love and hope and faith. And it had been intoxicating—*he* had been intoxicating. But she should have known then how it would end. With lies and confusion and regrets.

She looked away before he could see her tears. Before she could see his face change. She didn't want to go back to the way he had looked at her in London, with so much anger and contempt. So much distance.

'What was it that you wanted?'

He spoke so quietly that at first she thought she had imagined his voice. But then he said it again.

'What was it that you wanted?'

She wanted it still. More than she ever had. Because now she knew him. But she couldn't tell him that. There was too much history. Too much hurt.

'I wanted you. I wanted us. Before, I'd thought a relationship...marriage...was just a trap, a cage. But you made it feel like danger and freedom and safety all at once.'

It was only as he reached out and pulled her closer that she realised she had spoken the words out loud. She felt naked and young and stupid, and terrified that he would see too much—see the love she still felt for him. She buried her face against his shoulder.

'I felt the same way.'

His cheek was warm against her, and his body was strong and so, so comforting, but still she couldn't look at him.

'Dove—'

She felt him slide his hands into her hair, and then he tilted her face up to him, forcing her to look at him.

'I'm sorry. For making you work for me. For threatening you. Threatening Alistair. I shouldn't have done it. I knew it was wrong, but I was angry. With you. With myself. With everything and everyone.' He dropped his hands and his face twisted. 'I'm always angry. I don't want to be, but it's—'

He broke off and, seeing his pain, feeling his fatigue, she felt her heart crack in two.

'I'm so tired of feeling like this all the time. That's why I have to make this acquisition happen. So I can move on. And I *need* to move on. But I'm not going to force you to stay and do something you're not comfortable with.'

'Are you firing me?' she asked, struggling to keep her voice steady. To keep looking at him as if there was something more inside her than the terrible silent scream that was breaking her ribs apart.

His hands caught hers. 'No, but if you stay it has to be of your own free will. And if you choose to leave there won't be any repercussions. I don't think I made that clear before.'

There was a perfect stillness.

Did he really think that was why she had stayed?

He was holding her loosely, his thumbs resting against the soft white underside of her wrists. But she felt the press of his thumbs in every part of her body.

Her eyes found his. He was giving her a choice. Only there was no choice. Because she didn't want to leave. She didn't want to lose him. Not yet, anyway.

'I want to stay,' she said quietly.

Stretched between the silence and the drumming of his heart, Gabriel felt his body soften with relief. Only a few days ago he had asked Dove to stay.

'I don't want it to end like this. It feels wrong,' he had said.

And she had stayed.

Only he couldn't bear thinking that it was because of the threats he'd made back in London, and then again on the yacht. Nor could he bear the idea of her leaving, even though he knew that she had every right to go.

And yet, incredibly, she was choosing to stay. Even though he knew that she would never do this—seek revenge after so long. But he didn't know another way to finish what his birth mother had started.

All he knew was that Dove was here, and that he couldn't stop staring at the hollows of her collarbone and the pulse beating in her throat.

The air quivered around them.

She moved first, reaching up to brush her lips against his, so softly that if his eyes had been shut he would have thought it was nothing but his imagination. But then she leaned in and kissed him on his mouth, and all over his face, licking him, nipping his skin, her breath warm and sweet.

His pulse jolted as she pressed her hand to his trousers, flattening her fingers inside the waistband.

At first there was just the need for her…the need to taste her again and know that she was his. Only that wasn't enough. He wanted more.

Heart pummelling his ribs, he slid his hands under her robe and pulled her towards him. She made a soft, choking noise against his mouth, and the sound snagged all five senses and made his breath chafe in his throat.

Her skin was warm and smooth, like satin, and it seemed to melt under his touch. But still he wanted more.

He tugged the belt around her waist, loosening it so that the robe slipped from her shoulders, and now she was naked. Pulse accelerating, he stared at her, feeling her nakedness and her nearness go through him.

She was exquisite. If she were a drawing it would be nothing more than a few curving lines. His eyes lingered on her nipples, then dropped to her thighs. And some light shading, he thought, his body shuddering into a hardness that made his legs sway beneath him.

They kissed again and then she broke away. But she left her hand inside his trousers, stroking him, smoothing her thumb over the swollen heavy head of his erection, her touch igniting a blaze of need, her soft, hungry grey gaze sliding straight through him, undoing him, making him shake…

Grunting, he batted her hand away, pushing her back on the bed and stripping off his clothes. She lay there watching him, her limbs sprawled against the sun-soaked sheets, her hair spilling over the pillow like rays of sunlight, and all of her seemed to be golden and white.

And then her hand reached for him, and he stopped seeing, stopped thinking, and his mind was nothing but heat and need.

Lost in her beauty, scraped raw and aching with desire, he lowered his mouth to her breast, tasting her there, teasing first one nipple then the other, feeling them swell and harden, feeling her body squirming restlessly against him as her hands splayed against his back, and it was sweet and slow and irresistible…

Dove shivered inside all the way through. She felt as if Gabriel was tuning her body…each touch, each lick, each caress sounding out a different note inside her… and she was lost in the shimmering vibrations breaking over her skin in a lazy, sensual rhythm that lifted her outside herself.

She wanted, wanted, *wanted* him. Only Gabriel could make her feel so whole and yet so prised wide open.

'Do you like that?'

His voice, the hoarseness of it, prised her open a little more, just as if he was using his mouth, his tongue, to part her legs and tease the coiling heat that pulsed there.

'Yes…'

Her breasts felt heavy, the taut peaks of her nipples pulled so taut that it hurt when he touched them. But it hurt more when he didn't. She arched upwards, pushing against his hard, seeking mouth, and then he was rolling over, taking her with him so that she was on top.

'I want to see you. All of you,' he said, in that same hoarse way that made her breath spin out of her throat and her heart beat light and fast like the wings of a hummingbird.

His hands were flush against her hips and he lifted her up, moving her forward, then back, so that the blunt tip of his erection was rubbing her clitoris. It felt so good... made everything inside her swell and curl like a wave.

'Like that,' she whispered. 'Just like that.'

Her head tipped back. She couldn't get enough. And when he lifted her again she shifted her weight, her hands finding him, guiding him between her legs.

He sucked in a breath, sharply, and she felt his hunger sweep through her like a rolling sheet of flame.

'Yes. *Yes.*'

She tilted her hips to his, pushing down, feeling him fill her, arching her body. His blue eyes were dark with the heat that flooded her limbs. His fingers were pulling at her nipples, pinching them lightly, stroking the taut flesh, and all the time he was moving against her, his hardness filling her, his hands anchoring her against him as he pushed harder, deeper, harder, deeper...

Her nails dug into his arm.

'Let go.' He reached up and pulled her mouth to his, 'Let go,' he said again, and he pulled her closer, then closer still, and she tensed.

A bolt of lightning whipped through her, hot, stinging, making her body twitch and jerk over and over. She gasped, then cried out, and he licked the sounds from her trembling mouth. And then he was tensing, shuddering against her, dragging her hips down and thrusting up inside her, making her splinter and fly apart into a thousand glittering shards.

Breathing unsteadily, she folded against him. For a moment they lay together, panting, spent, and then he lifted her to one side, moving her under his hard, muscular body, stretching out above her.

The maleness of him set her alight. His hand was tight in her hair. His face was serious, his blue eyes blazing with a light that she could feel inside.

'I've never wanted any woman the way I want you—'

She felt his mouth on her throat, as if he needed her pulse to live, and she held him tight, wondering what it would take for that to be true.

Then he lifted his head, shifting his weight so that they were side by side.

'How would you feel about going to New York?' he asked. He stroked her tangled blonde hair away from her face. 'I'm supposed to be going to a dinner there on Friday—some charity event. I was going to cancel and just send in a donation, but why don't you come with me?'

'To New York?'

'Why not? We don't actually have to go to the event. We could just go out on our own,' he said softly. 'Have dinner…see a show.'

She stared at him, mesmerised by the softness in his eyes, terrified by the longing that had sneaked into her heart at his suggestion.

'Does that make me your date?' She gave a mock frown. 'Only I thought I was a distraction.'

'Can't you be both?'

She felt the press of his erection against her stomach, hard where she was soft, and instantly forgot the question.

'I don't know,' she said helplessly.

'But I do—and the answer is yes, you can. So come with me,' he said again. 'If you need an excuse for Alistair we could always drop in at my office. I can show you around. After you've finished distracting me,' he added.

And then he smiled, and she felt it ripple through her, making her yearn for him all over again.

Her hot, damp skin was sticking to his and she could feel his heart beating in time with hers. They were seamless…fused with need.

But it was not just need for her, she thought, and had to press her hand against her mouth to stop herself from declaring her love for him.

What would be the point? For Gabriel, this was sex. She knew he felt the familiarity of it, but he wasn't offering her a future, just dinner and show. And a personal tour of his office. Business and pleasure.

*But not love.*

'I don't need an excuse,' she said, smiling up at him casually, pretending that she wanted nothing more than to distract, and be distracted by him.

And then Gabriel leaned in and kissed her, and she didn't have to pretend any more.

# CHAPTER NINE

GAZING OUT OF the window of his private jet, Gabriel tried to let his thoughts drift in time to the clouds gliding past the glass.

It wasn't easy. The clouds passed by smoothly, like swans on water, but his thoughts were stop-start, jerking back and forth between the past and the present, between Dove and Fenella Ogilvy. He was running from the past, from the mother who had pushed him away not once but twice, and he hated it that he was the kind of man who did that.

But the idea of meeting her just yet was beyond him.

Better to concentrate on the present, and on the woman sitting beside him. The woman who had stayed with him when he'd pushed her away, and then stood by him, literally holding his hand, while he shared the secrets he had held close for so long.

He glanced to where Dove sat opposite him, her grey eyes lowered to the book in her lap. They had talked again, about her father and his mother, and he knew that she was still struggling to understand Oscar Cavendish's actions six years ago. But, unlike him, she wasn't fighting the truth. She had accepted it. Maybe because her father was gone.

No, he thought, his eyes seeking Dove again, as they

did roughly every two minutes. She didn't fight. She solved problems. If Oscar had still been alive, she would have been trying to find a way to live with the consequences, not dwelling on what couldn't be changed.

She hadn't tried to get him to talk to Fenella again. Instead, she had suggested that he write a letter.

'You don't have to send it,' she'd said. 'Just write down everything you want to say to her and maybe then, when everything's clear in your head, you could arrange to meet her on your terms.'

He understood the theory, and he'd half listened to her, but there had been a small indentation in her forehead that had kept distracting him. But then there seemed to be no end to the things about Dove which distracted him.

There was her voice.

That sweet smile that seemed to light up her skin and fill him with light too.

The softness of her hair.

And that hollow at the base of her neck. It was exactly the right size for his thumb, and he liked to rest it there, feeling her pulse.

His hand twitched and he wondered what she would do if he reached over and cupped her head and held her like that now and for ever—

*For ever?*

The words hovered in the cool cabin air, dancing in front of his eyes like light reflecting off water, and he felt a calmness that was also a kind of euphoria. *For ever with Dove.* Waking with her every day and taking her into his bed every night and all the hours in between...

But what was he thinking?

His chest tightened. There was no 'for ever' for him

and Dove. How could there be? She knew him too well to want anything beyond these few days and nights they had set aside to say goodbye properly. That was all he had to offer. And it was the least he could do to make up for the appalling way he had treated her.

For all the appalling things in her life.

He stared out of the window, his throat closing over. Listening to her talk about her parents' marriage, he had felt numb with shame and self-loathing. All the time they'd been together, and all the years that had followed, when he had condemned her without trial, right up to the moment when he had bullied her into working for him, he had been so certain that he alone had suffered.

But Dove had been hurting all this time. Everything he'd thought he'd known about her was wrong. She had suffered too.

And then there was the acquisition. Dove was right. Things were different now. He wasn't a penniless young man any more. He was fully grown, and very wealthy and successful.

His fingers tapped out a rhythm on the armrest. But she was wrong about other things. Outwardly he might have changed, but inside everything had stayed the same. The wound of his mother's rejection was as raw now as it had been seven years ago. And he couldn't do it. He couldn't go and talk to Fenella. He couldn't put himself in the position of being rejected again.

Unlike Dove.

Remembering how she had hidden away on *The Argentum* and confronted him, he stilled his fingers. She was brave in a way he simply couldn't be. That was why things had to be done his way. So that he could leave Fenella

Ogilvy and James Balfour behind for ever. It was what he had been working towards for almost a third of his life.

'What is it?'

He glanced up. Dove was staring at him, her grey eyes resting on his face, her expression a mix of confusion and concern.

'Nothing,' he lied. 'I was just thinking about which show we could go to.'

He knew she was worried about him. Knew, too, that she had agreed to stay because of the way he had spoken about his mother. He had seen the shock and fear in her eyes, and it sickened him that he'd scared her.

What he wanted was to take care of her, to protect her. Except that wouldn't work because he wanted to protect her from men like himself and her father. Men who were damaged irretrievably. Men whose anger at the world made them forget the rules.

'We don't have to do a show. I mean, we probably won't be able to get tickets at such short notice.'

'Don't worry about that. In fact, don't worry about anything. Just leave everything to me.'

He leaned forward and cupped the back of her head in his hand, his pulse jerking as he fitted his thumb into the hollow there. They had only been in the air an hour, and they had made love multiple times before they'd left. The last time he had dragged her upstairs to the bedroom, lifting her against the door, both of them panting and fully clothed. But, he wanted her still—always.

Leaning forward, he pulled her towards him, tilting her head up to meet his, fitting his mouth to hers. Her fingers fluttered against his arms and he knew that she wanted what he wanted.

They made it to the cabin, mouths fusing, hands pulling at each other as they fell onto the bed.

Somewhere nearby a phone started ringing. Not his, but he could feel Dove tensing. Groaning, he reached over and picked up the phone, frowning down at the screen. 'It's your mother.'

She hesitated. 'It's probably nothing. She just likes to catch up. I'll call her back.'

Her mouth found his as the ringing stopped and he pulled her closer, his fingers loosening around the phone as everything else tightened.

He swore under his breath as the ringing started again. But, catching sight of Dove's face, he tamped down his hunger.

'It's fine.' Shifting away from the soft, seductive warmth of her body, he handed her the phone. 'But just so you know…we have four hours of flight time left and I intend to spend every remaining minute of those hours in this bed with you.'

'Hi, Mum.' She kissed him lightly on the lips. *I won't be long*, she mouthed.

Given his current state of arousal, any amount of time was too long, he thought, rolling back against the pillow, his heartbeat slowing to match the pulse in his groin. He felt a burst of heat as she leaned forward and he caught a glimpse of the back of her neck. Four hours in bed wasn't going to be enough to satisfy his need for this woman. That would take several lifetimes. In fact, he would probably need until the end of time itself.

'But what did they say? Is he going to be all right?'

The breathless shock in Dove's voice cut across his musings like a guillotine. His eyes snapped over to where she was sitting, her hand clenched around the phone, the knuckles stark against her pale skin.

'What is it?' He was by her side in an instant. 'What's happened?' he asked gently.

'It's Alistair. He's been taken into hospital.' She pressed her hand against her mouth. 'My mum couldn't get him to wake up, and when she did his speech was all slurred.'

Dove was struggling to speak, and there were tears in her eyes.

'He must have had a stroke. Or maybe it's his diabetes.'

Her voice was muffled by her knuckles but still he could hear her pain.

'My dad died before I got to the hospital—'

'That won't happen.' The pain in her voice made him want to tear the plane apart with his bare hands. 'I won't let that happen.'

Staring down into her pale, desperate face, he felt his heart swell. Nothing mattered except making her happy and whole again. Not the acquisition. Not his own pain. There was only Dove.

He knew in that moment that he loved her, and the urgency of it filled his mouth—only this wasn't the right time. Dove needed him to step up. She needed someone she could rely on.

'It's okay.' He pulled her against him. 'Listen to me. It's going to be okay.'

He took the phone from her hand, deliberately slowing his mind, blanking out his love for her and her heart-wrenching panic.

'Mrs Cavendish? It's Gabriel Silva. I'm here with your daughter. Could you tell me which hospital Alistair was taken to?'

\* \* \*

For Dove, the next three hours were a nightmarish blend of time moving with agonising slowness and holding her breath, waiting for the phone to ring again.

She felt another wave of panic rise up inside her. Everything was jerky and disconnected. Her breath, her thoughts. And she couldn't stop the tears from rolling down her face.

If she had been on her own, she had no idea how she would have got back to London. But she wasn't on her own. Gabriel was with her.

After hanging up the phone, he'd taken charge immediately. Within minutes the plane had turned round and headed towards London. Next, he'd called ahead to arrange for a driver to meet them at the airport, and all the time he'd been making calls and organising people he'd been by her side, the quiet, solid strength of his body giving her strength.

And now they were heading towards the hospital in a limousine, and she was having to tense every muscle to stop herself crying out when the car stopped at a red traffic light.

'He's in good hands.'

She turned to where Gabriel sat beside her. His blue eyes were steady and calm on her face and she let out a long, slow breath. He sounded so sure, so certain.

'I just wish I knew what was going on.'

'You will. We're less than five minutes away from the hospital now. But in the meantime just try and focus on what you do know—which is that your mother acted very quickly. She didn't wait…she called an ambulance immediately.'

Remembering the sadness in her mother's voice on the phone, she felt her throat swell. Her mother and Alistair had grown up together. They had known each other their whole lives. Before Oscar, Olivia had been engaged to Alistair. After she married Oscar, she and Alistair went back to being friends—better friends than she had ever managed to be with her husband.

'I don't know what she'll do if anything happens.'

'She's stronger than you think,' he said quietly.

There was that certainty again, and it hit her then with a jolt that Gabriel had spoken to her mother. Obviously, she knew that—she'd been there when they'd talked—but somehow the knowledge had got swallowed up and swept aside in all the panic. But after all this time it had happened, and she sensed that her mother had liked him, and that probably she would always have liked him. Only now it was too late to matter.

She took a deep, shaky breath. 'She's never been very good at fighting back.'

There were a few seconds of silence, and then Gabriel said quietly, 'You don't need to be a fighter to have strength. But whatever happens, we'll face it together.' His fingers tightened around hers. 'I'm not going anywhere.'

Her heart felt as if it was being squeezed in a vice. It was the kind of thing people said in dramas on TV. It didn't mean anything. She tried not to think about how much she wanted it to mean something.

But there was no time to think about that anymore. They had arrived.

In the car, some of her panic had subsided. But now, breathing in the hospital smell of cleaning fluid and vending machine coffee, she felt it return. There were people everywhere. Sitting, shuffling, rushing… But somehow Gabriel seemed to know exactly which way to go, and she let him lead her through the corridors until finally they reached a pair of swing doors.

'Your mother's in there.' He gestured towards the doors. 'She's probably not had anything to eat or drink, so I'll go and see if I can find something.'

'Aren't you coming in with me?' She felt a rush of panic, although she wasn't sure if it was the thought of him leaving or the fact that the need in her was so close to the surface.

'Your mum will want to talk to you.' He put his arms around her, gathering her against him, and then gently pushed her away. 'I'll wait out here for you.'

His eyes were so very blue, like the sky above the island and the sea where the dolphins had ridden through the waves, and she felt a pang almost like homesickness as she pushed through the doors and walked into a waiting area.

'Dove!'

'Mum!'

'Oh, darling…'

Dove felt her face crumple as her mother stepped towards her and they hugged one another tightly. Olivia looked tired and pale, but she was still recognisably her mum.

'Have you seen him? Is he okay?' she asked.

Olivia nodded. 'They let me sit with him for about ten minutes. He's very weak, but he knew who I was, and he sent his love to you. He doesn't want you to worry.'

That was typical of Alistair. Even when he was lying in a hospital bed he was worrying about other people.

'Was it a stroke?'

Olivia shook her head. 'I thought it was, but it's something called sepsis.'

Dove felt her heartbeat punch upwards into her throat. 'What is that?'

For a moment her mother's face seemed to break up, but then she rallied. She *was* strong, Dove thought, just like Gabriel had said.

'I'm not really sure. They did try and explain, but I just couldn't take it in. I think it's when the body overreacts to an infection. Sit down, darling...' She guided Dove onto a chair.

'What kind of infection?' Dove asked as she sat down.

Olivia reached out and took her hands. 'Apparently he cut his foot the other week, when he was out in the garden, and it must have got infected. The nurse said that anyone can get sepsis, but apparently if you're diabetic you have trouble fighting it.'

'Is it dangerous?'

Olivia hesitated, then nodded. 'It can be. But he's responding to the antibiotics, and they've given him some other drugs, but I can't remember their names.'

Dove glanced across the waiting room. A nurse at the desk was talking to one of the porters. On the wall above their heads a clock was loudly ticking, marking the minutes. Nobody was wailing, and everything felt reassuringly calm, so she was able to say quite normally, 'He's going to get through this.'

'Yes, he is.' Her mother frowned and swallowed hard. 'He has to.'

Dove stared at her mother's bowed head. She looked as if she was praying. Or asking for forgiveness. And then, from nowhere, she remembered what Olivia had said earlier on the phone, about not being able to wake Alistair up.

Only why would her mother be waking him up?

Across the room the nurse was still talking, and the clock was still ticking, but inside her everything was still and silent, as if her heart had forgotten how to beat.

Her head was spinning, and old familiar shapes were turning around and upside down to form a new picture.

'You love him, don't you?' she said slowly. And as she spoke the words out loud it was like watching a film that seemed unfamiliar and then realising halfway through that you had seen it before and already knew the ending. 'You love Alistair—not just as a friend, I mean.'

There was a short silence, and then her mother nodded slowly, her eyes filling with tears. 'I'm so sorry, Dove. I should never have married your father. I knew it was a mistake almost immediately. We both did. But I was young and thoughtless and vain, and I didn't know the difference then between love and being in love. By the time I did it was too late. I know you must be shocked and angry and hurt and disappointed, and you have every right to be all of those things.'

Maybe she was a very strange person, Dove thought, searching inside herself, because she didn't feel any of those things. But maybe that was because Alistair was such a big part of their lives anyway. He was always there—helping, encouraging, listening...

'I'm not angry, Mum.' Reaching out, she took Olivia's hands. 'I suppose I'm confused. I don't understand why you and Dad stayed married.'

Her mother sighed. 'It's complicated.'

It was an echo of another conversation…with Gabriel. 'So simplify it, then,' she said softly. 'If you could sum up your reasons in three words, what would they be?'

There was a short silence. Olivia's face was strained and sad. 'I don't need three words,' she said, then hesitated, as if considering what she was about to say. 'I can do it in one,' she said finally. 'Blackmail.'

Dove stared at her mother. *Now* she was in shock. Around her, the walls of the waiting room seemed to be swaying.

'I don't… I don't understand.'

'Your father always needed money. My inheritance gave us a generous allowance, but he always needed more—only it was all tied up in a watertight trust for you and your sisters. Perhaps if he had joined his family's firm he would have known that,' Olivia said, and there was an exhaustion in her voice that cut through Dove's shock.

'So he found out about you and Alistair and blackmailed you?' Dove felt as if she was feeling her way in the dark, hands outstretched, each tentative step offering different, unknown choices. 'What did you do? Did you borrow money?'

Her mother was shaking her head. 'He did know about Alistair, but Oscar had multiple affairs, so he couldn't use that. He found out something else.' She bit her lip. 'Guessed, really. But it was enough.' She sounded very, very tired.

'What was enough?' Asking the question made Dove's back prickle. 'What did he guess?'

Olivia took a breath. Her shoulders were braced, as if for the impact of what she was about to say. 'That you weren't his daughter. That Alistair was your father.'

Later, Dove would wonder if she had always known. Now, though, she was just trying to pull her head together.

'Does Alistair know?' she asked.

Olivia nodded slowly, her eyes bright. 'I told him. And I told Oscar I was going to leave him.'

'But you didn't?'

Now she shook her head. 'Oscar went to see Alistair and threatened him. He said that he would go to court, make everything public and drag it out for as long as possible. Alistair was devastated. He felt so guilty—we both did—and he loved you girls.' Her face softened. 'Especially you.'

Dove swallowed past the lump in her throat. She could almost feel Alistair's love for her, vibrating in her mother's voice.

'So what happened?'

There was a brief silence, and she watched as her mother returned reluctantly to her story.

'Alistair told me that he didn't want to break up our marriage. And he agreed to subsidise Oscar's lifestyle. I only found that out after Oscar died that he left a mountain of debt that Alistair's been trying to clear for years. He's had to re-mortgage his house…the offices.' Her lip trembled 'I'm so sorry, Dove. None of this was meant to happen. One thing just led to another, and I was selfish and weak. I'm not expecting you to forgive me, because I don't deserve it—'

'There's nothing to forgive. We can't choose who we love.' Dove felt her heart contract. She was thinking not about Alistair, but Gabriel. She squeezed her mother's hands. 'Why now? Why did you decide to tell me all of this now?'

Olivia looked down at their hands. 'We've spent so much time not being the couple we could have been… the family we wanted to be. Seeing Alistair lying there, with all those tubes and wires, it felt like a sign for me to be brave. To stop living a half-life. Because life is shorter than you think. But it's also wonderful, too. Or it can be, if you let it.'

She was crying, and Dove was too, and suddenly they were clinging to one another.

Finally her mother let go of her. 'I know he wasn't a good person, but please don't think too harshly of Oscar. I don't think he knew how to love…but he did try. Strangely enough, he tried the hardest with you.'

They hugged again, for a long time. The clock ticked steadily above Dove's head, but she didn't hear it. She couldn't see the hands moving. All she could see was Gabriel's face…the curve of his jaw as he told the pilot to turn the plane around and the softness in his blue eyes as he pulled her into his arms.

She had thought it was too late for them, but her mother and Alistair had shown her that wasn't true.

She just had to be brave.

And find Gabriel.

The corridor was empty. Gabriel glanced at his watch. Probably some shift was changing, or maybe the hospital was always quieter after lunch. It was lucky he had only bought one coffee otherwise it would be cold by now. But the sandwiches and cold drinks should be good for a while.

His stomach clenched—not with hunger, but with an anxiety that seemed to be hotwired into all five senses.

He could feel it vibrating through his body, taste it in his mouth, hear it in the jerkiness of his heartbeat. Watching Dove push through those doors, he had wanted to follow her, to shield her with his body against what lay on the other side, and it had taken every ounce of his willpower not to go with her.

Only he'd known that it wasn't right for him to be there. He wasn't family. He was an outsider…a stranger.

There was a sudden unbearable ache in his chest. If he hadn't let the past get in the way it might have been so different. But it *was* different now, he thought, remembering how he and Dove had talked, and how she could be quiet and listen too.

He felt a beat of hope, and let it take shape into something light and elliptical, like a piece of surf-smoothed volcanic rock from the beach at Pico. And he could be different. He could do that for her. He could forget about the acquisition. Write that letter to Fenella. Send it or not send it and get on with his life. *With Dove.*

The doors swung open and he felt his body loosen and tense at the same time as Dove stepped out of the waiting room, and then he was on his feet and pulling her against him, breathing in the light, clean scent of her as if it was pure oxygen.

They stayed like that for as long as he could justify it, and then he let her go. 'How's Alistair?'

'Tired and a bit shaken. It wasn't a stroke—he has sepsis. But they think they've caught it in time.' She smiled weakly. 'He's loving having all the nurses fussing all over him.'

His hand tightened around hers. 'Thank goodness.'

There was a luminous quality to her skin that seemed

to light up the dingy corridor. She looked young and alive, almost eager.

'You care about him too?'

'Of course.' He spoke automatically, but it was true. He did care about Alistair. But why did that matter to Dove? 'So what happens now?' he asked.

'They said that he's got to stay in hospital for a couple of weeks, but everyone is really pleased with the progress he's made.'

She was watching him, waiting...

'But that's not all?' he said slowly.

There was a silence, and then she shook her head. 'My mum has just told me something. About Alistair.'

She met his gaze, and suddenly, looking down into her soft grey eyes, he knew what she was going to say.

'He's your father.'

His hands tightened around her waist as she stared up at him dazedly. 'How did you know that?'

'I didn't. But you have his eyes,' he said simply.

She blinked, then nodded. 'They love each other. They always have. And one night they gave in to their feelings. And...'

'And they still love each other?'

She nodded as he finished her sentence. 'They both feel as though they've waited so long to be together.'

There was another silence. 'Are you okay?' he asked finally.

She nodded. 'It's a lot to take in, but it makes sense of so much. And it feels right. It feels good. I feel like we can be a family.'

He could hear the hope in her voice, and he knew that

she was remembering that photo of his family, picturing something once so out of reach, now there for the taking.

'There are other things too… They can wait, though. Everything else can wait. You see, there's something I have to tell you. Something I need to tell you. Something I realised when my mum was talking about love and obstacles and having to fight to get back to where you want to be.'

Her eyes were so open and soft it almost blinded him.

'I love you,' she said. 'I always have. I didn't want to for so long, but I couldn't not. And I think you love me too.'

Gabriel stared at her, holding his breath. She loved him. And he loved her. There was nothing to stop him. He looked down at her beautiful, hopeful face, seeing the sweetness of her, and the goodness. And now she was whole too. But he had nothing to give her. Nothing good—not like his father or Alistair.

*But she wants you.*

It was like saying a prayer or a poem. And for a moment he hesitated. He could take her hand and let her love him. There was nothing to stop him.

So he would have to stop himself.

Because if he took her hand, and her love, he might ruin her life.

Because he didn't know how to be whole. He didn't know if he could ever be whole, and not knowing for sure meant that he couldn't be with her.

He couldn't take the risk and maybe hurt her again. Hurt her more. He would do anything to make sure that didn't happen. Even give up the chance to be with her.

She was waiting for him to speak, and he needed to

say something quickly, before he gave in to his need to be loved by this marvel of a woman.

'I'm sorry.' He lifted his hands from her waist carefully. 'I don't feel the same way,' he lied. 'I don't love you. Back on the island it felt brutal, just ending things between us, but I thought I'd made it clear that this was only ever a temporary arrangement.'

It hurt so much, watching her face change, and he knew then that she did love him. Because she couldn't hide her confusion and her pain.

'But we were going to New York—'

'For fun.' He frowned. 'Look, I'm sorry if you got the wrong idea—'

'So what was all this for?'

She took a step towards him, and he knew what it must have cost her to do it, because he knew what it cost him to stop himself doing the same.

'You and me on the yacht and the island? Going to New York? Coming with me to London?'

Her gaze was steady, and she looked so serious, so determined, he felt like a child. And he *was* a child—a damaged child—and she deserved so much better.

Forcing himself to meet her eyes, he frowned again. 'We were on my plane and we were in mid-air. I had no choice but to come with you. The rest of it was just sex,' he lied again. 'But I won't deny that I still want you, so if you want to keep things casual then we can hook up when I'm in town, but as for anything else...'

He remembered her confronting him on the deck of *The Argentum* and he hated himself. But he couldn't be who she needed him to be. Not for certain. And not sure wasn't enough.

'I'm sorry,' he said again—and he was.

But he needed to put her off, keep her at arm's length, because if he touched her, felt the beat of her heart, then he wouldn't be strong enough to push her away.

'I know you don't want to hear this, but all I care about is getting this acquisition over the line. You were there, and we had some fun. But all this was about putting the past behind me. All of the past. Including you.'

The lie felt seismic. He could feel it expanding in every direction, so that he half thought the walls would start to crumble and fall.

And he wanted to be crushed.

Anything would be better than seeing Dove's eyes.

For one terrible moment he thought she might tell him she loved him again, but instead, in a voice that tore at him inside, she said quietly, 'I thought you were a good man. But you're not. You're just anger and emptiness all wrapped up in a beautiful skin.'

He forced himself to meet her eyes. 'You'll get over it.'

She stared at him in silence, her face small and pale and stunned, and then she turned and pushed through the doors.

He had known it would be like this, but it was still unbearable. He stared after her for a moment, telling himself that it had been the right thing to do, and that he'd done it for her, and then he too turned and walked away.

# CHAPTER TEN

IN THE BOARDROOM of the Silva Group's headquarters in New York, Gabriel shifted back in his seat and gazed across the city skyline. It was eleven o'clock and the meeting had just broken up for coffee and the protein bars that were delivered every day by a local bakery.

But, unlike everyone else in the room, he wasn't interested in either. Nor was it eleven o'clock. For him, there was only one time. London time.

Picking up his phone, he turned it over in his hand.

It had been that way since the moment he'd returned to the States a month ago. At first he'd thought it was jet-lag. But then it had carried on, day after day, week after week. And now it was the fourth week, and it was just how he lived, mentally adding five hours on to the time that everyone else worked by.

Because despite the very real truth of his being here, in New York, his head and his heart had never left that hospital corridor in London.

He saw her face everywhere. Pale, devastated, crushed. And it hurt more than anything in his life. He wanted to put that part of himself away somewhere, so that he could forget her, but that would mean not seeing her face, and living was hard enough right now. He couldn't live in a world where he couldn't see Dove's face.

He missed her unbearably. It was continuous—an overwhelming, endless awareness of her absence.

And he didn't understand it. Every hour that passed should be easing his pain, but if anything it was getting worse. So many times he had almost picked up the phone and called her...

'Gabriel?'

He turned. His CFO Bill Brady was looking at him expectantly.

'Sorry...' He frowned. 'I was miles away.' *Three thousand four hundred and fifty-nine miles, to be precise.* 'Where are we at?'

'The acquisition.'

He stared at Bill blankly. What acquisition? The question echoed inside his head. And then he remembered, and he was stunned. How could he have forgotten? How could something that had been his purpose in life for so long suddenly be so unimportant?

His CFO cleared his throat. 'The Fairlight Holdings acquisition.'

Bill smiled at him, the kind of reassuring, placating smile you might use with someone who was lost. And he *was* lost, Gabriel thought, his fingers tightening around the phone. Lost for so many years...held in limbo between an unknown past and a present that should be enough but always felt incomplete, so that his whole life he'd felt as if he was missing something.

*Except with Dove.*

With her, he wasn't lost in himself, or in the pull of the past. He was present and whole and happy.

'There's still some pushback about the name-change.' Bill was speaking in that same, careful way. 'But I think they're tiring. So we'll stand firm. Unless, of course, you've changed your mind?'

He felt the combined stares of the ten people sitting round the boardroom table. He thought about Dove, and he could hear her voice telling him that things were different...that *he* was different.

Still holding his phone, he shifted back in his seat. 'No, nothing's changed.'

It was a hot day in London.

Too hot, Dove thought, to be dragging boxes around. But luckily she was going to have help. Having made a proper nuisance of herself, her mother had managed to persuade the removal company to turn up a day early.

Although she didn't really mind wrapping up her mother's teacups and saucers in old newspapers, Dove thought. There was something oddly comforting about it, and it gave her a chance to think. Not brood. That would be a bad idea. But so was ignoring things, burying them, pretending they didn't exist.

It was hard to change her ways. It was what she had done all her life.

But not this time.

This time she was trying something different. Being someone different.

And that meant thinking about her father and Gabriel.

She had forgiven her father—and she still thought of him as that. She accepted that she would probably never know why he had done what he had to Gabriel, but she believed her mother when she said that Oscar had loved her.

Just as she'd believed Gabriel when he'd said that he didn't. Not in the way she needed and wanted him to love her.

She hadn't wanted to believe it…

Her chest folded in on itself as she remembered that terrible conversation at the hospital four weeks ago, and Gabriel's quiet but adamantine assertion.

*'All this is about putting the past behind me. All of the past. Including you.'*

He could have hardly made it clearer, and yet even as she'd walked back towards her mother she had hoped he might follow her, grab her arm and spin her around, tell her that he didn't mean it, that he was just scared, that he loved her…

Only he had done none of those things.

He had left her, just as he had six years ago. Only this time there was no mix-up, no interference. He had gone because he'd wanted to go. Because she wasn't a reason to stay. She had made a fool of herself for nothing.

And yet she was glad she'd done it. It had been the right thing to do even if it had been the wrong man to do it for.

Her throat tightened momentarily. That was progress, at least. But then she wasn't alone this time.

Instead of hiding her pain, trying to cope, pretending that she was all right, she had walked straight back into that waiting room and burst into tears. She had cried for a long time, and then it had taken even longer to tell her mother everything.

Her mother had been amazing.

She had listened and comforted her, and then she had called the Silva Group in London and told them that her daughter was taking compassionate leave.

So now Dove was at home, organising her mother's house move. At first she had been worried that she wouldn't have enough to do, but every morning her mother handed her a list written in her neat, copperplate writing and she worked her way through it.

Most of the tasks required nothing more than a phone and a fair amount of determination, but everything took a surprising amount of time and effort, and the days had turned into weeks.

It was hard, getting used to Gabriel not being there in her heart, but one of these days she knew she would wake up from a Gabriel-free sleep and not think of him. It wouldn't always feel as if she'd had open heart surgery without an anaesthetic. Like he'd said, she would get over it—get over him.

In the meantime, there were other things—good things—to take the edge off the pain. Now that she was off the acquisition there was her job, and there was this new and entirely astonishingly effortless version of her family—and, best of all, Alistair was coming home this afternoon.

Alistair had recovered well. He was still tired, but he couldn't seem to stop smiling, and it was a joy to watch him and her mother laughing and teasing one another about their upcoming wedding. Their easy love for one another was building on her newfound faith in relationships, and she no longer imagined marriage as a trap or a cage. Rather, she could see how it could be a partnership, with boundaries, but also room to grow and be your best self.

She cut the packing tape and yanked it over the bulging box, and then sat on it quickly as it threatened to burst open.

Now that they were together officially there was no need for Olivia and Alistair to have a house each. Dove glanced around the kitchen, with its surfeit of cooking implements and spice jars. She had no idea how they were going to fit all of this in one house, though. But they would work it out, she thought, and it was a good feeling being able to think that.

She heard the doorbell ring and felt a rush of relief.

*Now, where was that list?*

Sticking her head through the open window, she shouted up to the man who was presumably joined to the pair of trainers she could see on the doorstep.

'It's open,' she called up. 'Just let yourself in. I'm downstairs.'

She heard the door open, then close, and footsteps on the staircase.

'Thanks for fitting us in today. I thought we'd start in the bedroom, if that's all right with you?'

'The bedroom sounds perfect.'

Her heartbeat faltered. Her mouth seemed to lose its shape and she felt her legs sway beneath her.

Gabriel was standing in the kitchen. Against her mother's pastel pink saucepans and delicate floral blinds and tablecloth he looked too big, too male, and she edged to the other side of the table as memories of facing him across another table jostled with her heartbeat for space inside her head. It was only six weeks ago, but it felt like a lifetime.

'What are you doing here?'

For a moment he didn't reply, and then he said quite calmly, as if he was in the habit of turning up in her mother's kitchen unannounced, 'I need to talk to you about the acquisition.'

She stared at him in disbelief, feeling the blood rushing to her head, and a kind of mindless anger that had no name swelling inside her. Was he insane? Did he actually think he could just walk in here and start talking to her about acquisitions after everything that had happened?

'Firstly, I'm off work,' she told him. 'On compassionate leave—not that I'd expect you to understand the concept of compassion. Secondly, I don't want to talk to you about anything. So I suggest you go back up the stairs you just came down. Oh, and shut the door on your way out,' she added.

He didn't move.

Obviously. Because he was delusional or utterly without empathy, or both.

'You have ten seconds to get out of this house.' She picked up her phone. 'And then I'm calling the police.'

Gabriel stared at the woman he loved, his heart beating like a drum in his chest. Walking up to the house, he'd felt more like himself, and hopeful. Now, though, he could feel his hope draining away.

Dove was furious. Beneath her obvious confusion and shock at having him turn up at her mother's home he could see her frustration in the clean, curving lines of her face and the storm clouds of her eyes, and he couldn't blame her. But nor could he do what she had told him to do.

'I will leave. But first you need to listen to what I have to say.'

She was staring at him as if he was mad. And maybe he was. His team certainly thought so. In his mind he replayed the meeting two days ago, when Bill Brady had asked him about the Fairlight acquisition. For so long it had been his goal, but sitting there in the boardroom it had suddenly seemed distant and irrelevant to him, almost as if it was happening to someone else. He had felt the way he had back in that hotel with Charles Lambton, when he had felt like a stranger to himself.

Only that hadn't been supposed to happen. He had wanted to buy out Fairlight Holdings so he could erase Fenella's family business, as she had erased him, but suddenly he had felt as if he was erasing himself.

To the complete astonishment of the men and women sitting round the table, he had got to his feet and cut short the meeting, striding out of the office without so much as one word of explanation.

'Or else what?' Dove's grey eyes narrowed on his face. 'What are you going to do? Threaten me? Threaten my family.'

'No, but I won't leave until you've heard me out. And you know me well enough to believe me when I say that.'

Dove glared at him. She should call the police, but the last thing Alistair needed was to come home to yet more flashing blue lights.

'Fine. You have five minutes—starting now.' She lifted

her chin. 'But I don't know why you're bothering. I'm not going to be working on the acquisition anymore.'

'No, you're not,' he said quietly. 'Because there isn't going to be one.'

She stared at him in confusion, her heart tight inside her chest, feeling worried despite herself. She knew how badly Gabriel had wanted the acquisition to happen.

'What happened? Was it the name-change? Did they pull out?'

There was silence.

'No, I did. I went to see Fenella, like you suggested.'

*He had?* Her head was spinning like a Waltzer. Why had he done that? More importantly, what had Fenella said?

'How was it?' she asked, choosing her words with care.

He tilted his head back and, seeing the strain around his eyes, she had to stop herself from reaching out and taking his hand. It wasn't hers to take, she reminded herself. And yet it hurt to leave him standing there alone.

'She was upset. Then angry. And then upset again.' He let out a breath. 'It didn't change anything between us.'

'I'm sorry.' She meant it. Even though he had hurt her, she didn't want him to be hurt.

He shook his head. 'Don't be. It wasn't easy, or enjoyable, but I'm glad I did it. It changed how I feel about her. Filled in a few fairly crucial gaps.'

There was a silence, and then he said quietly, 'It made me realise that my birth mother and father might have given me my genes, but my adoptive parents and my family gave me my identity. And I would never have worked that out without you.'

His blue eyes rested on her face, not blazing with anger or hurt any more, but light and calm.

'I wanted to thank you for making me see things differently.'

'You came all the way from New York to thank me?'

She stared at him in bewilderment, her earlier anger fading and morphing into something more dangerous.

*Why did he have to go and do that?*

For weeks now she had been telling herself that he was a monster, without a soul or a conscience, but now he was here in her mother's kitchen, apologising, looking young and serious and contrite, and making her feel things, want things…

'I have business in London.' He shrugged. 'A couple of new acquisitions.'

Of course he did, She swallowed, her skin tightening at her own stupidity. 'Well, don't let me stop you.'

He took a step closer. 'But that's the thing—you *have* stopped me. I can't do anything. I can't sleep. I'm not eating. My staff think I've lost my mind… What I'm trying to say is that I made a mistake.'

The strain in his voice made her stomach clench painfully, so that she had to grip the edge of the table to stop herself doubling up.

'We both made mistakes,' she said.

'I should never have left you in the hospital.'

*It's guilt, that's all*, she told herself. And that was a good thing. Because it meant that deep down he cared about things, and she was glad for him. Only it wasn't fair that she should find that out now, when she was trying so hard not to care about him.

She shook her head. 'You can't do this, Gabriel. You can't come here and say things like that to me. It's not fair—'

He took another step closer, and the blue of his eyes was like the sea and the sky, so that looking into them was like drowning and flying both together.

'It's love,' he said hoarsely. 'And everything's fair in love and war, Dove. Only I think we've done the war bit, don't you?'

Her heart was beating in her throat, so that it was hard to swallow, to speak, and she couldn't breathe past her hope and longing.

'But you don't love me.'

'But I do.'

His face shifted, his expression suddenly so sweet and sure and steady that she couldn't stop a sob from leaving her throat.

'I love you, and I need you, and I know I made a mess of things, and that it's probably too late, but I had to tell you. That's why I came to London.'

He reached over and took her hands in his.

'To tell you that you were right. I *am* different—because you changed me. I thought that punishing my mother, taking something from her, would make me feel whole, but it's you who makes me feel whole.'

His fingers tightened slightly. 'You remember when I told you I was angry? I was. All the time. Raging deep down. But I'm not angry anymore. And that's because of you. Because you're a good person. The way you see things makes them better. You've made me better.'

His expression, with all its need and hope, went straight into her, filling her like sunlight.

'You're a good person too,' she said shakily.

Her hands were shaking too now, and Gabriel reached

out and pulled her close, not kissing her, just holding her, slotting her body into his like a key in a lock.

'I'm sorry… I'm sorry,' he whispered into her soft clean hair. 'For what I said…for what I did…'

'I know.'

And now they kissed, soft and gentle at first, and then with heat and longing and love. So much love it seemed to fill the kitchen with sunlight.

'How did you know I was here?'

'I spoke to your mother.' He grimaced. 'She sounds like a debutante on the phone, but she was surprisingly fierce in person.'

'You've met my mother?' Dove's mouth dropped open. 'When?'

'Yesterday.'

His arms tightened around her, his gaze reaching inside her, warming her, caressing her.

'I wanted to talk to her first. About you. About us. I didn't want there to be any confusion. Or any secrets.' He hesitated. 'And then I spoke to Alistair.'

A great tangle of emotion was swirling inside her. 'You went to see him at the hospital?'

He nodded slowly. 'I needed to talk to him about the acquisitions. Actually, one of them is more of a merger.'

She felt his hands slide down to her hips, holding her gently but firmly.

'A very specific merger,' he said softly. 'The only merger that matters to me.'

He reached into his pocket and pulled out a small square box, his eyes blazing not with anger but with something that burned inside her too.

'Marry me, Dove. You have my heart. You are my life. Let me love you and care for you.'

Tears sliding down her cheeks, she nodded, and he slid the ring onto her finger and they kissed again. Some time later they broke apart, but they stayed close, their hands moving over one another in relief and wonder, as if neither of them could quite believe that they were there, together.

'You said there was an acquisition too.' Dove frowned. 'What is it?'

She watched his face change, tense a little.

'Cavendish and Cox.'

For a moment she didn't react, and Gabriel waited, his heart accelerating a little.

'And Alistair knows about this?'

He nodded, curving his hands round her body, anchoring her against him.

'Your mother told me what Oscar did.' He hesitated. 'And I know the sepsis could have happened to anybody, but Alistair's been pushing himself for years. This way he can slow down a little. Enjoy life with his new family.'

He felt her arms slide up around his neck. 'I said you were a good person.'

He smiled then, and she felt her whole body open up to him like a flower to the sun.

'Well, to be absolutely truthful, I have been looking into acquiring a law firm for a couple of years now, and it just so happens my fiancée works for one.'

Gabriel felt a jolt of astonishment and elation as he used the word, and the rightness of everything blossomed inside him.

'So you're going to buy us out?'

He shook his head. 'I'd invest in the business. But I would be more of a sleeping partner.'

She leaned into him, her heart somersaulting. 'I'm not sure that would work. I don't remember you doing much sleeping.'

His blue eyes were steady on her face, and there was a softness in them that she couldn't turn away from. With joy, she realised that she didn't have to, not now—or ever.

'That reminds me—didn't you say something about starting in the bedroom?' he said softly.

And then he laughed, and she laughed too, and then they were kissing as if the world was ending…but for them it was only just beginning.

\* \* \* \* \*

# COMING SOON!

We really hope you enjoyed reading this book. If you're looking for more romance be sure to head to the shops when new books are available on

# Thursday 1st April

To see which titles are coming soon, please visit

## millsandboon.co.uk/nextmonth

MILLS & BOON

# MILLS & BOON®

## Coming next month

### THE ITALIAN'S INNOCENT CINDERELLA
Cathy Williams

"Explain," Maude whispered, already predicting what he was about to say and dreading confirmation of her suspicions. "What…what was in the paper, Mateo?"

"I debated bringing it, but in the end, I thought better of it."

"Why?"

"Because we're engaged."

Maude's mouth fell open and she stared at him in utter shock.

"Sorry?"

"It would seem that I found the love of my life with you and we're engaged."

"No. No, no, no, no…no…"

*Continue reading*
THE ITALIAN'S INNOCENT CINDERELLA
Cathy Williams

*Available next month*
www.millsandboon.co.uk

# LET'S TALK

# *Romance*

For exclusive extracts, competitions
and special offers, find us online:

- **f**   facebook.com/millsandboon
- **𝕏**   @MillsandBoon
- **⊙**   @MillsandBoonUK
- **♪**   @MillsandBoonUK

Get in touch on 01413 063 232

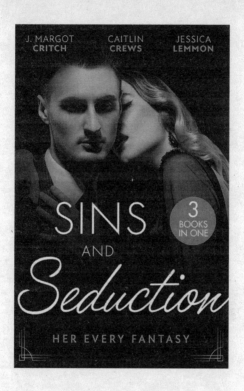

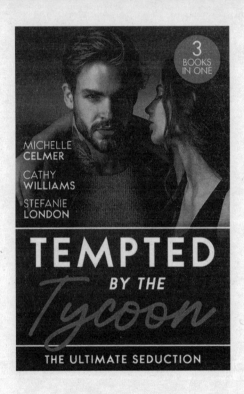

# MILLS & BOON

## THE HEART OF ROMANCE

---

## A ROMANCE FOR EVERY READER

---

### MODERN

Prepare to be swept off your feet by sophisticated, sexy and seductive heroes, in some of the world's most glamourous and romantic locations, where power and passion collide.

### HISTORICAL

Escape with historical heroes from time gone by. Whether your passion is for wicked Regency Rakes, muscled Vikings or rugged Highlanders, awaken the romance of the past.

### MEDICAL

Set your pulse racing with dedicated, delectable doctors in the high-pressure world of medicine, where emotions run high and passion, comfort and love are the best medicine.

### True Love

Celebrate true love with tender stories of heartfelt romance, from the rush of falling in love to the joy a new baby can bring, and a focus on the emotional heart of a relationship.

### Desire

Indulge in secrets and scandal, intense drama and plenty of sizzling hot action with powerful and passionate heroes who have it all: wealth, status, good looks…everything but the right woman.

### HEROES

Experience all the excitement of a gripping thriller, with an intense romance at its heart. Resourceful, true-to-life women and strong, fearless men face danger and desire - a killer combination!

To see which titles are coming soon, please visit

**millsandboon.co.uk/nextmonth**